CAN'T HIDE FROM ME

CORDELIA KINGSBRIDGE

I0563638

RIPTIDE
PUBLISHING

Riptide Publishing
PO Box 1537
Burnsville, NC 28714
www.riptidepublishing.com

Can't Hide from Me

Cover art: G.D. Leigh, blackjazzdesign.com
Editors: Sarah Lyons; Kate De Groot
Layout: L.C. Chase, lcchase.com/design.htm

ISBN: 978-1-62649-444-2

First edition
October, 2016

Also available in ebook:
ISBN: 978-1-62649-443-5

CAN'T
HIDE
FROM
ME

CORDELIA
KINGSBRIDGE

RIPTIDE
PUBLISHING

TABLE OF CONTENTS

CHAPTER ONE

"All right, comm check," Jade said, her honey-sweet voice coming clear and strong through Charles's earpiece. "Siren here. Everything looks good on my end. Valkyrie?"

"Online," said Eva. She slipped her arm into the crook of Charles's elbow as they strolled along a crowded sidewalk in downtown El Paso. A tall woman even while barefoot, Eva's strappy heels put her at height with Charles, a couple inches over six feet. The drape of her silky black dress over lean, hard muscles drew more than a few admiring glances. "We're approaching the restaurant now."

"Copy that. Griffin?"

"Online," Charles said. He scanned the hordes of Saturday night pleasure-seekers thronging both sides of the street, alert to any behavior out of the ordinary. Though only in his early thirties, he felt ancient next to the swarms of fresh-faced college kids who made up a big chunk of the population, compliments of the local branch of the University of Texas. Had he *ever* had that much energy?

"Fury?"

With a crackling sigh, Sakura said, "I'm sitting literally three feet away from you."

"Yeah, but I just love the way your forehead scrunches up when you're annoyed," Jade said. "This isn't only for *my* benefit, you know."

"Fury online. Wheels ready to go at extraction point."

"Thanks, sweetie. Sandman?"

"Online," Shane said. "I'm in position across the street. Someone want to remind me why I'm being relegated to lookout?"

"Because you're a young white man," said Charles, lowering his voice as he and Eva entered Bar Medianoche, joining the line for the hostess stand. "Nobody's going to harass you for sitting alone in your car on a busy city street."

"I don't know—some of these ladies walking by are looking *very* interested."

"I'm sure your wife would be thrilled to hear that."

Charles and Eva reached the front of the line, where the beleaguered hostess gave them a tight smile and said, "How many?"

"We'd like to just sit at the bar, if that's all right," Charles said.

"Of course," she said, her smile relaxing. "Go right ahead."

"Remember, people, this is an *extraction*," Eva said once they were clear of the hostess stand. "There will be no engagement or apprehension of any criminal suspects unless absolutely necessary. There will *certainly* be no shots fired. Is that understood, Sandman?"

"Ouch, Valkyrie, way to call a guy out," Sakura said.

"You shoot a mannequin *one time*," Shane grumbled.

Bar Medianoche was a large establishment, classy and upscale, packed to the rafters with a diverse clientele. An enormous three-sided bar dominated the center of the restaurant, with tables expanding outward in concentric arcs and booths lining the walls. Charles and Eva merged with the mob at the bar, where there wasn't a single empty seat; the din of conversation was so loud that people had to shout their orders to the bartender.

"I've got the camera feeds up," Jade said, accompanied by the sound of clicking keys. "Nice of the manager to let us piggyback, but if he thinks I couldn't take control in three seconds flat—"

"No," Eva said.

"I'm just pointing out that I *could*," said Jade, all wounded innocence. "Oh, I see you guys—damn, Griffin, you are looking *fine* in that suit. Hey, how come there's never been a black James Bond?"

Charles adjusted his tie, trying to catch the bartender's attention. "Do you really want me to answer that?"

"Well, you're way hotter than Daniel Craig. And that's saying something."

"*Siren*," Eva snapped, over Shane and Sakura's snickering.

"Sorry, Valkyrie. You look awesome too, as per usual. That dress is really working for—"

There came a loud *thud*, a yelp, and a sudden silence.

"Thanks, Fury," said Eva.

"No problem," Sakura said.

Eva lifted one hand and smiled in the direction of the bartender, who all but dropped the shaker he was holding to hurry toward them. She and Charles accepted their swiftly poured wine and stepped away from the bar.

"Now all we have to do is find one total stranger in a jam-packed restaurant," Charles said, directing his remark to Eva, though the other three could still hear him.

"Yeah, but on the plus side, we know he's a Latino man in his late twenties," Jade said. "Who could be easier to find in El Paso?"

Charles sighed. Their target, a fellow ATF agent who'd spent two years undercover with the Esparza cartel, had requested extraction when the cartel leader's sudden death destabilized the power structure. Straightforward enough—until the agent's handler, Paul Warner, had gone missing the night before the scheduled meet up.

As per protocol, Warner was the only person who knew the undercover agent's true identity; all of the agent's electronic records had been purged. The single paper copy of his file had been safeguarded in a secure room in the agency's Dallas office, tucked away in a lockbox to which Warner had sole access. When Warner's disappearance was confirmed, Dallas Division had instituted emergency protocols to break into the lockbox, only to find it empty.

Warner had filed a bare-bones report on the extraction request, including place and time. But with everything else missing, that was all the agency had to go on. Concerns of internal corruption had prompted Dallas Division to call in Eva's team from two divisions over to handle the extraction. For all they knew, the undercover agent was already dead.

"We're looking for high-level lieutenants of the Esparza cartel," said Eva. "Phoenix's communication indicated that he wouldn't be alone. It's the only hope we have of identifying him."

"Split up?" Charles suggested.

Eva nodded, and they went their separate ways. While Eva headed to the east side, Charles went south, making a slow circuit of the restaurant and sipping casually from his wineglass. He skimmed every table and booth he passed, but it was a losing proposition. The patrons were in a partying mood, milling back and forth between tables and many not sitting in their seats at all; the servers had a hard time getting through the crowded aisles. About half the men present were Latino and relatively young.

"Anything on those cameras, Siren?" Eva asked.

"I'm doing my best, but these are shitty restaurant security cams. The resolution is terrible, and it's not like I can run face-recognition software on this system."

Charles completed his perusal of the restaurant's south section and headed up the west wall, narrowly avoiding a collision with a server bearing a trayful of cocktails.

"Worst-case scenario, we could evacuate the restaurant," Sakura said. "Position someone at each exit, watch everyone who comes out."

"And risk collateral damage in the panic that would cause?"

Charles considered the tables he wove between. If he were cartel, he wouldn't sit in a wide-open space like this; he'd want something against the wall, with easy access to at least one of the exits. This restaurant was a logistical nightmare judged from any angle, and the only tables that offered real protection were the booths along the sides. Maybe by the kitchen, for the added possibility of escape through the back . . .

He turned his head, humming in thought, and met the eyes of a man he never thought he'd see again.

He stopped short right in the aisle, shock reverberating through his body. A woman bumped into him from behind, muttered something uncomplimentary, and skirted around him. Charles's hand spasmed around his glass.

Ángel was too good to give himself away. His jaw tightened, but he otherwise showed no reaction as his eyes slid naturally past Charles's and returned to his companions, two burly, bearded Latino men at least two decades his senior.

"I . . ." Charles cleared his throat and moved away, returning to the bar before he could call any unwanted attention to himself. "I found Phoenix. Booth in the far northwest corner."

"On my way to you," Eva said.

"I'll grab a visual," Jade said. "You're sure it's Phoenix?"

Setting his wine on the bar, Charles said, "I'm positive. I know him."

"You *know* him?" Shane said.

"We worked together in Tucson," Charles said, just as Eva rejoined him.

Her eyes widened; she was the only one on the squad who understood the full import of that statement. She glanced in Ángel's direction, then back at Charles with raised eyebrows. He pressed his lips together.

"All right," said Jade, "let's see what I can do here . . . Oh. Oh, wow. *Hot*. Super hot. Turn up the A/C, Fury."

Eva groaned in exasperation. "Siren, do you remember the conversation we had about not saying every single word that goes through your head?"

"Let me see that," Sakura said to Jade. There was a short scuffle over comms, a squawk of protest from Jade, and then Sakura said, "Looks like Oscar Palomo to me—Esparza's brother-in-law. What do you guys think?"

"Agreed," Charles said. Palomo's square jaw and cold eyes were easily recognizable from the dossiers Charles and his team had reviewed on the flight to El Paso.

"We've got more than enough for a positive ID, then," Jade said. "That's Phoenix."

"He's scared," Eva said quietly.

Charles nodded. Ángel was an excellent actor—the best Charles had ever met—but his shoulders were tense, his smile strained at the edges as he chatted with the two men. Palomo laughed at something Ángel said, clapping a hand over the back of his neck and squeezing, and Charles saw Ángel's harsh swallow all the way from where he stood.

"Take a look at that security," said Charles, jerking his chin toward the table diagonal to Ángel's booth. Four beefy, hard-eyed men occupied it, their plates untouched.

"Way to be inconspicuous," Jade said with a snort. "They might as well be wearing buttons that say 'I'm cartel, ask me how!'"

"We need to be careful about this," Eva said. "I don't think they'll risk gunfire in a public place, but you never know. Sandman, Fury, how are we looking?"

"All quiet out front," Shane reported. "Well, not *quiet*, but you know what I mean."

"Ditto in the back. I'm ready to move when you are."

"All right." Eva smoothed out her dress, flipped her long blonde hair over one shoulder, and lifted her glass of wine. "Siren, be prepared to scramble cell phones on Griffin's signal."

"Roger."

Eva started across the restaurant, heading for Ángel's table, teetering on her heels as if drunk. Charles set his own glass on the bar and moved in the opposite direction, though he kept an eye on her.

As Eva reached the booth, she stumbled over her own feet and lurched forward, dumping her red wine all over Ángel's front. Ángel jerked in surprise, reaching out to steady her with one hand. The guards at the next table shifted, wary, but all it took was batted eyelashes, a smile, and a few charming apologies on Eva's part to draw forth disarmed replies from Ángel's companions. Eva tottered off, and Ángel slid out of the booth.

"Now, Siren." Charles turned and walked as quickly as he could without drawing attention. The restaurant's kitchen was massive, spanning the entire north wall, with doors on either end—one by the cartel's booth, and the other opening into the same wide hallway that provided access to the restrooms. Palomo couldn't have chosen a table more convenient to their team's plan if he'd done it deliberately.

"Cell phones scrambled. Ninety seconds."

"Whoa, they're having *two* guys follow him," Sakura said. "I thought his cover hadn't been blown?"

"That was three days ago, and before his handler disappeared." Charles ducked out of the dining room and into the restroom hallway.

"If his cover had been blown, he'd be dead, not having dinner with Palomo and company in a nice restaurant," said Shane.

Sakura hummed agreement. "Either way, this is gonna get nasty. They're only fifteen feet behind him."

"I've got your back," Eva said. "Just get Phoenix out of here."

Ángel turned the corner into the hallway, pausing when he saw Charles. God, he was beautiful, as beautiful as the last day Charles had seen him—black hair falling loose into one eye, sensual mouth thin with anxiety, fine suit tailored to flatter every long line of his lithe, toned body.

Charles pushed open the kitchen door and tilted his head sharply. Ángel ran toward him.

They slammed into the kitchen together as the guards entered the hallway. The two men shouted in Spanish and gave chase, footsteps pounding behind Charles and Ángel as they bolted past the startled kitchen staff, dodging a cook coming off the back line. He dropped an armful of dishrags with a loud yelp.

"Palomo heard the shouting," Jade said, all business now. "He's realized his cell doesn't work; he's sending the other two guards after you. *Move your ass.*"

Charles grabbed Ángel's elbow and hauled him through the back exit into the staff parking lot. Their black Suburban idled ten feet away, the rear door standing open.

The guards caught up with them then, one leaping forward to wrap an arm around Ángel's throat. Without breaking stride, Ángel flipped the man over his shoulder so he landed hard on his back on the asphalt, then reached down and snatched his gun.

Charles drew his own gun as he spun to confront the second guard, who already had Charles in his sights. Eva came flying out of the restaurant, landing a hard kick to the back of the man's leg that sent him to his knees. The man half turned, startled, and Eva grabbed his head with both hands, slamming his face into her kneecap. His nose broke with a loud *crunch.*

"Get in the car!" Eva said.

Ángel pulled his cell phone out of his jacket pocket, whipped it at the ground with a choked, angry cry, and stomped on it. Then he dove into the Suburban's backseat with Charles right on his heels. Eva followed last, yanking the door shut. Sakura floored the accelerator and peeled out of the parking lot as the other two guards emerged from the restaurant at a dead run, firing off a few wild shots.

"Palomo came out the front; he's getting in his car," Shane said. "I'll follow."

Charles looked sideways at Ángel, silent beside him with a grim face and his hand tight around his stolen gun. Sakura swung the car onto the road that would lead them to the freeway.

"Uh, guys?" Shane said a couple of minutes later. "Palomo's heading right for you. Like, *right* for you. I don't know how, but he knows where you are."

"Shit," said Sakura. She changed lanes and made an abrupt right turn. "I'll reroute."

"What's wrong?" Ángel asked.

"Palomo knows our location somehow," Charles said. "You dumped your cell—is there another way he could be tracking you?"

"Fuck, I don't know. It could be anything." Gazing down at his own body, Ángel unbuckled his fancy watch, rolled down the window, and tossed it out onto the road. The watch was followed in short order by his suit jacket, his cufflinks, and—after a moment's hesitation—his shoes.

"Okay, they're slowing down," said Shane. "They're definitely confused."

"Maintain evasive maneuvers for now," Eva instructed Sakura.

Sakura nodded, taking them on a zigzagging route through a web of quiet residential streets with guidance from Jade, who sat in the front passenger seat with her computer open to a local map. Five tense, silent minutes later, Shane reported that Palomo had ceased pursuit. Everyone but Ángel let out a collective sigh of relief.

"Fury, get us to the airport ASAP," Eva said. "Sandman, meet us there."

"Wilco, Valkyrie."

"Looks like we lost them," Charles said to Ángel.

Ángel set his gun down with a shuddering exhale, running both of his hands through his hair. He buckled his seat belt, then turned in his seat to face Charles with a small smile.

"Hello, Charles," he said.

CHAPTER TWO

"Ángel," Charles said evenly. He was stiff in his seat, his handsome face unsmiling, dark eyes as piercing and intense as Ángel remembered. His broad shoulders took up more than his fair share of the back, edging into Ángel's space.

"*Charles*," he'd introduced himself when they'd first met, Ángel fresh out of training and assigned to his first post in Tucson. "*Never Charlie*." Ángel had spent a good six months after that greeting him as *Charles-Never-Charlie* just to watch him fight off one of his rare smiles.

"Dude, that was some intense littering," said the woman in the front passenger seat, redirecting Ángel's attention. Her voice was rich and sweet, pouring over his skin like molasses.

Ángel turned to her in surprise. "God," he said, "you have the most beautiful voice I've ever heard."

"Thanks," she said with a smile. Her brown hair was plaited in a simple braid, her skin smooth and white. She held a laptop on her thighs. "I'm—"

"No," Charles interrupted. "Code names only until he's been debriefed."

"Do you think I've gone native, Charles?" Ángel said softly.

Charles's nostrils flared, but all he said was, "I'm not qualified to make that assessment, which is why information will be compartmentalized until you've been debriefed by the appropriate professionals."

So composed, so proper. Even after everything that had happened between them, and everything that had come afterward, Ángel felt the old familiar urge to provoke Charles, to prick and sting him until all that careful self-control unraveled. He reined it in with difficulty.

"He's right, though obviously you already know *his* name," said the Scandinavian goddess on Charles's other side. She leaned around him to shake Ángel's hand. "I'm this team's supervisory special agent. Valkyrie."

Aptly named. "Ángel Medina."

The woman in the front seat lifted a hand. "Siren."

"Fury," said the Asian American woman driving the car. She was short but solidly built, the sleeves of her T-shirt clinging to the impressive muscles of her shoulders and biceps. Ángel caught a glimpse of the tail end of a tattoo peeking out beneath one: —ER FI. Former Marine, then.

"Thank you all very much for the extraction," Ángel said, "but where the hell is Paul?"

His stomach dropped at the uncomfortable silence that met his question.

"His wife reported him missing this morning," Valkyrie said. "Apparently he never came home last night."

Ángel sat back in his seat, blood roaring in his ears.

"We're not sure if it was foul play or if he, ah, went somewhere willingly. His car is gone, and there were no signs of struggle at his home or his office. When Dallas broke into your lockbox, your file was missing too."

Despite her insinuation, there was no chance on this earth that Paul had betrayed Ángel somehow and then made a run for it. If he was missing, he'd been taken. "Without Paul or my file, there's no way for me to prove I am who I say I am," Ángel said numbly.

"That's not true," said Charles. "*I* know you, and so does everyone who worked with us in Tucson."

Ángel rubbed his eyes. "That's not the same. There's no paper trail now."

"The FBI is looking for Warner," Siren said. "They'll find him."

"You're absolutely sure your cover wasn't compromised?" Charles asked.

Lowering his hand, Ángel said, "If it had been, I wouldn't be sitting here talking to you now, trust me."

"So your handler disappearing with the only copy of your file right before your extraction is just the biggest coincidence of all time?"

Ángel scowled at him. Charles glared right back.

With a slight cough, Valkyrie said, "I think we can table this discussion until we've had a chance to decompress a bit."

Breaking eye contact with Charles, Ángel turned to look out the window. He pulled his sticky, wine-soaked shirt away from his chest and grimaced. "You said we're going to the airport, right? Are we flying to Dallas?"

Valkyrie shook her head. "Given Warner's disappearance, Dallas Division is concerned for your safety, so we're taking you back to our own field office."

"Which is where?"

"San Diego," Charles said.

Ángel had been undercover for so long that he'd forgotten what it was like to not have to monitor and modify his behavior, speech, and body language every single moment. Over and over, he caught himself adjusting his responses to accommodate the others' perceived expectations, his brain no longer able to react with natural spontaneity. Underlying it all was his constant companion, fear, warning him that one wrong word, one single misstep, could end in his death.

That's over now, Ángel reminded himself. *You don't have to live like that anymore.*

They arrived at a private terminal at the airport, where Ángel met the fifth member of the team, a cute, preppy white guy code-named Sandman. Forty-five minutes later, they were in the air, en route to San Diego.

Ensconced in a comfortable window seat in one of the jet's four-top seating arrangements, Ángel accepted the bottle of water Siren passed him and gave her a grateful smile. She'd claimed the seat across from him, her face alight with curiosity; Fury and Sandman occupied the other two seats. Charles and Valkyrie sat across the aisle, the latter on the phone, reporting to the resident agent in charge of the San Diego field office.

"So, two years undercover," Siren said. "How are you feeling?"

"I think it'll take some time to adjust." Ángel sipped his water.

Fury gave him a considering look, rubbing a hand over her short, spiky hair. "All the trouble the Esparza cartel's been having the past couple of years—that was you, huh?"

"Well, it was a joint task force with the DEA. They had an agent undercover as well, though she wasn't as central to the operation. I'm pretty sure she requested extraction too, but I lost track of her a few days ago when things went crazy."

On the other side of the aisle, Valkyrie ended her call and started texting. Charles was reading his tablet, doing a pretty good job of pretending he wasn't listening to their conversation.

"How'd you even get undercover with them in the first place?" Sandman asked.

"I was Raúl Esparza's piece on the side," said Ángel.

He watched for Charles's reaction from the corner of his eye, and he wasn't disappointed. Charles went abruptly, absolutely still, his eyes fixed on his tablet screen.

"His . . . piece on the side?" Sandman said, as if that couldn't possibly mean what he thought it did.

"We were fucking," Ángel said, so there would be no confusion.

His three seatmates regarded him with open mouths. Charles's lips thinned out and his knuckles tightened around the edges of his tablet. Only Valkyrie showed no reaction, continuing to text without acknowledging that she'd heard anything out of the ordinary.

Old resentments flared to life as Ángel watched Charles. The wounds from their last fight had never healed, and knowing what Charles must be thinking now ripped them open further.

"You were Raúl Esparza's *boyfriend*?" Siren said, her eyes wide.

"More like his mistress. Kept man, I guess you could say."

Charles dropped his tablet on the table with a rattle and straightened his jacket, cracking his neck from side to side. Valkyrie glanced up from her phone to briefly meet his eyes.

Fuck, why was Ángel doing this to himself? There was no reason to be so blunt—except he *wanted* to upset Charles, to hurt him, even if it meant hurting himself as well.

Raising his eyebrows, Sandman asked, "How does a cartel boss get away with having a kept *man*?"

Ángel shrugged. "He also had a wife and several girlfriends. It was no threat to his *machismo* to fuck a man the same way he would a woman."

"Ah, I love the smell of misogyny in the morning," said Siren.

Fury nodded with a derisive snort. "Plus, I wouldn't want to be the one to tell Esparza he couldn't fuck whoever he wanted to fuck. Sounds like a good way to get your throat slit."

"You're not wrong," Ángel said.

"We heard about his assassination," Sandman said. "Rival cartel, right?"

"Yes. I was there when it happened. It was . . ." Ángel trailed off, not fighting the tide of memories—the *crack* of the bullet, Raúl's head exploding, the spray of blood that had drenched Ángel's hair and the back of his neck. "Unpleasant."

Siren tilted her head. "That's why you had to leave, even though your cover wasn't blown. You weren't safe without him."

Ángel nodded. She didn't need to know the gory details; besides, she could probably fill in the blanks well enough herself.

"The Esparza cartel doesn't operate in California." Siren reached across the table, resting her hand lightly atop Ángel's. "You'll be safe there."

Safe was a word Ángel had lost touch with a long time ago. How safe could he be, really, with Paul missing?

He glanced at Charles, who sat staring out his window with his arms folded across his chest. Ángel had burned that bridge thoroughly before he left, and what could have been a reassuring point of familiarity to ease his return was only another source of pain.

Refocusing on Siren, Ángel mustered a smile. "Tell me about San Diego," he said. "I've never been."

They touched down in San Diego around midnight. The team split up and headed in different directions, only Charles and Valkyrie remaining to escort Ángel to an ATF safe house. Charles didn't say a single word to Ángel as they handed him over to the waiting agents, and for once Ángel felt no desire to goad him. He was beyond exhausted, fraying at the edges from the stress of the past few days.

The safe house was a bland suburban ranch, no different from its neighbors if one didn't recognize the steel-reinforced doors and bulletproof glass in the windows. Ángel turned down the agents' offer of food and retired to the bedroom at the back of the house, where the windows were further barred with thick shutters. He stood in the center of the room for a moment, struggling with himself, before he gave in and checked under the bed and inside the closet.

Assured that he was alone, Ángel went into the attached bathroom and started the shower. He stood in front of the mirror as he stripped out of his clothes, examining the livid bruises Oscar had left on his arm that morning. They weren't as bad as the ones on his hips from the night before, or the bite mark just above his collarbone. Fucker had broken the skin.

Ángel frowned at his reflection and then turned away.

A hot shower did wonders to relax him. He changed into the boxers and T-shirt he'd been provided—both a couple of sizes too large—turned off the lights, and slid into bed, lying on his side so he faced the locked door. After a few minutes, he leaned over and switched the bedside lamp back on.

Hours later, he was still wide-awake, staring at that door.

CHAPTER THREE

After they dropped Ángel off at the safe house, Charles and Eva changed into street clothes and went to Susie's, a twenty-four-hour diner near their office. For Charles, there was something comforting about the way diners looked the same everywhere in America. He could just as easily have been back home in Indiana, hitting the greasy spoon a few blocks from his high school with his teammates after a football game.

Eva was kind enough not to address the proverbial elephant until they'd been served their food. "So," she said as the waitress walked away, "this must be weird for you."

"You could say that." Charles stabbed a link of breakfast sausage with his fork.

"Ángel is gorgeous."

"Yes, and he's *very* aware of it, believe me."

Eva squirted a healthy amount of ketchup onto her cheeseburger, then more onto her plate for her fries. "I'm trying to decide whether or not we need to disclose your history with him to Ed," she said, referring to the RAC of their field office.

"There's nothing to disclose," said Charles. "He and I had a sexual relationship *years* ago, and we haven't seen or spoken with each other since."

"You had a sexual relationship that blew up in your faces so badly it made him leave town."

"That wasn't my fault," Charles said, his voice tight.

Eva popped a fry into her mouth, her silence saying more than words could.

"He fucked my trainer, Eva."

"You told me you two weren't monogamous. It's not like Ángel was your boyfriend; you were sneaking around hooking up in secret."

Charles snapped a piece of bacon in half. "That's not the point. He fucked my trainer *on my birthday*. We'd made plans, he knew I was on my way over, and he just couldn't have cared less."

The stunned pain of the memory was still fresh—letting himself into Ángel's apartment, looking forward to the night they'd planned, and discovering Ángel bent over his couch, taking it up the ass from a guy Charles had introduced him to only days earlier. Charles had stood in the doorway for a full minute before either of them noticed he was there.

"He didn't even apologize," Charles said, dropping the bacon onto his plate. When he had recovered from his shock and started shouting, Ángel had shown no sign of remorse—he'd screamed back, and things had devolved quickly from there.

Their relationship had been tumultuous even before that point, a series of thrilling highs and wretched lows, and finding Ángel with Jared had pushed Charles over the edge. It had all come pouring out of him at once—all his frustration and pain and confusion, every insecurity that their secret affair had stirred within him, with Ángel the only viable target. His grandmother would have torn a strip off his hide if she'd heard the pure venom that had come out of Charles's mouth that night.

"I'm concerned that you won't be able to stay professional around him, given your history. And vice versa." Eva took a bite of her cheeseburger, regarding Charles with thoughtful eyes as she chewed and swallowed. "The way he told us what he'd been doing undercover—that was for your benefit, wasn't it? He was trying to get a rise out of you."

"Probably," Charles said. "He's like that—or he used to be, at least. I don't know him anymore. Two years is a long time, especially for someone who's been deep undercover."

"If your relationship had ended on good terms, or even neutral ones, I wouldn't give this a second thought. As it is . . ."

He suppressed a sharp remark about how Eva, with her trouble-free ten-year marriage and three beautiful, perfect children, couldn't possibly understand how things stood between Ángel and himself. It was petty, uncalled for; Ángel had always brought out the worst in him.

When he wasn't bringing out the best.

Charles twitched with irritation and shoved the thought away.

"I won't say anything to Ed for now," Eva said. "I know you don't want to come out at work, and I don't want to be the person who forces you into that position. But Ed does need you to come in tomorrow to give a statement about your history with Ángel at the Tucson office. It'll help establish his identity since all of his records are gone."

"That's fine."

Eva sipped her water. "It'll just be a couple of hours."

"I didn't have any plans," said Charles.

They ate in silence for a couple of minutes until Eva said, "He won't stay here. Once he's been reinstated, there's no way he'll want to stay in the same office as you. I wouldn't even want to be in the same division. He'll be gone in a few days."

Charles nodded. A few days, and everything would go back to normal.

Eva didn't mention Ángel again. Once they'd finished eating, she drove Charles home. He let himself into his quiet, dark apartment, dropped his keys and wallet in the bowl by the door, and slipped out of his shoes.

The apartment was all but empty; most of the furniture and all of the art and knickknacks had been Amy's, and she'd taken them with her when she left. A place this size was ridiculous for one person living alone, but it would be more expensive for Charles to break the lease than to just stick it out to the end.

The blinds over the sliding glass patio doors in the living room and master bedroom were drawn shut—Charles couldn't remember the last time he'd opened them. He didn't bother turning on any lights until he was in the bedroom, pulling his cell out of his pocket and heading for the charging station on his nightstand.

He'd deleted Ángel's number from his phone within minutes after leaving Ángel's apartment that day. When Ángel didn't show up for work the following Monday, Charles had assumed he'd requested transfer to another office. Charles hadn't just been relieved, he'd been *glad*—viciously, spitefully pleased that Ángel had been the one to run away, the one to feel like he couldn't show his face.

Except Ángel hadn't transferred offices. While Charles had been going about his daily life in Tucson, filled with self-righteous ire, Ángel had been in Mexico, fucking one of the most violent criminals in North America for access to information that had eventually crippled the cartel's operations and infrastructure.

Charles's phone creaked under the pressure of his grip. He shook his head, set the phone in the dock, and stretched out his aching fingers.

Just a few days.

"Looks good," Ed Campos said, skimming Charles's signed report. He was a Mexican American man in his early fifties, a bit stout with age but still powerfully muscular, his beard and moustache neatly groomed. "I've reached out to Tucson's RAC as well. She's new, but she put me in touch with the guy who was in charge when you and Medina worked there. I should hear back from him tomorrow."

"Has the FBI made any progress in the search for Warner?" Charles asked.

Ed shrugged and dropped Charles's report onto his desk. "They don't report to me."

Keeping a tight lid on his frustration, Charles said, "Medina could still be in danger. There's no way Warner's disappearance isn't linked to his extraction."

"I agree," Ed said, "but if Warner was rotten, either he waited too long to flip on Medina or he told the wrong people, because from what I've heard, there's just no way Oscar Palomo knew Medina was a mole at the time of his extraction."

Charles inclined his head, conceding Ed's point.

"The other alternative is that somebody figured out Warner knew the identity of a mole in the cartel, snatched him, and he held out long enough for Medina to get clear. That's bad news for Warner, but Medina should be fine. Even if the cartel got their hands on his file, Warner didn't know he'd end up in San Diego."

"Once they know his name, they'll be able to find him anywhere," said Charles.

Ed spread his hands. "That's true to an extent, and of course the agency will do everything within its power to protect him, but *we're* going to have trouble proving that Medina is who he says he is. The cartel was floundering before Esparza was assassinated; now they're fighting over succession on top of everything else. Tracking Medina down under the circumstances would take serious time and resources, not to mention the risks of crossing into other cartels' territory to confront him here, where he has the full support of the agency behind him."

He had a point, but Charles didn't like the loose thread created by Warner's unexplained absence. An undercover agent's life depended on a clean extraction.

Watching Charles's face, Ed's eyes softened. "Look, I get it," he said, leaning forward to prop his forearms on his desk. "You know this guy; you worked with him. We're not gonna just hang Medina out to dry. After he's been reinstated, I'll encourage him to choose a posting as far away from the US–Mexico border as possible. New York, Chicago, somewhere interesting."

"Thank you, sir," Charles said. Ángel would never go for that; he hated the cold.

"Anyway, he's taking his polygraph right now. Assuming everything checks out, we'll set him up in a motel for the time being, give him a stipend for food and clothing. Apparently all his stuff is in storage in Dallas, and only Warner had the key."

"He's on the box?" Charles said, his hands tightening around the arms of his chair. "Could I have permission to observe?"

"Sure, knock yourself out." Ed rose to his feet, gesturing for Charles to do the same. "I've gotta get home. I'm supposed to be watching my grandkids today, and my wife is going to kill me if I leave her alone with them any longer. Three-year-old twins are no joke."

On a Sunday afternoon, the office was quiet, only a few agents and administrative personnel scattered here and there. Charles headed for the interrogation suites in the back and let himself into the viewing room of Ángel's.

A bored agent—Ángel's escort—was slumped in a chair in the corner, his arms crossed over his chest. He barely glanced up at Charles's entrance.

"Campos gave me permission to observe," Charles said, just in case.

The agent shrugged, and Charles turned his attention to the two-way glass. Ángel sat on the other side, his chair facing away from the examiner's desk. He had a blood pressure cuff strapped around his right bicep, two corrugated rubber tubes placed over his chest and abdomen, and a couple of electrodes attached to the fingers of his left hand. His eyes were hollowed out with exhaustion, and his oversize clothing made him look deceptively vulnerable.

"Do you know the current location of Special Agent Paul Warner?" asked the examiner, a woman in a fluffy angora sweater and horn-rimmed glasses.

"No," Ángel said.

"Have you ever physically assaulted another person?" she said next, an irrelevant question designed to provoke a deliberate physiological reaction, so it could be compared against Ángel's reactions to the relevant questions.

"Yes."

"How long have they been at this?" Charles asked the observing agent.

"About twenty minutes. Shouldn't be too much longer."

Charles watched as the woman interrogated Ángel about his time undercover, based on questions he'd have answered in his pretest and interspersed with irrelevant comparison questions. While the polygraph was required of all returning undercover agents, it was pretty much bullshit, and there was no reason someone like Ángel—a natural-born liar backed up by a lifetime of experience and a master's degree in psychology—couldn't get around it if he wanted. After this, though, he'd be thoroughly questioned by a therapist trained to debrief agents who'd been undercover. Charles trusted that a lot more.

"During your time undercover, did you ever find yourself empathizing with Raúl Esparza?"

With a long, slow blink, Ángel said, "Yes."

"Did you ever provide Raúl Esparza with information you knew would aid him in his criminal activities?"

"No."

"Did you ever deliberately withhold information from your ATF handler that you knew would have prevented criminal activities from taking place?"

"Yes," Ángel said, frustration written all over his face. Charles had been there before, in that chair; the requirement to answer *yes* or *no* without elaboration could be maddening.

"Did you ever withhold such information in a situation where you did not believe its disclosure would compromise your cover?"

Ángel relaxed. "No."

"Have you ever told a lie to someone you cared about?"

"Yes."

"Were you in love with Raúl Esparza?"

Ángel's entire body jerked. "What the fuck kind of question is that?" he said, looking at the examiner over his shoulder. "That wasn't in the pretest."

"Agent Medina," the woman said primly, "please face forward and only answer yes or no. Were you in love with Raúl Esparza?"

"*No*," Ángel snapped.

"You're having a strong response to this question," she said, eyeing her laptop.

"Wow, I wonder why?" Ángel said. "Maybe it's because you're accusing me of being the kind of idiot who would fall in love with a murderous psychopath through sheer proximity!"

"It's a question, Agent Medina, not an accusation, and please—"

"Esparza once shot one of his own men right in front of me, just to make a point to his other lieutenants," said Ángel, talking over her. "Then he turned around and offered me more champagne like nothing had happened."

The examiner paled, her throat working, and Charles rolled his eyes. How could she not see how Ángel was manipulating her—deliberately making her uncomfortable so she'd lose her motivation to pursue this line of questioning?

"Why don't you ask me again if I was in love with the man who once fucked me while his hands were still bloody from gutting someone like a fish," Ángel said.

That clinched it. The examiner grimaced and shook her head, though Ángel couldn't see her. "Ah, no, that's all right. Let's move on."

Charles stepped away from the glass, noticing that the agent in the corner was no longer quite so bored. The examiner wasn't going to go anywhere near the subject of Ángel's personal relationship with Esparza again, though, not after Ángel's perfect little tantrum. She'd probably end the exam early.

Giving the window one last glance, Charles left the room. He wasn't going to get the answers he wanted this way.

Of course, it would help if he knew what his questions were.

Much to Ángel's amusement, the motel room was indistinguishable from the safe house—same oatmeal carpet, bland furniture, and absolute lack of anything resembling a soul. He set down the bags of groceries and clothing he'd bought at Target and gazed around the bleak room.

This was fucking ridiculous. All of his stuff was thirteen hundred miles away, and he couldn't get to it unless Paul's frantically worried wife managed to come up with the key to the storage unit. He couldn't access his own bank accounts because he didn't have his card or his ID. At least the San Diego office had supplied him with a cell phone—heavily guarded against external access, but linked back to the agency's servers so they could locate him through its GPS in case of emergency. Or, he supposed, in case he turned out to have gone native after all.

Not exactly the welcome home he'd been expecting.

Ángel was wrung out, worn down to the bone from his sleepless night, that inane polygraph, and the three-hour psych eval that had followed. Standing alone in the motel room, he couldn't decide whether he wanted to collapse into bed or use the little money he had left from his stipend to get drunk off his ass.

A soft knock sounded at the door. Ángel stiffened and spun around, staring at it with suspicion. He'd surrendered the gun he'd taken off Oscar's bodyguard, and he wouldn't be issued a service weapon until he'd been reinstated. The agency didn't have the manpower to give him a protective detail 24-7, so if the person outside wanted to do Ángel harm, he was pretty much fucked.

Ángel sidled up to the window, twitched back the curtain, and peeked outside. Drawing a sharp breath, he yanked the security chain off the door and wrenched it open.

"Jesenia?" he said incredulously, greeting the DEA agent who'd been undercover with him in the Esparza cartel.

"Ángel, *Dios mío*, you're really all right." Jesenia threw her arms around Ángel, and he returned the hug. "I couldn't believe it until I saw you myself."

"How did you know I was here?" Ángel asked as Jesenia stepped back.

"I got out myself a couple of days ago, and when you never showed up in Dallas, I went to Bauer. He told me about Paul and that you'd been diverted to San Diego. I may have pulled a couple of strings to get in touch with your office here."

"Well, come in, please." Ángel moved away from the door and shut it behind Jesenia as soon as she'd entered the room, slotting the security chain back in place.

Jesenia Santos had the kind of nondescript features that made her perfect for undercover work, attracting neither negative nor overly positive attention. She had her black hair up in a messy bun, and her lanky, athletic body was clad in a T-shirt and jeans that nobody would give a second glance.

Her role in the cartel had been minor, running drugs north across the border—but she'd been the one to introduce Ángel to one of Raúl Esparza's lackeys, enabling them to maintain regular contact under the pretext that they'd been friends before. Despite his momentary shock, Ángel couldn't have been happier to see her here. At least she'd understand some of what he was going through.

"I'm so sorry about Paul," Jesenia said, her eyes sympathetic. "I can't imagine what must be going through your mind right now."

"I'm trying not to think about it, honestly." There was nothing Ángel could do to help Paul now.

Jesenia frowned as she took in the motel room. "This is where they're putting you up?"

"It's just temporary."

"I have to fly back to Dallas tonight, unfortunately, but will you let me treat you to an early dinner?" Jesenia asked. "I hate the thought of you stranded in this city all alone."

Ángel smiled. "Sure, thanks."

There were few enticing options in the strip malls that populated the drab stretch of highway by his motel. Neither of them were in the mood for pizza, Ángel didn't like Thai, and Jesenia turned her nose up at the cheap, inauthentic Mexican joints.

It had been years since Ángel had eaten a genuine American hamburger, so they ended up at a casual burger restaurant, settling into a corner booth where Ángel could put his back against the wall. Jesenia didn't comment on his choice of seating.

"So how'd your debrief go?" she asked, skimming the laminated menu.

"About how you'd expect. You'd think I was the first federal agent to use sex to establish and maintain my cover."

"It *is* technically against protocol."

"Which of course has stopped everyone from doing it before," Ángel said.

Jesenia laughed.

Ángel put down his menu, restless, and looked out the window at the parking lot. It was that awkward period between lunch and dinner, and the restaurant was mostly empty. "If either Raúl or I had been a woman, nobody would say shit about it. Judgmental dicks."

"They'll get over it. Nobody can fault your results."

He sighed. "I wish I'd had more time; we were so close. If Raúl hadn't been shot . . ."

Jesenia dropped her menu and stared at him. "You *can't* be serious. Ángel, you—"

She was interrupted by the arrival of their server. They gave him their orders and handed over their menus, and when they were alone once more, Jesenia lowered her voice and switched to Spanish for good measure.

"You can't be serious," she said again. "You didn't *have* more time. Three months, tops, and that would have been pushing it. Esparza was falling in love with you."

"I had it under control," said Ángel.

Jesenia snorted. "No, you didn't. Everyone was talking about it. It was one thing for Esparza to keep a pretty boy toy, and a totally different thing for him to fall in love with one. That's crossing the line for men like that."

Ángel shifted, the vinyl of the booth creaking beneath his weight.

"A few more months, and you would never have gotten out of there alive," Jesenia continued, relentless. "Esparza would never have let you go. He'd have sent people after you to drag you back by the hair if he had to. And the other men in the cartel would have killed him *and* you for that."

"I don't think it would have been *that* dire," Ángel said, smoothing his hands over the chipped Formica table. He had let things go too far, though; by the time he recognized the shift in Raúl's feelings for him, it had been way too late to change them without endangering himself further.

"You weren't watching from the outside." Jesenia gave a one-shouldered shrug. "This is a terrible thing to say, but you're lucky Esparza died when he did."

"Yeah, I feel lucky," Ángel muttered.

Brushing her fingers over the back of Ángel's hand, Jesenia changed the subject, steering the conversation around to her family's relief at her return and her plans for the leave she'd been granted before going back to work. Ángel was content to listen, scarfing down his burger and imagining what it was like to return from years undercover to people who welcomed you with open arms. Besides Paul and Jesenia, Ángel had no real personal ties left; his friendships hadn't been the sort to survive an unexplained two-year absence, and his family was a sick joke. As far as Ángel knew, his parents hadn't even noticed he'd disappeared, and that was just fine with him.

Jesenia paid the check and brought Ángel back to his motel, where she lingered on the threshold. "I wish I didn't have to go back so soon," she said. "I could try to stay a little longer . . ."

"Don't be silly," Ángel said. "You have a life to get back to. I won't be here that long, anyway."

"All right. Here, let me text my phone from yours so we have each other's new numbers." Once Jesenia had done that, she handed Ángel's new cell back and squeezed his arm. "If you need me, I'm just a phone call away. Any time."

"Thank you so much for coming," Ángel said, unable to express the full depth of his gratitude. He felt worlds better now than he had that morning.

Jesenia kissed his cheek before she left, and Ángel locked the door behind her. He turned around to consider the tiny room.

The safest, smartest choice would be to stay in for the rest of the evening, watch some TV, and die a slow and painful death of boredom. Or he could go out—not to get drunk, like he'd been contemplating earlier, but to at least try to get back into the rhythm of a normal life.

Ángel stripped out of his shirt as he headed for the shower. He'd never been much of a guy for the safe, smart choice.

CHAPTER FOUR

"This is a terrible idea," Charles said out loud while sitting in his car in the motel parking lot.

Unfortunately, the common sense he prided himself on tended to go on vacation whenever Ángel was in the mix, and it wasn't going to stop him from knocking on that door any more than it had stopped him from hooking up with Ángel in the first place. He blew out a breath, grabbed the tote bag on the passenger seat, and got out of the car.

Ángel's room was the corner unit on the second floor. Charles rapped his knuckles against the door; a few moments later, the curtains over the window fluttered subtly, and Ángel swung the door open wide.

He was soaking wet, having clearly just gotten out of the shower, wearing only a threadbare motel towel low on his hips. Charles's brain short-circuited.

Ángel smirked.

"I would have waited for you to put some clothes on," Charles said, already so irritated that he had trouble getting the words out. This did not bode well.

"Doesn't bother me." Ángel leaned against the doorway, cocking one hip, and his towel slipped a little farther. Beads of water streamed down his chest and over his flat, ripped abdomen, begging to be licked off.

Charles jerked his eyes back to Ángel's face. "It's not safe for you to stand here with the door open."

Rolling his eyes, Ángel moved away from the door to let Charles inside. Charles made sure the door was bolted and the security chain had been thrown before he set the tote bag on the table.

"Ed told me about your situation," he said. "I brought you some food."

"How generous," said Ángel, his hands on his hips. "Why don't you tell me why you're *really* here?"

Calm. Professional. Deep breaths. "I . . ."

Ángel tugged off his towel, baring his sleek, beautiful body in all its slippery wet glory.

"Jesus *Christ*, Ángel," Charles snapped, turning his head aside. His resolve to stay calm and professional shattered like fine glass. "What's wrong with you?"

Ángel lifted the towel to scrub his hair. "So uptight, Charles. It's nothing you haven't seen before."

"It's nothing half the men you've met haven't seen before."

"Oh, so you've come to *slut-shame* me," Ángel said, flinging his arms wide. "What a shocker. I'd have thought you'd learned the words to a different song by now."

"That's not . . ." Charles clenched his hands into fists and breathed through his nose. He couldn't help a quick sideways glance at Ángel; his ass was a crime against man. "This isn't why I came here. Could you please get dressed?"

Ángel scooped a pair of boxer briefs off the bed and put them on. They were a marginal improvement over his nudity, the stretchy fabric outlining his cock in front and clinging to his narrow hips and lush ass in back. To have convinced Ángel to concede even that much was a victory though, so Charles didn't press for more.

"Your debrief went well," Charles said.

"They wouldn't have let me leave the office if it hadn't." Retrieving his towel from the floor, Ángel rubbed down his chest and arms. "What do you want, Charles?"

The question had been nagging at Charles all afternoon, refusing to allow him any peace. "I need to ask you about something you said during your polygraph."

Ángel went still, narrowing his eyes. "You read a transcript of my polygraph?"

"I was there, actually. I watched part of it."

Ángel flung his wet towel at Charles, who caught it with an exasperated grunt. "Are you fucking *kidding* me?"

"I had permission—"

"Should I get you a copy of my therapist's notes too, just to make sure you didn't miss anything?"

"Ángel, come on, I don't want to fight," Charles said, though that wasn't entirely true. That old familiar itch crawled beneath his skin, that low burn twisting in his gut. Fighting with Ángel was almost as good as fucking him. "Just hear me out."

Ángel crossed his arms and waited with a lifted eyebrow.

"When the examiner asked if you'd ever empathized with Esparza, you said yes."

"Of course I did," Ángel said. "It's impossible for an undercover agent to do their job if they can't empathize with their mark."

Charles shook his head, bewildered. "Esparza killed hundreds of people, and those are only the deaths he's *directly* responsible for."

"Yes, and he hated bananas, and he was embarrassed by the difficulty he had speaking English, and his daughter was the most important person in the world to him." Ángel sighed. "Human beings can't be boiled down to a single aspect of their personalities, no matter how heinous. Raúl was a terrible person—but he was still a *person*, and empathizing doesn't imply condoning. You've never been able to understand that."

Charles's heart clenched at the casual way Ángel referred to Esparza by his first name. "I know you told the examiner you didn't, but . . . did you love him?"

Ángel's face went blank, save for the lines of tension around his eyes and mouth. "Get the fuck out of here," he said with cold fury.

"I didn't think you did, but you completely overreacted to that question, even though you must have known they'd ask something like it," Charles said, barreling on despite the clear warning in Ángel's glare. "You put so much effort into making sure the examiner wouldn't go anywhere near those questions again. There was something you didn't want her to know, and that doesn't make sense, unless . . ." Oh. Oh, *obvious*. "He was in love with *you*."

Ángel's nostrils flared.

He had a bite mark on his collarbone, Charles noticed for the first time, now that he wasn't making such a pointed effort not to look at Ángel's body. Bruises on his hips in the shape of fingers.

Charles stepped toward him. "Ángel, please, I need to know if this is my fault," he said, giving voice to his anxiety for the first time.

"What are you talking about?"

"The fight we had, the way we ended things . . . Is that why you did this? Did I drive you to him?"

Ángel blinked, and all the rage went out of him, his shoulders slumping. "You don't know a single fucking thing about me, do you?" he said wearily.

Charles moved closer, close enough now that he could touch Ángel if he reached out. "If he hurt you—"

"I need you to leave."

"This isn't what I wanted," said Charles, his insides twisted with guilt and anger and pain that was almost as strong as it had been two years ago. "I was angry—I'm still angry, if I'm being honest—but it's driving me crazy, thinking about what he must have done to you, thinking I could be responsible for it—"

"It shouldn't," Ángel said, his voice low and dangerous. "I loved it."

Charles shut his mouth. Too late, he recognized the spiteful flash in Ángel's eyes. He should have left when Ángel asked him to, but he hadn't, and he'd pushed too far, and now Ángel was going to make him pay for that.

"Fucking Raúl was the only good part of that assignment." Ángel stalked toward him; Charles backed up, giving ground because he didn't want to engage Ángel in a physical confrontation. "I enjoyed it. I looked *forward* to it. He was the best I've ever had."

"Don't do this," Charles said. He knew, rationally, that Ángel was provoking him, trying to get under his skin. Knowing that should have meant it didn't work.

It was working. God, was it working. Charles's breath came short, his blood pumping with adrenaline. He couldn't look away from Ángel's face.

Ángel got Charles up against the wall and planted his hands on either side of Charles's shoulders. "Say what you will about Raúl, but the man knew how to use his cock. You can't imagine how good it felt inside me, fucking me, filling me up—"

Charles grabbed Ángel's forearms, intending to push him away. Ángel twisted out of his grip and shoved Charles hard, so that his back slammed into the wall. Charles exhaled harshly.

"How dare you come in here all prissy and sanctimonious and try to make the last two years of my life about *you*?" Ángel said. He fisted his hands in the collar of Charles's shirt, as if he was about to shove him again. Charles seized both his wrists, but Ángel didn't move, didn't try to free himself again. "I don't want your condescending pity, Charles, or your fake guilt. I don't want anything from you anym—"

Charles yanked him close and kissed him, their mouths crashing together. Ángel wrenched his wrists out of Charles's hands only to throw his arms around Charles's neck.

The kiss was messy and violent, Charles clutching at every inch of Ángel's warm, damp skin that he could reach, Ángel's nails digging into Charles's scalp through his short hair. Charles was hard—had been hard since Ángel had shoved him into the wall—and Ángel caught up quickly, his swelling cock pressed against Charles's.

Charles groaned low in his throat, ears ringing and body shaking with the intensity of his desire. He pushed one hand down the back of Ángel's underwear to grope his ass. Ángel grunted in response, dropping his own hands to Charles's shirt buttons. Together, they wrestled Charles out of his shirt, and Charles slipped an arm around Ángel's waist, herding him back toward the bed. They kissed as they stumbled along, biting at each other's mouths, Ángel tugging open Charles's belt and fly.

When Ángel's thighs hit the edge of the mattress, Charles broke the kiss and pushed him backward. Ángel sprawled, propping himself on his forearms, all long, lean limbs and smooth golden-brown skin. His cocksucking mouth was swollen, his tousled, wet hair in his eyes as he looked up at Charles.

Charles toed out of his shoes and hesitated with his hands on his waistband.

"Take your fucking pants off," Ángel said, kicking Charles's thigh.

Charles stripped off the rest of his clothes while Ángel shimmied out of his boxer briefs. Then Charles was on him again, crushing Ángel into the bed with his weight, kissing the fuck out of him and frotting their cocks together. Ángel's hands roamed Charles's sides, grasping at his shoulders, raking over his chest.

There were times it had been soft and sweet between them, bodies moving together languidly, Ángel gasping compliments into Charles's ear about his strength, the breadth of his shoulders, the rhythm of his hips.

This wasn't one of those times. Ángel scraped his fingernail over Charles's nipple, then pinched and twisted viciously. Charles bucked against him.

"Are you going to fuck me or what?" Ángel said.

Charles bit Ángel's throat, sucking until Ángel squirmed and cursed underneath him. Having successfully retaliated, Charles released his flesh and said, "I don't have anything."

"Bedside drawer."

Frowning, Charles reached over and opened the drawer in the nightstand. Sure enough, it contained a brand-new bottle of lube and an unopened box of condoms.

"When did you get this?" he asked as he dropped them on the bed.

"When I went to Target today." Ángel still rubbed his cock against Charles's, his eyes half-closed. "I was going to go out tonight."

Charles's jaw tightened. "Of course you were." He rose, grabbed Ángel's hips, and flipped him onto his stomach.

Far from protesting the new position, Ángel arranged himself on his knees, flexing his hips to present Charles with his delicious, round ass. Charles cracked open the lube and squirted it messily over his fingers without looking away.

The satisfied sigh Ángel let out when Charles slid a finger inside him unraveled Charles's self-control. "You can't even go a single day without this, can you?" he said, giving Ángel a second finger too soon. "How were you even going to get to a bar? Bus, cab? You don't have any money."

Ángel rocked back against Charles's hand, his ass tight but accommodating, taking the penetration with no problem. "I would have figured something out."

Deliberately avoiding Ángel's prostate, Charles corkscrewed his fingers in and out of his hole. "Probably wouldn't have made it past the parking lot before you were bending over the trunk of some guy's car."

Ángel's laugh was sharp and cruel. "Speaking from experience?"

Charles *hadn't* been thinking about that time, but now that Ángel had reminded him, he couldn't think of anything else. Though it had been illegal and stupid and so vulgar, he'd once taken Ángel over the trunk of his car in the parking lot of his apartment building—because when Ángel Medina wanted a cock up his ass, it was very difficult to refuse.

The fact that he hadn't wanted to refuse was beside the point.

He pushed his fingertips against Ángel's prostate and pulsed them until Ángel cried out, his smugness collapsing into a litany of breathless moans as his hands clawed at the comforter. Ángel's prostate was insanely sensitive; with enough stimulation, he could come without touching his cock, something that had always fascinated Charles.

"Fuck, fuck, you *asshole*," Ángel said when Charles pulled his fingers out. His entire body trembled.

Charles ripped open the box of condoms and fished one out, rolling it onto his cock with unsteady hands. Ángel turned onto his back. Annoyed, Charles took hold of his hip to flip him back over, but Ángel slapped his hand away.

"If you're going to fuck me, you're going to look me in the face when you do it," he said.

"Fine." Charles grabbed the backs of Ángel's knees and spread his legs wide, lifting Ángel's ass off the bed and settling it on his own thighs. He had to release one of Ángel's knees for a moment to guide his cock into place, but as soon as the head popped in, his hand was back in position, keeping Ángel splayed open for him. Charles rolled his hips, working his cock into Ángel's slick, tight hole with slow thrusts.

"Ah, fuck, I forgot how big your cock is." Ángel braced one hand against the headboard, turning his face aside and panting into the pillow. "*Shit.*"

Charles had to close his eyes, because if he watched the rapturous expression on Ángel's face as he was opened up by Charles's cock, Charles would blow his load right now. He gripped Ángel's legs and fucked into him until he bottomed out, then pulled back and slammed home again with one rough thrust. Sparks exploded behind his closed eyelids.

Ángel's free hand scrabbled at Charles's hip, pulling him forward. "Yeah, fuck me, come on. Come on."

"Oh, God," Charles said, surrendering to his body's—and Ángel's—demands. He snapped his hips, pounding into Ángel, thrilling to the way Ángel moaned and moved with him and accepted every aggressive stroke like he'd been made for it. "Take it. Fucking take it."

"Give it to me harder, then," Ángel ground out.

Charles opened his eyes, startled to find Ángel watching his face closely. Ángel stiffened and looked away, but Charles caught his chin and turned him back. Ángel's freed leg wrapped around Charles's waist without missing a beat, the rhythm of their hips never faltering.

"Did Esparza fuck you like this?" Charles said, hoarse.

Ángel met his eyes with a defiant glare. "Better."

Charles barked out a laugh. "You've always been a little fucking liar. If you ever tell the truth, it's completely by accident."

Before Ángel could respond, Charles dropped the other leg and lowered his body, leaning forward on his hands so he could drive his cock deeper into Ángel's ass. Ángel shouted, both of his legs clenching against Charles's sides, and grabbed for his own cock where it bobbed rigid and leaking between them.

Ángel's cock was as gorgeous as the rest of him, long and cut, the glistening head flushed dark with blood. Charles watched him stroke it, remembering how good that cock had felt in his mouth. Spurred by the memories, Charles changed his angle, fucking Ángel quick and shallow so he could catch his prostate over and over. Ángel's answering cry was high and thready; he writhed, biting his lip as he stared down at where their bodies came together.

"That's it," Charles said, speeding up. "That's it, you like that?"

Ángel pushed Charles's shoulders, knocking him backward, his cock slipping free of Ángel's ass. Charles hissed in discomfort, but before he could worry that he'd crossed the line, Ángel rolled them both over and climbed on top. He sank onto Charles's cock with a throaty moan.

"I like this better," he said, daring Charles to challenge him.

Fine by Charles. He planted his feet flat against the bed and held Ángel's hips, helping Ángel bounce on his cock. Ángel braced one hand on Charles's chest, jerking himself off with the other while he rode Charles, both of them exhaling punched-out breaths every time Ángel's ass smacked against Charles's hip bones.

Charles wasn't going to last long, watching Ángel so passionate and uninhibited on top of him. Once, he would have tried to hold out, determined for Ángel to come first, but now he didn't give a shit. He tightened his grip, rutting away, pumping up into Ángel's sleek heat until he came in hot, throbbing pulses that sucked all the energy out of the rest of his body.

"Ugh, you selfish dick," Ángel said when Charles sagged into the mattress. He pulled Charles's hand off his hip and wrapped it around his cock. "Get me off."

As Ángel circled his hips, rubbing his prostate against Charles's shaft, Charles tugged his cock tight and hard, just the way he liked it. Ángel sucked in a sharp breath, then slapped Charles's chest and threw his head back in orgasm, come spurting over Charles's hand and splattering onto his abdomen. Ángel's hole clenched around Charles's sensitive cock, and Charles let out a strangled groan, his spine arching and his hips coming right off the bed in a whole-body shudder.

When Ángel's body relaxed, Charles dropped down. Ángel slumped forward over him, catching himself on his hands. He was breathing as hard as Charles, his body glistening with sweat. Their eyes met.

Charles lifted his clean hand to brush Ángel's hair out of his face. Ángel's gaze shifted to Charles's mouth, and he leaned down a bit more. Charles's fingers stroked over Ángel's cheek, down his throat, and lingered over the bite mark above his collarbone.

It was then, with his tension purged and his mind working clearly for the first time since he'd seen Ángel again, that Charles realized the marks on Ángel's body were fresh, one or two days old at most.

Esparza had died six days ago.

CHAPTER FIVE

Ángel saw the pieces clicking together in Charles's mind too quickly for him to do anything to stop them. Shit.

He reached between their bodies and held on to the base of the condom as he lifted himself off Charles's cock. "Now I have to shower again," he said, rolling to the other side of the bed and standing up.

"Ángel." Charles sat upright, seeming not to care that his hand was smeared with Ángel's come and more was trickling down the rich, dark brown skin of his abdomen, catching in the hair around the base of his cock. "Who put those marks on you? It couldn't have been Esparza."

"I'm pretty sure that's none of your business." Ángel fetched his towel from the floor and tossed it to him.

Charles frowned at Ángel as he wiped off his hand and stomach. Just the sight of him sitting in the bed made Ángel want to fuck all over again: his ridiculous shoulders and broad chest tapering in a perfect V to his tight waist, so much power and strength coiled in those defined muscles. A hint of stubble shadowed his strong jaw.

"Did you go out last night?" Charles asked.

Ángel groaned. "Yes, Charles, I snuck out of an ATF safe house in the middle of the night after nearly being shot hours earlier, because I just needed to be fucked *that badly*."

Charles didn't rise to the bait this time—he was usually too relaxed after he came to respond to Ángel's needling. He stripped off the condom and tied it in a knot. "Where did you get them, then?"

What the hell. Ángel wasn't ashamed, and he already knew what Charles thought of him, anyway. Folding his arms across his chest, he said, "Oscar."

"Oscar . . ." Charles's brow furrowed, and then his eyes widened. "Oscar *Palomo*? Esparza's brother-in-law?"

"Yes."

Instead of the disgust Ángel had been expecting, Charles's face went slack with dismay. He stood up and threw the condom in the trash can without looking at it. "Oh my God, Ángel, why would you let me fuck you?" he said, grabbing his boxers and pulling them on.

"What?"

Charles put on his pants as well, fastening his belt with jerky movements. "Did you tell the psychologist about this?"

Ángel closed his eyes for a brief moment, exhaling a long, slow breath. "You think he raped me."

"Didn't he?" Charles gestured to Ángel's body. "Christ, look at your *arm*, I didn't even notice—"

"*No*," Ángel said. He scrubbed a hand over his face. "It was consensual. I went to Oscar myself; I initiated the sex."

Charles paused with his shirt half-on. "Why?"

"Because I needed his protection. The other men in the cartel . . . they tolerated Raúl fucking me, but once he'd been killed, it was a different story. Most of them wanted me dead or—or worse. I knew I could convince Oscar otherwise."

"I saw you with him in El Paso," said Charles. He flicked the last of his shirt buttons shut, but didn't bother tucking his shirttails in. "You were afraid of him."

"He's not exactly a gentle lamb," Ángel said.

"And Esparza was?"

"Raúl was predictable, and easy to control." Ángel tilted his hand from side to side. "Oscar, not so much."

That was understating the situation quite a bit. Oscar had only wanted Ángel because he'd been so jealous of Raúl; unlike his brother-in-law, he'd had no personal investment in Ángel. Once Oscar worked out his resentments, Ángel would have been in as much danger with him as any other man in the cartel.

Charles watched Ángel with tense shoulders, his mouth pursed.

"Just say it," Ángel said, lifting his chin. "Say what it is you're dying to say."

He could still hear the revulsion in Charles's voice the night he'd found Ángel with Jared, the vile accusations he'd flung Ángel's way. They'd run a nauseating loop in Ángel's brain for two years.

Charles shook his head. "I said those things because I was furious, and you have to admit I had good reason to be."

"There's no reason good enough for the things you said to me that night," Ángel said quietly.

"Whereas what you *did* was perfectly justifiable?"

Ángel looked away. "Just go, Charles. You got what you came here for, didn't you?"

With a sound of deep disgust, Charles said, "Don't worry, I'm gone." He snatched up his shoes and socks and stormed out of the motel room, though he didn't slam the door—no matter how angry, Charles wouldn't draw attention to Ángel when he knew Ángel might be in danger.

Left alone and naked, the echo of Charles's thick cock still aching inside him, Ángel covered his eyes with one hand. "God*damn* it," he said to the empty room.

"Whoa, what happened to you?" Eva said to Charles at six thirty the next morning. "You look like shit."

"I don't want to talk about it." If Charles told Eva he'd slept with Ángel, she would report it to Ed, and she wouldn't be wrong.

They checked in with the rest of their team, then split up, resuming surveillance on the case they'd been working before they were tasked to extract Ángel. For months, they'd been tracking a street gang called the Jackals who ran guns down the California coast and across the Mexican border through a combination of straw purchasers—US citizens with clean records who'd been paid or coerced to purchase firearms and hand them over to the gang—and stock "diverted" from gun shows and stores, both with and without the owners' collaboration. Their team had a good handle on the Jackals' supply and smuggling routes, but limited knowledge of the gang's internal hierarchy; they needed more evidence to nab the higher-level members and knock out the majority of the gang in one fell swoop.

As Charles and Eva leapfrogged each other, following one of the Jackals' key foot soldiers around the city, Charles lost himself in the mind-numbing tedium of surveillance. He'd been up half the night rehashing his encounter with Ángel until his brain had finally tapped out from sheer exhaustion. At least work gave him something else to focus on, no matter how boring.

They hooked up with Shane and Sakura in the late afternoon and returned to the office for lunch, greeting Jade where she sat at their cluster of desks.

"Anything interesting?" Eva asked as they sat down. Shane tossed Jade a wrapped sandwich.

Jade, a consummate multitasker, used three computers to monitor every electronic source of surveillance they'd been able to get a warrant for. "Shauna is cheating on Billy with Marcus."

"*Nooo*," Sakura and Shane said in unison.

"I don't blame her," said Jade. "Billy is so ratchet."

"Let me rephrase," Eva said with infinite patience. "Anything *pertinent to the investigation*?"

"That's gonna be pertinent when Billy blows Marcus's idiot head off," Sakura said.

Charles snorted, unwrapping his own Cuban sandwich and dousing it with hot sauce.

"It's just the same chatter we've been hearing for the past week." Jade popped open a bag of chips. "They're all worked up over this shipment they're expecting and some bigshot client who's coming into town to inspect the purchase."

"Any word on who the client is?"

Shaking her head, Jade said, "I don't think they even know—too low on the totem pole."

That meshed with what Charles and Eva had been picking up from their own targets, and a quick discussion confirmed the same with Shane and Sakura. "There's something different about this one," Charles said to Eva. "They've never had a client come in from Mexico to inspect the weapons before smuggling them. Think it's too premature for a raid?"

"I'm not sure," she said. "I'll discuss it with Ed."

Their conversation drifted away from work as they ate their lunches. Charles was settling into the groove of the familiar routine when Jade glanced beyond his shoulder and said, "Hottie with a body, two o'clock."

Charles wouldn't have looked—she could have been talking about literally anyone—but Shane and Sakura perked up as well. Eva's careful nonreaction confirmed it, and Charles turned around to see Ángel heading toward them, bearing a friendly smile and a long bakery box.

"Hey, Ángel," Jade said. "What's up?"

"I had to come in to teleconference with my old RAC from Tucson, and I thought I'd take the opportunity to thank you all properly for my extraction." Ángel leaned over to place the box in the middle of their desk cluster, brushing against Charles's shoulder.

He smelled like the woodsy shampoo scent he used to leave all over Charles's pillows—and his couch, his car, and on several memorable occasions, his living room carpet. Charles held himself still and tried not to breathe too deeply.

"Ooh, Reggie's!" Shane said, noting the box's retro pink-and-white design. He flipped up the top and revealed a dozen fresh gourmet doughnuts of various flavors. "Dude, you are a *god*. Reggie's is the best."

Ángel smiled. "I asked a local."

Don't say it don't say it don't say it—

"Did you buy these with your stipend?" Charles said.

Turning cool eyes on Charles, Ángel said with venomous sweetness, "No, I bought them with a blowjob. Is that a problem?"

This was met with an explosion of shocked snorts and giggles; even Eva's mouth twitched. Charles scowled.

"How come *he* doesn't get in trouble for stuff like that?" Jade said to Eva.

"Because he's not one of my agents," Eva said, "and he's also never had his entire team dragged to a sexual harassment workshop."

Jade said, "Okay, that was a total misunderstanding and very embarrassing for everyone involved—"

Sakura pegged her balled-up sandwich wrapper at Jade, receiving an indignant squawk in return. "You wanna sit down?" she asked Ángel.

To Charles's utter horror, Ángel said, "Sure, thanks."

As the closest person to Ángel, Charles should really have been the one to get up, but his legs refused to cooperate. Sakura stood instead, dragging a chair over from a nearby cluster and squeezing it into the space between Charles and Jade. When Ángel sat down, his thigh pressed right up against Charles's, and he couldn't have made it more obvious that he was doing it on purpose.

Charles inched his chair over, colliding with Sakura, who pushed him gently back into place. "I love you, Charles, but not enough for you to sit in my lap," she said.

"Sorry," he muttered, staring at his desk. Ángel's thigh radiated heat, scorching him even through two layers of clothing.

Eva stood up far enough to reach across the desks and shake Ángel's hand. "Eva Johansen," she said. "It's nice to meet you—for real, this time."

"Likewise."

Pointing around the cluster, Eva said, "Jade Montgomery, Shane Campbell, Sakura Matsui. And of course you know Charles Hunter."

"So, are you all set now that you and Ed spoke to your old RAC?" Shane asked as everyone but Charles helped themselves to the doughnuts.

"Not quite," said Ángel. "Metzger identified me, and he's going to submit a signed statement, but they're also waiting for the new Tucson RAC to send in whatever old records she can dig up. Obviously all my electronic records were purged when I went undercover, but there might still be some hard copies floating around that they missed."

"What a nightmare," Jade said.

Ángel huffed out a laugh. "Honestly, I'm more concerned about getting to my stuff. Campos is trying to get a warrant to break into the storage unit Paul kept for me in Dallas."

Jolted out of his self-imposed silence, Charles said, "You can't go back to Dallas. The cartel could be looking for you there."

Ángel's eyes searched Charles's face before he responded. "Then I'll hire movers," he said. He plucked a doughnut from the box and held it out to Charles. "Don't you want one?"

The doughnut he offered was maple-glazed—Charles's favorite. His teammates knew that as well as Ángel did, so there was no way for Charles to refuse without coming off like a total dick.

"Thanks," Charles said, accepting the doughnut. He could have happily punched Ángel right in his smug, beautiful mouth.

Fucking Ángel yesterday hadn't gotten him out of Charles's system. If anything, he'd burrowed even deeper inside, coursing through Charles's blood like the first hit of heroin after two years clean, all the more potent for having gone so long without. Charles had lost his tolerance.

"Any idea where your next placement will be?" Shane asked.

"Not yet. They'll let me choose instead of just assigning me, but Campos seems to be pushing New York pretty hard for some reason."

"New York?" Eva said, with a glance in Charles's direction. "Sounds exciting."

"I don't do well with the cold," said Ángel.

Charles broke off a piece of his doughnut and said nothing.

"Hey, Hunter, you've got mail," one of the admin assistants said, rolling past their cluster with a packed cart. He lobbed a bulging interoffice mail envelope onto Charles's desk and continued on his way without pausing.

Charles wiped his hands off on a napkin, picked up the envelope, and raised his eyebrows at the way it had been addressed.

Special Agent Ángel Medina
c/o Special Agent Charles Hunter

"It's for you," he said, passing the heavy envelope to Ángel. "From human resources. Must've figured I was the best way to get stuff to you, since you have no address on record." It would have been better protocol for them to send it through Ed, though.

"That was fast," Sakura said.

"*Too* fast. I only spoke to the RAC this morning." Ángel turned the envelope over, his brow creasing. "Maybe she faxed something over?"

He unwound the envelope's string, pulled out a sheaf of papers—and made a horrible choking noise Charles never wanted to hear again, his face draining of color. Ángel dropped the papers on the desk with a weighty *fwump*, shoving his chair back and stumbling to his feet. Charles snatched the papers up before anyone else could.

They were a hard copy of Ángel's file, the one that had been missing from the lockbox Paul Warner had kept for him. On the top sheet, Ángel's demographics, a message had been scrawled in what was unmistakably blood:

I KNOW WHO YOU ARE

CHAPTER SIX

"**N**eedless to say, human resources denies sending you that envelope," Campos said, sitting across from Ángel and Charles in his office with the door shut and the blinds closed.

Charles had flat-out insisted on being included in the meeting, and Ángel had been too shaken to protest. Besides, Charles had a steady, rock-solid presence that made him reassuring to have around in a crisis.

"We're reviewing security footage," Campos continued, "but it's like looking for a specific strand of hay in a haystack. Anyone with a legitimate reason to be in the building could have dropped an interoffice mail envelope into anyone's outbox. It's going to take the lab a couple of days to test the blood, too."

"They don't have to test it," Ángel said. He had his arms folded across his chest, hands tucked against his sides to hide their tremors. "The blood is Paul's."

"You don't know that," said Charles.

Ángel looked at him, unable to even muster a glare.

Charles sighed. "Though it probably is," he conceded. "Warner's the only one who had access to that file."

"The good news is that it wasn't much blood," Campos said. "Forensics said it wasn't any more than you'd have drawn at the doctor's for a few tests. He could easily still be alive."

"Yeah, he could be alive and *wishing* he were dead." Ángel straightened in his chair. "Sir, I need a gun."

Campos hesitated, clasping his hands together on his stomach. "For me to issue you a service weapon, you'd need to be an employee of this field office. Now that we have your records, I can push that through, but I'd strongly recommend that you get as far away from Mexico as possible instead. I'd even suggest witness protection—"

"I am not letting those assholes force me into hiding," Ángel said fiercely, "and anywhere I go under my real name, they'll be able to find me. No. I'm not leaving this office unarmed. I don't care what that takes."

"Ed," Charles said. "Come on. Send him out there without a gun, and you might as well kill him yourself."

Campos nodded and leaned forward, jogging his mouse to wake up his computer. "I'll start the paperwork. Medina, you'll need to change motels as a precaution, so I'll send another agent with you to get whatever stuff you have."

"I'll do it," Charles said. Ángel turned to him in surprise, but Charles didn't look at him.

Ed raised his eyebrows. "You sure? It'll be hours before I've got him set up and ready to leave."

Charles's face was expressionless. "That's fine. I'll run it by Eva, but I don't think she'll object."

"All right, go ahead."

Charles stood and left the office without acknowledging Ángel, who pushed his bewilderment aside and returned his attention to Campos.

"Are you absolutely sure you want to do this?" Campos asked. "I could have you on a plane tonight, anywhere you want to go. We always recommend that returning undercover agents take leave before going back to work, anyway."

"So I could wait there until they catch up to me?" Ángel shook his head. "Thank you, but no. My best option is to stand my ground and make sure they go down for good when they come."

"That's the spirit we like to see around here," Campos said with a chuckle. "By the way, the FBI wants to talk to you about this."

"Awesome," Ángel said.

Between one thing and another, it was after seven by the time Ángel and Charles left the office and headed for the parking garage. "Oh my God, I can't believe you still drive this piece of shit," Ángel said as they approached Charles's ten-year-old black Nissan. "There must be two hundred thousand miles on this thing by now."

Charles pulled his keys out of his jacket pocket. "Still runs."

Of course it did. The car was hopelessly out of style—had never been *in* style, really—and didn't even have power windows, but it was spotless inside and out and maintained as meticulously as if it were a classic Rolls-Royce.

There was no remote unlock, so Ángel had to wait by the passenger side for Charles to unlock the driver's side manually and reach in to pop the rest of the locks. The back of Ángel's neck prickled, unease creeping through him. Dark, near-empty parking garages were not traditionally the safest places for a person being pursued by an angry cartel.

A skittering noise sounded on the cement behind Ángel. He whipped around, heart pounding, hand flying to the butt of the new Glock settled in his shoulder holster, before he realized it had just been a foam coffee cup blown along the ground by a gust of wind.

Charles slammed the driver's side door shut and hurried around the car, his eyes alert and his hand resting on his own gun. "What is it?"

"Nothing." Ángel dropped his shaking hand. "It's nothing. I overreacted."

He leaned back against the car and closed his eyes, breathing out. Charles's footsteps moved closer to him.

"Paul is gonna die," Ángel said, the bleak truth overwhelming him. "Do you know what they would have had to do for him to give up access to that lockbox? They're torturing him, and eventually they'll kill him, and it'll be my fault."

"There is no universe in which what's happening to him is your fault." Charles took hold of Ángel's elbow and tugged him off the car, forcing him to open his eyes or lose his balance. "He accepted the risks of being your handler, the same way you accepted the risks of going undercover. This is on whoever took him, not you."

"He was one of the only people I could talk to for two years," said Ángel. "He listened to me, and he didn't judge me, and now . . ."

Ángel shuddered. Charles smoothed his hand from Ángel's elbow to his shoulder, then wrapped his arm around him and pulled him close. Ángel pressed his face into Charles's shoulder and gripped his jacket with both hands.

Charles was only an inch or so taller than Ángel, but he was much broader, thick through the shoulders and chest; leaning against him was like leaning on a brick wall, albeit one that smelled amazing. He stroked his free hand down Ángel's back.

"We probably shouldn't stand out in the open like this," Charles said quietly.

Ángel pulled away, clearing his throat. "You're right. Let's go."

His motel room was just as he'd left it, with no evidence of entry—not even by housekeeping, thanks to the Do Not Disturb sign he'd hung. Ángel packed his things in a few minutes, tossing them into the plastic Target bags and the tote bag Charles had left, and they continued on to the new motel where Campos had arranged a room for him under yet another alias.

"You gonna be okay here?" Charles asked, hovering in the doorway.

"Yeah." Ángel trailed his fingertips over the round wooden table by the door, hesitating before he said, "You, um . . . you don't have to leave."

"Yes, I do," said Charles.

When Ángel stepped toward him, Charles moved away, backing right up out of the room and into the exterior hallway.

"This isn't healthy, Ángel," he said. "This thing between us—it's never been a good idea, and it's an even worse one now."

"That never stopped you before."

Charles snorted. "That was . . . well, *before*."

Before things between them had imploded so spectacularly, he meant. Ángel pressed his lips together, propping one hip against the doorjamb.

More gently, Charles said, "You only want me to stay because you're upset. We'd both regret it right afterward. Let's just not, all right? We have to work in the same office again, even if it's only temporary."

It was a rational, mature response, the one anyone else would expect of Charles. But Ángel knew better. He saw the tension in Charles's shoulders, the quick darting glances that skated over Ángel's hips and thighs, the slight twitch of his hands at his sides. If Ángel pursued this, Charles would give in. It wouldn't even be that difficult.

Ángel nodded and pushed himself upright. "Good night, Charles. Thanks for the escort."

A brief hint of surprise flashed across Charles's face, and then he nodded in return. "No problem," he said. "See you tomorrow."

Charles turned and walked away. Ángel closed the door, locked it, and banged his forehead once against the peeling wood.

Entering the office the next morning to see Ángel sitting at their cluster with tired eyes, clutching a coffee, gave Charles such a powerful sense of déjà vu that he stopped walking midstride. Sakura, who had ridden the elevator with him from the parking garage, bounced off his back and just managed to save her own coffee from a fatal fall.

"*Charles*," she said, irritated. "I swear, you're a zombie in the morning."

Charles didn't even apologize, too preoccupied by the fact that another desk had been added to their cluster and *Ángel was sitting at it*, talking to Eva and Jade like he had every right to be there. Shoulders tensing, Charles sat at his own desk.

"What's going on?" he asked Eva, his voice even.

"Ángel is going to be joining us temporarily in an analyst capacity," she said. She rose to her feet and smiled at Charles. "Could you help me out with the coffeemaker, please? It's stuck again."

Charles followed Eva into the break room, pretending he didn't feel Ángel's eyes on his back. "What the hell?" he whispered to her once they were alone.

"Don't even start," she said, hands on her hips. "This is *your* fault. You were so eager to help Ángel out yesterday that Ed assumed you were good friends in Tucson, and he thought Ángel would feel safest and most comfortable working with our team while he's attached to this office. I couldn't correct him without telling him why."

"Shit," said Charles.

"If you disclosed the nature of your relationship now—"

"*No*."

Eva shrugged. "Then suck it up. Try to engage him as little as possible. He'll be stuck at that desk all day anyway."

She got herself a coffee—though Charles could have told her that her excuse hadn't fooled Ángel for a minute—and they returned to the cluster. When Shane finally showed up, late as usual, they spent a few minutes settling in before Eva tapped on her desk to get everyone's attention.

"Like I said earlier, Ángel will be working with our team for the time being," she said. "He'll be keeping the code name Phoenix from his extraction."

Shane leaned over the desks to offer Ángel a fist bump, which Ángel returned with some bemusement.

"The FBI is intensifying their search for Paul Warner and his possible abductors," Eva said, ignoring Shane's antics with an ease born of long practice. "We do *not* have jurisdiction in that case, and we've been ordered not to obstruct the investigation in any way. That includes rogue solo sleuthing."

She gave Ángel an arch glance as she spoke. He smiled sweetly.

"Ángel is on desk duty only, absolutely no fieldwork until the current situation is resolved. Jade, I'm giving you latitude to assign him whatever tasks you need done—"

Jade's eyes lit up as she opened her mouth. Sakura kicked her hard under the table.

"Ow, *fuck*," Jade said, scowling at her. "What I was *going* to say is that I could use your help translating some of the Spanish conversations we've got, Ángel. Charles and I are both certified translators, but we can never keep up with the backlog."

"I'd be happy to," said Ángel.

"Make sure you look through the case reports too, get a sense of the background," Eva said. "Now, as for our next steps—I'd like to get a lock on when and where this new shipment is coming into town. This is a departure from the Jackals' usual pattern, and that means there's something significant about this particular shipment, whether it's the client or the weapons or both. Ideally, we'll surveil the delivery and track the merchandise to the meet. Depending on intel, we may decide either to raid the meet or extend our surveillance."

"I'm meeting Amber today," Charles said, referring to one of his best confidential informants. "She may have some good info."

Half an hour of discussion and strategizing later, the team headed off on their individual assignments, and Charles and Ángel hadn't had a single personal interaction. So far, so good.

The bar Amber favored was a total dive, and not in a charming, rustic way. At 11 a.m. on a Tuesday, only the most hard-core drinkers were present, most of them older white men. A couple of them looked up at Charles's entrance, eyeing him up and down with hostile sneers before returning their attention to their drinks.

Charles reined in his contempt. Dress a large black man in a hoodie and jeans, and suddenly he was pure thug. Racist idiots.

He walked to the end of the bar, where Amber huddled against the wall, and sat on the derelict stool beside her.

"Hey," Amber said, flashing him a tight-lipped smile designed to hide her rotting teeth. Her skin was pasty white in the dim light filtering through the filthy windows, her stringy red hair pulled into a low ponytail. One foot bounced anxiously against the rung of her stool.

"Hey," said Charles. He kept his hands well away from the sticky bar. "How've you been?"

Amber shrugged and gestured to the bartender. "Mich Ultra," she said when he came over.

Charles ordered one as well—to do otherwise would invite unwanted attention. While they waited for their beers, Amber absently scratched at the open sores on her arm; her fingernails were flecked with blood.

Wincing, Charles took hold of her wrist and tugged her hand away. "You're bleeding," he said.

"Oh shit." Amber wiped her hand on her jeans. "Sorry."

As the bartender set two beers in front of them, Charles said, "At least let me get you something to eat with this."

Amber agreed, and Charles ordered her a basket of wings. She picked up her glass and drained half the beer in one long swallow.

"How's Johnny?" Charles asked. Amber was always reticent at first, but inquiring after her scumbag boyfriend was a foolproof way to fire her up.

Right on cue, Amber launched into an exhaustive account of Johnny's many faults, rambling on and on throughout the entire time it took the kitchen to send out the wings and her to work through two beers. Charles listened patiently and made commiserating noises when necessary.

"And he thinks I'm so fucking *stupid*, you know?" Amber said at length. She gestured with a half-eaten chicken wing, nearly clipping Charles's nose. "Like I don't hear him talking to his gangbanger friends, or I can't understand them. And if he thinks I don't know about that slut at the Big City Liquor—"

"What have he and his friends been talking about?" Charles said, steering her back on track.

"Ugh, *guns*." Amber gave an exaggerated roll of her eyes. "It's always fucking guns with those shitheads. 'S how they get their drugs, you know? I've told Johnny a thousand times he's getting in too deep with those Mexicans, but do you think he listens to me? No way. Just laughs right in my face!"

"What—"

"You know he's learning *Spanish*?" Ripping a hunk of chicken off the bone, Amber continued speaking with a full mouth. "Fucking Spanish! Says he doesn't like not knowing what they're saying around him. I told him, 'Johnny, those fuckers are gonna come to America, they gotta speak American.' You know?"

Jesus Christ. Charles put his hand on top of Amber's, met her eyes, and waited for her to focus on him before saying, "Have Johnny and his friends been talking about anything unusual lately? Something different from the normal way things are run—maybe something that's got them excited, or nervous?"

"Oh, yeah," said Amber. "Truck coming in from up north. Monterey, I think? Got them all worked up, just about shitting their pants. I don't know why."

A *truck*? Charles frowned. The Jackals rarely shipped their illicit merchandise in bulk, preferring the less risky approach of transporting it in bits and pieces, hidden in compartments inside personal cars. "Do you know where or when the truck will be here?"

Amber sucked buffalo sauce off her fingers. "Day after tomorrow, 'bout four o'clock, at one of those crappy warehouses in Chula Vista. I remember because Johnny and Buzz were arguing about it. Johnny thought the truck should come in the middle of the night, you know, and Buzz was saying it's safer to bring it in when the roads are busy and everyone's working." She snorted contemptuously. "Johnny's such a fucking idiot."

Charles questioned her more, but that was the extent of Amber's knowledge; she had no idea who the client was or what made this shipment unique. Still, learning the date and location of the delivery was a huge break and far more than Charles had allowed himself to hope for.

When he pulled out his wallet to pay the tab, Charles surreptitiously slid a couple of extra bills toward Amber. She snatched up the money and stuffed it in the pocket of her cutoff shorts.

Every time Charles paid Amber for her information, he struggled with an internal voice, that sounded a lot like his grandmother's, telling him how wrong this was. He could pretend all he wanted that Amber would spend that money on rent or food, but he knew the moment she walked out of this bar, all of it was going right to her meth dealer.

"Thanks, Amber," he said, hopping off his stool. He nudged his untouched beer in her direction, then added, "You know that if you ever want out—"

"Yeah, I know." Amber knuckled his arm, her smile genuine. "Got my knight in shining armor waiting for me, huh?"

Charles squeezed her shoulder and left the bar. It would be a cold day in hell before Amber left Johnny, but that never stopped him from offering.

He spent the rest of the afternoon making the rounds, checking in with his other sources. None of them were as well connected as Amber, but the scattered crumbs of information he picked up verified her story. Energized by the new lead, Charles returned to the office in a much-improved mood.

"I've got actionable intelligence," he said as soon as he reached Eva at their cluster. Jade and Ángel looked up from their computers with interest.

"Thank God," Eva said, "because we've got exactly nothing."

Charles filled them in, and when Shane and Sakura joined them, they sketched out a plan for surveilling the delivery. Unfortunately, there were plenty of crappy warehouses in Chula Vista, so they'd need to narrow the field somewhat before they could take real action.

"I'm on it," said Jade. "I'll look into the financials of the buildings in the area, search for any ties to the Jackals or the cartels they work with. Ángel, you have any experience with forensic accounting?"

Ángel smiled at her, tilting his head so his hair fell over one eye. "I'm a quick study."

Oh, please. Charles turned away, annoyed, and caught sight of Ed Campos walking toward them.

Generally speaking, Ed was an easygoing guy, cheerful and mild mannered, with a friendly smile for everyone. Right now, though, his face was grim and his jaw clenched tight. Charles straightened up in his chair.

The rest of the team fell silent with equal apprehension when Ed stopped at their cluster—including Ángel, who excelled at picking up social cues. Ed opened his mouth, closed it, then sighed. "The FBI found Paul Warner's car."

Ángel snapped to attention, not a hint of flirtatiousness left in his demeanor.

"It was in the long-term parking lot of the El Paso airport, keys tucked in the visor, no blood anywhere in the car or trunk, no signs of a struggle whatsoever."

"Then they didn't take him from his car," said Ángel. "They took him somewhere else and drove his car to the airport to draw out the search."

"That's quite possible, but that's not all they found." Blowing out a hard breath, Ed met Ángel's eyes and said, "The night Paul Warner disappeared, Raúl Esparza's passport was used to cross the Zaragoza Bridge from Mexico into El Paso."

CHAPTER SEVEN

"So somebody used Raúl's passport to get into the US," Ángel said, hyperaware of six pairs of eyes riveted to him. "It happens."

Sakura made a face. "Who would be stupid enough to use Esparza's passport? They'd have to know Customs and Border Protection tracks his movements like a helicopter mom."

"*Used* to track him. They don't anymore, or we would have known about this as soon as it happened." Ángel turned to Campos. "They canceled the alerts when he died, didn't they?"

"Yes."

Waving a hand, Ángel said, "Then someone else bet on that and took his passport—or sold it."

Where everyone at the cluster had been staring at him only moments before, now they were all just as carefully *not* looking at him. Silence reigned until Charles—of course Charles—took the lead.

"Ángel," he said. "How certain are you that Esparza is dead?"

"How . . ." Ángel blinked. "I was *with him* when he died. I had to take three showers to get his brain out of my hair!"

"Your hair?" Eva said, her gaze sharpening. "Were you not facing him when he was shot?"

Ángel's mouth worked open and shut before he said, with mounting frustration, "We were getting into a car. He was behind me." He groaned at the skepticism on their faces. "There is *no way* Raúl could have faked being shot at that distance. His blood was everywhere, it was all over me—"

"Would you know the difference between human's blood and, say, pig's blood?" Sakura asked.

Rendered speechless, Ángel could only gape at her.

Eva raised a hand, motioning for Sakura to hold back. "Ángel," she said, her tone calm and oh-so-rational, "did you touch Esparza's body after he died? Spend any time with him at all? Was it an open-casket funeral?"

The moment Raúl was shot, his bodyguards had wrestled Ángel into the car, shielding him with their bodies as they were paid to. Ángel had only caught a glimpse of Raúl's lifeless legs stretched out on the pavement before the door had slammed shut, but he'd been drenched with blood and bone fragments, matting his hair and dripping down the back of his shirt, filling the car with a sickly-sweet stench. Raúl had been shot with a sniper rifle with enough force to shatter his skull, so of course there hadn't been an open casket—

Agitated, Ángel leaped to his feet. "Oh my God, you people are insane," he said. "What possible reason would Raúl have for faking his own death that way?"

"He might if he knew you were an undercover agent," said Charles. When everyone turned to him, he shrugged and added, "Whose observations would have more credibility with the US and Mexican governments?"

Ángel clenched his fists by his sides, breathing hard, clinging to the last of his composure by the thinnest of threads. "You're implying that Paul revealed my identity to Raúl, who then faked his own death, and the two of them rode merrily off into the sunset?"

"Not *together*, obviously," Charles said. "But yes, I think it's possible that Esparza knew he had a mole in his operation, paid off Warner to find out who it was, and then used that information to make sure the law enforcement agencies trying to bust him thought he was dead."

Ángel had no words. There were simply no words in English *or* Spanish to encompass how absolutely fucking ludicrous that suggestion was—but there Charles sat, his expression all patient and understanding like *Ángel* was the one being illogical, and everyone else at the cluster appeared to agree with him.

Everyone, that is, except Jade. "Wait a minute, come on," she said. "Why would Esparza go to all that trouble and then risk blowing it by using his own passport just so he could come here and send Ángel a taunting message? Because I gotta tell you, that little delivery came off less like angry cartel boss seeking revenge and more like a crazy, jilted stalker . . ." She trailed off, realization dawning in her eyes, and winced. "Oh."

The others quickly picked up on Jade's assumption, becoming just as uncomfortable. Nothing Ángel could say would change their minds, but he knew the truth—though Raúl had been falling in love with him, he hadn't reached the point of obsession, and he certainly hadn't been an idiot.

"Paul would never betray me," Ángel said, his voice shaking. "*Never.* And Jade is right—if Raúl had pulled this off, he wouldn't be stupid enough to come after me at all, still less using his own passport. You're looking for connections where they don't exist."

He had to get out of here before he said something he'd regret. Grabbing his jacket off the back of his chair, he hurried out of the office, pulling his phone from his pocket to call a cab as he went. The office hadn't been able to issue him an agency vehicle because he *still* didn't have his fucking driver's license. Besides his new ATF badge, the only form of ID he had on him was the fake license he'd used for his alias with the cartel.

Charles caught up with him on the sidewalk outside. "Ángel, wait," he called. "I don't think it's safe for you to be alone right now—"

Ángel spun around to face him, his anger boiling over. "Why are you doing this?"

"Doing what?"

"Bending over backward to help me! If you want to fuck me again, that's fine, let's go. You don't have to pretend you don't hate me."

Charles recoiled, looking ill. "I wouldn't ever . . . That isn't . . ." He sighed. "I don't hate you."

Ángel's laugh grated his throat.

"I don't," Charles snapped. "And I don't want . . . that . . . from you."

What a fucking liar. "Really?" Ángel said. "Then why did you chase after me so dramatically?"

"Because I've never seen you this afraid before," said Charles.

Ángel stiffened.

"Until that night in El Paso, I'd never seen you afraid at all, not really. You were always fearless—stupidly, recklessly fearless. It used to drive me crazy." Charles made a helpless, abortive gesture. "You don't have that anymore."

Ángel's stomach churned like Charles had sucker punched him. He glanced to the side, relieved to see his cab approaching. "Well, I'm so sorry I don't measure up to your memories of me," he said.

Exasperation swamped the concern on Charles's face. "Christ, Ángel, you know that's not what I'm saying—"

"See you tomorrow, Charles." Ángel jumped into the cab, closing the door before Charles could speak again, and gave the driver the address of his motel.

Fuck Charles, anyway. Did he think Ángel was unaware of how he'd changed? Ángel would give anything to be back in his old life—surrounded by friends, with a job he loved, sneaking around to hook up with his hot coworker on the sly—instead of sitting alone in the back of this cab, all of his personal relationships fragmented, with a license in his pocket that didn't even have his real name on it.

Three hours of flipping channels and pacing his motel room later, Ángel was ready to tear his own hair out. The more time he spent alone, the worse his thoughts spiraled, anxiety for Paul duking it out with fury over Charles and his team's ridiculous theories. If the FBI backed off the search for Paul because of this . . .

All right, this was getting him nowhere. He could go out and hook up, except . . . he couldn't leave this room unarmed, and he couldn't exactly hit the club floor with a gun strapped under his arm.

If he kept his jacket buttoned, it would hide the gun well enough. He could hang out at a bar, keep it low-key, bring a guy back to the motel, and stash the gun before the guy noticed it and freaked out. That was the best he was going to get.

His mind made up, Ángel took the bus to Hillcrest, where he walked around the vibrant, busy neighborhood for a while, keeping an eye out for any signs he was being followed before slipping into a packed gay bar. He wrangled himself a seat in the corner, and it took less than two minutes for an older daddy type to approach him and offer to buy him a drink.

Ángel wasn't looking for a daddy tonight, but the guy was sweet and offering free booze, so Ángel accepted an Angry Orchard and drew him into a friendly conversation. Once the man realized that was as far as things were going to go, he wandered off amiably and was replaced at once by two college jocks.

Ángel paced himself on the alcohol; he couldn't risk compromising his judgment or reflexes. The guys here were hot, but nothing special—except for one guy across the bar who'd been cruising Ángel hard since walking in about half an hour after Ángel arrived. He was rough around the edges, tanned and athletic, with curly dark hair and artful stubble. Though he did nothing to hide his obvious attraction, he showed no signs of making a move, and that alone was enough to pique Ángel's interest.

After gently rejecting his latest hopeful suitor, Ángel crooked a finger at the man. A broad smile spread across the man's face as he headed for Ángel's high-top and sat down.

"You know, some guys wouldn't appreciate being stared at all night," Ángel said.

"You've been pretty popular," the man said. His voice was low and rumbly, sending shivers down Ángel's spine. "I didn't know if I could compete."

Ángel grinned at his terrible false modesty. "Well, why don't you buy me a drink, and we'll find out?"

The man introduced himself as Ian, and they made pleasant small talk over another round. Neither of them had come to the bar for conversation, though. A few minutes later, Ian had pulled his stool close to Ángel's and they were kissing, Ángel's hands buried in Ian's hair and Ian kneading his thighs.

"You want to get out of here?" Ángel asked breathlessly. "I'm staying in a motel not too far away."

"Fuck, yeah." Ian nipped his throat. "You got a car?"

"I took the bus."

"I'll drive, then."

Ian was a handsy guy, but Ángel managed to keep him from grabbing anywhere that would reveal the existence of his shoulder holster. When they reached the motel, Ian stood behind Ángel and rubbed his cock against Ángel's ass while he unlocked the door.

"That's not helping my motor skills," Ángel said, pushing back against him.

Ian's laugh ruffled Ángel's hair. "You won't need your hands for what I have in mind."

Ángel managed to get the door open, and they stumbled through it, kissing even as Ángel threw the dead bolt and security chain. It had been two years since Ángel fucked someone without ulterior motives, without literally pretending to be someone he wasn't. The other day with Charles, layered with anger and resentment and old hurts, didn't count. This was simply sex for the sheer pleasure of it, and fuck, Ángel *needed* this.

Ángel caught Ian's hands before they could slide up his sides, and stepped back from the kiss. Ian saved him the trouble of coming up with an excuse to separate for a couple of minutes by asking, "Okay if I use your bathroom?"

"Yeah, sure."

Ian gave him another lingering kiss and then walked into the bathroom, closing the door. Moving quickly, Ángel stripped out of his jacket and stashed his gun and holster in the top drawer of the bureau. By the time Ian returned, Ángel was checking his hair in the mirror, unfazed by the rush.

"You're sexy as hell," Ian said, running appreciative eyes over Ángel's chest and waist. He pulled Ángel close, nuzzling his neck, and grabbed his ass with both hands. "You want to bottom?"

Ángel rubbed up against him. "I really, really do."

Ian kissed him again, groaning into Ángel's mouth and kneading his ass. "I've got condoms," he said when they came up for air. "You have lube?"

Nodding, Ángel hooked a finger in Ian's waistband and led him to the nightstand, where he retrieved the bottle from the drawer and pressed it into Ian's hand. Ian turned it over with a thoughtful expression, then gave Ángel a wicked smile and tugged him away from the bed, toward the other side of the room. Ángel followed, intrigued.

Ian set the bottle on the desk and turned Ángel around, gently pushing him face-first into the wall beside it. Ángel caught his breath, aroused, and moaned when Ian kicked his legs apart.

"Could've fucked you like this right outside the bar," Ian said. He gripped Ángel's hips, pressing their bodies together and grinding his erection into Ángel's ass in small circles. "Taken you in the alley out back."

Ángel tilted his head to the side so Ian could kiss his neck. "That would have been very illegal," he said teasingly.

Ian chuckled. "Only if we'd gotten caught."

Rucking Ángel's shirt halfway up his stomach with one hand, Ian undid Ángel's fly with the other and pushed his jeans and boxer briefs down to midthigh. His mouth roamed over Ángel's neck and shoulders while he fingered him, quick and rough, murmuring compliments into his ear.

When Ian pushed inside him, Ángel braced his hands against the wall and arched his back in pleasure. Fucking standing up and fully dressed was dirty in a safe, exciting way; he could imagine they were really in the alley behind the bar, his hands sliding against rough brick instead of cheap motel wallpaper, asphalt beneath his feet instead of carpet.

"Oh, God, that's good," Ian said, bottoming out in Ángel's ass and giving him a few slow thrusts. "You're so fucking tight."

He was a great fuck, with a natural sense of rhythm and enough know-how to locate Ángel's prostate without needing step-by-step instructions. The only drawback was that he clearly had no intention of giving Ángel a reach-around, but whatever, Ángel had two hands.

Ángel propped his left forearm against the wall, let his forehead fall against it, and jerked himself off, taking every one of Ian's smooth, rolling thrusts with a soft gasp. "Right there, just like that," he said when Ian set a quick pace that hit him at the perfect angle. "Fuck, yeah, don't stop—"

He groaned as he came, shooting all over the stupid floral-print wallpaper. Ian grunted behind him and sped up, slamming through the last few thrusts, then shoving all the way in and burying his face in Ángel's shoulder.

Ángel panted, his shoulders relaxed and his body buzzing with warmth. There was a lot to be said for casual, friendly hookups with no strings attached.

Ian pulled out and got rid of the condom, and they cleaned themselves up, trading a few more lazy kisses as they put their clothing to rights. "You're welcome to stay," Ángel said, just to be polite.

"Thanks, but I've got an early morning tomorrow." Ian palmed Ángel's ass and gave it a greedy squeeze. "Maybe I could get your number, though?"

Ángel tore a scrap of paper off the notepad on the desk and scribbled the number to his cell. Ian tucked it into his pocket, playfully slapped Ángel's ass, and headed for the door. With a satisfied sigh, Ángel tipped his head back against the wall and closed his eyes.

"By the way," Ian said, and a strange shift in his tone made Ángel open his eyes again. Ian stood in the open doorway, smirking at him. "Raúl sends his love."

The door swung shut as Ian left. Ángel stood frozen, staring blankly at the door, Ian's words rattling around in his brain without sinking in.

Then he launched himself off the wall and ran after Ian, pausing only to grab his gun as he bolted out of the room.

It had taken Ángel too long to recover from his shock; Ian was already downstairs and halfway across the parking lot. He wasn't even running, apparently unconcerned that Ángel might pursue him.

Ángel took off down the exterior hallway, cursing his tight jeans as he rounded the top of the staircase. Five steps from the bottom, he jumped to the ground, landing lightly on his feet and springing up to continue the chase. Fortunately, there was nobody else around, though Ángel wasn't sure he'd have been able to hold himself back if there had been.

"Stop!" Ángel shouted as Ian hit the remote unlock button for his car.

Ian opened the door without turning around.

Ángel careened to a halt ten feet away and brought his gun up in a two-handed grip. He'd spent time at the range while with the cartel, letting Raúl "teach" him how to shoot so he had a handy excuse for keeping his skills sharp, but it had been years since he last aimed a gun at a human being. "I said *stop*," he said, the word reverberating with fury.

Ian glanced at him, annoyed—and then lurched backward, slamming hard against the side of his car. All of the arrogance in his body language collapsed.

"Who sent you?" Ángel asked.

Ian only had eyes for Ángel's gun, his breath coming in quick, sharp pants. His fear was gratifying, but not exactly helpful.

"Look at me," said Ángel. When Ian's eyes jerked up to his, he said, "Somebody told you to say that. Tell me who it was."

"Are you fucking insane?" Ian said, his gaze dragged back to Ángel's gun. "Why the hell do you have a gun?"

Oh, shit. Ángel transferred his gun to a one-handed grip, digging in his pocket for his badge. He flipped it open and waited for Ian to peer at it in the sickly-yellow haze of the streetlamps. Ian blanched and muttered a curse underneath his breath.

"I'm going to need you to come with me," Ángel said.

CHAPTER EIGHT

"**A**re you out of your goddamn mind?" Charles said, banging into the viewing room of the interrogation suite.

Ángel barely glanced away from the two-way glass. "Good morning, Charles."

He looked like he'd gotten two or three hours of sleep, tops. Charles shook his head, refusing to sympathize. "You had no right to drag that guy in here."

"I didn't drag him," said Ángel. "I didn't even arrest him. He came in willingly for questioning."

"Because you pulled a gun on him!"

"I felt threatened," Ángel said flatly.

"Oh, *bullshit*." Irritated that Ángel wouldn't look at him, Charles grabbed his elbow. Though Ángel shook him off with a disgruntled noise, he did turn around to face Charles. "You realize that whatever they might have been able to charge him with will never stick now, right? Not after the way you handled this. The second he decides to lawyer up, he's gone for good."

"Campos read me the riot act last night, thanks."

Now that Charles had Ángel's attention, he didn't want it; Ángel was agitated, clearly on the verge of exploding, and it would be best not to get caught in that blast radius. He stepped back to give Ángel some breathing room and looked through the window himself.

The man on the other side looked even worse for wear than Ángel, with tousled hair and deep bags under his eyes, but he was still very attractive in a dark, intense way. What the hell was his name again? Isaac, Ivan . . . no, Ian.

Mina Sadir, the FBI agent leading the search for Paul Warner, was in the interrogation room with him now. "He been saying anything?" Charles asked.

Ángel shrugged. "Just the same crap he said last night."

"I've told you people this a thousand times," Ian was saying to Sadir, raking both hands through his hair. "A guy came up to me in a club, offered me two hundred bucks to pick up his ex in a bar nearby and deliver a message. He said his ex had screwed him over, cheated on him, and he just wanted to rattle him a little."

"You accepted money in exchange for having sex with this man's ex-lover?" Sadir said with polite incredulity.

"What? No!" Ian backpedaled quickly, his eyes wide. "No way. I would have tried to pick up Ángel anyway—have you seen the ass on him? No, the money was just for delivering the message."

Charles risked a sideways glance at Ángel. He stood glowering through the window, his arms crossed, fingers digging into his biceps so hard they were going to leave marks.

"The man who approached you," Sadir said. "What did he look like?"

"I don't know, it was dark." Waving a hand, Ian said, "Early fifties, I guess? Big guy, not really fat, just solid. Definitely Latino—maybe Mexican, I'm not sure. He had a thick accent."

Charles's mouth fell open. "Ángel . . ."

"There are tens of thousands of men who fit that description," Ángel said, his voice tight.

Tens of thousands of men who fit that description *and* had motivation to fuck with Ángel's mind this way? Sure.

"I'm sorry, I just have to ask." Sadir leaned forward over the table, her sympathetic smile inviting confession. "It didn't strike you as odd that this man would be willing to pay you so much money to sleep with and then harass his ex?"

"Well, after he showed me a picture of Ángel, I figured it was one of those gold-digger situations, you know, and Ángel had gotten bored and started fucking around on the side. No way is a guy who looks like that going to stay in some old dude's bed for long, no matter how rich."

Ángel's nostrils flared. Charles took another step away from him, just to be safe.

"Look, I know it was a dick move, okay?" Ian said. "I'm sorry. I really needed the money. And obviously I had no idea he was a federal agent, or I wouldn't have done it. But I don't understand why this is such a big deal that I need to talk to the FBI, for God's sake. Is what I did even technically illegal?"

Sadir hesitated, drumming her fingers against the tabletop. Charles didn't need to see her face to infer her thoughts. He'd said it to Ángel himself just minutes earlier—after the way Ángel had brought Ian in, there was no way they could charge him with anything. Even a crappy lawyer would have the case thrown out in half an hour; a good lawyer could talk Ian into bringing charges against Ángel.

"There's a possibility that the man who approached you was Raúl Esparza," Sadir said carefully. "He's a criminal with strong ties to Mexican cartels, and if it *was* him, he's also wanted for questioning in connection with the disappearance of another ATF agent."

Ángel clenched his fist and lifted it, as if he were about to bang on the glass, but pulled his hand back at the last second. "Raúl is *dead*, you idiot," he muttered.

Deciding discretion was by far the better part of valor, Charles kept his mouth shut.

Ian, for his part, could not have looked more horrified. "Oh my God," he said, scrubbing his hands over his face. "I . . . I didn't . . ." Raising his head, he said, "I want a lawyer."

Ángel *did* bang his hand against the glass then, causing both Ian and Sadir to startle. With a sound of deep disgust, Ángel stormed out of the room, slamming the door behind himself.

Charles stayed for a few more minutes, listening to Sadir unsuccessfully try to talk Ian out of his request for a lawyer before she gave up. Then he sighed and left to fill Eva in on this latest debacle.

What a fantastic start to the day.

Behind the office was an open concrete space where some of the staff took their smoke breaks. Ángel stepped out into the sunlight, smiled at the group of three smokers who were chatting among themselves, and moved as far away from them as possible. Leaning against the side of the building, he drew a deep breath and then pulled his phone out of his pocket.

Jesenia answered on the second ring. "Ángel? *¿Como estás?*"

"*Pues más o menos.*" Ángel swallowed hard. "There's something you deserve to know."

"What is it?"

"There's a chance Raúl Esparza may be alive."

This was greeted by a long silence before Jesenia said, "What," with absolutely no inflection.

Ángel gave her a quick account of the events of the past few days, beginning with the bloody delivery of his personnel record and ending with Ian's confession. Laying it all out in a logical sequence calmed him down, and by the time he finished, he felt less like he was falling down the rabbit hole.

"Holy shit," Jesenia said. "Holy *shit.*"

"I don't think it's him," said Ángel. "I genuinely don't. You know I was with him when he died, and I just don't see how he could have faked that convincingly when I was so close to him. But I also can't come up with another explanation for what's been happening."

"You need to leave California."

"Jesenia—"

"*Lo digo en serio*, Ángel," Jesenia snapped. "This is crazy. What's your plan here, to wait around for this to keep escalating until whoever it is tries to kill you?"

Ángel scuffed his toe along a crack in the pavement.

Softening her tone, Jesenia said, "My uncle—well, my ex-uncle, really—has a hunting lodge in the forest in Canada. It's gorgeous and super private. I could talk him into letting you use it for a while, at least until the FBI finds Paul and this all gets straightened out. You should have had some time off before you jumped back into work, anyway. I think it would be great for you to go somewhere you can relax and be alone."

"That's very generous," Ángel said, touched. "But if I run now, I'll never be able to stop running. Here, I can be prepared; I have the office to back me up. Maybe the FBI will actually do their jobs for once, but if they don't, this is going to get nasty before it gets better. I'd rather face that on my own terms than have it hit me in the back while I'm running away."

Jesenia sighed. "This is the kind of nonsense that led to you going undercover in the first place, you know," she said, though she sounded fond.

"*¡Mira quién habla!*"

She laughed. "The offer still stands. When you realize what a terrible idea it is to stay there—and you will—I'll help you get out."

They talked a bit more, until Ángel could no longer put off returning to work. He slipped back into the building, walking up four flights of stairs instead of taking the elevator, and stopped in the break room to fill a travel mug with coffee. With no other way to delay joining his new team, he headed for their cluster.

Everyone else was already there, and one glance at their faces was enough to confirm that they knew all about what had happened last night and this morning. They had too much class to say anything to him about it, though, and greeted Ángel normally as he took his seat.

The plan for the day was to scout potential sites for the Jackals' expected weapons delivery. Jade had found a few possibilities the night before, and she and Ángel would continue the investigation, feeding information to the rest of the team on the ground in Chula Vista. Once assignments were made and the team broke up, Ángel's tension eased. A day spent on the computer in Jade's amiable company wouldn't be too taxing for his stressed-out, sleep-deprived brain. He lifted his coffee to his mouth.

"Try not to pull your gun on any civilians while we're gone," Charles sniped at him as he walked past.

Ángel slammed his mug down on his desk, gritting his teeth, but Charles was already gone.

Jade peered at him over her computer monitor. "Don't listen to him," she said as Ángel picked his coffee up again. "He's been super salty ever since his fiancée left him."

Ángel didn't quite do a spit take, but it was a near thing. "His *fiancée*?"

"Yeah, Amy. She moved out about a month ago."

Jade returned her attention to her computer, and Ángel wiped the back of his hand over his mouth, considering the timing. Charles had been in Tucson just two years ago; it was unlikely he'd been transferred to San Diego right after Ángel had left.

"When did Charles move here?" he asked.

"Um . . . a year and a half ago, I think?" At Ángel's answering silence, Jade met his eyes and said, "Yeah, it happened fast. Too fast, if you ask me. Honestly, I think it's why their relationship hit the rocks, but I don't know for sure. Charles isn't exactly chatty about his personal life."

Ángel snorted at the gross understatement, and Jade grinned. Knowing he couldn't pursue this any further without making her suspicious, he focused on the queue of lease agreements waiting for his inspection.

Charles had spent over a year with Ángel, refusing to even call what they were doing a relationship—but then he'd met, moved in with, and fucking *proposed* to some random woman in little more time than that.

They hit on the right warehouse in the late afternoon. It was owned by a cousin of one of the Jackals, used for what appeared to be a legitimate import-export business. A bit of digging revealed that most of the regular employees had been scheduled off the following afternoon, during which there was a suspicious and unexplained lack of officially scheduled deliveries.

The necessary warrants were obtained, and it was child's play for Jade to disable the warehouse's security after dark so that Charles and Eva could slip inside.

"This place is a maze." Eva clicked on her flashlight after they'd entered through the back door.

"That'll be good for us tomorrow," said Charles.

The two-story warehouse was jam-packed with movable shelving units that towered to the ceiling and were crammed with crates of iron and steel products. The few aisles between the units were narrow and claustrophobic.

Charles and Eva picked their way around the shelves, heading for the warehouse's docking bay. When they emerged from the maze, they both stopped short, and Charles let out a low whistle.

Over a dozen cars of various makes and models had been parked in the bay, taking up every inch of available space except for an area that was just big enough to squeeze in a good-sized truck. The cars were all popular, common sedans in neutral colors, worn in but not banged up—nothing a person would look at twice on the street.

"Guess they're going to split the shipment up right away," Eva said.

"Looks like it'll be a big one, too." Charles shone his flashlight through the windshield of the nearest car and glanced at the driver's side dashboard. "Siren, you ready for these VINs?"

"Roger."

While Charles read off each car's VIN and license plate, Eva moved silently around the loading bay, setting up a few tiny cameras in strategic positions. She rejoined him just as he finished with the last car.

"No point in tagging these cars now," she said. "They might scan them for trackers before they load them up."

Charles nodded. "What do you think they've got coming in, WASR-10s?" The Romanian knockoff of the AK-47 was a popular choice among Mexican cartels.

"Probably. Though I don't know why they'd break their MO and risk bringing them all this way by truck before splitting them up."

"So far all the cars are coming back clean," Jade said over comms. "I can see a couple of family connections to the Jackals without even trying."

The gang's favored method of smuggling was to conceal weapons in hidden compartments inside cars belonging to family members with clean records. One of their highest-volume smugglers was a Jackal's seventy-six-year-old grandmother.

"I think we're all set for tomorrow," said Eva. "But we're going to have to come up with another method of entry. We won't be able to just stroll in here in the middle of a workday while the warehouse is full of gangbangers."

Charles looked around the warehouse, his eyes lingering on the wide awning-style windows at the very tops of the walls. They were positioned close enough to the top shelves of the units to allow for a safe drop.

Following the direction of his gaze, Eva said, "Ugh. Okay, which one of us is going to climb up there and unlock one of those?"

Charles turned back to her. "Rock, Paper, Scissors?"

He went with scissors; Eva crushed him with rock. She crowed in quiet triumph.

"He throw scissors?" Jade asked.

"Yep."

"Every time, dude. Get some new moves."

Charles sighed, grabbed a grease-stained towel from a bench in the loading bay, and headed for the opposite side of the warehouse. He navigated the shelving units until he reached a movable staircase, then climbed all the way up and eased himself onto the top of the crates against the wall. Moving carefully, he walked along the crates to a corner where the shadows would provide decent cover even in daylight.

These windows hadn't been opened in years—if they'd ever been opened at all. Charles cranked the lever as much as he could, but he had to throw his shoulder against the window a few times before it finally popped out of its frame. He opened and closed the window until the hinge moved smoothly, then threaded the towel along the frame so that pieces of it stuck out at either end when he closed the window again. Tomorrow, he and Eva would be able to use the makeshift handles created by the towel to open the window from the outside.

Charles returned safely to the ground and met Eva by the back door. Once Jade had given the all clear, they left the warehouse and crossed the street, walking the three blocks to Eva's car.

"All good on our end," Eva said as she buckled her seat belt. "See you tomorrow, Siren."

"Roger that, Valkyrie. Siren out."

Charles took out his earpiece and dropped it into his pocket. Eva started the car and pulled away from the curb.

"Want to come over for dinner?" she asked. "Greg's making pot roast."

"I have plans," Charles lied.

Eva gave him a frankly incredulous look.

"I *do*," he said. He couldn't tell Eva that he couldn't bear to be around her, Greg, and the kids right now.

"With whom?"

"A woman I met at the gym."

That was Charles's only option for a cover story; he didn't *go* anywhere else besides work, which was obviously out. Eva raised her eyebrows but didn't push it.

After Eva dropped him at his car, Charles stopped by the grocery store to pick up a precooked rotisserie chicken and a bag of frozen vegetables. Back at his apartment, he settled on the couch with his dinner, cracked open a beer, and turned on the Indiana State football game he'd DVRed over the weekend.

He glanced at the clock on his cable box. Ángel wouldn't be stupid enough to go out again tonight, would he? Bored or not, he would know better than to risk it. Maybe Charles should check to make sure, though . . .

Charles had keyed in the pass code to his phone before he fully realized what he was doing. "Oh, for fuck's sake," he said, irritated with himself. Setting his plate aside, he took his phone into his bedroom and threw it into a drawer so he wouldn't be tempted to use it. All evidence to the contrary, Ángel didn't need a babysitter.

Charles's towel trick worked like a charm, and after creeping up the side of the warehouse the next day, he and Eva got the window open with little fuss. Eva lowered herself in first; Charles followed, dropping to his feet on the crates and immediately hunkering down into a crouch.

Their side of the warehouse was deserted, but the loading bay was chock-full of boisterous Jackals milling around and shooting the shit while they waited for the delivery. Charles and Eva had a relatively clear view of them from their perch, which meant there was a chance the Jackals could spot them too.

"We need to get on the ground," Eva whispered.

They crept along the crates to the nearest staircase and made it to the ground without incident. As they touched down, Jade said, "I count fourteen Jackals . . . no, fifteen. One just came out of the bathroom."

She and Ángel were monitoring the video feeds from a nearby van; Shane and Sakura were posted on either end of the block, monitoring the environment and prepared to lend tactical assistance if necessary.

"Hey, Marcus got a haircut," Jade said. "He looks pretty good."

"Which one is Marcus?" Ángel asked.

"That one there, with the neck tattoo."

"Hmm. Not bad."

"Is there anyone you're *not* attracted to, Siren?" Shane said with a laugh.

"Your mom," said Jade.

"*Guys.*" Eva's voice was no less fierce for its low volume. "Could we please concentrate a little more on the armed gang members?"

She and Charles inched through the warehouse. As they approached the loading bay, Shane said, "I've got a truck coming from the west."

There were no more jokes after that. A breathless, focused tension crackled over the line while Shane relayed the truck's information to Jade. Hunkered down close to the floor, Charles pressed his back against the shelves and peered around the corner.

The Jackals were a white gang, though they had friendly ties with a few Latino gangs with whom they had no territorial disputes. Most of the members present were men, with a couple of women mixed in, all tanned from the San Diego sun and tattooed with the esoteric symbols of gang communication. As would be expected of gunrunners, they were well and heavily armed.

The loading-bay door rumbled and rose. Snapping to attention, the Jackals moved out of the way of the large truck that backed inside, which was marked with the logo of a produce company.

Charles and Eva kept themselves hidden and silent as the Jackals shouted back and forth, opening up the truck and beginning to unload it.

"Only crates of produce for now," Jade reported, since Charles and Eva didn't have a clear sight line to the back of the truck. "Onions and garlic and stuff."

A couple of minutes later, there was a succession of thumping and rolling noises that had Charles frowning in confusion.

"Now they're just dumping the onions out on the floor. This is a terrible waste of— Oh hey, a gun case. Marcus is gonna check inside . . ."

Jade and Ángel gasped in unison.

"What is it?" Eva asked under her breath.

"That's not a WASR-10," said Ángel. "That's an M4 carbine. With a grenade launcher."

CHAPTER NINE

After a moment of startled silence, Sakura said, "A military M4 or a civilian replica?"

"Military," said Jade. "No doubt. Fully automatic, 14.5-inch barrel. Also, the grenade launcher kind of gives it away."

Charles and Eva exchanged a grim look.

"Where the hell would these punks get their hands on full-auto M4s?" Shane asked.

"Griffin, didn't your CI say this truck was coming from Monterey?" Sakura said. "There's an Army garrison there."

"Christ," Charles muttered. If a shipment of weapons had been diverted from an Army garrison, there was no way someone on the inside wasn't involved. This was going to devolve into a total clusterfuck very quickly.

"Maybe they aren't all M4s," Jade said.

Her optimism was proven unfounded as the Jackals continued unloading the truck, piling up case after case of identical weapons. They might not even have enough cars here to hide them all.

"If this much firepower gets into the hands of one of the cartels, the casualties are going to be off the charts," Ángel said.

"That's not going to happen." Eva shifted on the balls of her feet where she crouched beside Charles. "Sounds like they're finished unloading the weapons. Siren?"

"Affirmative."

"All right. Sandman, proceed."

A few seconds later, a burst of gunfire sounded nearby. The Jackals stiffened, most of them running for the open loading-bay door.

"The fuck was that?" said a short, skinny kid who couldn't be much older than fourteen.

"Probably those goddamn 66ers. They're always trying to poach these warehouses from the Espinas."

More gunshots cracked through the air from the opposite direction, courtesy of Sakura. Confused shouts rang out among the Jackals. Charles risked another peek and saw the whole group gathered by the door.

"Dance, puppets," Jade said gleefully.

"Go check it out," Marcus said to the others. "Those fucking cokeheads are gonna bring the cops down here, and that's the last thing we need right now. Go!"

The Jackals took off, heading in both directions. Marcus stayed behind with two men stationed by the truck's cab with their guns drawn, alert to any movement on the street—but not so much to the warehouse behind them.

"Valkyrie, Griffin, you're good to go," said Jade.

Charles and Eva slunk forward, staying low to the ground as they wove between the parked cars. They didn't have the resources to track every single car, so Eva would choose a selection at random to tag with GPS units. Charles, meanwhile, made his way to the gun cases stacked on the ground behind the open truck.

Checking to ensure that his position concealed him from the Jackals' sight, Charles rose to half height and eased open one of the top cases. He was greeted by the sight of a standard military-issue M4 assault rifle, packed along with seven magazines and an M203 grenade launcher nestled into their own cutouts in the foam lining. Jade was always right, and today was no exception—this was military equipment, no question.

Charles pulled a quarter-sized GPS tracker from his pocket. After stripping the backing off the tracker's adhesive, he peeled away a corner of the case's foam lining, pressed the tracker into place, and smoothed the lining flat again.

Though their intel suggested that all of these weapons were going to the same buyer, they couldn't be sure, and Charles only had three trackers. He couldn't risk making noise by moving the cases around to get a varied sample, but they were already sorted into three stacks, so his decision was made for him. He moved on to the next case over and tagged it the same way.

"I'm clear," Eva reported. "Griffin, hurry up."

Charles opened the gun case on top of the third stack, tried to pull on the lining—and found it glued to the side of the case too well to be tugged away like the others. Cursing internally, he grabbed his pocketknife and made two neat, surgical cuts in the corner.

"Just leave it!" Jade said, her voice tight with stress. "Marcus is on his way."

Sure enough, footsteps were heading right for him. Charles stuck the tracker inside, replaced the lining, and lowered the case's lid. He hit the ground and rolled beneath the nearest car just as Marcus rounded the truck, speaking on his cell phone.

"They must've run off," Marcus said, ambling toward the gun cases. "You see any cops? Okay, good. Call Ricky and get your ass back here so we can load up these cars."

He aimed an idle kick at one of the onions on the ground, sending it tumbling underneath Charles's car. Charles grabbed it a split second before it hit his face.

As he ended his call, Marcus turned around and opened the door of a Toyota two cars over, ducking into the driver's seat. The hiding places in these smuggling cars were well concealed, often rigged to require a complex sequence of actions performed from inside the car before they could be opened.

Charles exhaled a breath he'd been holding since he heard Marcus approaching. He army-crawled along the cement floor, trusting Jade to have his back as he moved from one car to another.

"You're good," she said. "Just go as fast as you can. I can set off all those car alarms at once if I need to disorient him."

Fortunately, such tactics weren't necessary. Charles made it to the shelving units undetected, though short of breath and aching from shoulders to hips. Once they'd retreated to the relative shelter of the far wall, Eva socked him hard in the arm. Coming from Eva, that was no joke, and Charles stumbled sideways with a pained hiss.

"*Pinche idiota*," Ángel said. He sounded shaken.

"Let's get out of here while we still can," said Eva.

When Ángel left Campos's office at the end of the day, Charles was the only one left at their cluster, still writing his report on the surveillance mission. He took one look at Ángel's face and said, "What's wrong?"

"The lab results came back on the blood that was on my personnel record." Ángel grabbed his jacket off the back of his chair and pulled it on. "It's Paul's."

"I'm sorry," Charles said.

Ángel shrugged. He'd never had a single doubt that the blood was Paul's, and—unlike Charles—he also had no doubts that it had been taken involuntarily. Someone out there had bled Paul so they could taunt and threaten Ángel. He wanted to vomit just thinking about it.

"The good news is that they got a warrant to break into my storage unit," Ángel said, seeking to distract them both. "The Dallas RAC said the agency will cover the costs of transporting my belongings here, given the circumstances."

"Great." Charles shut down his computer and set his desk in order, which took him about five seconds because it was never *out* of order. "It'll be a relief to have your own stuff back, right?"

"Honestly, what I'm looking forward to most is my driver's license. I'm getting really sick of cabbing it."

"Is that your passive-aggressive way of asking for a ride home?" Charles asked, rising to his feet and putting on his own jacket.

Ángel tilted his head. "Is that your passive-aggressive way of offering?"

With a snorting laugh, Charles said, "Fine, come on."

Ángel stared out the window the entire drive, utterly failing not to obsess over Paul. Were his captors just keeping him prisoner, isolated in a room somewhere, or were they actively torturing him? Was he even still alive? Once Ángel's true identity had been revealed, what use could Paul have to the people who had taken him?

"We're here," Charles said, startling Ángel out of his brooding.

The motel parking lot was full, its No Vacancy sign lit in neon. Ángel thought of the depressing evening awaiting him and couldn't bring himself to reach for the door handle.

"Why did you and your fiancée break up?" he asked, apropos of nothing.

Charles had been relaxed—as relaxed as he got around Ángel these days, anyway—but now he tensed, his hands tightening on the steering wheel. "That's none of your business," he said without looking at Ángel. "And Jade needs to learn to keep her mouth shut."

"Don't blame her. It's harmless workplace gossip." Ángel shifted around in his seat to face Charles. "You got engaged fast."

"I guess. Didn't seem fast at the time, though." Finally turning his head toward Ángel, Charles sighed and said, "You're not going to get out of the car until I answer your question, are you?"

"I just want to know."

"She said I didn't trust her." Charles released the steering wheel, flexing his fingers and lowering his hands to his lap. "She kept waiting and hoping for me to open up more, make myself vulnerable, but she realized that I was never going to lower my guard around her. She said it was like I was always waiting for the other shoe to drop."

"Why?" Ángel said with a sinking feeling.

Charles was silent for a moment. "How can you even ask me that?"

Ángel looked away, clenching his jaw. So Charles blamed his breakup on Ángel's indiscretion with Jared? Fantastic.

"Let me ask you another question," Ángel said, his blood humming with resentment. "Do you miss her, or do you miss being engaged?"

Charles dropped his head against the seat and closed his eyes, exhaling a harsh breath. "Fuck you, Ángel."

"I'm serious."

"Of course I miss her. I loved her."

Ángel narrowed his eyes. "I'm sure she's something really respectable and impressive, right? A lawyer, maybe—but not a trial lawyer. Taxes or estate law or something."

"She's an accountant," Charles said, shooting him a warning glare.

"Thrilling," said Ángel. "And she's probably into farmers' markets and antiquing and day hikes."

"I like all those things."

"No, you don't! You think you should, so you try to make yourself—"

"Amy is an amazing person," Charles snapped. He unbuckled his seat belt so he could twist around to fully confront Ángel. "She's reliable, grounded, level-headed . . ."

"All excellent qualities in an accountant," Ángel said. "Are those really the first adjectives you want to spring to mind when you're describing the person you'll spend the rest of your life with?" When Charles opened his mouth, Ángel added, "What *you* want, Charles. Not your grandmother."

"I swear to God—"

Charles broke off with a strangled groan as Ángel pushed a hand between his legs. As he'd expected, Charles's cock was swelling, the thick bulge of it heavy through the jeans he'd changed into after ruining his first pair of pants crawling along that warehouse floor.

"You're getting hard just sitting next to me and arguing." Ángel squeezed Charles's cock, massaging along the length of the shaft. "Did she ever do that to you?"

"You always make everything about sex," Charles said, but he didn't move Ángel's hand.

Ángel slid as close to Charles as he could get without sitting on the gearshift. "I'm not talking about sex; I'm talking about *passion*. They aren't the same."

Now Charles knocked Ángel's hand aside, huffing in exasperation. "Passion is all you and I ever had, and look where that got us."

Stung, Ángel drew back. Charles pulled the key out of the ignition and opened the door, stepping out of the car. He waited a moment and then leaned back in.

"You coming?" he asked impatiently.

Ángel blinked and grabbed his own door handle.

Charles had been obliged to park in the far corner of the packed lot. They walked up to Ángel's room in charged silence, and once Ángel had locked the door behind them, he stripped off his jacket and holster and waited for Charles's next move.

After a long, slow look around the room, Charles said, "Where did he fuck you?"

"What?" Ángel said, taken aback. "Who, Ian?"

"Has anyone else fucked you in this room?"

Interested to see where Charles planned on taking this, Ángel led him to the desk and gestured to the wall beside it. "Standing up, against that wall."

The bottle of lube was still out on the desk, as were a couple of condoms from the strip Ian had used. Charles took off his own jacket and holster, draped them on the back of the chair, and pulled it away from the desk. Then he grabbed Ángel and dragged him over, shoving him forward into the desk so his thighs hit the edge.

"He should've fucked you over the desk instead," Charles said into Ángel's ear. "Better leverage."

Ángel took a shuddering breath. When Charles reached for the hem of his shirt, he raised his arms to help Charles pull it off him.

"Ian didn't take off my shirt," Ángel said, just to be a dick.

"Then he was an idiot." Charles smoothed his hands up Ángel's chest, rubbing and plucking at Ángel's nipples until Ángel jerked against him. "He didn't get to see how sensitive you are here."

"*I'm* sensitive? I'm not the one who came so hard wearing nipple clamps that I blacked out."

It had taken weeks for Ángel to sweet-talk Charles into wearing the clamps. They'd fucked face-to-face, Ángel's legs in the air and his hand fisted in the chain between the clamps, yanking on it whenever he wanted Charles to give it to him harder.

"I didn't *black out*," Charles said, nettled.

"You almost suffocated me—"

Charles flicked both of Ángel's nipples hard enough to make him gasp. Ángel let his head fall back onto Charles's shoulder.

"I bet he never even touched your cock." Charles undid Ángel's pants and pushed his hand inside, caressing Ángel's erection through his underwear. "Just went straight for your ass, no foreplay at all."

Annoyed by Charles's perceptiveness, Ángel said, "Of course he touched my cock."

Charles laughed. "No, he didn't. Anyone who would take money to pull a stunt like that is too selfish to care about their partner's pleasure." He eased Ángel's cock out of his underwear, and his voice deepened as he said, "I don't know how anyone could not want to get their hands on this."

Rubbing his own erection against Ángel's ass, Charles slowly stroked Ángel's cock, his other hand cupping Ángel's balls. He nuzzled Ángel's neck and bit down with gentle pressure.

"Charles," Ángel said, breathless, watching Charles's hands work on him. Dangerous words hovered on the tip of his tongue, things he couldn't afford to say no matter how good this felt. "Take off your shirt," he said instead.

Once they were skin to skin, things progressed quickly. Charles pushed Ángel forward to brace his hands on the desk and reached for the lube; Ángel tugged his pants and underwear down his thighs with eager anticipation.

A few minutes later, Ángel was writhing flat against the desk, clawing at the wood as Charles fingered him into an incoherent mess with one hand and jerked him off with the other. He was more than ready to take Charles's cock, but Charles didn't seem to have any intention of stopping.

"Fuck, all right, Charles, I get it," Ángel said, panting. "You're great at foreplay. Congratulations, okay? I'll get you a trophy. Would you please put your dick in me now?"

Charles slowed his fingers but didn't pull them out. "Maybe I want to make you come this way."

"Really?" Ángel reached back with both hands to spread his ass cheeks apart, smirking at the audible catch in Charles's breath. "Are you sure about that?"

"Stay like that," Charles said, finally withdrawing his fingers.

His chest and cheek pressed to the desk, Ángel held his ass open while Charles rolled on a condom and nudged up against him. He groaned through his teeth when that thick, fat head pushed inside.

"Was Ian as big as I am?" Charles asked, working his cock into Ángel's ass.

"You know he wasn't."

Charles got in deeper, and then said, haltingly, "Was Esparza?"

"Oh, fuck you," said Ángel, caught off guard.

The mention of Raúl should have killed Ángel's erection—should have had him pulling off Charles's cock and demanding he get the hell out. Instead, his balls tightened and his cock leaped, his ass clenching greedily around Charles's shaft.

Charles was jealous. Charles was fucking *jealous*.

Burying himself to the root, Charles ground his hips in small circles that were guaranteed to drive Ángel insane in short order. "Was he?"

"He was . . . about as thick," Ángel said, struggling to think through the haze of lust clouding his mind. "Not as long."

Charles pulled all the way out and then slammed back in; Ángel gasped, jolting against the desk. "He couldn't give it to you this deep," Charles said.

"*Shit.*" Ángel's hands slipped in the sweat on his skin, and he firmed his grip, keeping his ass spread. "No. Nobody ever has." Pushing back, he said, "Come on, Charles, let me feel you. Come on."

Groaning low in his throat, Charles leaned forward, grabbed Ángel's shoulders for leverage, and pumped his hips, giving Ángel a brutal deep dicking. Ángel moaned and shook beneath the onslaught, overwhelmed by the pleasure of it. Charles fucked like he did everything else—with focused, single-minded determination, the same commitment and intensity of purpose that had resulted in him almost being shot up by a gangbanger that afternoon.

Ángel bit his lip, but as the pleasure continued to build, a low scream escaped him. Charles's thrusts sped up even more at the sound.

"Did Esparza make you scream like this?" Charles asked, his breathing ragged.

"S-sometimes," Ángel said. He hadn't been lying when he said he'd taken pleasure in sex with Raúl. In terms of technical skill, Raúl had been an extraordinary lover; it was everything else about him that had left much to be desired.

Charles grunted in dissatisfaction. Releasing Ángel's shoulders, he took hold of his hips and lifted them, driving in at an angle that lit up Ángel's prostate like the neon sign outside. Ángel's hands slipped off his ass, and he grabbed Charles's thighs instead, feeling the powerful muscles flexing beneath the skin.

"Fuck, right there," Ángel said, rising onto the balls of his feet.

"Yeah?"

"Yeah, God, don't stop."

When Ángel reached for his cock, Charles got there first, pushing his hand away. "Just take it," Charles said.

Ángel rested his arm on the desk and buried his face in the crook of his elbow, the fingers of his other hand still biting into Charles's thigh. He bucked his hips while Charles fucked his ass and jerked him off with perfect rhythm, crying out freely, surrendering every sense to the moment.

"You love this, don't you? You love it when I give it to you rough like this." Though Charles's words were domineering, his tone was anything but—his voice was pleading, cracking around the edges.

"Yes, I love it," said Ángel. "Make me come on your cock, Charles, do it—"

Squeezing Ángel's cock on every upstroke, Charles gave him a few particularly rapid, well-aimed thrusts, and Ángel's back snapped into a rigid arch as he came. His cock was still pulsing when Charles flattened his chest to Ángel's back and pushed all the way inside, humping Ángel's ass with quick, short jabs until he groaned through his own orgasm.

Ángel let go of Charles's thigh and pushed his hair off his sweat-damp forehead, his chest heaving, Charles's weight pinning him flat to the desk.

Charles must have some kind of illness. That was the only explanation for why he kept ending up balls-deep inside Ángel, despite all logic and common sense. He wasn't any better at controlling himself around Ángel now than he'd been in Tucson.

Weak-kneed from the strength of his orgasm, Charles straightened up and pulled out. He looked down at Ángel's flushed, swollen hole, gaping after the vigorous pounding Charles had given him. All Charles wanted to do was shove his fingers right back inside.

Yes. Definitely an illness.

Charles threw the condom in the trash, then turned away from Ángel to fasten his jeans and put his shirt on. When he turned back, Ángel had pulled up his own pants, though he'd left them undone. Still shirtless, Ángel stumbled across the room and collapsed on the bed.

Shifting awkwardly from foot to foot, Charles said, "Are you okay?"

"Mmm."

Ángel lay with his eyes closed, his face relaxed and content. Charles glanced at the door. As desperate as he was to get the hell out, he couldn't leave without saying . . . something.

After a minute of silence, Ángel opened his eyes and said, "I'm sorry, do you need me to pay attention so you can give me your whole 'This was a mistake, it can't happen again' speech?"

"You know we shouldn't be doing this," said Charles. "I'm not— I haven't forgiven you for what happened in Tucson."

Ángel shot upright, glaring at him. "Who said *I've* forgiven *you*?"

Bristling at the implication that he shared blame for how things had ended between them, Charles scowled and folded his arms. He'd said harsh words in anger that night, things he'd regretted later, but he'd been provoked beyond reason. "This is what I'm talking about. What we're doing is so fucked up, and if anyone found out—"

"They'd realize that you're bisexual?" Ángel widened his eyes in feigned dismay. "Oh, the horror."

"Don't mock me," Charles said, his back stiffening. Ángel had *always* done this, pressuring Charles to come out over and over again even though Charles wasn't ready. He acted so self-righteous about it, like any queer person who didn't want to come out was a selfish coward.

Ángel was gay, though, and when he came out, he had at least been assured of finding acceptance *somewhere*. He had never experienced the stigma of bisexuality—still less in black communities, where men on the down-low had long been blamed for increasing the spread of HIV.

Charles wasn't going to take this from Ángel again. "Just because being out is the right decision for you doesn't mean it's the right one for me," he said.

"You don't have to be ashamed—"

"I'm not ashamed of anything!" Frustrated, Charles rubbed a hand over his face. "Wanting to keep my sexuality private doesn't mean I'm ashamed of it, for Christ's sake. Eva knows. As for everyone else—it's just none of their business. You have no right to trivialize my feelings about this."

Ángel flopped back down on the bed. "That's not what I'm trying to do."

It was, though, and it was nothing new between them. Half their fights in Tucson had been about this very issue. Charles had made it clear from the first time they hooked up that he wasn't prepared to come out at work, and instead of accepting that, Ángel had pushed and pushed and pushed, making Charles feel guilty for a decision he'd had every right to make.

Charles shrugged into his shoulder holster and jacket. "I'll ask Sakura to give you a ride tomorrow morning; you're only a couple of minutes out of her way. Though we won't have much to do, anyway, until the Jackals start moving those weapons."

"They won't sit on them for long," said Ángel. His voice was still stiff with irritation. "If I had illegal M4s hidden underneath my trunk, I wouldn't be able to unload them fast enough."

"That should work in our favor."

Charles slid back the door's security chain and unlocked the dead bolt. As he was turning the knob, Ángel gave him one last parting shot. "You know, for someone who's so adamant about not wanting to fuck me, you sure can't seem to keep your dick out of my ass."

"Jesus, Ángel," Charles said wearily, and shut the door behind himself.

Moving out of view of both the peephole and the window, he waited until he heard Ángel get up and refasten the various locks. Then he headed for the stairs.

He was distracted on the walk to his car, berating himself for his utter lack of self-control. As he approached the far corner spot where he'd parked, he dug in his pocket for his keys.

Looking up, he stopped dead, the keys falling from his numb hand to clatter on the ground.

Someone had beaten the shit out of his car, cracking the windshield in three places so that fractures in the glass spiderwebbed out in each direction. The headlights, taillights, and all four windows had been smashed in, the side panels were dented, and every tire had been slashed to ribbons. Glittering chunks of glass and long peels of black rubber encircled the car, strewn across the ground like the mechanical version of arterial spray.

Dazed, Charles rounded the car to the other side. A message had been keyed into the doors in large, jagged letters:

STAY AWAY

CHAPTER TEN

The sound of a door closing startled Ángel from the doze he'd fallen into, slumped in an uncomfortable chair after yet another sleepless night in a safe house. He cleared his throat and pushed himself upright.

Charles and Eva sat on either side of him, the former stiff as a board and the latter calm as ever, her long legs crossed at the knee and her foot dangling at a perfect angle for Ángel to admire the red-lacquered sole of her Louboutin pump. Her husband must be raking in the cash, because no way did Eva make enough here to afford Louboutins—

Ángel's rambling thoughts derailed as Campos came around to sit behind his desk, dropping a couple of file folders onto its cluttered surface. "Sorry to keep you waiting," Campos said. "This week just keeps getting better and better."

Campos placed both hands on his desk, took a deep breath as if steeling himself, and looked Ángel in the eye.

"Your motel room was bugged to hell and back," he said.

"*What*?"

"That's not the worst of it. Forensics combed through your belongings, and there were GPS trackers in your shoes, bugs hidden in the lining of a couple of your jackets."

"Oh my God." Ángel's stomach cramped with nausea. "I bought those things here in San Diego." At least the clothing he wore now had been provided by the safe house.

"I know," said Campos. "You may have been under electronic surveillance this entire week."

This stalker, whoever they were, had known Ángel was in contact with the San Diego field office—this was where they'd sent his file.

It would have been difficult, but not impossible, to wait for Ángel here and follow him back to his motel room. After two years undercover, Ángel was paranoid about being followed and took every precaution, but without his own vehicle, he was limited in the evasive maneuvers he could employ.

Once the stalker knew where Ángel was staying, they could have broken in at their leisure to tamper with his belongings, negating the need for physical surveillance thereafter.

Ángel didn't dare glance at Charles, who he was pretty sure had stopped breathing. "So that's how they knew that Charles was with me last night."

"Seems like it." Campos turned to Charles. "Why were you in there long enough for someone to wreck your car, anyway?"

"Yes," Eva said, her tone glacial, "what an excellent question."

She knew. Ángel was certain she did; he just wasn't sure *how.* Even knowing Charles was bisexual, most people's first assumption wouldn't be that he and Ángel had slept together. Unless Charles had told Eva about Tucson . . .

"I didn't want to be alone," Ángel said smoothly, because Charles couldn't lie for shit when he was anxious. "Charles came in to keep me company, watch a movie."

Campos accepted this without question. "Well, I don't think whoever has it out for you appreciated that."

"You don't really think it's Raúl Esparza, do you?" Ángel asked.

"I won't believe Esparza is alive until I see concrete proof," Campos said. "But I think we need to keep our minds open to the possibility."

His voice short with impatience, Ángel said, "If Raúl wanted Charles to stay away from me, he wouldn't have keyed a nasty message into his car. He would have waited by the car, or *inside* it, and then killed Charles when he came out of the motel."

The other three absorbed this with thoughtful expressions, so Ángel pressed the point harder.

"If Raúl were alive and he wanted me dead, he would kill me," he said. "If he wanted me back, he would take me. He wouldn't send me threatening notes written in blood and pay men to freak me out and bug my motel room just so he could lurk around in the parking lot and fuck up Charles's car. This is *stalking.*"

"You don't think Esparza would stalk you?" Charles said, the first time he'd spoken since they'd entered Campos's office ten minutes earlier.

Ángel shrugged one shoulder. "I think Raúl's version of stalking would be much more straightforward, not to mention lethal. He didn't fuck around and he didn't play games, especially not when he was angry. This kind of sneaky, nonconfrontational behavior just doesn't fit his psychological profile."

"Maybe you didn't know him as well as you thought you did."

Pinning Charles with an incredulous glare, Ángel said, "I spent two years constantly at his side."

"He could say the same about you," said Charles, "and obviously he didn't know *you* very well."

As Ángel opened his mouth in outrage, Eva held up a hand. "I think we can all agree that, out of everyone in this room, Ángel knew Raúl Esparza best." She waited until they'd both settled down before speaking again. "Ángel, do you have any idea who other than Esparza could be responsible for this?"

"I . . . not really," Ángel said. "It's just that this behavior is so—"

"Creepy?" Campos suggested.

"Yeah. I could rattle off two dozen or more people who wouldn't bat an eye at abduction and murder, but this particular brand of psychopathology?" Ángel shook his head. "I don't know. I'll have to think about it."

"I want to encourage you again to take some time off and get out of San Diego," Campos said. "Leave the country, maybe."

"You sound like Jesenia."

"Who?"

"My friend Jesenia, the DEA agent who was undercover with me in the cartel." Leaning back in his chair, Ángel raked a hand through his hair. "She wants me to stay at her uncle's cabin in Canada."

Charles hummed. "That's not a bad idea."

"I'm not running away," Ángel snapped.

"Because staying here to risk death is so much more exciting?"

"How dare you—"

"*Boys,*" said Eva. "I understand that you're both running on very little sleep, but could we maintain a little professionalism, please?"

Ángel flushed and mumbled an apology, which Charles echoed. Eva gave Ángel's forearm a gentle squeeze.

"You'll need to change motels again, obviously," Campos said. "I want you to choose it yourself this time, under an alias you've never used before, and don't tell anyone where you're staying—not any members of your team, not even me. Your cell phone was clean—no bugs, no evidence of hacking—so you can pick it up from forensics whenever you're ready."

Ángel nodded.

"Charles, I've arranged an agency vehicle for you. You'll need to fill out the paperwork downstairs before you leave."

"Thank you, sir."

"Eva, what's the status on the Jackals' weapons?"

"The vehicles transporting the M4s are all parked at residences belonging to their legally registered owners," she said. "The ones we don't have trackers on are being monitored by local police via license plates. We're not sure when the meet with the buyer is scheduled, but chatter on the street suggests it'll be within a day or so."

"Fuck," Ángel said abruptly, as realization set in. "Sorry, it's just— Charles and I talked about the case in my motel room. Not in a lot of detail, but enough to tip off anyone who was listening. And if I've been bugged while at work . . . the stalker could know as much about this case as we do. More, even, if they have their own connections to the cartels."

"I considered that," Campos said, frustration written all over his face, "but we absolutely can't allow this hardware to make its way into Mexico. Up to this point, whoever's targeting you has only seemed interested in you personally, and our window of opportunity is so small here that we'll have to risk moving ahead with the raid once the weapons are en route to the buyer. Eva, set up whatever you need to, get your preparations in place, and then you and your team take the rest of the day off so you're fresh and ready to move when you're called. Understood?"

"Yes, sir," Eva said.

Campos dismissed them, and once they were in the hall, Eva breezed between Ángel and Charles.

"You two come with me," she said as she passed. She disappeared into a nearby conference room without a single backward glance.

Charles sighed, but didn't hesitate to go after her. Ángel followed, closing the door to the conference room with some trepidation.

Eva rounded on them with her arms crossed, a frown darkening her lovely face. "You slept together last night."

"It was a mistake," said Charles.

"A *mistake*?" Eva said. "Leaving aside your prior relationship, and the fact that you're coworkers—you knew Ángel was being stalked by someone who's dangerously obsessed with him, and thought the wisest course of action was to have sex with him? It never occurred to you that might be throwing gasoline on a fire?"

Charles opened his mouth, closed it, and shot Ángel a helpless glance.

"We got caught up in the moment," Ángel said. "We weren't thinking."

Eva raised her eyebrows. "And is this the first time since you've been back that the two of you 'got caught up in the moment'?"

"Yes," Charles said at once.

Ángel kept his mouth shut and his face blank as Eva gave him a searching look. She was perceptive, but he'd fooled some of the most suspicious men in the world for years.

"This cannot happen again," Eva said, stressing every word. "There are half a dozen reasons the two of you shouldn't be fooling around, and if I find out you've been having any more *moments*, Ed is going to hear about it too."

"It's nobody's business—" Ángel started.

"It is when it's putting the two of you in danger. Besides, coworkers engaging in a romantic relationship have a responsibility to disclose that relationship to HR. There could be serious professional consequences for you both, you know."

Charles grimaced, though Ángel wasn't sure if he was objecting more to the word *romantic* or *relationship*. "It won't happen again," Ángel said, and he was so angry with Charles in that moment that he actually meant it.

"Good." Eva uncrossed her arms, her face softening. "I understand that the two of you have a lot of history together, and I can imagine the temptation that presents. All I'm asking is that you think about the consequences of your decisions before you make them. Okay?"

"It's not going to be a problem," Charles said.

Eva nodded and left the room, clapping Charles's shoulder on her way out. She rather pointedly left the door wide open.

"When did you tell her about Tucson?" Ángel asked, wondering if Charles had confessed everything to Eva in some kind of panic after they'd extracted him.

Charles shoved his hands into his pockets. "About a year ago, I guess."

"Oh." Ángel blinked. If that was the case, Charles and Eva were closer friends than he'd assumed. "Does she know about . . ."

"Yes."

Meaning Eva had heard about their disastrous fight on Charles's birthday—or Charles's version, at least, in which Ángel wasn't presented in a sparkling light. No doubt he'd left out significant chunks of the story, because Ángel was certain that Charles still considered his own behavior to have been one hundred percent excusable.

"We should get to work," Ángel said, and hurried out of the conference room before he could give in to the urge to punch Charles in the face.

They spent the morning making all the necessary arrangements to launch a multitarget tactical assault at a moment's notice. Because the meet up was an inspection, not an actual hand over of goods, it was likely the Jackals would only bring two or three cars at most. All the weapons had to be seized at the same time, however, which meant liaising with local law enforcement for backup on top of everything else.

Jade was the first to finish up her tasks and leave, followed soon after by Eva and Charles. Ángel remained at his desk, in part because he wanted to be sure Charles was gone before he left, but also because he really wasn't looking forward to changing motels yet again.

"So, you've had a rough week," said Sakura, coming to lean against Ángel's desk with Shane by her side.

"You could say that." Ángel shut down his computer and pushed back his chair.

"Wanna come shoot stuff with us?" Shane asked.

Ángel grinned.

They spent a couple of hours shredding paper targets at a private range, which did wonders to melt away Ángel's tension. When Shane and Sakura invited him out for a drink afterward, he was happy to accept.

At the casual sports bar they ended up in, neither remarked on Ángel's request to be seated in a corner booth. They ordered a round of drinks and a few greasy appetizers to share, and settled in for the duration.

Ángel had always been a people person; even the defenses he'd built up over the past couple of years hadn't changed that. He easily got Sakura and Shane talking, inquiring after Sakura's boyfriend, with whom she'd just moved in, and Shane's four-months-pregnant wife.

"Do you think you'll stay in San Diego after this is all over?" Sakura asked him after an hour or so of friendly conversation.

"Maybe," Ángel said, though there was no way he was going to stay here, falling back into old patterns and letting Charles jerk him around. The last time had been difficult enough to recover from. "Or I might take the paid leave I'm owed, head up the coast a little."

"That's probably a good idea," Shane said. "I'm sure you could use a break after, you know, everything you've been through . . ."

Sakura shot him an exasperated look across the table, and Shane flushed, dropping his eyes to his beer.

"It's all right, you can talk about it," said Ángel. They'd gone out of their way to include him in their plans that afternoon and treat him like any regular newcomer to their team; he was impressed they'd lasted this long without giving in to their curiosity.

"I'm sorry." Shane looked back up at Ángel, rolling his bottle between his palms. "It's just . . . you seem so *normal*. If I'd spent that long with the cartel, so close to someone like Raúl Esparza, I'd be a hot mess. I don't know how you're keeping your shit together."

Ángel considered this as he savored his last sip of hard cider. "I don't *feel* normal," he said eventually. "You didn't know me before, but I used to be more . . . carefree, I guess. Less guarded. Now I'm too used to watching every word that comes out of my mouth; I'm inside my head in a way I never was before. It makes me uncomfortable when I think about it. I don't feel like myself anymore."

He would never regret taking the assignment. Ángel's work within the cartel had saved lives—maybe not in any direct, dramatic way, but by disrupting the cartel's operations, interfering in their business, dismantling their infrastructure piece by piece. Whatever the cost to himself, it had been worth it.

There were days, however, when Ángel ached to reclaim his old self, who he'd been before learning what it meant to live in constant fear and completely alone in every way that mattered.

"Then how can you not be angry with Esparza?" Sakura said.

"It wasn't *his* idea for me to go undercover." Ángel balled up his napkin and dropped it on his plate. "Raúl didn't respect me—his particular concept of masculinity meant he couldn't treat me as an equal if he was going to fuck me—but he liked me, genuinely wanted to make me happy. Most of the time, he was very sweet and affectionate with me. I don't know that I can really articulate how I felt about him."

He'd tried to, with Paul. It had been Paul who'd listened to Ángel's frantic confession the first time he called Raúl to come over simply because he'd been so lonely, Paul who had talked Ángel down when he was tied up in guilty knots, Paul who had helped Ángel unpack the complex and twisted emotions created by repeatedly betraying someone who cared for him.

It was Paul who was suffering now because someone in the cartel wouldn't let Ángel go.

In a soft voice, Sakura said, "What if Esparza is the one who's stalking you?"

"He's not," Ángel said firmly.

"Then who is?" asked Shane.

Ángel didn't have an answer for that.

The call came just after midnight. Instantly awake, Charles rolled over in bed and snatched his phone off the nightstand. "Hunter," he said.

"The weapons are on the move," said Eva.

"On my way."

Charles was out the door in minutes, headed for the temporary command post they'd set up in a foreclosed house roughly central to the various smugglers' cars. Though dark and silent on the outside, the house buzzed with quiet activity within, blackout drapes drawn over every window hiding the light and dampening the noise.

He met the rest of his team in the kitchen, where Jade and Ángel sat at a table amid a mess of computers and electronic equipment.

"What's our status?" Charles asked as he suited up in his tactical gear along with the others.

"Two of the cars are moving west," Jade said, eyes on her computer monitor. "One of the tagged weapons is with them. The other vehicles haven't moved; we have eyes on all of them, and teams are moving into place."

Eva strapped down her vest. "Jade and Ángel will stay here to coordinate. The rest of our team will be taking point on the meet, with Baerger's team as backup. It's essential that we do everything we can to avoid fatalities—we need the targets alive for interrogation."

A few minutes later, they were bundled into two vans en route to the Jackals' location and keeping in touch with Jade over comms. "They stopped in a gas station parking lot in Point Loma," she said. "I don't know if that's their final destination or if they're really just getting gas, but I'll send you satellite images."

Charles leaned over Eva's shoulder to look at her tablet. The parking lot in question was shared by a gas station and a convenience store that faced each other over the expanse of asphalt; the property backed up against a marine conservation area that was mostly marshy wetland with some tree cover.

"I'll want a man up on each of those roofs and a team across the street," Eva said. "Everyone else will approach in a diffuse formation from the rear. Siren, let me know if there's any movement."

The Jackals were still holding position when they arrived. One of their vans cruised down the street, past the parking lot, to drop off Sakura and a couple of Baerger's guys out of sight; Herbenick, Baerger's best shooter, circled around to get up on the convenience-store roof. Meanwhile, Charles, Eva, and the rest of the agents entered the wetland from the north, taking a roundabout route toward the back of the lot. Shane split off halfway for the gas station.

Guided by Jade, they slogged along carefully, the wet, muddy ground sucking at their boots with every step. Though the tree line at the edge of the parking lot wasn't thick, it provided reasonable cover in the dark so long as they stayed low. Fortunately, there was no fence separating the lot from the wetland, just a short brick wall that could be easily mounted. Charles kept himself spaced evenly between Eva and the agent on his other side and crept into position at Eva's signal, crouching against the wall.

The Jackals had parked their cars near the rear of the lot—six of them, by Charles's count—leaning against the cars and smoking while they chatted quietly. As the ATF agents reported in to Jade from their various positions, three more cars pulled into the lot. The Jackals' body language became tense and wary; they tossed their cigarettes on the ground, clustering together to face the new cars, their hands not-so-subtly resting on their guns.

"All teams ready to move at your go-ahead, Valkyrie," Ángel said.

"Roger that, Phoenix. All teams hold positions for now. I want eyes on the weapons before we move."

Eight Latino men spilled out of the newly arrived cars. The best dressed among them, a tall, lean man with a distinct vulpine quality, strode forward to meet the Jackal who broke away from the pack. Charles recognized Buzz, friend to Amber's boyfriend Johnny—thick and stocky, his sandy-blond hair shaved in his eponymous style.

Buzz and the Latino leader shook hands and spoke a few words before Buzz gestured to the nearest car. As the men moved toward the trunk, one of the other Jackals jumped into the driver's seat. Both entourages shifted sideways, carefully keeping an equal distance between the two leaders.

"Be prepared to move," Eva said.

Charles firmed his grip on his rifle, his pulse quick but steady. He drew deliberate breaths through his nose and exhaled through his mouth, the muscles in his legs tensing in anticipation.

The car's trunk popped open, and after the Jackal inside the car worked his magic, the hidden compartment was revealed. Buzz retrieved the gun case, opened it up, and stepped aside so the other man could take a look.

"Go!"

Charles leaped over the wall, bringing his rifle to bear as the team from across the street closed in, flanking the meet from all sides within seconds. Members of both gangs shouted in alarm, drawing their own weapons.

"Freeze! Federal agents, you are under arrest. Lower your weapons!"

One of the Jackals whirled around and took a panicked shot at Eva, who ducked and rolled out of the way. The *crack* of a sniper rifle rang out from the gas station, and the shooter went down screaming with a bullet to his right shoulder.

At the fire from above, the gangs crouched instinctively, pressing against the sides of the cars for cover. Buzz looked between the two roofs, his eyes wild and his gun shaking as he aimed it at the nearest agent. His well-known reputation for an itchy trigger finger could blow this up into a full-out firefight.

Charles squeezed his own trigger and put a bullet through Buzz's knee. Buzz collapsed with a wail of pain.

"Lower your weapons!" Eva repeated. "We have you surrounded."

An expression of utter, frustrated rage twisted the Latino leader's face. He slashed his hand through the air and called out in Spanish for his men to comply. As guns clattered to the asphalt and the men lowered themselves to their knees, the Jackals followed suit, lifting their hands in the air.

Charles rushed forward with the rest of his team, kicking away the gun from the closest Jackal and slapping a pair of handcuffs on him.

Their vans roared into the parking lot, followed closely by three police cars with lights flashing and sirens blaring. While the police barricaded the parking lot, Charles and his fellow agents rounded up the gang members, loading them into the vans one by one. Ambulances arrived for the men who had been shot, necessitating a pair of officers be assigned to escort each one.

Half an hour of controlled chaos later, the scene had been contained, and the guilty parties were on their way to the ATF office to be processed. Charles checked in with Eva and was pleased to hear that all of the weapons had been secured and accounted for by the auxiliary teams.

"We just need to open up the second car the Jackals brought with them, and we'll be set," Eva said. She waved over one of the crime-scene photographers. "Would you mind?"

"No problem." Heading for the car with the photographer in tow, Charles switched to a private channel so he could communicate directly with the command post instead of every agent present. "Hey, Siren, I need you to walk me through the steps to get to this car's stash."

"She's occupied," Ángel's voice said a few seconds later. "I'll help you. Which car is it?"

Charles hesitated briefly before saying, "Ford Focus, license plate six-Lima-Victor-Romeo-four-four-eight."

The video surveillance from the Jackals' warehouse included footage of them loading the weapons into each car, providing handy instructions for how to access their smuggling compartments. While they waited for Ángel to find the relevant recording, the photographer snapped shots of the car from every angle.

"I've got it. You need to sit in the driver's seat with all the doors shut."

That was a common first step—there was likely a pressure plate beneath the seat, and requiring the doors to be shut to activate the sequence would stymie most law enforcement during a standard search. "All right, what's next?" Charles said once he'd gotten in the car.

"Do you have the keys?" Ángel asked.

"Yeah, they're on the dashboard."

"Turn on the car and . . . well, he presses one of the buttons on the climate-control panel on the dashboard. I can't tell exactly which one, though. The angle of the camera isn't ideal for seeing inside the car."

Charles shrugged and hit the button that directed the airflow toward the footwells. "And?"

"Open the glove compartment and lower the front driver's- and passenger-side windows simultaneously," Ángel said. "From what I can make out, that should reveal some kind of mechanism inside the glove compartment."

Though Charles did as instructed, it had no effect. "Nothing's happening."

"Try a different button on the dashboard, then."

Charles studied the climate control panel, thinking it through this time instead of choosing a button at random. They'd want something less frequently used, right? No point risking the compartment being revealed accidentally.

He pressed the defroster button and lowered the windows again. This time, a loud *click* sounded from the glove compartment as a small panel sprang back to reveal a discreet black button.

"Can you imagine the good that people who do this shit could accomplish if they used their creativity to solve problems instead of create them?" Charles muttered.

"They believe they *are* solving problems," said Ángel.

Rolling his eyes, Charles said, "Just tell me what I'm supposed to do now."

"Pop the trunk before you press the button. After that, you should be fine to leave the driver's seat."

When Charles got out of the car, he was unsurprised to find the trunk crammed full of random crap. He had to call for another agent to help him and the photographer sort, label, and document each item as it was removed until the trunk was finally empty.

"You need to press down on the bottom of the trunk," Ángel said. "The button in the glove compartment should have unlocked it, so it'll slide right open."

Charles smoothed his gloved hands along the carpeted trunk floor until he found an area with a slight rebound. He applied some pressure, and the panel snapped back and retracted. The bottom of the trunk had been hollowed out all the way to the backseat and loaded up with gun cases.

Charles hefted the first case out of the trunk, frowning when a Ziploc bag fluttered and fell over from where it had been stuffed in between the two cases. He set the gun aside and picked up the bag, turning it over in his hand.

"This is weird," he said. "Looks like the Jackals were smuggling a set of fake papers along with the guns. I've got a birth certificate here, social security card, US passport . . ."

"What's the name?" Ángel asked.

"Manuel Juarez." Charles pulled the passport out of the bag and flipped it open.

Raúl Esparza's photograph glared back at him.

"Let me talk to him," Ángel said, pacing the viewing room floor.

"Absolutely not," said Ed.

"Ángel, you can't go in there," Eva said. "If this man is really working with Esparza, we have to limit your exposure—"

"*Raúl is dead*," Ángel spat.

"I can handle this," Charles said, stepping forward to intervene before Ángel really lost his temper. "Please trust me, Ángel."

Ángel narrowed his eyes and opened his mouth.

"*Please*," Charles said again. "You're way too personally invested in this to conduct an appropriate interrogation. If he knows anything about what's going on, I'll get it out of him."

"Fine," Ángel said with poor grace. He crossed his arms and turned to face the two-way glass.

At a nod from Ed, Charles left the room and headed next door. The leader of the Jackals' business associates had proven to be Felix Torres, a US lawful permanent resident with ties to the Alvarado cartel, which was a growing player in southern California. Every other man arrested in the raid had steadfastly denied any knowledge of the false papers Charles had found; Torres was their last hope for a break.

Inside the interrogation room, Torres sat handcuffed to the metal table, the sharp, thin lines of his face thrown into harsh relief by the fluorescent lighting. He met Charles's eyes with confidence as Charles crossed the room and dropped the fake passport onto the table, opening it to the first page.

"Do you recognize this man?" Charles asked.

Torres glanced down at the picture, then back at Charles. "No English," he said, his accent thick and heavy.

"*Así está bien*," said Charles. "*Hablo español.*"

Torres's nostrils flared with displeasure. He considered the passport photograph once more, and when he spoke again, his accent was miraculously much lighter. "I know *of* this man. I also know that he is dead, so I don't see why you're interested in his passport."

"This passport was found with a set of false papers along with the military weaponry you were inspecting for purchase from the Jackals."

"I have no idea what you're talking about," Torres said smoothly. "And as for this . . ." He gestured to the passport. "What is your concern? A dead man has no need for a passport, false or otherwise."

"That's a great point." Charles pulled out the other chair at the table and sat down across from Torres. "Which raises the question of why a brand-new passport with a dead man's photograph was in a car all packed up to smuggle guns into Mexico."

"For all I know, you planted it there."

"Uh-huh," Charles said. "Or maybe rumors of Raúl Esparza's death have been exaggerated."

Torres blinked, seeming genuinely taken aback, and then snorted out a laugh. "You federal agents. Always searching for conspiracies where none exist."

Charles propped his forearms on the table. "You said it yourself—dead men don't need passports."

"The Esparzas have never had friends in Western Mexico or California," said Torres, unimpressed. "If Raúl Esparza were indeed alive and in need of assistance, he would find no help here."

"He might," Charles said, "in exchange for, say, enough money to bribe military officials to divert a shipment of fully automatic M4s."

Torres tightened his jaw, regarding Charles with flat, cold eyes. "That's a very serious accusation, agent."

"About as serious as being caught red-handed with said weapons."

"No money was exchanged," Torres said. "I had no idea my business associates would have illegal firearms in their cars. I would, of course, have informed the appropriate authorities at the earliest opportunity."

"Of course." Charles smiled. "I'm sure your *business associates* will corroborate your story."

They were interrupted by muffled raised voices from the other room. Charles shot an irritated glance at the two-way mirror, which gave Torres the moments he needed to regain his self-assurance.

"You're very interested in why this passport was in that car," Torres said when Charles turned back. "Have you considered *how*?"

Charles raised his eyebrows, inviting Torres to continue.

"Someone paid to have the papers made. Someone put them inside the car. And you can be certain that neither of those people were me. Wouldn't your questions serve better pointed in a different direction?"

Of course they'd considered how the papers had gotten into the car, but Buzz—the highest-ranking Jackal present at the meet—was in the hospital, undergoing surgery on his shot-up knee. Every other Jackal had flat-out insisted that they had no idea the papers were even in the car, let alone where such documents could have come from.

Charles opened his mouth only to be interrupted yet again by an angry shout coming through the wall. He exhaled slowly and then rose to his feet. "Excuse me for a minute."

"Certainly," Torres said with a smirk.

Thrumming with irritation, Charles returned to the viewing room to find an incensed Ángel facing off against Ed and Eva, who both looked like they were at their absolute wit's end. Charles could empathize.

"What the hell is going on in here?" he snapped. "You understand I'm trying to conduct an interrogation next door, right?"

"I understand that nobody here is interested in listening to a single fucking thing I have to say," Ángel said.

"That's not true, Medina," said Ed. "I appreciate that you have good reason to have such a strong emotional reaction to all this, but it's not helpful. We have to consider all angles—"

"Oh, do we?" Ángel's tone was so sarcastic it bordered on insubordination. "Then why don't you consider this? If Raúl used his real passport to enter America and is hanging around here to stalk me, why would he have a fake passport smuggled *back* into Mexico when he's not even there?"

They all fell silent.

"Raúl Esparza is not alive," Ángel said, a little calmer now that he had their full attention. "The stalker got their nose into this investigation through the surveillance they had on me, which we already knew was a possibility, and they're fucking with me—with all of us. If we focus on searching for Raúl instead of what possible reasons someone could have for perpetrating this ruse, we'll miss important details."

"Nobody's saying we can't consider the case from multiple angles simultaneously," said Eva.

As she and Ángel fell back into arguing, Ed gestured for Charles to step out into the hall with him.

"I need you to take Medina home right now," he said once he and Charles were alone.

"What? Why?"

"He's exhausted and distraught." Ed rubbed the bridge of his nose, looking pretty exhausted himself. "I'm happy to give him a little leeway, considering the circumstances, but soon he's going to say or do something stupid I can't ignore."

"No, I understand why you want him gone," Charles said. "And I agree. Why have *me* take him, though? I thought nobody was supposed to know where he's staying anymore."

"Honestly? I don't trust that he'll actually go home if I make him leave right now." Ed shrugged. "But you know him better than I do. What do you think?"

Charles paused, debating his options, though he didn't have any real choice but to tell the truth. "He won't go home. He'll go looking for whoever he thinks can answer his questions."

"That's exactly what I'm afraid of. Even leaving aside Medina's personal involvement, our jurisdiction here is murky at best. The last thing I want is to start a turf war with the FBI."

"All right, I'll take him to his motel," Charles said. "I can't guarantee he'll stay there, though."

"That's all I can ask," Ed said, slapping Charles's back.

It took ten minutes and a threat of suspension from Ed to get Ángel into Charles's car. Ángel spent the entire drive in moody silence, which Charles appreciated. There were certain conversations he wasn't equipped to have at 5 a.m.

When Charles parked at Ángel's new motel—managing a spot up in front this time—Ángel finally said, "We have to talk to Buzz. There's no way it was a coincidence that those papers just happened to be in one of the dozen cars he could have brought to the meet.

Someone put them there on purpose, and he's the most likely suspect. He may have even had direct contact with the stalker."

"He's in the hospital, Ángel. He'll be questioned as soon as it's feasible. And I can tell you now that it won't be by you."

With a noise of deep disgust, Ángel unbuckled his seat belt and reached for the door. Charles grabbed his arm.

"Promise me you're going to stay here and get some sleep," he said.

Ángel looked at him steadily and said nothing.

"Christ," said Charles. "You can't be serious. You'd be risking your life; you'd *definitely* lose your job—"

"So fucking what?"

Charles was startled into silence. "You love this job," he said a moment later.

"I *loved* this job," Ángel said. "Past tense." He yanked his arm out of Charles's grip and got out of the car.

Charles didn't even think before pulling the keys from the ignition and hurrying after him. He caught up with Ángel at the door to a first-floor room not far from where he'd parked.

"I'm not letting you leave this motel," he said.

"What are you going to do, tie me up?" Ángel said as he slipped the key card into the lock.

"Wouldn't be the first time."

Rolling his eyes, Ángel opened the door and flipped on the lights. Charles followed him into the room—and Ángel leaped back against him with a shriek, even as Charles's heart slammed against his rib cage and all the air in his lungs deserted him in one sickening rush.

Paul Warner lay dead in Ángel's blood-soaked bed, wrists and ankles bound to the posts, his sightless eyes staring up at the ceiling and his mouth half-open in a scream.

CHAPTER ELEVEN

"Oh my God." Ángel lurched toward the bed, stumbling over his feet until he fell gracelessly onto his knees beside it. "Paul. Paul!"

He pressed his hands to Paul's face and then his throat, searching for a pulse even though he *knew* Paul was dead. Paul's skin was as white as the sheets beneath him had once been; now they were drenched red with his blood, and more was spattered over the floor and walls. His bound, half-naked body was scored with deep cuts, mottled with bruises and burns.

Nobody could survive this.

A harsh sob tore Ángel's throat. "No. Paul, no, please—"

"Ángel," Charles said, crouching beside him and taking hold of his shoulders.

Ángel shook him off violently and reached for the ropes slicing into Paul's wrists. Charles grabbed his hands, pulling him back.

"Baby, you can't touch him. You're contaminating his crime scene. We need to leave right now."

That got through to Ángel as little else would have. He let Charles haul him to his feet; when Charles drew a sharp, sudden breath, Ángel glanced at his stricken face and followed his eyes to the far wall, which had been painted with Paul's blood.

YOU CAN'T HIDE FROM ME

Ángel let out a low moan and slumped against Charles's chest. Charles half carried him backward, retracing the path they'd taken out of the room and onto the sidewalk outside.

As the fresh predawn air hit his face, Ángel shoved Charles away, staggered to a nearby trash can, and collapsed against it seconds before he vomited. The brutal spasms shook his entire body, bile scorching his mouth and throat. He clung to the metal edge once it was over, not trusting himself to stand.

"Come here." Charles slipped an arm around Ángel's waist and led him to a bench at the edge of the parking lot. "Sit here for a minute. Don't move, okay?"

Charles stepped away, pulling his phone from his pocket. Ángel propped his elbows on his knees and buried his face in his hands.

Paul's dead. Paul's dead. Paul's dead Paul's dead Paul's—

You can't hide from me.

The next thing Ángel knew, a blanket settled over his shoulders. "You're shivering," Charles said when Ángel looked up at him incredulously.

"*¿De dónde sacaste esto?*" Ángel said, not realizing the words were in Spanish until they'd already left his mouth. It didn't matter with Charles, though, so he just pulled the edges of the blanket tighter around himself.

"It's part of a standard car emergency kit."

"Charles," said Ángel. "*Nobody* actually has a car emergency kit."

Charles shrugged and offered him a bottle of water. Ángel accepted it, using the first mouthful to rinse and spit onto the pavement.

"I knew Paul was going to die," he said. "The moment Eva first told me he was missing, I knew. I just— I'd hoped it wouldn't be like . . . like that."

"I'm so sorry," Charles said, sitting beside Ángel on the bench.

Ángel picked at the bottle's plastic label with his fingernail. "It would have taken him a long time to die that way."

"You don't know—"

"None of those wounds would have been fatal in and of themselves," Ángel said. He met Charles's eyes. "Some of those injuries were days old, and the ones that were fresh . . . He died of cumulative blood loss over time. It was slow, and it *hurt*, and he would have been so afraid—"

"Don't," said Charles, wrapping an arm around Ángel and pulling him close. "Don't do this to yourself, Ángel, please."

Ángel rested his head on Charles's shoulder and closed his eyes, silent tears sliding down his cheeks.

The police showed up minutes later, the FBI right on their heels. Soon afterward, the motel parking lot was a jumble of swirling red and blue lights, shouted voices, and bodies rushing back and forth. The motel's other residents spilled out of their rooms to cluster around the police barricades.

Throughout it all, Ángel remained on his bench, answering questions with a numb sense of depersonalization. The only detail he held on to was that Charles stuck by his side the entire time.

Charles shook Ángel's shoulder gently, and Ángel lifted his head, startled to find Charles standing in front of him and the parking lot bathed in early-morning sunlight.

"We're free to go," Charles said.

"Really?" Ángel looked over to where Mina Sadir was deep in conversation with two San Diego Police Department detectives. "They don't want to arrest me?"

"No, of course not." Charles squatted down so they were at eye level. "The coroner's early estimate for Warner's time of death is between 2 and 3 a.m. You've been in the company of dozens of federal agents since just after midnight. Alibis don't get much more rock solid than that."

"Oh," Ángel said, dazed. "Okay."

He was walking away from the scene of Paul's murder. Paul had been killed for the sole purpose of tormenting Ángel, and whoever had done it was still out there, and Ángel was literally turning his back on him and walking away. He was—

Ángel blinked, and found himself sitting in Charles's agency-issued car, his seat belt buckled, already on the road. He rubbed his eyes and asked, "Where are we going?"

"Back to the office," said Charles. "Ed called an emergency team meeting."

"I need coffee."

Charles frowned. "I don't think it's a great idea to put caffeine in your body right now."

"Then I guess it's a good thing you're not in charge of what I put in my body," Ángel said.

Sighing, Charles hit the blinker and pulled into the right-hand lane, heading for a nearby McDonald's.

"Ángel," Charles said as he turned off the car and unbuckled his seat belt. "We're here."

Ángel didn't respond. He hadn't moved for the past ten minutes—hadn't even sipped his coffee once, just held it in his lap while staring off into space with glazed eyes.

Charles leaned over and took the coffee out of Ángel's hands, setting it in the cupholder. Ángel didn't so much as twitch.

"*Ángel,*" Charles repeated, snapping his fingers in front of Ángel's face.

Gasping, Ángel jerked backward, then glanced around in bewilderment. He clearly had no idea where they were.

"That's it, I'm taking you to the hospital," Charles said, already reaching for the keys.

"No." Ángel's blank voice didn't do anything to allay Charles's concerns. "I'll be okay. I'm just . . . dissociating a little. It's not an uncommon response to trauma."

"I know what dissociation is," Charles said. Ángel might be the one with the master's in psychology, but Charles had at least been trained to handle victims and witnesses of violent crime.

Charles unbuckled Ángel's seat belt and took both his hands, squeezing until Ángel looked at his face.

"Tell me where you are right now."

"Um . . ." Ángel cleared his throat, then said, "The parking garage at the office."

"What day is today?"

"Friday—no, I guess it's Saturday now."

"The date?"

"September 12, 2015," Ángel said, his voice much stronger.

Charles stroked his thumbs over the back of Ángel's hands, watching his eyes sharpen and focus. "And who am I?"

"Charles." Ángel's mouth tilted in a half smile. "Never Charlie."

Charles's throat ached, but he swallowed past it and said, "Now, I'm not gonna ask you if you can do this, because I know you can. We're just going to have a brief meeting, and then you'll be able to rest. All right?"

Ángel nodded.

They were the last ones to arrive in the conference room, where Ed and their team sat at one end of the long rectangular table. The others' greetings were uncharacteristically subdued, and they regarded Ángel with sympathy as he took a seat. Charles sat next to him, keeping an eye out in case he started to dissociate again.

Jade slid a box of pastries down the table toward them. Charles shook his head, but Ángel plucked a cinnamon roll out of the box, placing it on a napkin and toying with the crust.

"We were all very sorry to hear about Agent Warner," Ed said to him.

"Thanks," Ángel said, staring down at his pastry.

"Agent Sadir has promised to keep me updated on the progress of her investigation. While we have no jurisdiction to investigate Agent Warner's murder or abduction, we *can* pursue the lead created by the papers Charles found, since it's tied directly to our own case."

"We'll put feelers out to the local forgers," Eva said.

"Good. And the weapons?"

"I'm tracing them now," said Jade. "If they did come from a military installation, I'll find out which one."

Ed turned to Ángel. "Medina—Ángel. My first concern here is how the murderer managed to find your new motel so quickly when nobody but you knew where you were staying."

Ángel pulled his cell phone out of his pocket and tossed it onto the table.

"Your phone was clean," Ed said, frowning. "Forensics literally took it apart. It hadn't been bugged or hacked."

"They didn't need to do either of those things," Ángel said. "This phone can be accessed from the ATF servers."

A frisson of tension went around the table. "Are you suggesting there's a mole in the agency?" Eva asked.

Peeling away a layer of his cinnamon roll, Ángel said, "No. I think the stalker has been using Paul's access to track my cell phone."

Ed waved a hand. "That's impossible. Agent Warner's access was suspended the moment the agency knew he was missing."

"Um . . ." Jade said.

Everyone turned toward her. The nape of Charles's neck prickled at the expression on her face.

"At least twelve hours passed between the time Agent Warner went missing and when it was reported," she said. "I hadn't considered this before because it's so unlikely, but *technically*, that would be enough time for someone with the skills or resources to use his server access to create a backdoor they could continue using after the access had been suspended. Tricky, but it could be done. It's just . . ." Jade hesitated, glancing at Ángel. "They would have had to get the information out of Warner first. And they would have had to—to keep him alive, to show them how to use it. The database isn't intuitive; agents' names and their cell phone IDs aren't directly linked."

"Paul was tortured," Ángel said flatly. "The stalker tortured him for access to the servers, to my lockbox, and then kept on torturing him for God knows what other reasons. The trackers in my clothing were either for redundancy or to throw us off. They've been using Paul against me this whole time."

"Christ." Ed scrubbed a hand through his neat beard. "All right. I'll have this phone destroyed, but I can't have you wandering around out there with no way for us to locate you in an emergency. If I issued you a new agency phone with access restricted to Jade alone, would you be comfortable with that?"

"Sure," Ángel said, with a small smile for Jade.

Ed made a note for himself and said, "You're still certain that Raúl Esparza isn't behind all this?"

"Yes."

"Then I'd like to hear your thoughts on alternative suspects."

Ángel looked surprised, but he recovered quickly. "Stalking is often a way for a person to relieve the intolerable psychological pressure created by an intense obsession with the subject. It doesn't have to be love—it can be rage, fear, jealousy, any overwhelming emotion that demands release. But the relief is only temporary, because the stalking behaviors themselves feed into and strengthen the obsession. That's why stalking tends to—to escalate."

His breath stuttered on the last word. Charles started to reach out to him and caught himself just in time, drawing back his hand.

"If Raúl were alive and knew that I'd betrayed him, I could see him having me killed, maybe abducted," Ángel went on. "He *wouldn't* behave like this. Raúl was jealous and possessive, and he had a temper, but he wasn't obsessed with me. If Raúl had successfully faked his own death, we'd never hear from him again. I definitely wasn't more important to him than his own life."

"Do you have any idea who *was* that obsessed with you, then?" Sakura asked.

"It's gotta be someone in the cartel, right?" Shane said. "If they knew enough to take Warner and create doubt about Esparza's death . . ."

"It has to be someone in the cartel for the simple reason that I haven't had contact with anyone else for two years." Drumming his fingers against the table, Ángel said, "I can't think of anyone who exactly fits a profile like this, but there are a couple of people I'd look at first."

Jade swiped her fingers over her tablet. "Give me their names and I'll run them down."

"There's Roberto Ibarra, one of my bodyguards before Raúl died. He, ah . . ." Ángel paused. "Let's just say he coveted his employer's possessions."

Charles's stomach twisted. He believed Ángel that the sex with Oscar Palomo had been consensual, and from the way Ángel spoke about Esparza, it didn't sound like he'd experienced any sexual violence there either—but Charles didn't know that for a fact. He didn't really know *anything* about what had happened to Ángel while he was with the cartel. There could easily have been occasions on which Ángel had "consented" to sex he didn't want in order to protect his cover or even his life. A handsy bodyguard, for example, could have caused a lot of problems between Ángel and Esparza if left unchecked—

"And the other one?" Jade asked, cutting through Charles's whirling thoughts.

"Mercedes Salazar, one of Raúl's mistresses," Ángel said. "She was his favorite before I arrived on the scene, and she loathed me beyond all rationality. I wouldn't have thought her capable of the stealth and intelligence to pull this off, but she does have a cunning streak, so maybe with enough motivation."

"You'd suspect Esparza's mistress before his wife?" Eva said, tilting her head.

"Maria Elena?" Ángel smiled. "She's not even on the list. Maria Elena and I got along very well. If she found out who I really was, she'd probably think it was hilarious more than anything else."

Everyone at the table stared at him with varying degrees of astonishment.

"Her and Raúl's marriage was a formality," Ángel said patiently. "They'd been living apart for years by the time I came along. There was no love lost between them, trust me."

"All right, so we've got Roberto and Mercedes," said Jade. "Anyone else?"

"Well . . . there's a second possibility for what's happening."

"Which is?"

"I'm being tortured, not stalked, by someone who's well aware of what they're doing and completely in control of their actions," Ángel said, his face grim. "Maybe they chose this particular MO to redirect suspicion, or just because they find it amusing, but the emotions implied by their behavior aren't genuine. They're simply inflicting maximum pain before moving in for the kill."

Shane slumped in his chair. "Shit," he said, echoing the sentiment expressed by every face around the table.

"Yeah," said Ángel. "I'm leaning more toward the first explanation—so far, the stalker hasn't caused me any direct physical harm even though they've had tons of opportunity, which would suggest a measure of concern or possessiveness, or at least a desire to avoid personal confrontation. But it could just be that the perpetrator is playing with their food, so to speak. In that case, we're dealing with an entirely different profile. It could be almost anyone with a serious grievance against me, which is a very long list these days."

"Faking a stalking still indicates a certain degree of fixation, though," Charles said. "Abducting a federal agent, following you all the way out here, placing you under surveillance, setting up these creepy stunts—that requires a serious commitment of time and resources, even if the base motivation isn't the same."

"True."

"What about Oscar Palomo?" Sakura said. "Could he be doing this?"

"He'd be at the top of my list for the second explanation." Ángel had shredded his entire cinnamon roll to bits without taking a single bite; he wiped his hands off on his napkin and pushed his hair out of his eyes in a gesture of exhaustion Charles knew well. "My escaping under his watch would have damaged his standing with the cartel, especially if it were known or later discovered that I was an undercover agent. He didn't have any emotional investment in me, but he's very proud and more than a little sadistic. It's possible he would go to these lengths for revenge."

"All right," Ed said, leaning forward. "This is enough for now. We'll pursue our current leads and then reassess. But *you* . . ." He turned to Ángel. "You're taking the rest of the weekend off. No arguments."

Ángel opened his mouth, but Ed preempted him with a stern pointed finger.

"*¡Basta!*" he said. "*No quiero oír nada más.* You won't be doing yourself or Agent Warner any favors if you compromise this investigation because you burned yourself out. You are not to set foot inside this office for the next forty-eight hours. I'll have you moved to a safe house—"

"We can't do that," said Charles. He'd been thinking about this since they found Warner's body, and no matter which angle he approached it from, he always came to the same conclusion.

"Beg pardon?"

"The stalker has been able to find Ángel wherever he goes—even if the cell phone is how he was doing it, there's no guarantee he won't find another way now. If we keep moving Ángel, all we'll accomplish is burning our safe houses one after the other and putting the custodial agents at risk."

Ed sighed and said, "Do you have another suggestion?"

Steeling himself, Charles said, "He can stay with me."

"*What?*" Ángel and Eva said in unison.

"We obviously can't hide you," Charles said to Ángel, uncomfortably aware of how his words recalled the message left on the motel room's wall. "The best we can do is ensure you're well defended while minimizing the risk of collateral damage."

Eva glared daggers at him across the table. "I'm this team's SSA. If anyone's going to take responsibility for Ángel's safety, it should be me."

"Your husband and kids need to be your first priority. Shane has his wife, Sakura has her boyfriend, Jade has her . . ."

"I dare you to call them my roommates," Jade said, her eyes flashing.

"Partners," Charles finished. He didn't really understand Jade's polyamorous relationships, so it seemed the most diplomatic response. "I'm the only one who doesn't have anyone else to worry about, and I have plenty of room in my apartment. Besides, the stalker is already pissed with me; I'm sure he knows where I live by now. I couldn't be making myself much more of a target."

"Are you okay with this?" Ed asked Ángel.

"I . . ." Ángel glanced at Charles's face, his lips pursed. "Yeah, sure."

"All right, then." Ed clapped his hands on the table. "That's the plan. Charles, I want you to stick with Ángel for now, but I'll call you if we need you to come in."

"Yes, sir."

"Dismissed."

They managed to make it out of the office without being waylaid by Eva again. Once they were back in Charles's car, Ángel said, "So are we going to talk about what a spectacularly bad idea this is, or just kind of glide right past it?"

"I don't know what you mean," Charles said without taking his eyes off the road.

"Come on, Charles. If I stay at your place, we're going to end up fucking, and you know it."

"I can control myself."

"In general? Sure. Around me? History has pretty conclusively proven otherwise."

Charles's hands tightened on the steering wheel, the leather squeaking in protest. "I can't be sure you'll be safe if you stay anywhere else."

"Oh." Ángel's eyes traveled from Charles's tense knuckles to his rigid shoulders to the way he absolutely refused to turn his head. "Okay," Ángel said, deciding to leave it alone.

He closed his eyes and leaned against the headrest, the exhaustion of the past twelve hours—hell, the past two *weeks*—weighing heavily on him. Though he'd gotten a grip on the dissociation, it had been replaced by a pounding headache and a roiling nausea that left a bad taste in his mouth.

Charles lived in an attractive complex of red-roofed, stuccoed apartments clustered around lush courtyards. Ángel got out of the car and trudged after him to the door of a first-floor unit, concentrating on putting one foot after the other without tripping. He'd never needed sleep so badly in his life, but he wasn't sure he'd be able to get there with the image of Paul's body seared into his brain.

Charles opened the door and gestured for Ángel to precede him. Once in the entryway, Ángel stopped short, blinking. Behind him, Charles locked the door and dropped his keys and wallet into a waiting bowl without noticing Ángel's shock.

"Oh my God, Charles," Ángel said. "Were you robbed?"

"What? No, of course not." Charles slipped out of his shoes and lined them up by the door.

Ángel followed suit, looking around with growing unease. They'd entered into one large, long room designed to serve as both living room and dining room, with a U-shaped kitchen tucked in one corner and blinds drawn over a sliding glass door at the far end. The apartment itself was quite lovely—wide open space, pale hardwood floors and fresh white walls, cute electric fireplace set in one wall—but it was empty.

As in, *empty*. The only furniture in the whole room was a couch, an end table with a single lamp, and a television set up on a slim console table. There were no photographs, no books, nothing on the walls—no personal effects at all. Ángel turned in a slow circle and peeked into the kitchen. The spotless granite countertops were entirely bare except for a coffeemaker sitting all by its lonesome.

"So you're going for Great Depression chic, then," said Ángel. "Bold choice."

With a roll of his eyes, Charles headed into the kitchen and opened the refrigerator. "I've never had a lot of stuff."

That was true, though Charles's minimalist style in Tucson had been an actual *style*, sleek and low-key and comfortable. This was just a bare-bones assortment of crap he could have bought off Craigslist.

Ángel waved off the water bottle Charles offered him. "Your apartment in Tucson didn't look like this."

"When Amy and I moved in together, I got rid of a lot of my things," Charles said. He sipped his own water. "She took her stuff with her when she moved out, and I just haven't gotten around to replacing anything yet."

"She left you with nothing even though she was the reason you had nothing left to begin with?"

"You're taking this out of context—"

"You don't even have a kitchen table."

"I eat on the couch," Charles said, his voice sharp. He closed his eyes for a moment and breathed out, then said more calmly, "I've got a futon in the second bedroom. I'll sleep there, and you can have my bed."

"No way," Ángel said. "I'm not putting you out of your bed, Charles, come on."

"Ángel—"

"I'm too tired to argue about this. Please."

Charles led Ángel to the second bedroom, where the chocolate-brown futon was in its sofa configuration, its only companion in the room a floor lamp that wasn't even plugged in. The cord trailed aimlessly across the carpet, far from any of the outlets.

This would be bleak for a broke grad student living off a tiny stipend. For a grown-ass man with a steady, fairly well-paying job, it was beyond depressing.

Charles lowered the back of the futon so it lay flat, then left the room and came back a minute later with an armload of sheets, blankets, and pillows that he dropped on top of the lumpy mattress.

"You don't have any chairs, but you have eighteen thousand blankets?" said Ángel.

"You're still shivering," Charles said brusquely. "I turned the air conditioning down too."

Ángel folded his arms across his chest, embarrassed and a little ashamed of himself. "Thanks." When Charles started shaking out the sheets, Ángel caught his arm and said, "I can do it."

Charles stepped back from the futon. "Good night, then," he said, though it was almost nine in the morning.

"Night."

Once Charles left, Ángel closed the door, opened the blinds over the window to let in some sunlight, and made up the bed. He did a sloppy job of it, but he was worn out and it wasn't like he had to impress anyone with hospital corners or whatever.

Ángel collapsed onto the futon, curling around one of the pillows and pulling the blankets up to his chin. Relentless images of his blood-spattered motel room whirled around in his head and chased him even into sleep.

Ángel heard the door open and close in the distance, but he stayed where he was, leaning over the balcony railing of his villa on the grounds of Raúl's compound. He listened to the heavy footsteps approach, letting Raúl think he'd caught him by surprise.

"There's my beautiful boy," Raúl said as he stepped onto the balcony.

Ángel turned around with a pleased smile. He was careful not to pay attention to the laptop case Raúl lowered to the ground, keeping his eyes on Raúl's face instead. "You're back," he said, and held out his hands. "How was Torreón?"

Raúl took Ángel's hands in his and pressed a kiss to each one before pulling him into his arms. "Very dull without you there."

He kissed Ángel deeply, greedy after a week spent apart. Wrapping his arms around Raúl's neck, Ángel melted into it, giving Raúl the enthusiastic welcome home he was expecting. Raúl slid a hand inside Ángel's robe and groaned when he found Ángel naked underneath.

"Aren't you going to ask if I brought you anything?" Raúl said, breaking the kiss to nuzzle Ángel's neck.

"Oh, I know you brought me something." Ángel dropped his own hand to Raúl's hardening cock and gave him a devilish smile.

Raúl laughed, smacking Ángel's ass beneath his robe. "Then I suppose you don't want the original Dalí I purchased with your bedroom in mind?"

"You're joking," Ángel said with genuine surprise.

"Not at all." Raúl pulled his hand back to brush Ángel's hair out of his eyes, then traced his thumb down the side of Ángel's face and over his mouth, eyes warm and expression soft. "The next time I go out of town on business, you're coming with me."

"I'd love to," said Ángel. Finally. Six goddamn months just to get to the point where he'd be able to travel with Raúl.

They kissed again, Raúl untying the belt of Ángel's robe and spreading it open, bending his head to run his mouth over Ángel's chest. Ángel glanced over Raúl's shoulder at the laptop case that lay forgotten by the door.

When Raúl made to pull Ángel inside, Ángel resisted. "Wait," he said, and shrugged out of his robe, letting it puddle at his feet. He leaned back against the railing, giving Raúl a good long look at his naked body in the afternoon sunlight. "Why don't you just fuck me here?"

"Really?" Raúl arched an eyebrow, gesturing toward the grounds. Though very private, they were regularly patrolled by teams of armed guards. "Someone could see."

"I don't care." Ángel seized the lapels of Raúl's jacket and tugged him closer, playfully biting at his lower lip. "I want them all to know I belong to you."

Raúl was almost too easy. He moaned, turning Ángel around to bend him over the railing and already reaching for the packets of lube he kept in his wallet. Ángel braced himself on the wrought iron, restraining an eyeroll.

Indulging Raúl's exhibitionism would have him in a good mood for days, and a few rounds of vigorous, energetic sex would knock him out long enough for Ángel to spend some quality time alone with his laptop. He'd have to get in touch with Paul, update him on his progress—

A strong hand gripped Ángel's shoulder. With a panicked shout, Ángel flailed out blindly, grabbing the man by the throat and throwing him sideways. He rolled with the momentum, crouching atop his assailant, and pulled back his free hand in a fist.

Charles grabbed Ángel's fist before it could smash into his face, the fingers of his other hand tight around Ángel's strangling wrist.

Ángel shook his head, his mind clearing as Charles came into focus beneath him and he remembered where he was. "Sorry," he said. He released Charles's throat and sat back on his heels.

That proved to be a terrible idea, because Charles wasn't wearing anything but sleep pants, and Ángel had stripped down to his underwear before going to bed; the new position pushed Charles's soft, heavy cock right into the crease of Ángel's ass.

"Shit, sorry," Ángel said again, and scrambled off Charles altogether.

Charles sat up, rubbing his throat. "It's okay; I shouldn't have touched you. I heard you muttering and I was worried there might be someone in here, and then when I realized you were asleep, you just seemed so upset . . . Nightmare?"

"Not really," Ángel said. "I don't know." He flopped down on his back.

"This mattress is shit," Charles said with a grimace. He rolled off the far edge of the futon and came around to look down at Ángel. "You'll never be able to sleep well in here after last night. We're switching."

"No."

"Get up or I'm gonna carry you."

"Yeah, right— *Hey*!"

Charles scooped Ángel off the futon and carried him out of the room. After his initial shocked jerk, Ángel held still; impressively strong though Charles was, he wouldn't be able to restrain a struggling man of Ángel's own strength and size in this precarious position without dropping him.

All of the blinds were drawn in the master bedroom, casting it in the pale glow of what sunlight managed to filter through. Charles dumped Ángel on the bed, said, "Go to sleep," and turned to leave.

"Wait." Ángel sat up, absently noting that this room was as Spartan as all the others, though at least the bedding was of high quality. "Charles, wait."

Charles turned back with his eyebrows raised.

"Stay."

His face twisting, Charles said, "You're twelve kinds of messed up right now. I would never take advantage of—"

"I've never wanted sex less, believe me," Ángel said, cutting Charles off before he could work up any steam. "I just don't want to be alone. Stay and sleep here." He saw Charles's resolve weakening, so although it stung his pride, he added a quiet, "Please."

Charles hesitated a moment more before giving in. "Yeah, okay. Just this once."

Ángel was on Charles's side of the bed, so he slid over on the queen-size mattress. Slipping under the covers, he turned to face the wall. The bed shifted beneath Charles's weight as he lay down beside him.

The ensuing silence was anything but comfortable. Ángel could *feel* Charles's tension creeping across the space between their bodies.

"You called me 'baby,'" Ángel said, because apparently his exhausted brain had decided this wasn't awkward enough.

"What?"

"When we found . . ." Ángel swallowed harshly, staring at the blank white wall. "When we found Paul, you called me 'baby.' Like you used to."

"I didn't realize," said Charles. "I'm sorry."

Ángel closed his eyes. "It's fine."

He heard Charles shifting around, and then Charles's hand settled on his shoulder. "Ángel—"

"Don't."

Charles sighed and withdrew his hand. Ángel burrowed deeper into the covers, and he did eventually fall asleep again, to the sound of Charles's steady breathing and the radiating warmth of his body.

This time, he didn't dream.

CHAPTER TWELVE

C harles had never been able to sleep well during the day, even after pulling an all-nighter. His sleep was broken and restless as he tossed and turned in search of a comfortable position, resurfacing every thirty minutes to gaze blearily at the clock on his phone.

Around two in the afternoon, he gave up and dragged himself out of bed and into the shower. When he emerged, Ángel was still sacked out on the bed, so Charles closed the bedroom door as he headed for the kitchen to make coffee. Lots of coffee.

He was slumped on the couch, sipping his second mug and watching *SportsCenter*, when Ángel came out of the bedroom. Charles fixed his eyes firmly on Ángel's face, rather than the tiny scrap of stretchy fabric he insisted on wearing instead of real underwear.

"Hey," Ángel said, grinding his eyes with the heel of his hand.

"Hey," Charles said with a frown. "You sure you got enough sleep?" Ángel looked like a hot mess, his face drawn and his eyes shadowed with grief and stress.

"If I sleep any more, I won't be able to sleep tonight. Okay if I shower?"

Charles realized that, once again, Ángel was without access to his own clothes and toiletries. "Sure. Use the master—there's nothing in the other one."

"Okay. I'm just gonna . . ." Ángel gestured vaguely to his half-naked body and then to the second bedroom. "Grab my clothes."

"Just get your pants. I'll leave a clean shirt out for you."

"Thanks." Ángel took a few steps toward the other bedroom, hesitated, and said, "Have you heard anything?"

"Not yet," said Charles.

Ángel nodded and shuffled off into the second bedroom. Charles watched him go, a sick pit forming in his stomach. He'd never seen Ángel beaten down like this before, and he'd never hated anyone as much as the person who had managed it.

Charles's soft, worn Indiana State T-shirt was a little too big on Ángel, but not ridiculously so—just some extra fabric in the chest and shoulders. Ángel returned to the main room of the apartment and paused, glancing between the patio door and Charles's position on the couch.

"Why haven't you opened the blinds?" Ángel said, heading for the door.

"No point when I'll just have to close them again in a few hours."

Ángel made a face, his back safely turned toward Charles as he reached for the cord. Granted, Ángel had only been around Charles for a week, but it was becoming clear that this was more than grieving a lost relationship—he was genuinely depressed.

That wasn't Ángel's responsibility to take on, though, and Charles wouldn't welcome his observations anyway. Blinds open, he rummaged around in Charles's kitchen cabinets until he found a mug printed with the words *I Don't Do Mornings*, filled it to the brim with coffee, and brought it out onto the patio along with his new cell phone.

Unsurprisingly, there was no furniture out here, but there *was* a gorgeous Weber grill that was completely out of place. Ángel checked it out with admiration as he dialed Jesenia's number from memory.

"Hello?" she answered, her tone polite but cautious.

"It's me; I got a new phone." That was all Ángel got out before he choked up; he set his coffee on the ground so he wouldn't drop it and braced his free hand against the waist-high railing.

"*Ay, Ángel, ¿qué te pasa?*"

"It's Paul," Ángel said. He kicked the railing with one foot, clearing his throat. "*Está muerto.*"

"No," said Jesenia. "The FBI found him?"

"I did. Someone . . . left him for me."

He told her as much of the story as he could bear, though he left out the message that had been painted on the wall. Talking about it was like reliving the whole thing, and he was shaking by the time he finished, his eyes hot and itchy.

"Holy shit, Ángel," Jesenia said, sounding horrified. "Please tell me you're going to get out of there now. *Please*."

"I can't—"

"Yes, you can. How are you going to get through this surrounded by strangers?"

"They're not all strangers," said Ángel. "I don't think I mentioned this before, but Charles Hunter works for the San Diego field office now. He was part of my extraction team; I'm actually staying with him for the time being."

"Charles Hunter," Jesenia said. "The same Charles Hunter from Tucson who used you as a booty call for over a year and then kicked you to the curb when he'd had enough?"

"*Ey, bájale.*" Ángel retrieved his mug and took a deep gulp, finding the coffee as strong as he'd hoped. "It was a lot more complicated than that."

"Not from what you told me, it wasn't." With new resolve, Jesenia said, "This settles it—if you're not going to leave, I'm coming back out there. I . . . Well, shit, I can't come tonight because I've got my nephew's birthday party, but I can be on the first flight out tomorrow."

"You don't have to—"

"I want to. I'm on leave, and it's not like it'll be any hardship for me to spend a few days in *San Diego*, for God's sake."

Ángel hesitated. As guilty as he felt about inconveniencing Jesenia, he *did* want her to come. She was the only person he knew was on his side no matter what, a phenomenon that had been rare for him his entire life. Growing up, he'd known better than to trust his abusive parents, the hellfire-and-damnation church that dominated his neighborhood, the teachers who pretended to care but were only interested in pushing poor Latino kids through the public school system as effortlessly as possible. Even today, though his teammates were good people, they were little more than strangers.

Charles . . . Charles, he trusted with his life. But their relationship was too inconsistent and fraught with extremes to provide Ángel the reassurance he craved right now.

"Okay," he said. "If you're sure it won't be a problem."

"You were there for me when things got rough," Jesenia said softly. "Now it's my turn. I'll text you my flight details as soon as I make a reservation."

Ángel was on the patio for a long time. When he came back inside, he looked steadier, less on the edge of a tearful meltdown.

"My friend Jesenia is flying in tomorrow to visit for a few days," he said, tucking his cell phone into his pocket.

"That's good," said Charles. "Did she know Agent Warner?"

"Not personally, but she knew how I felt about him." Ángel perched on the opposite arm of the couch, which was as far as he could get from Charles without sitting on the floor, and cradled his mug in his hands. "Looks like the truck with my stuff should get here sometime tomorrow too. Dallas PD went through all of it in case the stalker left me any nasty surprises, but it was clean."

Charles muted the TV to give Ángel his full attention. "What are you going to do with it?"

"I guess I'll just take whatever I need for now and put the rest in storage until I figure out where I'm going to land after this is all over."

"If I don't have to go in to work tomorrow, I'll help you move it."

"Thanks."

There. Casual, friendly, no lingering tension. Maybe it hadn't been the best idea for them to share a bed earlier, but it would have been worse for Charles to abandon Ángel while he was so raw. They could coexist in the same space for a few days without being constantly at each other's throats. Or dicks.

Charles turned the volume back on. A couple of minutes later, Ángel slid off the arm of the couch to sit properly on the cushion.

"How's your grandmother?" he asked.

"She . . ." Charles paused, coming to the startled realization that he hadn't spoken to his grandmother in a couple of weeks. She'd raised him like a son, and for most of his adult life, he'd never gone more than a few days without calling her. She would chat about the new drama in her Bible-study group or who in the neighborhood was popping out kids now—and where was *her* great-grandchild, Charles, because she wasn't getting any younger . . .

Ángel was still waiting for an answer. Charles cleared his throat.

"She's doing all right," he said. "Had her hip replaced last year, and she's been feeling better ever since."

"That's good." Ángel shifted, restless, and glanced toward the patio door. "Where'd you get the grill?"

"Hm?" Following Ángel's eyes, Charles said, "Oh, that thing. It was an engagement present from some friends, and when Amy and I broke it off, they wouldn't take it back. Amy didn't want it, so she left it here. I'd forgotten it was out there, to be honest."

"You could probably get good money for it on Craigslist."

"You can have it if you want."

"That's not what . . ." Ángel sighed, fiddling with his mug. "I thought I could grill some steak tonight, as a thank-you for letting me crash here."

"Sure, thanks," Charles said, and returned his gaze to the television.

Beside him, Ángel wound up tighter and tighter as the minutes ticked by, his fingers tapping against his mug. Charles ignored it as long as he could, but all the fidgeting was driving him to distraction.

"*What*?" he finally said. "If there's something you want to say, just say it."

"Are you going to sit here watching TV all day?" said Ángel.

"Well, we'll have to go to the grocery store at some point—"

Ángel jumped off the couch and hit the power button on the television.

"What the fuck," Charles said, too tired to work up real indignation.

"I can't sit in this apartment all day long with nothing to do," Ángel said. "I'll literally go crazy, and honestly, I don't think it's a great idea for you either. Can we just . . . I don't know, go to the gym or something?"

Charles didn't really want to get off the couch, but if Ángel couldn't settle down and ended up roaming the apartment like a squirmy puppy, *he* would go crazy. "Yeah, fine," he said, rising to his feet. "I've got a guest pass you can use."

They had to stop at Target first so Ángel could pick up some gym-appropriate clothing, as his motel room was still an active crime scene. At the gym, they went their separate ways, and Charles appreciated the break. The more time he spent in Ángel's company, the more confused he became; his anger and pain were still unresolved, but so was his attraction, sexual and otherwise.

He and Ángel kept acting like they'd ended things with that blowout fight. Since Ángel had left so abruptly afterward, though, the truth was that they'd just pressed Pause.

Charles made sure he finished his workout first—he wasn't going to risk being tempted into fooling around with Ángel in the gym showers, as he had on certain past occasions. Waiting in the smoothie bar with a recovery shake, Charles had to admit that he did feel much better than he would have if he'd stayed at home. He was still tired, but now his fatigue felt well earned, rather than the bleak cumulative effects of a sleepless night, an unsatisfying nap, and emotional exhaustion.

They stopped at the grocery store by Charles's apartment on the way home, splitting up once again to get it done faster. "Can you grab me some ice cream while you're in the frozen food aisle?" Ángel asked.

"Sure," Charles said. It was beyond him how Ángel managed to maintain such a great body while stuffing it full of junk food at every opportunity.

When they met back up at the checkout, Charles tossed Ángel the pint of cookie dough ice cream he'd grabbed. Ángel caught it and turned it over, a strange expression crossing his face.

"What?" Charles started unloading the rest of his groceries onto the conveyor belt.

"You know you never asked me what flavor I wanted, right?"

"Did I get the wrong one?"

"No," Ángel said with a small smile. "It's exactly right."

Charles gave an uncomfortable shrug and turned away, digging his wallet out of his pocket.

Back at his apartment, Charles threw together a salad and some baked potatoes while Ángel grilled the steaks. They ate on the couch with a couple of beers, watching *Let's Be Cops* on demand—Ángel had been in Mexico when it came out, and Charles had never gotten around to seeing it either, because goofy comedy hadn't appealed to Amy. The whole evening was easy, familiar.

Too familiar. Ángel had cooked Charles's steak just the way he preferred it without ever asking; Charles had bought a new six-pack of beer at the store because he'd known Ángel wouldn't like the dark stout he already had in his refrigerator. Even though Ángel wasn't as free with his laughter as he'd been two years ago, Charles could anticipate each moment when the movie would make him chuckle, and he was right every single time.

They were falling right back into old habits. Charles tried to hold on to the hurt Ángel had caused him, the anger he still felt, but after the rough few days he'd had, that all seemed less important than how good it felt just to have someone in the apartment with him again.

Instead of focusing on the painful parts of their history, Charles's brain spilled over with memories of the good times. There had been a lot of those—Ángel's body sliding against his on the dance floor, Ángel drunk and giggly and handsy in the back of a cab, Ángel soft-eyed and sleepy in his bed the next morning...

"I'm going to the kitchen," Ángel said, startling him. "Do you want another beer?"

"No, thanks." More alcohol was the last thing Charles's fading self-control needed right now.

Ángel took both their plates to the kitchen, returning with his pint of ice cream and a spoon. He settled back onto the couch and dug right into the carton.

"You're not going to put that in a bowl?" Charles said, before realizing they'd had this argument before.

This *exact* argument. He could have mouthed Ángel's response along with him.

"Why would I get a bowl dirty when I'm the only one who's going to eat out of the container?" Ángel lifted another spoonful of ice cream to his lips.

Charles glanced sideways, watching Ángel curled up comfortably on his couch, barefoot and wearing Charles's T-shirt. How could he have ever talked himself into believing this was going to work? He'd never been able to spend any length of time in Ángel's company without fucking him, fighting with him, or doing both simultaneously.

Ángel had set Charles on fire the moment they'd met, and while those flames had banked and flared over the years, they'd never been extinguished.

Ángel noticed Charles looking and held out the carton. "What, do you want some?"

"I'm good," Charles said, jerking his eyes back to the TV.

The silence between them charged with thoughtful tension. A few moments later, Ángel shifted over on the couch, closing the distance between their bodies. Charles took a shaky breath and continued staring at the screen. He had no idea what the fuck was going on—what movie were they watching?

"Charles," Ángel said, and his voice had acquired the low, smoky quality that meant he was turned on. "A few bites of ice cream won't ruin your body, you know."

"I don't like cookie dough." Charles turned his head anyway, heart pounding as he met Ángel's dark eyes. He opened his mouth for the spoonful Ángel offered him and swallowed it down.

Ángel licked his own lips, gazing at Charles's mouth. He was sitting way too close, kneeling on the couch with both knees pressed against Charles's thigh. Charles could hear each one of his heavy breaths.

Ángel spooned up more ice cream, started for Charles's mouth— and flipped the spoon over halfway, dropping the ice cream onto Charles's chest. Charles jumped at the sudden shock of cold.

"Oops," Ángel said.

Charles could no longer keep his hands off Ángel. He stroked Ángel's hip, then snagged the waistband of Ángel's jeans. "If you wanted me to take my shirt off, you could have just asked. You didn't have to ruin it."

"It's not ruined. That'll come right off." Ángel smirked. "I'm sorry, did I say *off*? Obviously I meant *out*."

Charles laughed; he couldn't help himself, and the delighted smile he got in return was well worth it. "Obviously," he said. He stripped out of his shirt, tossed it aside, and leaned back, letting Ángel ogle him.

Ángel fed Charles more ice cream, then dropped another spoonful onto his bare chest. This time, Charles was prepared, and he held himself still as the cold liquid slid down his skin. He *wasn't* prepared for Ángel's hot, sinful mouth to follow, licking along the path the ice cream had taken until he found Charles's nipple and sucked hard. Charles groaned aloud at the slight nip of Ángel's teeth.

"C'mere," Charles said, hooking his fingers under Ángel's chin. He pulled Ángel upright and into the kiss he'd been wanting to seize all evening.

Ángel swung his leg over Charles's thighs, settling on Charles's lap and deepening the kiss, pushing Charles hard against the back of the couch. He braced one hand on Charles's shoulder, the other still holding the ice cream carton. Charles yanked open the fly of Ángel's jeans and shoved his own hands down the back to grab Ángel's ass and help him grind their cocks together.

They were both flushed and panting when they came up for air, Ángel appearing as dazed as Charles felt. Ángel sat back on Charles's thighs and looked at his groin.

"Don't even think about getting ice cream on these jeans," Charles said.

"Get your cock out, then."

Charles opened his jeans, then shifted around and tugged them down far enough to free his balls as well as his cock. He was aching, standing at full attention, his cock straining toward Ángel like it knew who was responsible for its current state.

Though Charles braced himself, he hissed through his teeth and clutched at the couch for support when Ángel dripped ice cream onto his cock. For a few seconds, Ángel watched with a half-open mouth as the ice cream trickled down Charles's shaft; then he slid back and knelt between Charles's legs. He set the carton on the floor, got rid of his own shirt, and bent his head, lapping up all of the ice cream before he took Charles's cock into his mouth and let it glide right into his throat.

"God, that feels good." Charles threaded his fingers through Ángel's silky hair and closed his eyes.

Ángel was so fucking good at this, every bit as enthusiastic as he was skilled. He alternated between fast, shallow sucking and deep, slow strokes that brought his mouth all the way to where his hand gripped tight at the base of Charles's cock, working Charles into a fever pitch in no time. Charles was moments away from blowing his load when his cell phone rang, startling them both.

"Fuck," he said, fumbling for his phone and glancing at the caller ID. "It's Eva. If I don't answer, she's gonna get suspicious."

Ángel pulled back. "Take it."

Grimacing in discomfort, Charles swiped his thumb across the screen and lifted the phone to his ear. "Hey, what's— *Fuck*!"

Ángel's mouth was back around him, wet and tight and searing hot, his head bobbing in Charles's lap without a care in the world.

"Shit, sorry, Eva, hang on a second." Charles pressed the Mute button, glaring down at Ángel. "What the hell are you doing? If she figures out what's going on—"

With a slick *pop*, Ángel slid off Charles's cock, though he continued lazily stroking him with one hand. "How would she? Can't you control yourself?"

Oh, so that was how it was? Charles's blood fired up at the challenge. "You think you're that good of a cocksucker, huh?"

Ángel flicked his tongue against the tip of Charles's cock, grinning when Charles's hips twitched. "I know I'm that good of a cocksucker."

Charles's eyes narrowed. Holding Ángel's gaze, he picked up his phone, unmuted it, and said, "Sorry, Eva, I dropped something heavy on my foot."

Ángel's grin widened in the moments before he descended on Charles's cock once more.

"Are you okay?" Eva asked.

"I'm fine." Charles gritted his teeth against the hitch in his breath when Ángel's tongue dragged along the underside of his shaft. "What's up?"

"I'm just calling to check in," she said. "The cops in custody of Buzz gave us an update—he came through his surgery fine and he's recovering well, but with all the painkillers he's on right now, it would be too easy for a lawyer to challenge any statement he made."

"Buzz is too doped up to be questioned tonight," Charles said to Ángel.

Ángel rolled his eyes. His mouth was still stuffed with Charles's cock, his full, pretty lips stretched wide. As he took Charles deeper into his throat, his eyes fluttered shut, long lashes sweeping his flushed cheeks. He moaned softly around his mouthful.

"...hear me?" Eva was saying, sounding irritated. "*Charles.*"

"Uh, sorry, what?"

"We're going to send someone out to interrogate him tomorrow morning. I was thinking Buzz would respond best to Shane."

"Yeah, sounds like a plan." Charles stared down at his lap, watching Ángel going to town. He enjoyed giving head himself, but Ángel turned it into performance art, fucking his mouth on Charles's cock and moaning and squirming around like he'd never had it so good.

"You sure you're okay? You sound out of breath."

Coming up for air, Ángel met Charles's eyes and nursed languidly at the head of his cock. His mouth was already swollen, glistening with saliva and a bit of Charles's pre-come.

Charles clawed his free hand around the edge of the couch to keep from reaching for Ángel's head. He looked away, training his eyes on the far wall—there was no rule that said he had to watch.

"I bruised my foot up pretty bad," he said into the phone. "I'll ice it in a minute. Was there anything else?"

Eva paused, then said, "The other Jackals in custody have been spilling some good stuff, trying to cut themselves deals all over the place. We're going to be knocking down some doors tomorrow—I may need you to come in."

"That's fine. Just let me know."

Ángel's hand snuck between Charles's legs, caressing his balls while he sucked hard on Charles's shaft. Charles made a noise that was definitely *not* a whimper and clapped one hand over his eyes, struggling for control.

"How's Ángel doing?" said Eva.

So good, Charles thought nonsensically. He lowered his hand, his attention drawn helplessly back to the sight of his cock sliding in and out of Ángel's mouth. "He's, um ... he could handle a lot more than this before he'd give up."

Ángel's choked laugh reverberated through Charles's cock and balls. Charles slapped his free hand against the couch cushions and hunched over, breathing through it.

"Okay," Eva said. "I'm not going to ask anything else, because I know you're not the kind of man who would have sex with someone who just experienced a loss in one of the most traumatic ways possible and is under the stress of being stalked by a psychotic murderer who likes to paint with blood. Right?"

Charles winced. "Right."

"I'll call in the morning and let you know what's going on. Tell Ángel I said hi."

"I will. Have a good night." Charles hung up and dropped the phone on the end table; the second his hands were free, they landed on Ángel's shoulders, stroking his bare skin. "Eva says hello."

"Mmm." Ángel lifted his head. "You held it together better than I expected. I'm impressed."

His voice was so hoarse. It was all low and scratchy because he'd had Charles's *cock* in his *throat*, and God, Charles had to get back in there.

Cupping Ángel's head with one hand, Charles guided him to his cock, but Ángel turned his face at the last second so the tip skated over his cheek instead. Charles groaned.

"I'd rather have you finish inside me," Ángel said.

Charles's balls throbbed at the thought of the time it would take to prep Ángel and get him caught up to where Charles was.

"I'll never last that long," Charles said. He smoothed his hand down to the nape of Ángel's neck and rubbed his muscles, eliciting a pleased hum. "Can't we finish like this?"

Ángel tilted his head back against Charles's massaging hand. "What's in it for me?"

"I'll do you afterward."

"You won't be too tired?" Ángel said dubiously.

Charles glared at him. "That happened one time."

"*Three* times."

Despite his show of reluctance, Ángel pressed a line of kisses to the side of Charles's shaft, working his way down. He could be convinced, but Charles would have to offer him something he wanted more than a blowjob, something to make up for not being fucked.

Ángel rubbed the head of Charles's cock back and forth over his lower lip. Charles's jaw went slack as he watched.

"I'll eat you out," Charles said.

"*Really*," said Ángel, sitting back on his heels.

"Really." It was a tempting offer, Charles knew; he'd always had to be talked into rimming Ángel before.

"Without a dental dam?"

"*Yes.*" Charles took hold of Ángel's head with both hands but didn't pull. "Now will you get your mouth back on my cock?"

"That's not very nice, Charles," Ángel said, his mild scolding tone going straight to Charles's balls.

"I'm sorry," Charles said, light-headed. "Please."

Ángel lowered his head until Charles's cock was grazing his lips. "Please what?"

"Please suck my cock."

Ángel swallowed him down, and Charles moaned in relief.

He gave a small, experimental thrust of his hips; when Ángel didn't object, Charles thrust harder, fucking up into Ángel's mouth. Ángel took it like a champion, bracing his hands on Charles's thighs, shifting himself into a better position for having his throat fucked.

"Oh God," Charles said. He tugged gently on Ángel's head in time with his pumping hips, taking complete control of the blowjob.

Ángel relaxed into it. Reaching into his open jeans, he pulled his cock out of his underwear and stroked himself while Charles used his mouth.

"Such a gorgeous fucking cocksucker," said Charles, mesmerized. "Take a little more for me."

Though Ángel was right at his limits, gagging a little on every deep thrust, he never backed off. It was Charles who couldn't sustain that rough pace for long, urging Ángel's face up and out of his lap.

"I'm gonna come," he said.

Ángel climbed up onto Charles's lap again, straddling his legs and jerking him off. Charles clutched Ángel's thighs, pleasure spiraling tighter and tighter, and watched Ángel's hand flying on his wet, swollen cock.

At this angle, Charles was going to shoot all over Ángel's stomach when he came. Back in Tucson, Ángel had allowed Charles to give him a comeshot every so often, but Charles would have thought that privilege had been revoked.

"I'll come on you like this," Charles said, as if Ángel could have failed to notice.

"Yeah, you're gonna blow your load all over me." Ángel's own cock bobbed between them, knocking against Charles's.

"I'd rather come on your face," Charles said with raw honesty.

"I'm sure you would." Ángel leaned forward, brushing the head of Charles's cock against the hard muscles of his abdomen, his hand speeding up even more. "I'll tell you what. If you're a good boy when you're eating me out, I'll let you come on my face next time—"

Charles came with a strangled groan, his back bowing away from the couch. His hips jerked with every pulse as he painted Ángel's skin. Ángel coaxed out a few last drops, his hand lingering near the head of Charles's cock.

Only then did Charles realize they didn't have anything at hand to clean up the mess. He made a feeble attempt to get up, but Ángel pushed him back down and swung himself off Charles's lap.

"I'll be right back," Ángel said, and headed for the kitchen. He returned a minute later, scrubbing his stomach with a damp dishcloth, his hard cock still hanging out of his jeans.

Ángel tossed the cloth to Charles, who wiped himself down before hitching his pants and underwear back up. He zipped his jeans as he watched Ángel do the exact opposite, stripping out of the rest of his clothes until he stood buck naked in Charles's living room.

Charles slid off the couch and knelt in front of Ángel. Smoothing his hands up Ángel's thighs, he nuzzled the crease of Ángel's hip, breathing him in. Then he licked a broad stripe up the side of Ángel's cock and sucked it into his mouth, bobbing his head, reacquainting himself with the taste and texture.

Ángel's nails scritched along his scalp. "This isn't what you promised," he said, though he seemed disinclined to stop him.

Ignoring him for the moment, Charles continued sucking his cock, kneading Ángel's ass cheeks with both hands. He hadn't given head since—well, since the last time he'd done it for Ángel, over two years ago. He was out of practice, unable to take as much as he remembered.

Pulling off, Charles said, "Get on the couch."

Ángel arranged himself on the couch with his arms propped on the back, his knees spread wide and his back arched to present his ass. Charles knelt behind him and admired the picture he made, those firm round cheeks parted just enough to give him a good look at Ángel's hole.

Ángel had been the first lover, male or female, who had been able to convince Charles to rim him. Charles had been so unenthusiastic that first time, assuming he would hate it, thinking he was doing Ángel some enormous favor—and then had been so embarrassed by how much he enjoyed it that he'd still been reluctant to repeat the experience afterward.

Charles massaged Ángel's ass, indulging himself in the give of the supple flesh, then parted Ángel's cheeks farther, using his thumbs to spread the rim just a bit. He worked up a mouthful of saliva and spat right onto Ángel's hole; Ángel's entire body jerked in response.

"Fuck, I love it when you do that," Ángel said.

"Really?" Charles said, surprised.

"It's so fucking dirty."

"Well, I have to get you wet," Charles said, and then smirked at the shudder that ran down Ángel's back.

Holding Ángel open, he leaned forward and kissed him gently, his breath gusting against Ángel's skin. His lips traveled down to Ángel's balls and back up, soft and clinging. By the time he returned to kissing Ángel's hole, Ángel's thighs were quivering.

"*Charles*," he said.

"What, you don't like this?" Charles asked, all innocence.

"Use your tongue!"

Throwing his earlier words back at him, Charles said, "That's not very nice, Ángel."

Ángel twisted around to glare at Charles over his shoulder. He looked so sexy scowling, with his ass still up in the air, that Charles couldn't resist sinking his teeth into one lush ass cheek. Gasping, Ángel dropped his head to his arms.

Charles soothed the bite mark with his tongue and gave Ángel what he wanted, licking along his perineum and over his hole. With a firm grip on Ángel's ass, Charles shifted into a more comfortable position on his knees and settled in for a good, long rimjob.

Ángel wasn't shy about being eaten out—he rocked back and forth, pushing his ass against Charles's face, urging him on with filthy encouragement. Charles savored every grunt and groan, every shaking muscle as his exploring tongue pushed Ángel closer to the point of incoherence.

When Charles worked his tongue into Ángel's hole, Ángel moaned loud enough to echo off the walls and said, "Yeah, fuck me with your tongue, come on—"

Charles plunged his tongue in and out, getting as deep as he could; he pulled back for a moment, lapping around Ángel's hole while he rested his aching jaw, then dove back in. Ángel came undone underneath the attention, squirming around and scrabbling at the back of the couch. His cock dripped pre-come all over the upholstery.

Charles made to give Ángel a reach-around, but Ángel pushed his hand away. "You're not coordinated enough to do both," said Ángel. "Just focus on my ass."

Rolling his eyes, Charles smacked said ass in reproof. Ángel yelped and arched his back, just about begging for more—so Charles gave it to him, slapping both cheeks pink before he got back to work. This time, Ángel jerked himself off while Charles cored him open on his tongue.

"I need . . . I need more inside me," Ángel said, sounding wrecked.

His hole was slack and relaxed, drenched with Charles's saliva. One finger should be fine, *maybe* two, but that was as far as Charles would go without real lube. He slid one finger in up to the third knuckle and was greeted with a deep-throated groan.

Charles leaned in and licked around his finger as he fucked Ángel with it. He grunted in surprise when one of Ángel's hands landed on his head, pressing Charles's face against his ass.

"I'm so close," Ángel said. "Don't stop."

Though Charles couldn't see for himself, he could imagine the lewd picture Ángel must be making—bent over on his knees, one hand on his cock and the other stretched back to hold Charles in place. He had to be resting his forehead on the back of the couch to keep his balance, more concerned about having his ass played with than his own comfort—

His groan muffled by Ángel's skin, Charles hooked his finger toward the front of Ángel's body and found his prostate, massaging it in a brisk circle. Ángel cried out, his body quaking and muscles rippling as he came hard onto the couch. Charles helped him along, milking his prostate to prolong his orgasm, until Ángel gave a weak moan, his hand falling limply from Charles's head.

Charles withdrew his finger and sat back, wiping his mouth. His jaw was on fire and his lips were numb, but it was well worth it to see Ángel so fucked out.

Ángel shifted sideways, sprawling on one side of the couch. Charles picked up the dish towel and cleaned his hand before scrubbing Ángel's come off the upholstery.

"Sorry about your couch," Ángel said, watching him through half-lidded eyes.

"It's seen worse," said Charles, though that wasn't quite true. Now, the couch he'd had in Tucson—*that* thing had seen some shit.

He finished cleaning and went to his bathroom to drop the cloth in the hamper. Pausing in front of the mirror, Charles forced himself to own up to the truth of the situation. Yes, being with Ángel felt good; it always had. That didn't mean it was the right thing to do, or that he wouldn't end up hurting. Ángel had never apologized for Tucson, and Charles wasn't sure he could forgive him even if Ángel did. Plus, Ángel was all screwed up from the stalker, not to mention his time undercover. This wasn't fair to either of them.

When Charles returned to the living room, Ángel was half-dressed. "You don't have to say anything," Ángel said before Charles could speak. He pulled his T-shirt over his head. "We both knew this was going to happen, and if we try to talk about it, we'll only end up fighting. Can we please just accept that we've never been good at not fucking each other and leave it at that?"

"Yeah," Charles said, shamefully relieved. If Ángel wasn't going to make a big deal out of this, neither would he.

Ángel flopped down onto the couch. Charles glanced at the television, where the movie credits were rolling.

"I know it's early, but I'm going to hit the sack," he said. "I didn't really sleep earlier, and I'm totally beat."

"Okay, good night." Ángel picked up the remote control.

Halfway to his room, Charles turned. "Are you going to . . ."

"I'll sleep on the futon," Ángel said with a small smile.

Charles nodded and stepped into his bedroom, shutting the door behind himself. He exhaled heavily and considered the interaction they'd just had. The aftermath of hooking up with Ángel yet again could have been much worse—shouting, insults, thrown objects. A calm exchange of words and immediate disengagement was the best he could have hoped for.

So why did he feel so uneasy?

Ángel bided his time, flipping through the channels with the volume low enough that he could keep an ear out for any sounds from Charles's bedroom. Charles could have been telling the truth about going straight to bed—or he could have just wanted to get away from Ángel.

After half an hour of silence, Ángel padded over to the bedroom door and cracked it open. Charles lay on his back, twisted up in the covers, one arm flung out to the side. Ángel watched the steady rise and fall of his chest for perhaps longer than was necessary to be sure he was really asleep.

Closing the door with a quiet *click*, Ángel turned off the television, killed the lights, and shut the door to the second bedroom as well. Then he hurried toward the front door, where he shoved his feet into his shoes, helped himself to one of Charles's sweatshirts, and grabbed Charles's keys from their bowl before letting himself out of the apartment and into the cool night air.

He had a hospitalized gangbanger to confront.

CHAPTER THIRTEEN

"**I**'m sorry, sir, visiting hours are about to end," said the woman at the reception desk when Ángel entered the hospital lobby. The main entrance was on the opposite side of the building from the emergency room, and at this time of night, the lobby was quiet and deserted. A metal grate had been pulled down to lock up its small coffee shop.

Ángel flashed his ATF badge as he approached, casually hooking his thumb over the name on the ID card. "I'm checking on a prisoner," he said, his voice clipped. "Mark Cooper?" He hovered at the edge of her desk, bouncing on the balls of his feet as if he were in a rush and irritated by the delay.

Though Ángel wasn't one hundred percent sure this was the right hospital, it was the closest facility to the site of the raid that was equipped with a trauma unit. The receptionist's reaction confirmed his hunch.

Her face alight with curiosity, she said, "Oh, you mean the guy in 415? I heard he got shot up in some kind of gang fight!"

"That's the one," said Ángel, blessing human nature. Privacy regulations always fell by the wayside when gossip this salacious was involved.

The woman gestured to the log on the counter. "I just need you to fill out—"

"Look, I don't want to alarm you," Ángel said with a significant glance, "but I *really* don't have time for this."

Her eyes went wide, then darted furtively to the elevator bank like Buzz was going to come flying out any minute with guns blazing. "Should I call security?"

"That would just escalate the situation. I don't want to panic the other patients if there's no need."

"Of course." The woman handed him a visitor's badge and said, "I guess it wouldn't be a problem if you signed the log on your way out instead."

"Thanks," Ángel said. He clipped the badge to his sweatshirt pocket and strode toward the elevators, hitting the call button. The elevator arrived within seconds; once inside, Ángel made an educated guess and pressed the button for the fourth floor.

Sure enough, he emerged into the trauma unit—a standard layout of two long corridors of patient rooms with the nurses' station in the center. From where Ángel was standing, he had a clear view of the SDPD officer seated outside a room on the far end of the left hallway. The whiteboard in the nurses' station that displayed the nursing assignments didn't contain patient names, of course, but it did have initials.

415—M.C.

Mark Cooper was Buzz's real name; this was as much corroboration as Ángel was going to get without seeing the man face-to-face.

He considered the police officer guarding the room. She was sitting with her arms and ankles crossed, slumped a bit in her plastic chair. As Ángel watched, her eyes drifted shut and her chin nodded toward her chest before she startled and gave her head a hard shake. Ángel turned in a slow circle, checking out the rest of the unit, and smiled when he saw a small, comfortably furnished room of the kind used to hold family meetings.

A few minutes later, Ángel walked up to the officer with a cup of fresh coffee. "I think you could use this more than I could," he said, showing her his badge at the same time that he held out the coffee, ensuring that her focus was too divided to pick up any details.

"Thanks," she said. She gave Ángel a pretty subtle once-over as she accepted the coffee, but it was enough to convey her appreciation for his looks.

Letting a hint of flirtatiousness creep into his tone, Ángel said, "I promise my mouth hadn't touched it yet."

The officer grinned. "I guess I'll just have to take your word for it."

"Okay if I have a quick chat with the prisoner?" Ángel asked, jerking his thumb toward the closed door.

"Sure, knock yourself out." She sipped the coffee. "Don't think you're going to get anything out of him though."

"As long as I can tell the boss I tried." Ángel gave her a conspiratorial wink and let himself into the room.

He was relieved to see that the patient was indeed Buzz, asleep in his bed with the lights dimmed low. It was a private room, and Buzz wasn't on any heart-rate monitoring equipment, both of which were good things for Ángel and not so great for Buzz.

Ángel brightened the lights and dragged the visitor's chair to Buzz's bedside, taking a seat. Grimacing, Buzz stirred underneath his covers, lifting one hand to block the light from his eyes. He turned his head and frowned at Ángel.

"Who're you?" he asked, his voice slurred with sleep and narcotics.

"My name is Gael Flores," said Ángel, giving him the alias he'd used as Raúl's boy toy. "Have you heard of me?"

Buzz rubbed his eyes. "No."

"How about Raúl Esparza?"

"No, dude," Buzz said. He dropped his hand to the bed. "What do you—"

"Manuel Juarez?"

A frisson of tension ran through Buzz, and he was suddenly looking everywhere but Ángel's face. Ángel smiled.

"Why'd you put those papers in that car, Buzz?" he said.

"I don't know what the fuck you're talking about."

Buzz reached for his call button, but Ángel knocked it out of his hand. It fell off the far side of the bed and clattered to the floor.

"I think you do," Ángel said. "You stashed a set of false papers for a Manuel Juarez among the guns you brought for Felix Torres to inspect. I want to know why, and I want to know where you got them from."

"I'm not telling you shit," Buzz said, all fired up now. "You a cop? I'm not saying anything without a lawyer—"

"Do I look like a cop to you?" Ángel snapped.

Buzz hesitated, his eyes raking over Ángel's body—his casual hoodie and jeans, the obvious lack of a gun, his slouched posture, the long hair falling into his eyes. "Well, what the hell do you care, then?"

"You don't need to worry about that. Just tell me who contacted you and what they said."

"Fuck this." Buzz braced his hands on the mattress and tried to heave himself upright, getting about halfway before he swayed and slumped sideways with a pained expression. "Get the hell out of—"

Ángel grabbed Buzz's throat, forcing him flat on his back and holding him there. Letting out a choked gasp, Buzz slapped at Ángel's hand and pushed at his shoulder, but he was too out of it to have any effect. Ángel didn't even need to use both hands to keep him down.

"Do you have any idea how easy it would be for me to kill you right now?" Ángel said, retreating into the cold detachment that had allowed Gael to watch Raúl beat the shit out of some hapless victim with no reaction other than boredom. "You're weak, in pain, drugged up on narcotics. You couldn't be more vulnerable."

Buzz's frightened eyes shot toward the door.

"Think you could call out loud enough to get her attention before I managed to crush your windpipe?" Ángel tightened his grip just a bit. Though the hold he had on Buzz's throat was certainly enough to be painful, and it would prevent him from speaking, this wasn't near enough pressure to strangle him. "More to the point, is whatever you're hiding worth that risk?"

Buzz wet his lips anxiously, his eyes darting back and forth, then lifted his trembling hands in surrender. Ángel loosened his fingers but kept his hand placed over Buzz's throat in a clear threat. He wouldn't kill Buzz, obviously, but he was prepared to choke the man into unconsciousness if he had to.

After clearing his throat a few times, Buzz said, "Night before the meet, I had a voice mail on my cell when I came home from the bar. It was some guy who works with Felix Torres, said he'd pay me to call him from a pay phone at a gas station near my house." He snorted. "Didn't even know those still existed. When I got there, there was a hundred-dollar bill taped up underneath the phone box, so I figured what the hell, I might as well call the guy."

"And?"

"And it was the same guy who answered," said Buzz. "He had to get some papers to Torres, but the feds were all over him and he couldn't risk direct contact. Offered me five hundred bucks to put the papers in one of the cars we brought to the meet."

"He specified that exactly?" Ángel said. "That you needed to bring the papers to the meet with you?"

"Yeah, man."

Meaning, as Ángel had suggested to Ed, that the stalker had gotten his nose into the ATF's investigation through his surveillance of Ángel. That he'd figured out the meet was with Torres before the ATF had was troubling, but not all that surprising if the stalker were cartel himself—he'd have had a different set of contacts and his own extralegal avenues of investigation.

"Anyway," Buzz said, "I got home and the papers were in my mailbox with the cash. Easiest money I've ever made."

Ángel shook his head with reluctant amusement. "So you didn't tell any of your buddies, because you didn't want to split the payout."

Buzz scowled, his fear fading now that Ángel had made no further violent moves against him. "Why should I? They didn't do shit."

"You're sure it was a man on the phone?" Ángel asked.

"Yeah."

"Did he have an accent?"

"Uh, yeah—he sounded kind of Western. Like a cowboy, you know?"

"Western . . ." Ángel sat back, startled, his slack hand sliding from Buzz's throat to his collarbone. "You mean he sounded *American*?"

Buzz nodded.

This was unexpected. None of the men Ángel knew from the cartel would have been able to speak English with an American Western accent, at least none who also had motivation to pursue him this way. Oscar and Roberto definitely wouldn't have been capable of it.

Getting himself back on track, Ángel said, "You never met this man, then."

"No."

"Did you delete the voice mail?"

"No, I've still got it," Buzz said. "Don't have my cell, though. Cops took it."

Access to Buzz's cell phone wouldn't be a problem; Ángel would just have to make sure he subtly nudged the team into checking his voice mails. They might even do that of their own initiative and save him the trouble.

"This conversation stays between you and me, do you understand?" said Ángel. He placed his palm gently over Buzz's throat once more.

Buzz's Adam's apple bobbed against Ángel's palm as he swallowed hard. "Sure, dude. I don't want any trouble with the cartels, okay?"

Ángel considered Buzz for a long moment, decided he was sincere, and let go, rising to his feet. Buzz watched Ángel warily as he returned the chair to its rightful place and left the room, but didn't call out for help.

After bidding the cop a flirty goodnight, Ángel left the hospital through the packed emergency room, tossing his visitor's badge into the trash on his way out.

Had the information he'd gained from Buzz been worth leaving Charles's apartment alone and unarmed, jeopardizing his life as well as his career? Probably not in the long run. But Ángel wouldn't have been able to sleep tonight if he hadn't known that for sure. At least now he had an actual, concrete lead.

The next morning, Ángel emerged from Charles's guest bedroom marginally better rested than he'd been for the past few days. He rubbed sleep from his eyes as he shambled into the kitchen, where Charles was on the phone, his forehead creased in a deep frown. Ángel poured himself some coffee and listened to Charles's conversation with half an ear.

"So what are we going to do now, then?" Charles said. "Uh-huh. Yeah, okay. No, I'll tell him myself. That's fine. All right, see you later."

Charles hung up and put down his phone, his brow still furrowed.

Warming his hands on his mug, Ángel leaned one hip against the counter. "Was that Eva?"

"Yeah." Charles turned toward him, and the nape of Ángel's neck prickled at the grim expression on his face. "Ángel, I . . . I don't know how to tell you this, but . . . Buzz is dead."

The mug slipped out of Ángel's hands and crashed on the floor.

Hot coffee splashed over his feet, ceramic shards scraping his skin, but Ángel felt none of it. He stood motionless while Charles cursed and grabbed a dish towel, crouching to wipe the coffee off Ángel's feet.

"Get up on the counter before you slice your feet open," Charles said.

Moving as though he were submerged in molasses, Ángel reached back and lifted himself to sit on the counter. He gazed blankly at his reddened skin, his mind reeling.

Charles mopped up the rest of the coffee and then swept the shattered mug into a dustpan. "I know this is bad," he said. "We'll figure something out, okay? We'll . . ."

As Charles straightened up and met Ángel's eyes, his voice trailed off. Ángel stared back at him, too horrified to bother hiding his reaction.

Charles set the dustpan down and said, very quietly, "What the hell did you do?"

"I didn't kill him," Ángel said.

"Oh my God." Charles took two quick steps backward. "But you *saw* him?"

Ángel compressed his lips and nodded.

"When?" Charles said, and then shook his head. "Shit, you went out last night after I fell asleep, didn't you? Is that . . ." His eyes widened and he stepped even farther away from Ángel. "Is that why we had sex?"

"No!" Ángel jumped off the counter, wincing at the sting of his feet. "Charles, no, I would never do that to you. But . . . if I'm being honest, that's why I didn't want to talk about it afterward."

Closing his eyes, Charles pressed one hand to his forehead and breathed deeply through his nose.

Ángel wrapped his arms around himself. "How did he die?" he asked.

"There was an error with his insulin," Charles said, dropping his hand to his side. "He got ten times the dosage he was supposed to and went into diabetic shock. They couldn't resuscitate him."

"That wasn't an accident."

"It would be a pretty enormous coincidence if it were."

Ángel steeled himself. "I'll call Campos and tell him what I did—"

"No way," said Charles. "You can't do that, Ángel. He'll have no choice but to suspend you. You'll probably end up getting fired."

"It'll be worse for me if someone else finds out than if I come forward now," Ángel said. "I'll look like a suspect in his death!"

Charles was silent for a moment, worrying his bottom lip. "Walk me through exactly what happened last night."

Ángel described his visit to the hospital step-by-step, leaving nothing out, even the way he'd threatened Buzz.

When he finished, Charles asked, "Did you grab his throat hard enough to leave bruises?"

"I doubt it. It was only for a few seconds, and not much more force than you'd use sparring."

Charles nodded, his eyes thoughtful. "So you didn't tell anyone your real name, didn't sign anything. There's no solid evidence you were there at all."

"The two women I spoke to would be able to describe me," said Ángel, though he already felt much steadier.

"They won't have any reason to. You were there at 10 p.m.; Buzz didn't die until early this morning when he got his shot before breakfast. Even if the investigation reaches back that far, they'll be asking about people who were out of place, which you weren't."

"What about the security cameras?" Ángel asked. He hadn't been too concerned about them last night, since he hadn't been behaving suspiciously and nobody would go back to check them unless something went wrong.

Well, something *had* gone very, very wrong, and now he was rebuking himself for not being more careful.

"Wiped," Charles said.

Ángel raised his eyebrows. "Far enough back to cover me?"

"For the entire twelve hours preceding Buzz's death."

"That's . . . convenient."

"Maybe it was easier to erase the recordings in one huge chunk," Charles said with a shrug.

"Maybe." His skin crawling, Ángel said, "Or maybe the stalker knew I went to the hospital and deliberately got rid of the recordings to protect me from being implicated in Buzz's death."

He and Charles looked at each other with shared unease. "That's a very disturbing thought," Charles finally said.

"God, I could have led the stalker right to him," Ángel said. "I could be the reason Buzz is dead."

Charles shook his head. "The stalker wouldn't have needed you to track Buzz down, and he was probably planning to kill him no matter what. Otherwise there wouldn't have been any point in killing him after you'd already talked to him."

"True." Ángel shifted from foot to foot, starting and stopping his next sentence several times before he said, "So what now—I just pretend I was never there?"

"Yes."

"And you're okay with that?"

"I'm not okay with any of this," Charles said sharply. "You snuck around behind my back, put yourself in danger, and took stupid, senseless risks to do something you'd been specifically ordered *not* to do. None of that is okay, Ángel."

Ángel lowered his eyes to the floor. Charles was right, but even if Ángel could rewind time, he wouldn't make a different decision. He'd done what he believed he had to do.

"But absolutely no good will come out of you telling anyone else that you went to see Buzz," said Charles. "The stalker will already be the primary suspect, so we'll just make sure it stays that way."

If anyone found out that Charles had helped Ángel cover this up, it would be his ass on the line as well. Ángel would never throw Charles under the bus, but there were other ways his complicity could be discovered. Involving Charles in this was Ángel's only real regret; he should have controlled his reaction to the news of Buzz's death.

"All right," Ángel said. "I'll follow your lead."

Charles glanced at the clock on the microwave and sighed. "Turns out I have to work today, after all—we've got a ton of arrest warrants ready to go and they need the bodies. I won't be able to help you unload your stuff."

"Don't worry about it. I'm going to take a cab to the airport to pick up Jesenia; she should be more than enough help."

"Ángel," Charles said, closing the distance between them, "if you pull shit like this again, I might not be able to help you."

Annoyed, Ángel snapped back, "I didn't ask you to help me *now*. Maybe I do tend to take certain risks, but when have you ever known me not to take responsibility for their consequences?"

Charles blinked, and his shoulders slumped just a bit. "Never. But *I* can't accept the consequences for these particular decisions, okay? So please try to keep a cool head."

He turned and walked out of the kitchen, leaving Ángel at a loss for words.

"I'll make sure Jade gets Buzz's voice mails," Charles said over his shoulder when he reached his bedroom.

"Thanks," Ángel said, but Charles had already closed the door.

"Are you sure you want to take point?" Sakura asked, sitting shotgun beside Charles. "Maybe you should sit this one out."

"No, it has to be me," said Charles.

The house he'd parked in front of had peeling yellow paint and a sagging, rotted-through front porch; the lawn was dried-out and patchy, showing through to bare earth in more places than not. Its rusted mailbox listed precariously on its post, the door long gone.

Steeling himself for the unpleasantness to come, Charles got out of the car and pushed through the squeaky gate in the yard's chain-link fence. He cautiously mounted the porch steps, half expecting them to give out at any moment, and knocked on the screen door. Sakura lent silent support at his right shoulder.

Charles had to knock several more times before Amber finally opened the front door, her head tilted so her hair covered half her face. Her dull eyes swept Charles from head to foot, taking in his gun and ATF windbreaker.

"He's not here," she said before Charles could speak. "He took off yesterday as soon as he heard about the raid."

That was a chance they'd had to take. Most of the Jackals arrested in the raid had been convinced to snitch on their fellows to reduce their own charges, and the ATF's first priority had been to reel in the big fish, the ones higher up in the chain of command who had been previously untouchable. The delay had given some of the foot soldiers a chance to scatter, leading to Charles and Sakura being charged with cleanup detail.

Charles opened the screen door as well so there was nothing between them. "Do you know where he went?"

Amber shook her bowed head, anxiously picking at the sores on her left arm.

"Amber," Charles said, and waited for her to look him in the eye. Very slowly, giving her plenty of time to pull away, he reached out and tipped up her chin. Amber didn't protest as her hair fell back to reveal the massive bruise purpling her eye and cheek.

Charles withdrew his hand, biting back the first words that sprang to his lips.

"I know you love Johnny," he said instead. "It's in his best interests if we bring him in as soon as possible. He can't hide forever, and the longer he runs, the greater the chance that this will end badly for him."

"Is he gonna . . ." Amber blinked away tears. "Will he find out about all the things I told you about him?"

"Never," Charles said firmly. He and Amber had been over this dozens of times before, but reassurance never hurt. "You won't be named in any court documents, and you'll never have to testify. You can tell your neighbors that you told us to go straight to hell, and they won't have any reason to doubt you. But you know that it's better if I'm the one to arrest Johnny than a random cop he runs into on the street."

Amber scratched her arm harder. "I really don't know where he is, but he took my car. He barely has any cash, and there's nobody he trusts outside the city, so he couldn't have gotten that far."

"Thank you." Turning to Sakura, Charles said, "Could you give us a minute?"

Sakura hesitated, eyes flicking between Charles and Amber, before she nodded and stepped off the porch. She only went as far as the fence—out of earshot, but well within range to intervene if Amber made a threatening move.

Charles dug a wad of folded bills out of his pocket and pressed it into Amber's nonbloody hand. She looked down in surprise.

"You can still call me if you need anything, okay?" Charles said. "Anything at all."

"Thanks," Amber mumbled, giving him a watery smile.

Charles squeezed her hand. "I'm sorry," he said, then released her and let the screen door swing shut. As he rejoined Sakura, the front door closed behind him with a thump.

"I'll drive," said Sakura.

Charles tossed her the keys without argument.

Once they were inside the car, she said, "You know this isn't your fault."

"I know I'm not responsible for Johnny's decisions, or Amber's," Charles said, buckling his seat belt. "And I know I couldn't have warned her. But it still feels like I betrayed her somehow."

Sakura sighed, turning the key in the ignition and shifting the car into drive. "There's plenty of things in life to feel bad about that actually *are* your fault—what's the point in taking on more?"

They put out an APB on Amber's car, and in less than two hours, local police had tracked it down at a Motel 6 in La Mesa. The sun was setting when Charles and Sakura pulled into the motel parking lot, but it was still plenty light enough for Charles to see the man hurrying down the exterior stairs with a panicked look on his face.

Sure enough, it was skinny, raggedy-ass Johnny, making a beeline for Amber's white Honda Civic.

"Amber called him," Charles said, unbuckling his seat belt and popping the door open before the car had even stopped moving.

"Still feel guilty?" Sakura asked.

"Stay in the car!" Charles snapped as he jumped out. At least Amber had waited as long as she had.

The sound drew Johnny's attention; he took one glance at Charles's jacket, blanched, and spun on his heel, bolting in the opposite direction. Charles cursed and gave chase.

"Johnny Sinclair!" he shouted, pursuing Johnny around the corner of the motel. "ATF! Freeze, you're under arrest!"

That didn't work, of course—it rarely did—but Charles had to say it anyway. With the formalities out of the way, Charles focused on controlling his breathing while he pounded after Johnny, who vaulted the low fence that separated the Motel 6 from the Chevy dealership behind it.

"Siren, we need you," Sakura said over Charles's earpiece.

"I'm here," came Jade's bone-melting voice a few seconds later.

Johnny tore down a lane of gleaming trucks and SUVs, startling a salesman and the couple he was showing around. They yelled in alarm and jumped back when Charles came barreling right after him.

"Griffin and I are in pursuit of a suspect," Sakura said to Jade. "He's on foot and I'm on wheels. Get a lock on our positions and give us an idea of what we're looking at here."

Though the dealership lot wasn't exactly jam-packed with civilians, pulling his gun at this distance would be an unacceptable risk. Charles had to close the gap, but Johnny had a significant head start and was running on the adrenaline of fear.

Johnny's straight route took him right between the narrow aisles of parked cars—not a true barrier, but still a hindrance. Charles scanned the lot as he ran, noting a broad, empty lane that curved around to the side. Banking on the probability that the lane encircled the entire lot, Charles changed course and put on a burst of speed as he was freed from the worry of pinballing between the cars.

"I've got you," said Jade. "His only choice is to keep running east to west. Past the access road to the north is a four-lane highway, and the embankment to the south is way too steep to climb."

"Should I stay on the access road?" Sakura said.

"Yes, definitely. You should be able to cut him off in the RV resort coming up."

Charles rounded the final curve of the lane just as Johnny emerged from the mass of cars, a small stretch of flat asphalt all that remained between them. Johnny's eyes widened, and he threw himself at the tall chain-link fence at the end of the lot, scrambling up and over like a squirrel.

"Goddamn it," Charles said on a groan. He jumped up and grabbed the fence as well, hissing as the thin wires bit into his flesh. Heaving himself over the top, Charles tucked and rolled when he hit the ground, then leaped to his feet and continued the chase.

They'd entered the RV resort Jade had mentioned, a tidy grid of tight rectangular lots, most of which were occupied. Charles spared little attention for the shocked residents he and Johnny blew past; his breathing was labored now, his legs aching and his pulse thundering in his ears. He focused on Johnny's back and pushed himself a little harder.

Johnny veered south, into the wooded area that bordered the resort. Charles was close enough that he heard Johnny's dismayed curse when he realized that the sheer grade of the slope offered no hope of escape.

"Fury, turn into the resort on Beach Street," Jade said.

Racing back onto the street, Johnny cut through a few tiny yards and ended up on a long road that was one straight shot through the resort. Charles pumped his arms harder and ran at a dead sprint.

Sakura roared out of a side street, tires screeching as she swung the SUV in a neat semicircle, blocking the road. Johnny skidded to a halt mere feet from the front tire, his arms windmilling, and whirled around just in time to see Charles bearing down on him. Though Johnny lashed out with a wild punch, Charles blocked it easily and drove his own fist into Johnny's face. He felt a very unprofessional surge of satisfaction at the crunch of bone beneath his knuckles.

Johnny staggered backward, falling to his knees. Charles kicked him in the chest, sending him sprawling, then bent down and flipped him onto his stomach. He yanked Johnny's arms behind his back and slapped a pair of handcuffs on him. Sakura jumped out of the car and ran toward them with her gun drawn.

With Johnny safely restrained, Charles stumbled off to the side and doubled over, his chest heaving. His throat burned, his vision was graying, and it was through pure force of will that he didn't vomit all over the ground.

"You okay?" Sakura asked, resting a hand on Charles's back.

"I need to start doing more cardio," Charles gasped.

CHAPTER FOURTEEN

At the end of the day, once they'd tied up as many loose ends as possible and put out alerts to neighboring law enforcement agencies about the few Jackals who'd managed to slip the net, Charles's team headed out to a local bar for celebratory drinks.

"By the way, I called Ángel," Jade said in the elevator. "He's going to meet us there with his friend."

Charles grunted noncommittally; he himself hadn't heard a single word from Ángel all day. Then again, *he* hadn't reached out to Ángel, either.

Charles volunteered to be the designated driver—his judgment was impaired enough these days as it was—so everyone piled into his car. As they unloaded in the bar's parking lot, his teammates in giddy high spirits, Charles's attention was caught by the approaching rumble of a motorcycle engine.

"Oh no," he muttered.

They all fell silent as a sculptural red Kawasaki Ninja zoomed into the parking lot with two riders on board. The bike parked not far from Charles's car, and the rear rider hopped off first, removing her helmet to reveal a lanky Latina woman who had to be Jesenia.

Ángel switched off the bike and dismounted as well, shaking out his hair as he pulled off his own helmet, his eyes crinkling with amusement at whatever Jesenia was saying to him. He wore a black leather jacket that Charles hadn't seen since Tucson, and his face was glowing with exhilaration.

"Oh God, I'm not coming back from this," Jade said, staring at Ángel with a half-open mouth.

"*I'm* not coming back from this," said Shane, his eyes wide.

Ángel gave them a wave and headed in their direction, stripping off his leather gloves as he walked. Charles watched in astonishment; it seemed that a thousand pounds of pressure had been lifted off Ángel since that morning. *This* was the Ángel of Charles's past, all sparkling eyes and easy smile, his posture loose and relaxed. Was it getting his stuff back that had brought such a change, or had it been spending time with Jesenia?

"Hey, guys," Ángel said when he and Jesenia joined their group. "This is Special Agent Jesenia Santos of the DEA."

"Just 'Jesenia' is fine," she said with a laugh.

She shook hands all around as Ángel introduced her to everyone, but her friendly smile cooled when she came around to Charles. He wasn't surprised, if she knew about his and Ángel's history.

"Sweet bike," Sakura said to Ángel. "She handling okay after two years in storage?"

"Just needed a little TLC."

Charles tuned out their ensuing conversation—he'd never shared Ángel's fascination with motorcycles and cars—and trailed along at the back of the group as they entered the bar, thrown off-kilter by the improvement in Ángel's mental state. Unless this was all an act, Jesenia had been able to comfort and cheer Ángel up after spending only a day in his company, something Charles hadn't been able to accomplish in a full week.

Well, of course he hadn't. He'd been too busy fucking Ángel and then pushing him away in a vicious cycle, more selfishly concerned with how Ángel's return had affected *him* than how it was affecting Ángel. No wonder Ángel was doing better with Jesenia in town.

Their group finagled one of the larger high-tops, and everyone settled in except for Ángel, who unzipped his leather jacket but kept it on over his shoulder holster. "First round's on me," he said, digging out his wallet and flashing a credit card. "Not only do I *finally* have access to my bank accounts again, I just got paid two years' back salary, plus hazard pay and an undercover bonus."

Cheers went up around the table. Charles didn't join in, too distracted by his memories of that soft worn leather under his fingertips. He'd fucked Ángel wearing that jacket and nothing else—

Eva elbowed him hard in the side. "Ow, what?" Charles said, glancing around. None of the others were paying attention, busy giving Ángel their drink orders.

"What's the matter with you?" she whispered. "You're totally zoning out."

"I'm fine. Just tired."

Eva narrowed her eyes, but she was interrupted by Ángel.

"Eva, what's your poison, *querida*?"

"Manhattan, please," she said.

"Nice," said Ángel. "Charles?"

"Just a cranberry juice."

"Boo," Ángel said, wrinkling his nose.

Charles scowled at him. "I'm the designated driver."

"Whatever. Be right back." Ángel turned and strolled away into the crowd.

Charles struggled with himself for a few moments, gave up, and said, "He'll probably need help carrying." He jumped off his stool and followed Ángel, ignoring Eva's searching look.

The bar was halfway across the room, out of their table's direct line of sight. Charles caught up with Ángel as he was waiting for the bartender and put a hand on his shoulder.

"Hey," Ángel said, startled.

"Thought you might need help," Charles said. He made a vague gesture to encompass Ángel's entire body. "You look like you're feeling better. Good day?"

"Well, having possessions again does make me feel less like a vagrant drifter, even if I did put most of them right back in storage."

"Of course." Charles shifted on the balls of his feet. "And . . . Jesenia. Having her here is helping?"

"Yeah, it is," Ángel said with a soft smile.

Charles had no suspicions that Ángel and Jesenia had a sexual relationship; he knew Ángel had never touched a woman that way since his disappointing first-and-only fumblings with a girl in the seventh grade. They shared a connection much deeper than sex, though—they'd been undercover together, seen and experienced things that Charles couldn't imagine and would never truly understand. Jesenia could be there for Ángel in ways Charles couldn't, and he hadn't realized that would bother him until this very moment.

Ángel tilted his head, meeting Charles's eyes. He smoothed one hand up Charles's chest, then fisted Charles's shirtfront and yanked him into a kiss. Charles groaned, instinctively grabbing Ángel's hips and deepening the kiss, his tongue stroking into Ángel's demanding mouth. Ángel pressed up against him with a quiet moan.

The kiss went on for a while before Charles got control of himself, pulling away and taking a few steps backward for good measure. He couldn't help a fleeting look in the direction of their table, but none of his teammates were in sight. Though a few people nearby regarded them with raised eyebrows, nobody seemed inclined to start shit.

"What are you doing?" Charles said to Ángel. "Someone could see us!"

"You know, if I had a dollar for every time you've said that to me, I could pay for this entire round," Ángel said, more resigned than irritated. He turned back to the bar.

Shit. "I didn't mean . . ." Charles said, but it was too late.

"Go sit down, Charles. I worked in bars all through college and grad school; I can handle drinks for seven people."

Charles returned to their table without argument. It had been disrespectful for Ángel to kiss him in public when he knew Charles wasn't out, but Charles could have handled it better. Everything he did just muddied the waters more—unsurprising, since he had no idea what the fuck he was doing or what he wanted from this situation. He should be happy that Ángel had a friend he could rely on, a support system for when he left San Diego. Because Ángel would leave eventually, and Charles's life would go back to normal, and that . . . *that* was what Charles wanted.

Wasn't it?

"I thought you were helping Ángel," Eva said when Charles sat down.

"Says he doesn't need it."

Jesenia studied Charles from across the table, but she said nothing.

Ángel did end up needing help, enlisting a cocktail server to carry a second tray—because in addition to everyone's drinks, he'd bought seven shots of Fireball.

"*Yes*," Shane said, drumming his hands on the table.

"I told you I'm not drinking tonight," Charles said when the server placed one of the shots in front of him.

"What, you think you won't metabolize a single shot of whiskey in the two or three hours we'll probably be here?" said Ángel. He hopped up on his stool. "Just one shot, Charles."

In Charles's experience, *Just one shot, Charles*, tended to lead to five or six and Charles bending Ángel over any convenient horizontal surface. He had Eva to keep him in check this time, though, so he rolled his eyes and picked up his shot glass along with everyone else.

"To the completion of a successful operation," Ángel said in a toast.

"To Ángel getting his shit back," said Jade.

Ángel laughed, and everyone tossed back their shots. Charles grimaced as the cinnamon-flavored whiskey burned his throat.

"What happened to your hand?" Ángel asked Charles, dropping his shot glass and reaching for his hard cider.

"He socked this woman-beating piece of shit right in the jaw," Sakura answered for him. "Put the guy on his knees in one punch."

"Really?" Ángel said, intrigued. "Sounds like I missed all the excitement."

Sakura and Shane were eager to recount the exploits of the day, continuing an earlier argument over which of them deserved credit for more arrests. Charles nursed his cranberry juice and listened quietly as they whiled away an hour or so, the conversation flowing from the various Jackals' arrests to Ángel and Jesenia's travails with his movers. To Charles's surprise, Ángel switched to water after he finished his first drink, even though everyone else hit up the bar for seconds and thirds.

When discussion came around to partners and families, Charles excused himself to the restroom. He splashed cold water on his face as he washed his hands, stalling for time, unwilling to acknowledge the real reason he didn't want to go back out there. It was too ridiculous that he was jealous of Ángel's friendship with a woman he'd just met.

Charles left the men's room and almost ran over the object of said jealousy, who was hovering right outside.

"I was just about to head out for a smoke," Jesenia said. "Do you have a minute to talk?"

"Uh..." Try as he might, Charles couldn't think of a way to refuse gracefully. "Sure, I guess."

They slipped out the side door, standing against the brick wall while Jesenia pulled a pack of cigarettes from her jacket pocket and lit one. She took a deep drag, then glanced at the expression on Charles's face.

"It's gross, I know," she said ruefully. "I picked it up with the cartel to help my cover, and I've been having trouble quitting. Ángel hates it."

"I don't mind," said Charles, feeling guilty now about being so judgmental. "What did you want to talk about?"

"I think it's only fair to be honest and tell you that I know about what happened between you and Ángel in Tucson, and that you've been sleeping together again since he got back." Jesenia exhaled another slow stream of smoke. "Ángel said you don't want your coworkers to know, so I wanted to make it clear you don't have anything to worry about from me. I can keep a secret."

"Thanks." Beyond uncomfortable, Charles longed to reach for the door, but he held himself still. "Was that all?"

"No," Jesenia said. She fiddled with her cigarette, flicking a bit of ash off the end. "It's just... are you being careful with him?"

"Careful?" Charles said, incredulous. "With *Ángel*?"

Jesenia's smile was crooked. "Yeah, I know. He acts like most things just slide right off him. And he's an adult; he can make his own decisions, and he'd kill me if he knew I was talking to you about this. Considering how easily you fell back in bed with him, though, I have to wonder if he hasn't been honest with you about what happened with Esparza."

A chill ran down Charles's spine. "What do you mean?"

"I mean I hope you're not the kind of guy who'd fuck around with Ángel after what he's been through—"

"No," Charles said, "what do you mean, 'what happened with Esparza'?"

"Oh," Jesenia said, her eyes widening. "I guess he *hasn't* been honest, then. Shit." She dropped her cigarette on the ground and stubbed it out. "This is something you should really talk to him about, not me. It's not my place."

She turned for the door. Charles reached out to grab her arm, then decided that would come off as too aggressive and dropped his hand to his side.

"Jesenia, wait," he said. "Please. Ángel won't talk to me about this."

Jesenia raised her eyebrows. "Have you ever asked?"

Fair enough. "I'm asking you now."

Crossing her arms, Jesenia faced Charles. "Ángel can reason his way around this all he wants, but the truth is that Esparza treated him like his personal whore. The things Esparza did to him—word got around, you know. What Ángel didn't tell me himself, I heard from other people in the cartel, from the guys Esparza let watch or join in—"

"*What*?" Charles caught himself with one hand on the wall.

"It was awful," Jesenia said, hunching her shoulders. "And there wasn't anything I or anyone else could do about it. You can't stop a man like Raúl Esparza from smacking his boy toy around."

"Esparza hit him?" Charles said. His stomach churned.

Jesenia looked at Charles as if he were the stupidest person alive. "Yeah."

How could Charles not have known any of this? He should have asked—he should have at least suspected. He'd been interacting with Ángel the same way he would have in Tucson, but Ángel had been through hell and back since then, and Charles had just been ignoring it.

"I don't know that Ángel would even be ready for a healthy, loving relationship yet," said Jesenia. "He's definitely not ready to be your dirty little secret again."

Charles stiffened. *Dirty little secret?* Christ. If Ángel hadn't wanted to see a guy who wasn't out, he could have broken it off at any time. Charles had always been up-front about wanting to keep his sexuality private at work.

"Like I said—be careful with him." Jesenia pulled the door open and went back inside, leaving Charles alone in the quiet alley.

Charles had a hard time pretending everything was normal once he returned to the table, and he was relieved when they decided to call it a night around ten. Despite Jade's and Shane's protests, the fact remained that it was a Sunday night, and everyone except Jesenia had to be at work the next morning.

Even though Charles had to make four stops on the way home and Ángel only had to drive Jesenia to her motel, Charles still got to his apartment first. Like a coward, he considered going straight to bed and putting everything off until tomorrow, but he was already so disgusted with himself that he couldn't do anything other than sit on the couch and wait for Ángel.

He jumped up the second he heard his spare key in the lock to meet Ángel at the front door.

"Hey," Ángel said, putting his keys in the bowl with Charles's and setting his helmet next to it on the table. He was still upbeat, smiling and calm, and Charles was about to take that away from him. Again.

He *had* to, though, before things between them progressed any further. "We need to talk," Charles said.

Ángel tucked his gloves into the pockets of his jacket and hung it up. "About what?"

"About what happened to you in Mexico."

"What happened to me in Mexico?" Ángel repeated, bemused. He crouched down to unlace his boots.

Charles huffed out an exasperated breath. Was Ángel being purposely obtuse? "With Esparza."

"Why? God, is this why you were in such a weird mood tonight?" Straightening up, Ángel yanked off his boots, then pushed them against the wall. "Jesenia said the two of you didn't talk about anything important."

Feeling awkward, Charles folded his arms across his chest. "I'm worried I might be hurting you."

Ángel spread his hands and said, "Hurting me how?"

"By starting things up with you again after . . ." He couldn't say it. "After."

"After *what*, Charles?" Ángel's voice was slow and dangerous.

Charles didn't answer.

Ángel glared at him in disgust and then stalked around him, heading for the kitchen. Charles turned and followed.

"It's not a weird thing to be concerned about," he said. "We picked up right where we left off after that last night in Tucson, which would be fucked up even if you hadn't spent the past two years undercover. I don't know what happened to you there, Ángel, or what Esparza might have done to you—"

"Why now?" Ángel asked. He stopped with his hand resting on the refrigerator handle. "I've been back for a week. Why didn't you ask me about this before?"

"Because I didn't really want to know," Charles said, determined to be frank about his own selfishness. "It's been easier for me not to think about where you've been and what you've been doing since Tucson. And it seemed like you didn't want to talk about it."

"I didn't. I *don't*." Ángel wrenched the refrigerator door open with unnecessary force and retrieved a bottle of water. "I thought you were respecting that."

"I . . ." Charles hesitated. The thing was, if Ángel had ever initiated a conversation about his experiences undercover, Charles would have been more than willing to listen. He just hadn't seen the point in pushing Ángel into discussing something neither of them wanted to talk about. Should he be pushing Ángel *now*?

Shit. What was the right thing to do here?

"Look, I don't know what Jesenia said to you, but whatever it was, you have to take it with a grain of salt. Most of what she heard about Raúl and me would have been filtered through other people in the cartel, and a lot of them would have been exaggerating for effect."

"She said Esparza let people watch the two of you together," Charles said bluntly. "That he let other men touch you."

Ángel took a long sip of water before he answered. "I consented to that."

Charles swallowed past the horrible taste in his mouth and said, "She said he used to hit you."

Ángel tipped his head back with an irritated groan but didn't deny it.

"Jesus, Ángel—"

"He slapped my face sometimes when I was too disrespectful," Ángel said. "I was usually very good at knowing where that line was, but every now and then he was more on edge than I realized, and I'd cross it by accident. He'd smack me to put me in my place, and then he'd be fine."

Charles stared at him, openmouthed with horror.

"He didn't *beat* me, if that's what you're thinking. Raúl wasn't like that."

"Yeah, it's a huge relief to know the man you were sleeping with only hit you with an open hand," Charles snapped. "I don't know what I was worried about."

Ángel slammed his water bottle on the counter so hard that water sloshed out the top and splashed everywhere. "Would you give me a little fucking credit, please? Do you think I wasn't prepared for what it would mean to seduce a notorious criminal? Do you think I infiltrated a violent cartel expecting wine and roses and Pablo Neruda?"

Charles opened his mouth, but Ángel kept right on talking.

"I went in there knowing that Raúl would never respect me—men like him can't respect anyone they put their cocks in. I understood what that would mean, and I decided that the payoff was worth it. A few slaps to the face and some rough sex isn't anything I wasn't prepared to accept."

"Ángel—"

So worked up now that he was trembling, Ángel said, "Raúl never, *ever* laid a hand on me without my consent, and he never let anyone else do so either. If you ever suggest otherwise again, I will make sure you regret it."

"I didn't mean to imply you didn't know what you were doing," Charles said, taken aback by Ángel's ferocity. "I'm sorry."

Ángel regarded him with narrowed eyes, seemed to conclude that he was sincere, and relaxed a bit. He wiped his wet hand off on his jeans. "When I told you I'd slept with Oscar Palomo, you jumped right to the assumption that I'd been raped then too. Why are you so eager to think of me as a victim?"

"I'm *not*," Charles said, and then trailed off. Why *was* he so quick to believe Ángel had experienced sexual violence, when Ángel had never said or done anything to insinuate that? It wasn't just that he'd spent time around violent men; Ángel was more than capable of holding his own, defending himself not only physically but with skilled manipulation. "I guess I . . . I know that I would back right off if I found out you'd experienced something like that, and then I wouldn't be so confused around you."

Ángel blinked.

"We're furious with each other," said Charles. "You can't deny that, Ángel. It's always there, right under the surface, even when we manage to pretend it's not for a little while. We'll never get past that unless we talk about why—but we *can't*, because there's the risk that it would go so badly we wouldn't be able to be around each other at all, and that wouldn't be safe for you right now. So we're stuck in this horrible holding pattern where we lash out at each other and then fuck and then lash out again, and . . . what if I'm making everything worse? What if I'm making *you* worse?"

"How could you possibly be making me worse?" Ángel asked. "Worse how?"

Charles shrugged, his shoulders drawing together. "Look how much happier you are after spending the day with Jesenia. I don't do that for you. All I ever do is upset you."

"Charles . . ." Ángel took a slow step toward him. "I don't need you to cheer me up. I need you to help me keep my head above water when I can't do it by myself anymore."

Charles shook his head, not understanding.

"What do you think would have happened to me if you hadn't been there when I found Paul?" said Ángel. "What if I'd been alone? Or with someone who didn't know exactly what to say to make sure I didn't touch his body, and sat with me for hours afterward, and helped me stop dissociating?" Ángel's voice cracked, and he cleared his throat, looking away. "That was one of the worst moments of my life, and even after everything, there's nobody else I would have rather had with me than you."

Struck speechless, Charles scrambled for a response, but Ángel wasn't done.

"I feel safer staying here with you than I've felt in a long time," he said, meeting Charles's eyes again. "I didn't realize you didn't know that, or I would have said something. There are tons of people in the world who can make me laugh and have a good time, Charles. There's a very short list of people who make me feel safe. That's what you do for me; that's . . . that's how you make me better."

Charles held out a hand. Ángel took it, and Charles drew him close, slipping his arms around Ángel's waist.

"One day, we'll have that conversation about what happened," Ángel said as he rested his forehead on Charles's shoulder. "But not now, not while I'm being stalked by someone who might want to kill me. I can't handle both at once. Please."

"Okay." Charles kissed Ángel's cheek, overwhelmed, his throat sore and aching. "Okay."

They stood in that embrace for a long minute, until Ángel pulled back far enough to brush his lips over Charles's. "Come take a shower with me," he said, and that was that.

Showering together segued into a marathon sex session that traveled from the bathroom counter to the bedroom floor, broke for a quick snack in the kitchen, resumed over the kitchen counter, and traveled back to the bedroom wall before ending with Ángel on his hands and knees in Charles's bed, clinging to the rattling headboard as Charles pounded him vigorously from behind.

Most of Charles's life force left him along with that last orgasm. He toppled off of Ángel and landed on his back beside him; it took several tries to remove the condom with his shaking hands, and even then it was all he could do to tie the thing in a sloppy knot and drop it off the side of the bed.

Groaning, Ángel collapsed onto his stomach without apparent concern for the come-soaked sheets. They lay in sated silence for a while, Charles wavering in and out of sleep.

"God, I feel like I just took an entire college football team," Ángel said some unknown time later.

"Why a *college* team?" Charles said, affronted.

Though Ángel still lay on his stomach, his head was turned toward Charles on the pillow. He cracked open one eye and said, "What, you think you're good enough to go pro?"

Stifling a smile, Charles smacked his ass, and Ángel laughed. Rather than withdraw his hand, Charles rolled onto his side, trailing his fingers up and down the sweat-damp skin of Ángel's back.

Ángel made a soft purring noise, watching Charles's face. "Can I ask you a question?"

"Sure."

"What is it about me that's always scared you so much?"

At any other point in time, Charles would have brushed him off, pretended incredulity. But here, in the intimacy of his dark bedroom, his body warm and humming with bliss, he was able to say, "You make me want to break the rules."

Ángel's brow furrowed. "What rules?"

"Don't sleep with a coworker, for one." Charles gently kneaded the muscles at the base of Ángel's spine. "Don't get drunk on a weeknight. Don't eat ice cream for breakfast. Don't accept rides on motorcycles. Don't take off for a weekend in Mexico on the spur of the moment and end up staying with total strangers you meet in a bar."

"Those are stupid rules," Ángel said, and then paused. "Except for the last one. That was an error in judgment on our parts."

Charles snorted agreement; they were lucky the Gonzalezes had turned out to be good people.

"You know I don't *make* you break these 'rules' you made up for yourself, right?" Ángel arched his back into Charles's caress. "I might present the opportunities, but you decide to take them. You want to break your own ridiculous rules."

"No, I don't," Charles said mildly.

"Mm-hmm. You can't be happy living inside the rigid lines you've drawn all around yourself. Some people could be, but not you. You need a little excitement, a little danger. It's why you chose the career you did."

Charles's hand stilled on Ángel's back. "You know why I chose this."

Ángel was one of the few people he'd ever told the full story about how his parents had died, gunned down in a convenience-store robbery gone wrong when he was eight years old. Charles hadn't been the first or last child in his community to lose loved ones to guns, either, but things had never changed for the better.

"Yeah," said Ángel. He reached out and brushed the backs of his fingers over Charles's jaw. "There are lots of ways you could have worked against gun violence, though. You could have gone into law, or politics—you chose federal law enforcement. That's not a choice people make lightly."

Considering this, Charles moved his hand again, stroking along Ángel's spine.

Ángel's dark eyes gleamed in what little light filtered through the closed blinds. "You don't have to make up for the fact that your grandmother lost her son, you know. She'll still love you even if you don't force yourself into some arbitrary ideal of perfection."

His stomach twisting as the shot hit home, Charles said, "You're one to talk. Like the way you live your life isn't a deliberate *fuck you* to your parents."

"My parents were abusive garbage," Ángel said. "I don't live my life for them; I live it the way that feels right for me." His hand slid from Charles's jaw to the hollow of his throat. "I don't think you feel right, Charles. I don't think you've felt right for a long time."

Charles's first instinct was to deny it, but then he thought about all the days he'd come home from work or the gym and just sat numbly in front of the television for hours on end before dragging himself to bed, waking up the next morning feeling just as empty. The activities he'd once enjoyed, whether meeting the guys for a pickup basketball game or hitting happy hour with colleagues after work, had fallen by the wayside. He wouldn't say he'd been *sad*, exactly, but he hadn't looked forward to anything for a while.

Since Ángel returned, he'd woken up every morning knowing the day promised to be interesting, even if it annoyed the ever-loving shit out of him.

"I feel okay right now," Charles said.

Ángel's smile was breathtaking.

Charles smoothed his fingers down over the curve of Ángel's pert ass, seeking out his slick, relaxed hole. "You're really swollen," he said, tracing the rim with his fingertips.

"That's what happens when you get your ass reamed out for . . ." Ángel turned his head, picking Charles's phone up off the nightstand. "Christ, three *hours*."

"It wasn't three continuous hours," Charles said, though his chest swelled with pride nonetheless.

"Still." Ángel dropped the phone and turned his face back toward Charles.

His eyelids fluttered when Charles carefully slid one finger inside, savoring the easy give of his body. Charles added a second finger and watched, mesmerized, as they sank in and out.

"Charles . . ." Ángel parted his thighs, canting his hips. "I can't come again."

"I think you could," Charles said, hoarse. "I think if I milked your prostate, you'd come for me again—even if you couldn't ejaculate, even if you couldn't get hard. You'd still feel it inside."

Ángel moaned brokenly.

Charles curled his fingers, shifting closer to Ángel—and they both froze at a soft *thump* on the patio outside.

They met each other's eyes for a breathless moment, then disengaged without speaking, rolled off opposite sides of the bed, and gathered their scattered clothes, dressing in silence. The thumps and rustling continued, accompanied by a familiar hissing noise that Charles couldn't quite put his finger on.

Ángel retrieved their guns from the drawer where they'd stashed them before their shower, handing Charles his. There were two sliding glass doors to the patio—one in the living room and one here in the master bedroom—so Charles eased himself against the wall, Ángel at his shoulder, and twitched back the blinds.

A slight hooded figure stood in profile to them, spray-painting the other door. Charles flipped the lock and wrenched open the door, his gun held in a two-handed grip as he pushed through the blinds.

"Freeze!" he said.

The tagger yelped, dropped the paint can with a clatter, and sprang over the patio railing, rabbiting away into the apartment complex. Ángel took after him like a shot, not even taking the time to consult with Charles before he vaulted the railing as well and disappeared into the night.

"Ángel!" Charles cried in exasperation. He glanced at the message that had been sprayed onto the glass with blood-red paint.

I KNOW YOU'RE IN THERE

Groaning, Charles slid the bedroom door shut and went after Ángel, finding himself in his second goddamn foot chase of the day.

Fortunately for his sore legs, this one was shorter. The tagger was fast, but Ángel was much faster, or maybe just more determined. He gained steadily as they raced across courtyards and crashed through banks of flowering bushes; when they emerged from a cluster of buildings into the grassy area beside the complex's pool, Ángel leaped and grabbed the tagger around the waist, bringing them both to the ground.

By the time Charles caught up, Ángel had the thrashing tagger on his back, pinned by his hips and wrists. Charles leaned down to yank off the tagger's hood, then stepped back in surprise.

It was a skinny Latino kid, maybe twelve or thirteen years old, nobody Charles had ever seen before. He glared up at them both with the fuming defiance common to adolescents everywhere.

"Who is this?" Charles asked, though from the expression on Ángel's face, he already knew the answer.

"I have no idea," Ángel said.

CHAPTER FIFTEEN

They had to take the kid back to Charles's place so Charles could duck inside and grab his cell phone to call the cops—and clear the apartment, in case anyone had snuck inside when they'd been gone. While they waited, Ángel sat the kid on the parking-lot curb and settled beside him, keeping a sharp eye for any sign that he'd make another run for it.

"What's your name?" Ángel asked.

The kid wrapped his arms around his knees and didn't answer.

Ángel watched him for a moment, then said, "*¿Cómo te llamas?*" Even if the kid spoke English, speaking Spanish might create a sense of solidarity and get him to let down his guard a little.

"Marco," the kid muttered, his tone bleeding resentment.

"Why'd you tag my friend's door, Marco?" Ángel asked, continuing the conversation in Spanish.

Marco shrugged without looking up. "Just something to do."

"That was a pretty personal message," said Ángel. "Was it meant for anyone in particular?"

"Not really," Marco said. He toyed with his shoelaces, eyes glued to them like they were the most fascinating things he'd ever seen.

Charles emerged from the apartment and came around to stand in front of them. "It's clear. Cops are on their way."

Marco lifted his head just enough to glare at Charles with purest loathing.

"Can I tell you what I think, Marco?" Ángel said, drawing his attention away from Charles. "I think someone else put you up to this—paid you, or maybe threatened you—and you're afraid to tell us who it was."

"I'm not *afraid*." Marco's scornful eyes traveled back to Charles. "I just don't like cops," he said, clearly operating on two mistaken assumptions—first, that Charles couldn't speak Spanish, and second, that Ángel wasn't a cop himself.

Charles recognized the advantage at the same time Ángel did. He kept his face blank, betraying no indication that he'd understood. The poor guy had that distinct cop vibe seeping out of his pores, though, and there wasn't anything he could do about that.

Ángel, on the other hand, had always been able to pass for a civilian; he wouldn't have lasted long undercover otherwise. "He's not just a cop," he said, capitalizing on the opportunity Marco had handed him. "He's a special agent with the ATF. Do you know what that is?"

Marco's eyes widened, and he nodded.

"He's a good guy, though. He doesn't want to see you get in trouble for this any more than I do."

"Yeah, right," said Marco. "They're all the same."

Ángel looked up at Charles and switched to English. "He's worried about what'll happen when the cops show up."

"Tell him I won't press charges if he comes clean about who sent him here," Charles said.

Ángel relayed the message to Marco, though he'd seen enough comprehension on Marco's face to be certain that he did indeed speak English. Marco mulled it over for a minute, still eyeing Charles with distrust.

"You promise?" he said to Ángel. "I been in trouble for tagging before."

"I promise."

Marco huffed out a breath and said, "Me and my friends were hanging out in the park, just chilling, and some guy came up and asked if anyone would be willing to tag for him for a hundred bucks."

Ángel raised his eyebrows. "Does that happen a lot?"

"Sure. Everyone around here knows we're the best, and we're not ganged up, so we can get around without starting wars or shit. Anyway, I said I'd do it, and he told me the address and what he wanted. Figured his girl was sneaking around with some other guy." Marco gave Ángel a sudden startled look. "*You* his girl?"

"Something like that," said Ángel. "What did he look like?"

"Kind of skinny, not really tall or short. Other than that, I dunno." Marco raised his hands at Ángel's answering expression. "Seriously. He was wearing a hoodie and sunglasses and a scarf, the whole deal. I couldn't see anything but his nose."

"How about his hands?"

"Gloves."

"Then how do you know it was a man?" Ángel asked.

"No tits," Marco said, with all the confidence of a teenage boy keen on the subject. "Plus, his voice was pretty deep."

"Could you tell what race he was?"

"Latino—Mexican, for sure. Spoke to us in Spanish, didn't seem like he understood English."

Ángel sat back, frustrated. Was this the stalker, or just an intermediary? It couldn't be the same person who had approached Ian in the club—the physical descriptions were too different. And neither of those descriptions matched the voice Buzz had heard on the phone. Were *any* of them the actual stalker, or was he playing some kind of shell game?

A police car pulled into the parking lot then, thankfully without lights or sirens. After a brief discussion with Charles, the officers agreed to give Marco a warning and escort him home—though not before Ángel got his address and phone number in case they needed to contact him again.

As he and Charles stood on the sidewalk, watching the car drive off, Ángel said, "What if the stalker goes after Marco the same way he went after Buzz?"

"He might," Charles said. "I had a word with the cops about it and asked them to keep an eye on Marco's house tonight. Ed can discuss the situation with their captain tomorrow."

Ángel sighed unhappily, but there wasn't much more they could do.

"Did Marco's description sound like any of your suspects?" Charles asked.

"No. Roberto is even bigger than you are, and Mercedes could never be described as skinny either. It could just be a middleman."

"Then why cover up so much? Why not send another guy who kind of looks like Esparza, like with Ian?"

"For all we know, the person who approached Ian *was* the stalker," Ángel said. "Oscar could have fit that description just as well."

"And none of the people we're talking about could have spoken English with an American accent."

"Not to my knowledge."

Charles palmed his face, rubbing the bridge of his nose. Ángel took a step closer, and Charles reached out at once, pulling Ángel in against his side. Exhaling a slow breath, Ángel leaned into him and allowed himself a moment to appreciate Charles's calm strength. He gave Charles a lot of shit, but sometimes Ángel craved a little order and stability too.

"We've got to get at least some sleep tonight," Ángel said a few moments later. "Come on."

"There's just one more thing I'm worried about," Charles said as he closed and locked the front door behind them.

"What?"

"How the fuck do you get red spray paint off a glass door?"

"That's not a super-helpful description," Jade said the next morning.

"Tell me about it," said Ángel.

Due to the sensitive nature of their discussions, they'd taken a conference room for their team meeting rather than hold it out in the bullpen. Charles sat beside Ángel, who looked tired but not on the edge of collapse. They'd both managed a few hours of sleep last night—in separate beds.

"Well, I'll see what I can do, but don't expect any miracles," Jade said. "Maybe there were surveillance cameras near the park . . ." She trailed off, tapping away at the tablet that was never far from her hand.

"Where are we on the guns?" Charles asked.

"They hadn't been scrubbed, so it was easy to trace them," Eva said from the head of the table, where she had several thick file folders spread out in front of her. "The shipment was destined for the Presidio of Monterey, but the garrison's paperwork said the guns were coming in next week. They weren't missing them yet."

"Inside job," Sakura said.

"Yes. There's been no sign of the original transport vehicle, and the guards on the manufacturer's official record weren't actually the ones who left with it. It seems the Alvarado cartel had agents on both ends."

Shane swallowed a mouthful of cruller and made a face. "Not exactly a confidence booster to think that they can get to people inside our own military."

Nodding, Eva said, "Top brass took this out of our hands, and I was happy to let them. We're not paid enough to get involved in whatever political firestorm this is going to ignite."

"Political cover-up, you mean," Sakura said, dumping a packet of sugar into her coffee.

"Either way." Eva sighed. "People are going to go down for this. Let's make sure they don't take us with them, all right?"

"As long as we're browsing in the bad news department," said Jade, "I've had a look into the Alvarados' financials, and I can't find any suspiciously large or unexplained sources of funds. Which kind of puts a pin in the theory that Raúl Esparza paid them to help fake his death."

"He didn't," Ángel said, much more calmly than he'd objected to this discussion in the past. "What's happening to me now doesn't have anything to do with this case—the stalker just took the opportunity where he saw it. Even if Raúl weren't dead, he couldn't have known I would end up here; this would be too much of a coincidence. If I hadn't gotten involved with you guys, everything would have happened exactly the same, except there wouldn't have been any fake papers in that car and Buzz would still be alive."

Jade perked up and said, "Speak of the devil. I got hold of Buzz's cell phone like you suggested, Charles, and downloaded his voice mails. It was mostly nonsense, but there was one interesting message."

While Jade plugged her tablet into the speaker at the center of the table, Charles glanced sideways at Ángel. Ángel met his eyes with perfect composure, as if this were the first time either of them had heard of any suspicious voice mail.

Jade pressed Play.

"Mr. Cooper," said a man with a drawling Texan accent, "you don't know me, but I'm an associate of Felix Torres. I was hoping you might . . ."

The rest of the message was white noise to Charles, who was preoccupied with Ángel's immediate reaction. His face had gone a sickly gray, and he gripped the edge of the table with both hands, breathing shallowly through his mouth.

"That's Paul," Ángel said dazedly.

A ripple of reaction went around the table. Charles's stomach lurched.

"*That's* what's off about his voice," Jade said. She started the message over from the beginning and pursed her lips in thought. "There's kind of a tremor there, but it's indistinct, like he's trying to hide that he's afraid—"

"*Jade*," Sakura said. She inclined her head toward Ángel, and Jade turned the voice mail off at once.

"A cowboy," Ángel murmured, more to himself than anyone else. "Fuck, how could I not . . ."

Charles tensed, worried Ángel was going to give the game away, but he should have known better. Ángel pushed his chair away from the table and left the room without another word.

"Should someone go after him?" Shane asked.

Charles shook his head. "Give him a few minutes. When he's this upset, he tends to lash out at whoever's nearby."

"So the stalker forced Warner to be his middleman with Buzz," said Sakura. "That's beyond fucked up."

"Jade, have you had any luck locating the suspects Ángel named?" Eva said.

"Mercedes Salazar is living the high life in Mexico City—I guess Esparza left her a bunch of money. There's no official record of her leaving Mexico, and having seen her credit card statements, I'm confident that she never left under the radar either." Jade unplugged her tablet from the speaker and pulled it back toward herself. "I'm more concerned about Oscar Palomo."

"How so?" Charles said.

"A couple of days after we extracted Ángel, there was a bloody coup inside the cartel, and Palomo barely got away with his life. He hasn't been seen or heard from since."

Eva grimaced. "That *is* concerning."

"What about Roberto Ibarra?" Charles asked. "The ex-bodyguard?"

"Dead," said Jade.

"*Dead*?" Eva repeated.

"Shot in his apartment shortly after Palomo kicked him out of the cartel." Jade shrugged. "He's not the only one, either. At least a half-dozen of Esparza's flunkies have been executed in a similar way. Unofficial consensus in the PFM is that Palomo had them taken out."

The Policía Federal Ministerial was sure to have their own agents inside the Esparza cartel; in fact, Paul Warner had probably liaised with them to keep Ángel safe undercover. If anyone knew what was going on down there, it was the PFM. Still, something about all this didn't sit right with Charles.

"Man, poor Ángel," Shane said, tipping back in his chair. "Bodies are just dropping like flies around him."

"That's not his fault," Charles said, too harshly.

Shane blinked at him. "I never said it was."

"All right, let's table this for now," said Eva. "We have other work to do, and the FBI is still investigating Warner's abduction and homicide. We'll see if they come up with any leads."

"We're just going to sit around and wait for the FBI?" Charles said.

"They have more evidence to work with than we do." Eva propped her forearms on the table and leaned forward. "You *know* how difficult it is to catch stalkers, Charles. Leaving a body was a misstep on the stalker's part, but we can't touch that crime scene, so what else do you want me to do?"

"Nothing." Realizing his hands were clenched into fists underneath the table, Charles stretched out his fingers and laid them flat against his thighs. "Sorry."

Their conversation turned to new business, but Charles couldn't focus for the rest of the meeting.

It took him a few minutes to track Ángel down afterward, out on the smokers' patio on the ground floor. "Are you okay?" Charles asked, joining him against the wall.

Staring off into space, Ángel said, "What am I doing here?"

Charles opened his mouth, but since he wasn't sure what Ángel meant, he didn't have an answer.

"I brought the stalker here with me," Ángel said. "I dragged him into your case, something you've been working on for months. He could have ruined everything."

"He didn't. Everything worked out fine."

"*This* time. What about the next one? If I'd left when Campos suggested it—"

Charles took hold of Ángel's elbow, exerting light pressure until Ángel looked at him. "That wouldn't have been you."

"No," Ángel said bitterly. "No, it wouldn't. I'm the guy who sticks around and puts everyone in danger because I'm too proud to hide from a fight I know I can't win." He turned around and kicked the wall.

"You *can* win," Charles said, alarmed by this uncharacteristically defeatist attitude. "We'll find him, Ángel. We've all got your back."

"You shouldn't have to." Ángel gestured toward the building. "They've known me for a week. It's not fair to expect them to take risks for me."

"It doesn't matter how long they've known you. You're an agent, you're one of us—"

"He could kill you, Charles," Ángel interrupted. "Or Jade, or Eva, or anybody else around me." Ángel drew a shuddering breath. "He won't just stand by and let me live my life. He'll interfere in any case I work on, threaten anyone I care about. He'll poison everything I touch."

"What are you saying?" Charles asked.

Ángel closed his eyes. "I have to leave San Diego."

Charles stared at him. This was what he'd wanted, wasn't it? He'd genuinely had no desire to see Ángel again after their last fight in Tucson. Ángel's return had brought extremes of anger and confusion Charles hadn't felt in years. He'd been consistently deprived of sleep; his car had been destroyed and his apartment tagged by a nutjob out for his blood. He'd found a dead body in one of the most gruesome tableaus he'd ever seen.

He was so much more present and invested in his life than he'd been before.

"I don't think you should make any decisions right now," Charles managed to say. "You just had a nasty shock."

"My life has been a series of nasty shocks for the past two years," said Ángel. "I've had enough. I can't do this anymore."

He started walking away, toward the door. "Ángel," Charles called out, astonished. Never in a million years would he have expected to see Ángel Medina surrender. It was *wrong*, unnatural, and it left a bad taste in his mouth.

Ángel stopped and turned back, studying Charles's face for a moment. "I'll wait to discuss it with Campos until tomorrow," he said.

Charles nodded. He watched Ángel go inside the building, then just stood there, his brain whirling.

He wasn't sure he wanted Ángel to stay, not forever. But Charles *knew* he didn't want this to be the way Ángel left.

"So how private is your uncle's cabin in Canada, exactly?" Ángel asked Jesenia that night in her motel room.

"Really?" she said, pausing with her hands full of Chinese takeout containers. "You're considering it?"

"I don't know if I can justify staying here any longer." Ángel snagged an egg roll from the bag and dropped it on his paper plate. "I'm putting everyone near me at risk, not to mention endangering my office's cases. The stalker got involved in the Jackals raid just to fuck with me—if he'd wanted to, he could have blown the whole thing."

"That's a good point." Jesenia opened the rest of the containers and sat down at the table, spooning out orange chicken for them both.

Reaching for a pair of chopsticks, Ángel said, "I don't want to run away, but . . . isn't that a little selfish?"

"I don't know," said Jesenia. "I'm sure the rest of your team doesn't think so."

Ángel dragged his chopsticks discontentedly through his rice.

"What exactly is holding you back here?" Jesenia held up a hand before Ángel could answer. "I mean besides your natural-born stubbornness and pride. I've never known you to have trouble setting those aside to protect people before. So what's different now? What's making you want to stay even though you know it's a bad idea?"

Ángel took his time chewing and swallowing a bite of chicken. "Charles," he admitted, when he could no longer stall.

"*Ay*," Jesenia said, sighing heavily.

"I know, I know it's stupid—"

"It's not stupid, honey, it's just not going to do you any good." Stretching her arm across the table, Jesenia took Ángel's hand in hers. "Let's talk about this honestly, okay? What was your relationship like with Charles in Tucson?"

Ángel turned aside, disgruntled, but Jesenia held fast to his hand. "*Ángel*," she said.

"We had to sneak around because Charles didn't want anyone to know about us," Ángel said reluctantly.

"And here in San Diego?"

Ángel scowled at her, though it wasn't her fault she was right. "We're sneaking around because Charles doesn't want anyone to know about us."

Jesenia gave him a pointed look and released his hand.

"Something's different this time," Ángel said. Charles was more raw than the last time Ángel had seen him, less sure of himself— the breakup with Amy had shaken him. He just wasn't sure if those changes were enough to do them any good.

"I'm sure it is. It's been two years, after all." Jesenia picked up her chopsticks. "Let me ask you this, though: do you really believe Charles can forgive you for what you did to him?"

Shit. "No," Ángel whispered.

"There you go, then," she said. "For what it's worth, I don't think you should forgive him for the way he treated you, either. I'm not saying Charles is a bad guy; you're just not right for each other. It's obvious you want different things."

Jesenia let Ángel stew in his thoughts as they ate. Eventually he said, "I'll talk to Campos tomorrow about taking a sabbatical."

"All right." Jesenia gave him a sympathetic smile. "Whatever you want to do, I'll support you. *Cuenta conmigo.*"

Ángel spent the rest of the evening hanging out with Jesenia, hoping Charles would be in bed by the time he got back. No such luck—when Ángel entered the apartment, Charles was sitting on the couch, watching TV, which Ángel was willing to bet good money he'd been doing since he got home from the gym after work.

"Hey," Ángel said, stopping in the living room.

Charles hit the mute button on the remote. "Hey."

The blinds were drawn over the patio door, as always, so Ángel couldn't see if Charles had made any attempt to get the paint off the glass. "No more visitors tonight?"

"Nope."

All right. There was no point in delaying this, or skirting around the issue. At the very least, Charles deserved Ángel's honesty now.

"I decided to take Jesenia up on her offer," said Ángel. "With any luck, the stalker will be too lazy to follow me all the way to Canada."

His weak humor fell flat between them. Charles just gazed back at him steadily.

"Cold up there," was all he said.

"Yeah, I know."

"It's your decision." Charles unmuted the TV.

Ángel frowned. Though Charles's tone hadn't been judgmental, Ángel still felt he'd been dismissed—like he'd disappointed Charles somehow, which was beyond unfair. He turned and locked himself into the guest bedroom without saying good night.

Ángel showered and went right to bed, but he tossed and turned for hours, unable to find any peace. The last time he and Charles had separated, it had been devastating, ripping deep wounds into his very core that still hurt years later. He didn't want to leave things that way again. Not after what they'd been through this time.

Rolling over on the futon, Ángel rummaged in the duffel bag on the floor until he came up with a bottle of lube. He tossed back his blankets, stripped out of his underwear, and pulled his knees up to his chest, reaching down to tease his hole.

Ángel fingered himself slowly, easing his hole open and stroking his cock to hardness. Once he'd gotten himself nice and slick, he grabbed a condom from the bag and padded naked from his bedroom to Charles's.

Charles was asleep on his side, one arm curled beneath his head and the other flung out across the mattress. Not wanting to startle him, Ángel kept his distance from the bed as he said, "Charles. Charles, wake up."

With a sleepy groan, Charles blinked his eyes open and raised his head. "Ángel? Is something wr . . ." His voice cut off abruptly, and when he spoke again, he no longer sounded quite so drowsy. "What are you doing?"

Ángel said nothing, just approached the bed and pulled back the blankets. Charles shifted onto his back and watched him; he took a deep, slow breath when Ángel straddled his waist, dropping the condom onto the mattress.

"Wh—"

Ángel pressed his clean fingers to Charles's mouth. "*Cielito*," he murmured, leaning forward. "*Bésame*."

The second Ángel withdrew his hand, Charles's own were threading through Ángel's hair, pulling him into a hungry kiss. Ángel moaned into it, squirming atop Charles, pressing every inch of their bodies together and squeezing his knees against Charles's sides.

He just wanted one more night—one night setting aside their anger and bitterness and resentment, one good memory to take with him. If Charles made him ask for it, though . . .

He didn't. Charles lifted his hips just enough to wriggle out of his boxers, never dislodging Ángel from his seat or breaking the kiss. Ángel took hold of Charles's cock with his lube-slick hand, thrilling at the sensation of that thick shaft coming to life against his palm.

It wasn't long before Charles was swollen and straining. Ángel pulled back from the kiss, a little dizzy from oxygen deprivation, and got the condom into place. He lifted himself on his knees and held Charles's cock steady.

"Ángel, wait," Charles said, his hands flying to Ángel's hips. "Are you—"

His eyes rolled back in his head as Ángel's eager hole sank onto his cock. Ángel closed his own eyes, working his way down inch by inch, biting his lip when his ass settled against Charles's pelvis.

God, Charles's fucking *cock*, it always filled him up exactly the way he needed—

Ángel gave a few gentle bounces to make sure his body was ready, then folded forward, resting his chest flat against Charles's, and took his mouth again. They kissed languidly while Ángel alternated between rocking back and forth and swiveling his hips, grinding Charles's cock in circles inside his hole. Charles's hips rolled beneath him, matching Ángel's lazy pace; his hands grazed light patterns over Ángel's back and sides.

Eventually, Charles's hands found their way to Ángel's ass. He kneaded the cheeks, spreading them wide and then pushing them together around his cock.

Too turned on to focus on kissing anymore, Ángel lifted his head and said, "Fuck, that feels good."

"Mmm." Charles rubbed a finger against Ángel's hole, tracing the stretched, sensitive rim.

Ángel dropped his head into the crook of Charles's shoulder. "Put it in."

Charles's chest jerked underneath him with a sudden deep breath. "Yeah?"

Ángel nodded, his face hidden against Charles's neck. He sucked Charles's finger when it tapped against his lips, laving it with his tongue and getting it nice and wet, though there was already plenty of lube in play for what he had in mind.

Pulling out halfway, Charles hooked his finger inside Ángel's hole and tugged, coaxing the muscle to relax still more. Then he pushed all the way in and bottomed out, giving Ángel both his finger and his cock at once.

"*God*," Ángel said, letting out a deep groan. He writhed atop Charles, pushing back against the penetration, savoring the sweet ache of being so full.

Charles kept his finger in place as he thrust slowly in and out. He was struggling for breath, his body trembling against Ángel's, but his rhythm remained steady and measured.

Mouthing sloppily along Charles's shoulder, Ángel said, "Give me another one."

"Shit." Charles's hips bucked, just once, before he settled back down. "Are you sure? I don't think you're wet enough—"

"I can take it."

Being stuffed with two of Charles's fingers along with his sizable cock pushed Ángel close to his limits. He moaned throughout Charles's careful incursion, trembling uncontrollably once he had it all inside.

Bouncing or thrusting was out of the question, so Ángel gripped Charles's shoulders and swung his hips in lewd circles, pressing every inch of Charles's fingers and cock right where he needed them, rubbing his erection against Charles's abdomen. Charles grunted punched-out breaths, his free hand clutching Ángel's thigh like a lifeline.

"Kiss me," Charles said, echoing Ángel's earlier command.

Ángel did his best, but he was too overwhelmed. All he could manage was to pant against Charles's open mouth, their lips clinging together but barely moving otherwise.

"Can you come like this?" Charles murmured into the intimate space between them.

Ángel nodded. Releasing Charles's shoulders, he pushed himself up a bit on his hands, arching his back until he found the right angle. He quickened his pace, grinding his hips, his cock skidding against Charles's soft, warm skin. Charles gazed up at him, entranced, and Ángel couldn't tear his own eyes away.

As the pleasure swelled and neared its peak, Ángel squeezed all his muscles at once, clenching down around Charles's fingers and cock. The sudden pressure sent him over the edge; his orgasm wrenched a sob from his throat, his entire body wracked with crashing waves of pure release. Ángel spent himself all over Charles's stomach and slumped onto his elbows.

Charles gently withdrew his fingers, grasped Ángel's hips with both hands, and thrust up into him.

Ángel splayed his legs wider to give Charles more room to work. "You don't have to hold back," he said, sensing Charles's fraying self-control in his shaking muscles, his ragged breathing.

"I don't want to hurt you," said Charles.

"I'm fine." Ángel nipped at Charles's jaw. "I'm fine. Come on, I want you to feel as good as I do."

Charles snapped his hips, plunging harder into Ángel's ass. Ángel cried out as aftershocks zinged up his spine.

Charles was still watching his face intently. Ángel smiled at him, and when one of Charles's hands cupped his jaw, Ángel leaned into the caress.

"Don't give up," Charles burst out, startling him. "Stay here, Ángel, stay here and fight. I won't let anything happen to you. Please."

Ángel stared at him, eyes wide and astonished.

"Please," Charles said again, his voice choked with pleasure as much as desperation. The movement of his hips was frenzied now. "Please, I can't watch you give up, please . . ."

"All right," said Ángel. "I'll stay."

Charles's shoulders curled up off the bed; he pressed his face to Ángel's shoulder and wrapped an arm around his waist, squeezing tightly, as he came hard with a muffled groan. Ángel rode it out, rolling with every twitch of Charles's body until Charles fell back to the mattress.

He looked dazed, shattered. Ángel brushed a hand over Charles's cheek and leaned down to kiss him.

Whenever Charles asked Ángel to stay, Ángel wasn't able to leave.

CHAPTER SIXTEEN

"Á ngel, we're gonna be late!" Charles called from the kitchen. Ángel came out of the bedroom still buckling his belt, one sock on his foot and the other clutched in his hand. "You could go without me, you know. I've got my bike."

"It's ridiculous for us to drive separately when we're going to the same place," said Charles. "And that thing is a death trap."

"What are you, ninety?" Ángel pulled his other sock on.

When he straightened up, he was surprised by Charles grabbing his waist and pulling him into a deep, passionate kiss. Ángel wrapped his arms around Charles's neck and sank into it, kissing Charles there in his kitchen for several long minutes.

"That's some good stuff, Grandpa," he said once they separated, then smacked Charles's ass and scurried away before Charles could do more than sputter indignantly. "Come on, I thought you were worried about being late?"

After Ángel put on his shoes, they headed out to Charles's car. Ángel was in a much lighter mood than the day before; he'd spent the night in Charles's bed, and Charles hadn't pushed him away once, either literally or figuratively. In fact, Charles kept reaching out to touch him, fingers brushing over Ángel's hair and face and back as if reassuring himself of Ángel's presence.

Ángel's chest ached whenever he thought about Paul, but with Charles on his side, he could be strong enough to see this through to the end.

Still feeling giddy as they buckled their seat belts, Ángel snuck a hand into Charles's lap and squeezed his inner thigh, his knuckles grazing Charles's cock. Charles yelped and dropped the keys into the footwell.

"You little shit," Charles said, failing to hide his smile. He bent down to retrieve the keys.

A bullet tore through the windshield with an explosive *crack* and slammed into the headrest of Charles's seat.

Charles and Ángel both shouted, Ángel instinctively hunching forward and Charles staying down where he was. Their eyes met over the gearshift.

"Is someone *shooting* at us?" Charles said.

A second bullet ripped into the headrest centimeters from the first. Chunks of glass rained down on the dashboard from the shattered windshield.

"That would be a yes," said Ángel, digging his cell out of his pocket. Charles scooped up the keys and jammed them into the ignition.

"Nine-one-one, what's your emergency?"

"This is Special Agent Ángel Medina with the San Diego office of the ATF." Ángel winced as Charles swung them backward out of their parking spot without looking, banging their rear bumper hard into another parked car. "My partner and I are taking fire in our car from a sniper in the Bella Vista apartment complex off of South 89th Street."

"A . . . I'm sorry, did you say a sniper?" the operator asked.

Charles shifted the car into drive and stomped on the accelerator, driving blind through the parking lot.

"Yes," Ángel said. Another shot rang out, smashing the rear windshield this time, once more unerringly targeting the driver's side headrest. "Only rifle rounds could break this glass. They must be positioned on the roof of one of the buildings, but I can't tell which. We're attempting to leave the scene."

Their car clipped another parked vehicle; Charles overcorrected, bringing their right-hand wheels up on the curb. "Mother*fucker*," he spat.

As they fled, a fourth bullet took one of the rear tires. This was an agency vehicle, though, equipped with bullet-resistant tire inserts— after the first lurch, Charles was able to maintain control and speed, peeling out of the apartment complex's gate. He lifted his head just enough over the dashboard to make a right turn without driving into oncoming traffic.

"You need to dispatch officers to the scene immediately," Ángel said to the operator. "I don't think there was any collateral damage, but I can't be sure."

"Yes, sir. Please stay on the line."

A short way down the road, Charles risked sitting up higher. When no more shots were forthcoming, he drew his own gun and used it to knock the rest of the fractured glass out of the windshield on the driver's side, giving himself a clear view.

While they drove, Ángel provided the operator with all the necessary details, including his own number and the number for their office. Once he'd been assured that officers were on their way, he ended the call.

"I'm going to pull off at the next gas station," Charles said. "These tires are supposed to be able to go sixty miles after taking a hit, but I'd really rather not test that."

Ángel nodded, already dialing Ed Campos.

Campos sent agents to retrieve them, and Ángel and Charles spent the next two hours giving statements to both their own people and the SDPD. The responding officers hadn't found any trace of a sniper, not even shell casings; the only evidence left behind were the bullets in Charles's car and the damage they'd caused while escaping. Forensics would extract and analyze the bullets, but Ángel had little confidence they'd find anything useful.

Once the police had left and things had quieted down, Ángel and Charles joined their team at their desk cluster. The adrenaline of the attack and its aftermath began to wear off, leaving Ángel nauseous in its wake and too agitated to sit.

"You would have died," he said to Charles.

Charles remained standing as well. "You could have died too."

"No," said Ángel. "The sniper wasn't shooting at us; he was shooting at *you*. Just you. If you hadn't bent down to get the keys at that exact moment, you would be dead right now."

"I'm not," Charles said calmly.

Ángel shook his head in frustration. This was never going to stop. Stalking always escalated, and he *knew* that. God, why had he let Charles talk him into staying?

A cacophony of dings, whistles, beeps, and chimes resounded through the office as every cell phone present received a text message simultaneously.

Every phone, that is, except for Ángel's. He frowned at his empty screen, then looked at Charles, who shrugged and showed Ángel his own blank phone.

Gasps and whispers broke out across the room. Jade clapped a hand over her mouth; Eva uttered a low curse. One by one, every head in the room turned toward Ángel and Charles.

"What?" Ángel said, breaking out in goose bumps. "What is it?"

Jade handed Ángel her phone. Blazing on the screen was a photo of Charles and Ángel kissing—kissing *that morning*, in Charles's kitchen, completely absorbed in each other. Cross hairs had been superimposed over Charles's head, and a message printed along the bottom of the photograph:

IF I CAN'T HAVE HIM NO ONE CAN

Charles took the phone out of Ángel's hand and then sucked in a breath, his skin going numb as a buzzing started up in his ears. Dozens of stares burned into him from every direction, and he couldn't bring himself to look up. His eyes wandered from himself and Ángel to the cross hairs to the threatening message, his brain scrambling to process all the disturbing implications at once.

"So when you said you knew Ángel in Tucson," Shane said, breaking the office-wide silence, "you really meant you *knew* him in Tucson."

Charles couldn't deny it. The picture radiated a familiar, intimate vibe; it clearly wasn't the kiss of two people new to each other's bodies.

He returned Jade's phone and looked at Eva, whose expression was a struggle between anger and anxiety. Before she could say anything, though, Ed strode out of his office and into the bullpen.

"I need to see you two in my office," he said to Charles and Ángel. He held his own cell phone in one hand.

Ángel started after him; when he realized Charles wasn't following, he turned back and hissed, "*Charles*," under his breath.

Giving his head a hard shake, Charles trailed after Ángel and Ed. He avoided the eyes of everyone they passed, doing his best to block out their shocked whispers.

This isn't happening.

Inside his office, Ed shut the door, closed the blinds, and gestured for Charles and Ángel to sit down. He took a seat behind his desk and set his phone out on top.

"Is this a real photograph?" Ed asked.

It hadn't even occurred to Charles to suggest the photo had been doctored. Ángel was silent next to him, gazing down at his clasped hands, allowing Charles to take the lead.

Charles couldn't lie about this, not if he ever wanted to face himself in the mirror again. "Yes, it's real."

His brow furrowing, Ed said, "Were the two of you romantically involved in Tucson?"

Charles's hands spasmed on the arms of his chair. He tried to speak, but his dry throat only made a sort of clicking noise.

"He's objecting to your use of the word *romantically*," Ángel said, his glacial tone lowering the temperature in the room several degrees.

"What?" Charles said, recovering his voice. "No, I'm not . . . I'm just trying to catch up with what's happening here."

"You never disclosed your relationship to the agency back then." Ángel's face was wooden. "It wasn't serious."

"Serious enough to start things up again," Ed said. He turned to Charles. "I understand wanting to keep your relationships private, but for God's sake, once we realized Ángel was being stalked by someone with a vested interest in his personal life, this became a very dangerous secret. You should have at least told *me*, even if it was off the record. Did you think it would matter to me that you're gay?"

"I'm bisexual," Charles snapped. Jesus Christ. Ed had known Amy, had been around her and Charles together—had come to their *engagement* party—but his first assumption upon seeing a photo of Charles kissing another man was that Charles had been on the down-low all along, rather than the much simpler and more rational explanation that he was attracted to men as well as women.

This was why Charles allowed people to assume he was straight. Come out as bisexual, and suddenly everyone and their mother had a fucking opinion they were eager to share. Charles wasn't ashamed of his sexuality, but it was exhausting to be constantly forced to defend it, as if the matter were up for debate. He had zero interest in fending off accusations that he was in denial or going through a phase or somehow confused about what got his own dick hard.

"Oh." Ed hesitated, seeming thrown, before he soldiered on. "Well, regardless, you've angered the stalker enough for him to make a serious attempt on your life." He tapped his phone. "When was this picture taken?"

"This morning."

"But it couldn't have been taken from outside," said Ángel. "The blinds were closed over the sliding glass door, and there aren't any windows in that room." Glancing sideways at Charles, he said, "There must be cameras in your apartment."

"Goddamn it," Charles said, knowing at once that Ángel was right. He knew how the stalker had pulled it off too. "The other night, when Marco tagged the door—I cleared the apartment when we got back, but I didn't look for surveillance devices. I was too distracted."

"Why today, though?" Ed asked. "Why didn't he take a shot at you until this morning, when he must have had plenty of opportunities before this?"

"Because I changed my mind," Ángel said quietly.

Charles closed his eyes.

"If there are cameras in your apartment, you can bet your ass there are bugs." Ángel's voice grew more strained as he spoke. "I told you I was going to leave San Diego, and then you convinced me not to, Charles. He must blame you for that."

"This is exactly why you *can't* leave," Charles said, opening his eyes. "He wants you alone, unsupported, so it'll be easier to take you—"

"It'll be easier for him to take me after he picks off everyone around me here too," Ángel shot back.

Ed reached for his desk phone. "I'll send a team out to sweep your apartment, Charles. As for next steps . . ." He sighed. "I honestly don't know. You've got a literal target painted on your head. I don't think either of you should leave the office for the time being."

"If I leave, he'll follow me," Ángel said. "Charles won't be in danger then."

"You don't know that," said Charles, clenching his right hand into a fist. "What's to stop him from taking me out before he leaves? Or coming back later for revenge? If you go off alone, the only thing you'll be doing for sure is making yourself more vulnerable."

"So I'm just supposed to sit around with my thumb up my ass and wait for whatever he decides to do next? We aren't any closer to catching him than we were a week ago!" Ángel took a deep breath and looked at Ed. "May I please be excused, sir?"

Ed nodded. Ángel jumped up and hurried out of the room, closing the door behind himself. Charles scowled at it, his body strung tight with frustration.

"Go after him if you're going," Ed said, raising the phone receiver to his ear.

Charles didn't need to be told twice. He left the office and found Ángel moments later, pacing the same conference room where they'd promised Eva they wouldn't sleep together again.

"You're not going anywhere," Charles said once he shut the door.

"Why not?" Ángel said, whirling to face him. "Won't you be glad to get rid of me, now that your horrible secret is out?"

Charles frowned. "Horrible secret?"

"Everybody knows you're bisexual now."

"Uh, no, I'm pretty sure everybody now thinks I've been secretly gay all this time, which is gonna drive me up the fucking wall." Charles rubbed a hand down his face. "I don't know how many times I have to tell you this, Ángel, but my sexuality isn't a horrible secret to me. I just prefer not to tell people, especially at work. You know how most people react to anyone saying they're bisexual, let alone a black man. It's going to cause me problems here, and I'm beyond upset about being outed this way, but it isn't going to ruin my life."

Ángel stopped pacing and gave him an odd look. "That's it? After all of the fights we had about this in Tucson, I thought you'd be having a panic attack right now."

"We had those fights because you wouldn't stop *pressuring* me," Charles said. "When somebody tells you they don't want to come out, that's the end of the conversation. You don't argue with them about it.

Sometimes it felt like you were trying to shame me into coming out, and yeah, that made me angry."

Ángel grimaced. "That isn't how I meant it."

His hackles rising at the memories, Charles arched an eyebrow. "Really? Because I kept telling you I wasn't ready, and you mocked me for it. You can't rush a person into that decision, Ángel. It wasn't the right time for me."

"It wasn't the right time?" Ángel asked, his eyes narrowing. "Or it wasn't the right person?"

Uh-oh. Charles clenched his jaw, unwilling to lie to Ángel's face about this but knowing the truth would hurt him.

"God." Ángel raked his hands through his hair. "That's why you're not freaking out as much as I thought you would. It isn't that you didn't want to come out, period. It's that you didn't think it was worth coming out for *me*. But now that somebody's forced your hand, well, you'll just deal with the consequences."

Those weren't the words Charles would have chosen, but he couldn't refute the line of reasoning. He hadn't seen the point in going through all the bullshit of coming out at work for a relationship that had no future.

"We were always going to be temporary," Charles said wearily. "We're too different, we want different things—"

Crossing his arms, Ángel said, "You don't know shit about what I want."

"No?" Charles said, knowing he was treading into dangerous waters. "Let's say I had come out, we'd disclosed our relationship to HR, and everyone knew we were seeing each other. If I'd asked you to move in a few months later, started talking about getting married someday, maybe having kids—you expect me to believe you wouldn't have run as fast as you could in the opposite direction?"

Ángel's nostrils flared, but he didn't deny it.

"How many times had I heard you joke about marriage being a prison, or kids ruining people's lives?"

"For God's sake, Charles—"

"And there's nothing wrong with that," said Charles. He needed to get all of this out before Ángel interrupted him. "*I* want those things, though. You just wanted me to come out so that we didn't have to sneak around; you never thought of me as a long-term partner. Nothing in your life has ever been long-term."

Ángel blinked and took a step back, as if Charles had pushed him.

Charles lifted his hands. "I couldn't do it. I couldn't come out and go through all that bullshit just to have you leave me a few months down the line when you got bored, or scared of the commitment."

"You don't know that's what would have happened," Ángel said.

His eyebrows climbing up his forehead, Charles said, "Are you kidding me? That's exactly what *did* happen."

Everything they'd been dancing around for a week, everything they'd refused to confront directly, was suddenly standing right there in the room with them. Ángel glared at him as the tension in the air ratcheted up. "We're really going to do this right now?" he said.

"I just want to know why," Charles said, unable to hold himself back anymore.

"I told you from the beginning that I wouldn't stop fucking other guys as long as you wanted to keep us a secret," said Ángel. "You said that was fair—"

"I didn't mean why you fucked someone else," Charles said in exasperation. He'd known he had no right to expect monogamy from Ángel, given the circumstances. "Why a friend of mine, why on my birthday, why when you knew I was about to show up any minute? I know you didn't forget. You'd wrapped my present and it was sitting out on the counter. Did you just . . . not give a shit?"

Ángel's stiff shoulders crept up toward his ears, but he was strangely quiet.

Well, if Ángel wasn't going to say anything, there was more Charles wanted to get off his chest. "You never apologized," Charles said. "You pulled that selfish stunt, and then you ran away like a coward and threw yourself into bed with a goddamn Mexican cartel!"

"You're wrong." Ángel's voice was quiet, but in the dangerous way that meant things had already gone too far. His body trembled minutely, his hands fisted at his sides.

"About what?"

"I didn't go undercover because we had that fight." Ángel looked Charles in the eye. "We had that fight because I was about to go undercover."

"I . . ." Charles swallowed. "I don't understand."

He *did*, though. The pieces clicked together in the back of his mind, no matter how furiously he tried to deny them.

Ángel didn't look away, didn't lower his eyes or do anything to soften the blow. "The Esparza operation was my idea from the beginning. I'd heard chatter about Raúl's interests, and I knew I had a shot. I knew I could get in there where we'd always failed before. I designed the operation myself; I proposed it to Dallas. I had known I was leaving for weeks before that night."

Charles leaned sideways, bracing one hand on the conference table to keep himself upright. He shook his head, begging Ángel not to say what was sure to be coming next.

"I set things up so you would find me with Jared that night," Ángel said, relentless. "That wrapped present was just an empty box."

Charles hunched forward, his entire body curling around the sick pain lancing his guts. "You put me through that on *purpose*?" he whispered. "Why?"

"I wasn't allowed to tell anyone where I was really going," Ángel said. The tone of his voice had shifted, now ragged with pain. "I couldn't get an exemption for you, because our relationship was a secret. If I'd made up some bullshit story about transferring to another field office, you would have asked me to stay—and I would have stayed, Charles, because that's how pathetic I am. I would have stayed and kept panting after you, grateful for every scrap of attention you threw my way, knowing you'd never come out. I would have given up what could have been our only shot at the Esparzas, and I would have been left with nothing to show for it."

"Are you a fucking sociopath?" Charles stood up straight, though he didn't trust himself to let go of the table. "You can't just fuck with people's heads because you're too weak to say no to them!"

Ángel shrugged helplessly. "I thought about just taking off, letting you hear about my 'transfer' from the others in the office. But I was afraid you'd look for me, try to track me down, and I couldn't take the risk that the agency wouldn't be able to head you off before you'd compromised my cover."

Charles could only stare at him.

"Do you think I didn't get what I deserved for doing it? The things you said to me that night . . ." Ángel pressed his lips together and turned his face aside. "A *filthy fucking slut*, that's what you called me. So desperate for attention and approval that I'd bend over for anyone, crawl on the ground and beg for it like a dog if that's what it took to get someone to like me—"

"Stop," Charles said, nauseated. "Stop."

God, he'd spent two years trying to forget that words like that had come out of his mouth; it was one of the most shameful moments of his life. But the enormity of Ángel's manipulation was too fresh for Charles to apologize.

"You could have found a better way," he said.

"Maybe," said Ángel. "I just knew that I had to cut all ties in a way that would keep us both safe. And . . ." With a groan, Ángel threw his hands in the air. "And I was so fucking in love with you, Charles, and you wouldn't even admit we were in a relationship. I *wanted* to hurt you for that."

Charles sat down abruptly. *What?*

They looked at each other in silence. Charles had to say something, had to acknowledge what had been laid out between them. He needed to say— He should—

Too late. Ángel's face shut down, every trace of emotion wiped clean. "I'm sorry, I can't do this," he said, and slipped out of the room.

Charles wanted to follow him, but he physically couldn't move. He sat frozen at the conference table, his entire world knocked on its axis, Ángel's words echoing over and over again in his head.

Nobody tried to stop Ángel from leaving the building—though to be fair, it wasn't like he announced it. He just walked out the front door and called a cab, uncaring of the potential danger. If the stalker wanted to take him, he could give it his best fucking shot.

Ángel made it back to Charles's apartment without incident, got his bike, and took it out on the road. He drove for hours—winding through highways, cruising along the coast, doing his best to lose himself in the unfamiliar environs.

Of course, these days it was pretty hard to get lost in any area with decent 4G. Once he'd taken the edge off his roiling emotions, Ángel used his cell to find his way back to Jesenia's motel, ignoring his multiple missed calls from Charles, Campos, and Eva. He parked his bike in the lot and knocked on Jesenia's door, hoping she'd be in even though he hadn't called first.

"You look like hell," Jesenia said when she opened the door.

"I don't know what to do," Ángel choked out without preamble, though he hadn't intended to fall apart right there on the threshold. "I feel like—like I always make the wrong choices. I don't know what I should do next."

"Come in, sit down." Jesenia moved out of the doorway and guided Ángel to the small table in the corner of the room. "Do you want some coffee?"

Collapsing into the chair, Ángel peeled off his gloves and jacket. "Yes, please."

"What happened this time?" Jesenia asked as she headed for the coffeemaker.

Ángel told her about the sniper and the photograph, then about his confrontation with Charles. Hearing himself describe their argument had him cringing all over again. God, he'd told Charles he loved him and admitted to betraying and manipulating him in practically the same breath.

"And now what?" Ángel said after he'd taken a few deep gulps of coffee. It wasn't bad, though the bar for motel-room coffee was pretty low to begin with. "I don't know if I can ever look Charles in the face again. And no matter what I do—if I stay, if I go—people could get hurt. How am I supposed to live with that? Whatever decision I make, I'll always be second-guessing it."

"Nothing that's happening is your fault," said Jesenia, who had come to sit with him at the table. "Charles knew it was dangerous to get involved with you again, and he chose to anyway. That's on him."

"No, that's . . ." Ángel put down his mug and cradled his head in his hands. He'd been out on the road under the sun for too long; he was exhausted and dehydrated, his body heavy. "That's not fair. Were we supposed to let the stalker intimidate us? Let him dictate how we lived our lives?"

"You didn't have to provoke him," Jesenia said.

Ángel frowned. "Provoke . . ." He grunted as his elbow slipped out from under him, and he caught himself just before his forehead hit the table. Though he tried to push himself up again, his muscles were too watery, and his balance was all off, his vision swimming with sudden disorientation. "Jesenia, something's wrong, I feel sick—"

"I know, *cariño, lo siento.*" Jesenia stroked a hand through his hair, her fingers lingering on the nape of Ángel's neck. "It's just the sedatives taking effect."

CHAPTER SEVENTEEN

By the time anyone realized Ángel had left the building, it was too late to bring him back. Charles called him several times, as did Ed and Eva, but all their calls went unanswered.

Charles worked through the day on autopilot, his thoughts a scattered mess. He didn't even know what he'd say if Ángel *did* answer the phone. All Charles knew was that he couldn't let Ángel put himself in danger by taking off on his own.

Midafternoon, Charles called Ángel once more. The phone rang a few times before going to voice mail, as had all his previous calls, and Charles hung up without leaving a message. As he set the phone on his desk, however, he received a text from Ángel.

Stop calling me. I'm not coming back.

Charles scowled at his phone. What could he do to stop Ángel, really? Chase him down and drag him back by his hair? Ángel was a grown-ass man, and if he'd rather run away from Charles than face him again the way he had in Tucson—

Except Ángel *hadn't* run away in Tucson, as Charles had always assumed. His departure had been planned and deliberate.

Charles sat back in his chair, dazed, as he considered the possibility that Ángel had planned *this* as well. Had he revealed what he'd done in Tucson in an attempt to make Charles so angry that he wouldn't try to stop him from leaving? How the hell was Charles supposed to know which of Ángel's actions were honest and which were manipulation?

Groaning, he rubbed his aching temples and forced his attention back to his paperwork.

He stayed late, wanting to avoid his curious coworkers and their inevitable barrage of questions. As afternoon faded into evening,

Charles and Jade were the last ones left at their cluster. The rest of the office had emptied out except for a few agents here and there.

After he'd shut down his computer and sorted out his desk, Charles couldn't resist calling Ángel one more time. This time, the call went directly to voice mail without ringing, which meant Ángel had either declined the call right away or turned his phone off altogether.

Charles hesitated, then said, "Hey, Jade."

"Yeah?" she said, looking up in surprise. His entire team had been tiptoeing around him all day, even Eva, and Charles couldn't blame them.

"Can you track Ángel's phone for me and tell me where he is now?" Charles asked.

"I was tracking him earlier for Ed," said Jade. "He was just roaming around San Diego; he wasn't making any moves to leave the city."

"Just one more time. Please."

"What are you gonna do with this information, anyway?" Jade said while her fingers tapped across her keyboard. "You've still got a crazy person out there gunning for you, and you're not supposed to leave the office without an agency escort."

"It's just for my peace of mind," Charles said.

"Huh," Jade said, her forehead wrinkling. "There's no signal. Ángel must have taken the battery out of his phone."

His suspicions confirmed, Charles said, "Where was he last?"

"Um . . . the last time I pinged him, he was at a Super 8 in Hillcrest."

"That's Jesenia's motel," Charles said, relieved. At least Ángel wasn't alone. "I'll call her instead. Can you give me the number to the motel?"

"You don't have her cell?"

"Ángel left it on my refrigerator at home, but I can't go back there."

Jade read the number off to him, then said, "I only met Ángel a week ago, and even I know he's going to hate you doing this."

"Then he should have answered his own phone like a goddamn adult," said Charles.

"Super 8, this is Ben speaking," said a cheerful voice that picked up after a couple of rings. "How may I help you?"

"Could you connect me to Jesenia Santos's room, please?" Charles ignored Jade, who was shaking her head at him across their desks.

"One moment, please." Over the soft clacking of keys in the background, Ben said, "I'm sorry, sir, Ms. Santos already checked out."

"What?" Charles said, bolting upright. "When?"

"About half an hour ago."

"All right. Thanks." Charles ended the call and lowered his phone, looking up at Jade in bewilderment. "Jesenia checked out."

"And?" Heaving an exasperated sigh, Jade said, "Come on, Charles, you know what's going on here. Jesenia offered to let Ángel use her family's cabin. Obviously he took her up on that, and they already left."

"Sure," Charles said. "Or the stalker followed Ángel to Jesenia's motel and now they're both in danger."

Jade bit her lower lip. "Shit," she said after a long pause.

"Can you get—"

She slid a piece of paper across their desks. "I hunted down her cell number while you were on the phone."

"You're amazing," said Charles.

Jesenia's phone went straight to voice mail, just like Ángel's. Charles hung up and shook his head.

"Nothing," he said.

"Okay, that's not good," Jade said. "I can understand Ángel turning his phone off, but there's no reason for Jesenia to turn hers off too."

Charles stood up, grabbing his jacket. "I'm going down there. No way could the stalker have taken out two trained agents without leaving some kind of sign."

"You can't go alone, Charles, you're not— Charles, *wait*!"

He was already gone, eschewing the elevator for the stairwell. Ed hadn't issued him a new vehicle after the first agency car was destroyed that morning, and Charles couldn't sign one out without alerting the agency to what he was doing, which would cause a lengthy delay he couldn't afford. Instead, Charles called a cab as he dashed down the four flights of stairs.

Traffic slowed him down even more, and it was over twenty minutes before the cab finally pulled into the Super 8 parking lot.

"Can you stick around for a bit?" Charles asked as he handed the cabbie a few bills. "I may need to leave in a hurry."

"Sure, but I'll have to keep the meter running."

"That's fine. Thanks." Charles got out of the cab and headed for the office, scanning the parking lot as he went. He didn't see anything out of the ordinary, though he did note a couple of security cameras that could come in handy.

The motel was a plain two-story concrete block shaped in an L, and the small lobby, while utilitarian, was clean and well organized. Charles smiled as he approached the young man at the front desk.

"Hi," he said. "You wouldn't happen to be Ben, would you?"

"Yes, sir," said Ben, straightening up. "Can I help you?"

"My name is Charles Hunter. I called earlier looking for Jesenia Santos." Charles dug his badge out of his jacket pocket, banking on the hope that Ben was the type to cooperate with friendly law enforcement without demanding a warrant. "I'm actually with the ATF—is there any way I could get a look at the room she was staying in?"

Ben's eyes went wide. "Is something wrong?"

"I hope not, but I do have some concerns that Ms. Santos might be in danger."

That was enough to get Ben moving. He coded a key card and got someone to cover the desk, then led Charles outside and to the first-floor room at the farthest corner of the motel. One quick swipe, and Charles stepped inside, flipping the lights on.

Nothing seemed out of place at first glance, though the bed was still unmade, the covers rumpled. "Housekeeping hasn't been in yet?" Charles asked.

"No, not yet—Ms. Santos left way after even our late checkout time. She had to pay a fee, actually."

Charles walked slowly around the room, hunting for any small detail that might tell him what had happened here. "She checked out in person?"

Still hovering by the doorway, Ben said, "Yes, sir."

"Did she seem nervous at all? Frightened?" The stalker had forced Paul Warner to make those phone calls to Buzz; if he'd taken Ángel hostage, he could have forced Jesenia to check out without making a fuss.

"I don't know," Ben said. "I didn't check her out myself, but I think someone would have said something if she'd been acting weird.

I do know that she didn't complain about the late fee, though, which is pretty unusual."

Charles checked the bathroom, where a couple of damp towels hung on the rack, and returned to the bedroom. Everything looked normal. There was no blood, nothing damaged or broken, no personal effects left behind. "How full is the motel?" he asked.

"We're at about eighty-five percent capacity."

"And nobody saw or heard anything suspicious around this room? Loud noises, shouting?"

Ben shook his head.

Charles frowned, making one more slow, frustrated turn in the middle of the room. Even if the stalker had caught Jesenia and Ángel by surprise, how could he possibly have incapacitated them both without any noise or mess? For that matter, why have Jesenia check out of the room at all—why not leave her behind, or simply kill her?

Loath though he was to admit it, Charles was coming around to Jade's conclusion. Ángel must have asked Jesenia to take him to her family's cabin.

As he followed Ben back out to the parking lot, Charles said, "Could I see the footage from those security cameras?"

"Sure," Ben said, "but I don't know how helpful it'll be. They're not working."

"What do you mean?" Charles said, his skin prickling.

"They went on the fritz a few hours ago. Just static."

Charles raised his eyebrows. "And they haven't been fixed?"

"We're waiting for a technician to come out." Ben glanced around the lot like his boss was lurking behind one of the parked cars, then lowered his voice. "Between you and me, the cameras are just there to lower our insurance premiums. Management doesn't care about them."

Ángel's and Jesenia's phones both turned off *and* the security cameras out of commission? This couldn't be a coincidence. Charles swung firmly back into the *something's wrong* camp—he just wasn't sure what it was.

"Thanks for your help," he said, shaking Ben's hand. "I'm going to look around a bit more, if that's all right."

"Of course, sir. Let me know if there's anything else I can do." Ben headed back to the office, bubbling over with poorly concealed excitement, no doubt looking forward to sharing this story with his coworkers.

Charles stood on the sidewalk for a moment, staring thoughtfully at the motel-room door. Then he turned around and swept his eyes over the parking lot. He knew in his gut that something had gone wrong here—too many things didn't add up. Without hard evidence, though, he was dead in the water. Nobody at the ATF was going to be swayed by his hunches alone.

He didn't know what kind of car Jesenia had rented, so he wouldn't be able to ascertain if it was still here. But there had to be *something*, some trail left behind. Blood spatter, broken glass—he'd even take tire treads at this point.

As Charles walked along the sidewalk in front of the motel, inspecting the ground and the passing rooms, he called Jade on her cell.

"Do you realize what kind of position you put me in?" Jade said when she answered, not bothering with a greeting. "I had to tell Ed and Eva where you went! The only reason they haven't come after you is because they don't want to panic the civilians."

"I'll be fine," Charles said absently.

"A sniper shot at you in your own apartment complex this morning."

"I don't think he's interested in me anymore," said Charles. "Look, Jade, something's not right here, but I won't be able to convince anyone to mount a search for Ángel unless I can prove he didn't leave this motel willingly. I need to get in touch with Jesenia's family—her parents, or whoever is her next of kin. Even if they don't have another way of contacting her, at least I can speak to whoever owns the cabin in Canada and find out if Ángel and Jesenia are really headed out that way."

Jade groaned long and loud, then said, "All right, I'll get the info and text it to you. But after that, you'd better get your fine ass back to the office, Charles."

"I promise," he said. "Thank you."

While Charles waited for Jade's text, he stood at the corner of the building and called the local police precinct, double-checking for any reports of disturbances in or around the motel. Ben was right—the area had been calm all day. He hung up with a creeping sense of foreboding.

A text popped up on his screen with the name and phone number of Jesenia's mother, and Charles made a note to buy Jade something outrageously expensive when this was all over. Stepping off the sidewalk, he rounded the side of the motel as he listened to the phone ring.

"Hello?" said a pleasant woman's voice with a light Mexican accent.

"Hello, may I speak with Ramona Santos, please?"

"This is she."

"Hi, Mrs. Santos, my name is Charles Hunter." Charles walked along the back of the motel—there was more parking out here, plus a few dumpsters up against the wall. "I'm a friend of Jesenia's out in San Diego."

"Is everything all right?" Mrs. Santos said with a note of anxiety.

"Everything's fine. I'm just having some trouble getting in touch with her—I think she may have forgotten to charge her phone."

The sun was setting, bathing the lot in a rich orange glow, and the exterior lamps had switched on as well, adding their hazy yellow light. As Charles passed one of the dumpsters, a bright metallic glint caught his attention. He frowned and backed up a few steps. The flash of light had come from the space between the dumpster and the wall, mostly blocked by a mass of boxes. Why stack boxes beside a dumpster instead of throwing them inside?

"Anyway, Jesenia mentioned she was thinking about visiting a family cabin in Canada," Charles said, heading over. "I was wondering if she might have already left."

"Canada?" said Mrs. Santos. "Are you sure? I don't think anyone in our family has ever even *been* to Canada. We definitely don't own any property there."

"Really?" Charles said. "Maybe I misheard—"

He pushed aside the top box and sucked in a breath as he revealed the gleaming chrome and bright-red paint of Ángel's motorcycle.

Heart pounding in his throat, Charles hurriedly shoved and kicked the rest of the boxes out of the way, then stared at the gap behind the dumpster. This was Ángel's bike, no question. Ángel loved this fucking thing—if he was going to take off of his own volition, he wouldn't leave it behind, and he certainly wouldn't stash it behind a dumpster to hide it.

Unaware of Charles's distraction, Mrs. Santos was still chatting away on the other end of the line. "—and she's just been having the time of her life out there this past week," she said, finishing a sentence Charles hadn't heard the beginning of.

Charles's attention snapped back to the phone. "I'm sorry, did you say the past *week*?" Jesenia had flown into San Diego the day before yesterday.

"Yes, of course. She's been out there visiting her boyfriend—you must know him—"

Suddenly short of breath, Charles staggered away from the motorcycle. Jesenia had been trying to convince Ángel to leave San Diego from day one. She'd had a front-row seat to Ángel's experiences in the cartel and his relationship with Raúl Esparza; she'd known Paul Warner's identity and would have been able to lure him into a trap. She had the skills and training to track a target, break into motel rooms, infiltrate a hospital, wield a sniper rifle, fuck up security cameras. Her straight, narrow body could easily be interpreted as male in the right clothing.

She would have been able to abduct Ángel from this motel without causing a disturbance, because Ángel trusted her.

Charles turned and ran, ending his call to Mrs. Santos and hitting the speed dial for Eva as he raced toward the front parking lot.

"Do you have any idea how much trouble you're in—" Eva started.

"It's Jesenia," Charles said, throwing himself into the back of the waiting cab. "Jesenia is the stalker."

Ángel's struggle toward consciousness was like clawing his way out of quicksand. He woke long before he could move or open his eyes, his body a heavy, useless weight. All he was aware of was a quiet murmur of staticky voices and a sense of gentle movement.

Eventually, Ángel pried his eyes open, blinking groggily at his surroundings. There was a marked delay between his sensory input and his brain's reactions, the connection between the two sluggish. He'd felt this same way when he woke up after his appendectomy in college.

He was in a car; he could tell that much. The sky was darkening outside, and the headlights of the oncoming cars blurred together in a nightmarish haze as they rushed past. Ángel groaned, rolling his head away from the window and toward the driver's seat, noting the active police scanner mounted on the dashboard.

Jesenia was driving. Ángel wet his cracked lips and said, "What . . ." That was all he could get out, though, his tongue too thick for his mouth.

She glanced sideways, giving him a sympathetic smile. "I'm so sorry, you're going to feel like shit for a while. I had to keep you sedated for longer than I would have wanted while I got some things straightened out."

"You . . ." He shook his head, confused. Why were they in a car? Where were they going? The last thing he remembered . . . he'd been upset, he'd gone to Jesenia's motel, he'd felt sick after he drank that cup of coffee . . .

He looked down at his body, which was draped with a fluffy blanket that covered him from shoulders to feet. The thick material was stifling in the warm car, and he tried to push it off, only to be stymied when he found he couldn't separate his hands. Whining low in his throat, he squirmed in his seat, wriggling around until the blanket fell into his lap.

His wrists were bound with zip ties. He stared at them stupidly for a moment, then tested his legs. His ankles were tied together as well.

"Oh God," Ángel said as his drugged brain finally caught up. "Oh my God."

"Stay calm," said Jesenia.

"It was you," he mumbled, his speech still slurred. "It's been you the whole time?"

"Just let me explain—"

Ángel doubled over, his head spinning and his body wracked with nausea. He couldn't think, he couldn't— *How could this be happening?*

He tugged on the zip ties binding his wrists. When he found not a single inch of give, he was swept with an abrupt, overpowering surge of fury. He thrashed, yanking on the bonds, slamming his feet against the footboard over and over.

"Let me go," he spat, working himself into a frenzy. "Let me go, let me go, *let me go*—"

"Calm down, Ángel," Jesenia said sharply. Keeping one hand on the wheel, she withdrew a loaded syringe from her jacket pocket. "I don't want to drug you again, but I will if I have to."

He slumped in his seat, his chest heaving, and eyed the syringe with trepidation. The truth was, his fit had used up every bit of energy he had; he felt even worse now than he had before.

"*Why?*" he said, his voice choked with despair.

"It wasn't supposed to go this far." Jesenia put the syringe back in her pocket, though her posture remained wary, prepared for any sudden movement on Ángel's part. "I thought taking out Esparza would be enough."

Ángel's mouth fell open. "*You* killed Raúl? You were the sniper?"

Jesenia gave him a pleading look. "I had to save you, Ángel. Things kept getting worse for you there, and you *refused to leave*." She took a deep breath and returned her attention to the road. "I knew it would be a few days before you could be extracted, so I took care of some of the other men who had abused you, too—Roberto, Javier, Enrique . . . I put them down like the dogs they were so they could never hurt anyone again."

"Jesus," Ángel whispered.

"I should have been the one you turned to after you got out," Jesenia said, her hands tightening on the steering wheel. "With Paul missing, I was your only real friend left. I couldn't have known that *he* would be on the extraction team."

She was talking about Charles. A spike of terror left Ángel breathless—it had been hours since Jesenia knocked him out, hours in which she could have done anything, including removing Charles from the picture permanently.

No. Jesenia wouldn't have risked it. If her primary objective had been to abduct Ángel quietly, she wouldn't have endangered that by murdering a federal agent while she had Ángel unconscious in her motel room.

"Is that why you killed Paul?" Ángel asked. A blank, dead weight settled in his stomach. "You *tortured* him, Jesenia, tortured and murdered him and left his children without a father. Did you do that just so I wouldn't have anyone to depend on but you?"

"No, of course not," said Jesenia. "He deserved to die that way—he was the worst of all of them. Paul knew what was happening to you in that place, but he never pulled you out. He just let you keep going back, let them hurt you. He sacrificed you for the mission."

"I chose to make those sacrifices myself." Ángel inched sideways, shifting as far away from Jesenia as his weak muscles and bound limbs allowed. A splitting headache throbbed behind his eyes.

"I know that. And Paul had a responsibility to stop you. You said it yourself earlier, Ángel—you make bad decisions."

Jesenia reached over and readjusted his blanket, tugging it back up over Ángel's wrists. He flinched when her hand brushed his arm, but she didn't comment on this reaction.

"It's not your fault," she said. "Your parents hurt you when you were younger, so you think that's normal. You think you deserve to be abused, and you let men take advantage of you."

"That is *not* true," Ángel said, dumbfounded. Though he knew it was pointless to reason with her—obsession knew no rationality, no logic—he couldn't help defending himself against the way she'd twisted his past and his personality to suit her own ends.

Jesenia ignored his protests, her eyes bright as she spun out the narrative she'd created. "You just need somebody to take care of you, somebody to make sure you make the right choices. I won't let anyone hurt you again, Ángel, I swear."

His breathing came fast and shallow, his fear increasing with every passing moment. "You're hurting me now," he said, striving to remain calm.

Glancing at his lap, Jesenia said, "Are the zip ties too—"

"That's not what I mean!" Ángel glared at her, but even his rage wasn't enough to stop the shaking that had set in. "You've been torturing me, Jesenia. Do you not understand that? You've kept me in a constant state of terror for over a week. You murdered someone I cared about and tried to kill another, and you made me feel responsible for it!"

"I wouldn't have had to do most of those things if you'd just *left*," Jesenia snapped. "For fuck's sake, who sticks around in a strange city when they know they're being stalked? Just the possibility that Esparza was alive should have sent you running for the hills."

"I never believed that," said Ángel.

"I know," she said, frustrated. "And after all the trouble I went to—using his passport, recruiting that actor to send Ian after you, getting those false papers made." She shook her head. "I tried to be gentle at first; I tried to scare you just a little, just enough to make you accept my help. Then I could have taken you quietly, and all this would have been avoided. But you dug your heels in and I had to apply more and more pressure."

"You are fucking insane," Ángel said, more an expression of utter astonishment than an accusation.

"It was because of *him*. Charles." She said his name like it was something ugly and poisonous. "He messed with your head and strung you along and disappointed you again and again in Tucson, but you were still willing to risk your life to stay with him. That's exactly your problem."

Unable to bear looking at her a moment longer, Ángel turned his face aside, gazing through the window instead. He rested his forehead against the cool glass and forced himself to get a grip.

As horrifying as this situation was, he was certain he wasn't in immediate life-threatening danger. Jesenia had expressed a desire to protect him, and while her obsession would escalate over time—likely to the point of lethality—that could take months or even years. That might change in an instant, though, if she perceived his rejection to be absolute. Cooperating with her for now, at least nominally, could buy him some time until his body and mind recovered from the lingering sedation.

"So what now?" he asked. "Are you taking me to Canada?"

Even as he said it, he realized that couldn't be the case. Jesenia wouldn't have told him there was a cabin in Canada if she'd really been planning to take him there after she abducted him. Besides, it would be too difficult for her to get him across the border.

"There's nothing in Canada," Jesenia said, validating his thought process. "I have a nice private place set aside for us in Wyoming. You'll be safe there, and once you understand that this is for your own good, you'll be happy there too."

Ángel swallowed the bile that crept up the back of his throat. He kept his voice steady as he said, "You know that I—that I can't return your feelings, right? You're a woman, I can't . . ."

He trailed off then—because while he'd never contemplated the possibility of being raped by a woman, it occurred to him now that it *was* possible, and his brain was providing him with several creative scenarios.

"Sex doesn't define a loving relationship," Jesenia said, in a light scolding tone that was beyond bizarre, given the circumstances. "I just want to protect you, make sure you're taken care of. There's no other way for me to keep you safe, Ángel. You're too self-destructive."

Ángel watched the passing scenery, seeking any indication of how far they'd come or which route they were taking. There were no signs, though, no mile markers—they were on a two-lane road winding through a rural area, not a major highway. Jesenia would want to avoid law enforcement, cameras, and tolls as much as possible.

While the disadvantages to Ángel were obvious, there was also an upside—the more circuitous their route, the slower their progress, giving more time for the others in San Diego to figure out what had happened and track them down. Ángel had to believe that Charles wouldn't be content to let him just disappear without a word this time.

Jesenia drove exactly the speed limit, taking them deeper into the California hinterlands, the police scanner crackling softly in the background. Ángel kept himself turned toward the window, refusing to interact, but eventually, a need arose that he could no longer deny.

"Jesenia," he said reluctantly, "I have to go to the bathroom."

Without taking her eyes off the road, Jesenia reached into a bag in the backseat, withdrew an empty water bottle, and dropped it into Ángel's lap.

Ángel stared at the bottle in horror. "You're not serious," he said after a moment.

"I can pull over to the side of the road to help you, but I'm not stopping anywhere," said Jesenia.

After everything that had happened—everything Jesenia had done to him, every dark secret she'd revealed—it was this humiliation that came closest to breaking him. "Please," he said, tears stinging his eyes. "Please don't do this to me."

Her resolve clearly wavered, and it struck Ángel that she *liked* him needy, enjoyed him pathetic and helpless. It fed into her self-image as his caretaker.

He had no qualms about taking advantage of that. "I'll be good," he said. He curled himself into a smaller ball in his seat. "I promise. Please."

Jesenia sighed and then nodded. "All right. I guess it wouldn't hurt to top off the gas tank, anyway."

A few miles down the road, she pulled into a small gas station with only four pumps out front. She parked by the building, unbuckled her seat belt, and turned to face him.

"I want to make some things very clear," she said. From her other pocket, the one not storing the syringe, she pulled a stun gun. Ángel recoiled instinctively, but she made no further threatening movements. "First, I won't hesitate to use this on you if it looks like you're about to do something stupid."

"I won't," he said. He'd only get one real chance to escape; if he failed, she would either kill him or become so restrictive that he'd never have another opportunity. He wouldn't waste an escape attempt while he was still lethargic and fuzzy-headed from the drugs.

Jesenia tucked the stun gun away and lifted one side of her jacket, showing him the pistol in her shoulder holster. "If you try to communicate with anyone, or signal for help, I'll only hurt you a little—but I'll kill whoever you came in contact with. *¿Me explico?*"

"*Claro.*" He had not an ounce of doubt that she was serious. She knew him well; he'd never endanger innocent civilians to try to save himself.

She withdrew a pocketknife from her jeans, bringing her personal weapon count up to four. After cutting him free from his zip ties, she instructed him to stay still while she came around to the passenger-side door. He assumed it was another way for her to assert control—until he tried to stand up, and his knees gave right out from under him. She caught him around the waist and helped him away from the car before slamming the door shut.

As much as he hated to touch her, Ángel had no choice but to sling an arm around her shoulders and lean on her for support. Jesenia pulled up the hood of her jacket and then kept her free hand in the pocket with the stun gun as they shuffled along toward the restroom.

A man emerging from the shop crossed their path and stopped, looking Ángel over with concern. "Hey, man, you okay?"

"He had a little too much to drink," Jesenia said.

If Ángel had truly intended to reassure the man, he would have met his eyes, smiled, offered a friendly and self-deprecating comment. Instead, Ángel ducked his head and deliberately avoided eye contact—obeying Jesenia's order to not communicate while ensuring that the man would leave their encounter feeling uneasy. That internal sense of *not right* would stick with him, nagging at him; he would remember this, even if he didn't do anything about it.

The man continued on his way, and so did they. Jesenia propped Ángel up against the wall of the building while she quickly checked inside the single restroom.

"Don't lock the door," she said, gesturing for him to proceed. "You have three minutes, and then I'm coming in after you."

He staggered into the bathroom, gripping the walls and then the sink to balance himself on his shaky legs. Behind him, Jesenia rattled the doorknob to be sure he hadn't locked it, but she didn't open the door.

After Ángel relieved himself, he stood at the sink to wash his hands, studying his reflection in the mirror. No wonder the man had asked after him—he looked like hell, his eyes sunken and hollowed out, his skin drawn tight over his face, his dry lips visibly cracked. In case the man did mention what he'd seen to someone, Ángel had to leave some kind of sign behind. But what?

His eyes caught and lingered on the cracked, jagged edge of the mirror. Impulsively taking a page from Jesenia's playbook, he slashed his fingertip against the glass, then squeezed until several drops of bright red blood welled to the surface.

Jesenia wasn't the only person who could paint with blood.

Though he couldn't discount the possibility that she'd check the restroom for messages, people tended to have one significant blind spot while searching their environment—they rarely looked up. He was taller than Jesenia, and if he stretched his arm to its limit, he'd be able to reach the very top corner of the mirror.

He did exactly that, smearing his blood on the glass to form a discreet WY. Then he washed his hands again, scrubbing the cut with soap and putting pressure on it to stop the bleeding.

Jesenia opened the door just as Ángel grasped the doorknob. "Sorry," he said, leaning against the threshold and breathing heavily. "I feel a little dizzy . . ."

He stumbled and pitched forward, obliging her to grab for him. As he'd hoped, his distress proved an excellent diversion.

"*Ay, pobrecito*," Jesenia said, smoothing his hair. "Come on, let's get you back in the car."

They walked away, leaving Ángel's message undisturbed. It was the smallest of breadcrumbs, barely worth pinning his hopes on, but it was better than nothing.

He had to believe that someone was searching for him, or he might as well give up now.

CHAPTER EIGHTEEN

"I've got all of Jesenia's financials," said Jade. Her long brown hair was pulled up in a messy bun, and she still wore the sweatpants and tank top she'd been in when she rushed back to the office. "I'll put out an APB on her rental car—"

"She wouldn't have taken that car." Charles paced the length of the conference room as he spoke. At Eva's emergency summons, the entire team as well as Ed had returned to work, but he couldn't relax enough to join them at the table. "Jesenia's too smart. She would have had an alternate vehicle ready, and she would have dumped her legitimate car somewhere to distract us, the same way she did with Agent Warner's car at the El Paso airport."

"If Jesenia's so smart, why didn't she dump Ángel's bike far from her motel too?" Shane asked.

"She probably couldn't drive it," Sakura said. "You can't just hop on a motorcycle and take off if you've never driven one before. It takes time to learn how to balance and steer them."

"Charles," Eva said, watching him from her seat at the head of the table. Unlike Jade, Sakura, and Shane, who were all casually dressed and looked a little rough around the edges after a long day, she was still as crisp and fresh as she'd been that morning. "We've got Jesenia's and Ángel's faces splashed across every news outlet statewide, and Ed is on the phone right now liaising with the FBI to take this national. We'll find them."

Charles opened his mouth to respond, but was distracted by a soft chime from his computer. He practically leaped across the room and clicked on the new email in his inbox.

"Ben from the Super 8 sent me their parking lot security footage from the past couple of days," Charles said as he started downloading the compressed files. "At some point, Jesenia brought another car to that motel, and we need to find it. We have to review the—"

He stumbled to a halt, abruptly aware that Eva was regarding him with one arched eyebrow.

"Sorry," Charles said, rolling his tense shoulders. "Fuck, sorry, I just . . ."

"What were you planning?" Eva asked.

"We need to review the security footage going backward from the time when the cameras went out today. And we also have to break down every alias Jesenia Santos has ever used and find something to help us figure out where she would take Ángel—safe houses, contacts, financial assets, anything."

"Agreed," said Eva. "It's probably best if Jade and I take the research angle. You three split up the video files and see if you come up with anything."

With a grateful nod, Charles sank into his seat.

Sakura knocked back the rest of her energy drink and crumpled the empty can. "All right, let's do this."

The Super 8 cameras had cut to static less than thirty minutes after Ángel arrived. Charles watched from his bird's-eye view as Ángel hopped off his motorcycle and approached Jesenia's door, completely unaware that the friend he trusted had been the one tormenting him. This grainy image could be the last anyone ever saw Ángel—

Charles exhaled one hard breath and shook out his hands. Ángel didn't need Charles to wallow around in fear and regret right now; he needed Charles to fucking *focus*.

He, Shane, and Sakura chose different time stamps in the footage and worked their way backward, keeping an eye on Jesenia's corner room. It was tedious work, but it required close concentration, which helped keep Charles's panic at bay. He had little mental energy to spare for obsessing over what Jesenia might be doing to Ángel at this very moment.

"This is weird," Shane said after about half an hour of tense silence.

"What?" Charles jumped up and circled the table to lean over Shane's shoulder.

"Jesenia's entering her motel room here . . ." Shane tapped the figure on the screen, then pointed to the lot. "But her rental car is all the way over here. I went back and found the point where she left the room, a couple hours earlier, and she never gets into or out of that car—but she never gets in or out of any *other* car either."

Charles narrowed his eyes, watching Jesenia saunter out of her motel room on Monday morning. The angles of the security cameras were terrible, especially since Jesenia had that far-corner room, but he could see enough to figure out she was heading for the main road. "Okay, looks like she's planning to take a cab, maybe catch a bus. Show me when she comes back again?"

Shane clicked forward to the appropriate time stamp. Again, the poor sight lines of the cameras made it difficult to tell why Jesenia would approach her room from this direction—at least, for someone who'd never been to that motel before.

"She's coming from behind the building," Charles said, cursing his own idiocy. "There's more parking out there, but no cameras. She went out and got herself a new car somehow and then parked it in the back lot."

"Craigslist," said Sakura.

"What?"

Sakura spread her hands wide. "If I needed a vehicle to use in an abduction, that's how I'd do it. I'd pay cash for a used car off Craigslist, not change the registration, and slap on some plates from another car I knew wouldn't be used for a while."

That was exactly what Charles would do too. "*Fuck*," he said with feeling, and then turned back to Shane's computer. "We may not have cameras from behind the motel, but we do have a camera at the entrance. Let's see if we get lucky."

They did. In the five minutes preceding Jesenia's return to the motel, only one car had entered the lot, a silver Toyota Prius. Unfortunately, their luck ran out when it came to the license plate—the first three characters were all that were visible, the rest indecipherable thanks to a combination of low-quality equipment and bad angles.

Jade's quick search revealed that no silver Priuses registered in California had license plates beginning with 5GE. Sakura was right;

Jesenia had swapped the plates with some unknown car, making it impossible for them to fill in the blanks.

"And there's nothing you can do to enhance the image?" Charles asked Jade.

"I'm sorry," she said, shaking her head. "These are cheap motel parking lot cameras. I'm good, but I'm not a magician."

"A make and model with a partial plate is still good progress, man," Shane said. "We'll add it to the APB—"

The panic Charles had been ruthlessly tamping down welled up with a vengeance, threatening to burst free. He spun on his heel and strode out of the room, ignoring Eva calling his name.

Charles hurried down the hallway and into the empty break room. Swinging the door halfway shut behind himself, he collapsed into a hard plastic chair and gripped the edge of the table with shaking hands, closing his eyes. He didn't bother opening them when someone else entered the room; he knew it was Eva from the clicking of her high heels.

"Charles," she said, her voice soft. Another chair creaked as she joined him at the table. "We're gonna find him."

Opening his eyes, Charles said, "What if Jesenia kills him?"

"She won't do that. Look at everything she's done—she's obsessed with Ángel. She must love him in some warped way. Ángel will know how to handle her."

Eva always spoke with utter self-assurance, as if she knew that everything she said was the absolute truth. Her cool, unflappable confidence was what had drawn Charles to her the moment they'd met, and after a few short months, she'd earned his trust enough for him to confide things in her that he'd never told anyone else. But there were things he'd never shared even with Eva.

"We fought," Charles said. "The last time we saw each other, we fought. And now he's alone and afraid and maybe hurting, and he's going through all that . . ." Charles swallowed harshly. "He's going through that thinking I don't love him."

"Oh, Charles," said Eva. She covered his hand with her own.

Charles had never said that aloud before, not ever, not even to himself, but Eva didn't seem fazed in the least. "You're not surprised," he said.

"When you first came to San Diego, you'd been gutshot," Eva said. "You were bleeding out all over the place and insisting it was just a flesh wound. I've never seen a human being more determined to deny they'd just had their heart broken. So, no, I'm not surprised you love Ángel. If anything, I'm surprised you're willing to admit it."

"I didn't want to love him." Charles turned his hand palm-up beneath Eva's. "Love by itself isn't enough to sustain a relationship over the long term. You have to share goals, values, and I knew— I *thought* that the things Ángel and I wanted out of life were too different. I knew it couldn't last; I knew he'd get bored of me sooner or later. I didn't want to get too invested in him, build my life around him, and then have it all fall apart because we were walking down two different roads."

Eva tilted her head. "I'd be more inclined to approve of that decision if I weren't sure you made it unilaterally, without ever actually talking to Ángel about any of this."

Charles groaned and slumped back in his chair. Eva squeezed his hand, then released him.

"I promised him that if he stayed here, I wouldn't let anything happen to him," Charles said quietly.

Before Eva could respond, her cell phone chirped with an incoming text message. She fished it out of her jacket pocket and raised her eyebrows. "Jade says we've got a break."

They returned to the conference room, where it was all Charles could do not to grab Jade and shake the news right out of her. "What happened?" he asked.

"We just got a call from the Riverside County Sheriff's Department," Jade said, pretty much vibrating in her seat. "Some guy out in the desert around Palm Springs saw Jesenia's and Ángel's pictures on the news and reported that he saw them at a gas station near I-10 around eight thirty. He actually stopped to talk to them because Ángel looked sick, but Ángel wouldn't even look at him."

Charles's stomach leaped and did several nauseating somersaults; he breathed deeply and rolled his shoulders to release their sudden tension. "Did he see where they went?"

"No, he was leaving as they were coming in. He saw Jesenia help Ángel into the bathroom, and then he left. He didn't think about it again until he saw the news report."

"Jesenia let Ángel go into the bathroom by himself?" Charles said, his pulse pounding.

Jade shrugged. "Yeah, I guess."

"I need to use your car," he said to Eva.

"Why?" she asked, even as she tossed him her keys. "You're not seriously thinking of—"

"Tell the sheriff's department to go out to that gas station and tear the bathroom apart piece by piece," Charles said as he started for the door. "They need to look in the trash can, inside the toilet tank, even on the ceiling if they have to. If Jesenia left Ángel by himself for even a second, I guarantee you he left behind some kind of sign to help us. He wouldn't have wasted an opportunity like that."

"Are you going after them?" Sakura said, astonished. "We have no idea where they went from the gas station, and besides, they left the motel at least an hour before you even figured out what was happening. That gives them like a four-hour head start."

"Ángel will lead us in the right direction, and Jesenia would have had to take back roads and obey the speed limit." Charles clenched his fist around the keys, relishing the sting of the metal as it bit into his palm. "I'm not planning on doing either."

Jesenia didn't falter when the first APB came over the police scanner with their descriptions, but when it was updated an hour later with the model of their car and a partial license plate, she slammed one hand against the steering wheel, loosing an enraged shout so loud that Ángel cringed.

"Goddamn Charles," she said, in what was little more than a snarl. "I should have killed him before we left. Nobody else would have noticed you were gone for *days*."

This was the first concrete proof Ángel had that Charles was indeed still alive; he'd been too afraid to ask Jesenia directly. He turned his face aside so she wouldn't catch any indication of his relief.

"It's all right; it's fine," Jesenia said. She readjusted her grip on the steering wheel, her face smoothing into calmer lines. "We'll just have to stop earlier tonight than I'd planned, that's all. I'll ditch this car and get us a new one, and we'll head back out at rush hour tomorrow."

He said nothing. He hadn't spoken since they left the gas station, sitting silently and conserving his strength. His mind was clearing, his body recovering as the sedatives loosened their hold on him a bit, but he didn't feel normal yet, and he couldn't risk antagonizing Jesenia while he was still at such a disadvantage.

Eager to get off the road, Jesenia chose a dinky little motel in the middle of nowhere—independently owned, not a member of any national chain. Its only neighbor was a roadside diner a quarter mile south, its parking lot dotted with pickup trucks and motorcycles. Everything else was rolling desert wasteland as far as the eye could see.

She parked some distance from the front office, then turned to him and said, "Lay your seat all the way back."

"Why?" Ángel asked, immediately wary.

She hefted the stun gun in one hand. "Just do it."

Reaching the lever with his hands zip-tied in front of him was awkward, but it wasn't impossible. He lowered the seat all the way, then lay down with great reluctance, his breath quickening instinctively at exposing his belly and throat to an enemy. Jesenia used two sets of handcuffs linked together to chain his zip ties to the metal bars beneath the seat, making it impossible for him to lift his shoulders more than a few inches.

She rearranged his blanket and rummaged in the glove compartment, coming up with a roll of shiny black tape. Ángel's eyes widened as he pressed himself harder against the seat.

"Don't," he said, his intention not to antagonize her abandoned at the prospect of being gagged. "Don't you dare—"

"It's just bondage tape." Jesenia began unwinding the roll. "It won't hurt coming off, I promise."

"I don't care! Don't you fucking put that on me, you crazy bitch—*no*!"

Ángel tossed his head from side to side, evading her reaching hands. Bondage tape only stuck to itself, so she couldn't just tear off a piece and slap it over his mouth; she'd have to wind it at least once around his head. He struggled against her, caught in a frenzied panic that no rational long-term plans could subdue.

Jesenia's free hand cracked hard against his cheek. It barely stung, but Ángel was so stunned that she had *hit* him that he went still, giving her the opening she needed to wrap the roll of tape around him several times and secure it tightly over his mouth.

"Please, Ángel, I hate hurting you," she said, on the verge of tears. "Please don't make me hurt you anymore. Why don't you understand that I'm trying to help you?"

She returned the tape to the glove compartment, wiping the back of one hand over her eyes. Ángel breathed hard through his nose as he watched her; he flinched and whined low in his throat when she smoothed back his hair, bending to kiss his forehead.

"I'll just be a few minutes, *cariño*," she said. "Sit tight."

She tugged the blanket up to cover his mouth before she got out of the car. Ángel sobbed once, and only once, before reining himself in. His entire body trembled, and he had to swallow repeatedly to keep his gorge from rising. He'd choke if he threw up with his mouth taped shut.

When Jesenia returned, she kept him bound and gagged while she drove closer to the room she'd rented. After she turned off the ignition, she pulled the blanket down and said, "Do I have to knock you out and carry you inside, or are you going to behave?"

Ángel nodded, his eyes downcast.

"Same rules apply as before—anyone you try to make contact with dies. Do you understand?"

He nodded again.

Using her pocketknife, she sawed through the zip ties binding his ankles, then released the handcuffs and allowed him to bring the seat up. Instructing him to remain still, she got out and retrieved a large duffel bag from the trunk before rounding the car to the passenger side and opening the door.

Stun gun at the ready, she handed him the room's key card and said, "Hold this."

Though Ángel accepted the card, he lifted his hands to his mouth with a questioning noise, bringing her attention to the fact that his wrists were still bound and his mouth taped.

"There's nobody around, and it's ten feet to the door," said Jesenia. "I think I'll risk it."

Frustrated, he swung his legs out of the car and stood up. She pressed the stun gun to the small of his back and walked him to the motel room, where she made him unlock the door, turn on the lights, and precede her inside.

"Turn around," she said. The moment she had cut his wrists free of their zip ties, she added, "Back up to the middle of the room and take off your shoes."

Ángel did as she ordered. Now that he was unbound, Jesenia was much more guarded—watching his every movement with sharp eyes, stun gun held in anticipation of a possible attack. He wasn't stupid enough to bum-rush an opponent with four weapons when he himself was unarmed, though, so he just kicked his shoes and socks across the room when she told him to and waited for her next command. He could have removed the tape from his mouth, of course, but it seemed a pointless provocation when he had no intention of calling out for help.

Without ever taking her eyes off him, Jesenia dropped the duffel bag to the ground, unzipped it, and pulled out a few items, tossing them at his feet. "Put these on."

Ángel took one look at the stuff on the ground and glowered, shaking his head furiously.

"I know you know how to use these things, Ángel," she said. "Put them on."

Eyeing the pile with disgust, Ángel stayed right where he was.

Jesenia sighed, growing impatient. "You have two choices—you can put them on yourself, or I can stun you, sedate you, and put them on you anyway. Which is it gonna be?"

His body stiff with anger, he picked the spreader bar up first and sat on the edge of the bed to fasten the cuffs around his ankles. The bar was contracted to its shortest width, keeping his legs no more than shoulders-width apart, and the sturdy leather cuffs were lined with high-quality suede, so the physical discomfort would be minimal. The humiliation, however, grew more nauseating by the moment.

Jesenia had provided a bag of small bondage padlocks as well. Ángel snapped one around each cuff's buckle, any hope for freedom destroyed by their tiny *clicks*. She could leave him alone like this, with his hands completely free, and he still wouldn't be able to get out of the spreader bar without the key to those locks.

Naturally, she *wasn't* going to leave him like this, as there was still one item left—a bondage belt with wrist cuffs. The one very minor consolation was that generous lengths of chain attached the cuffs to the sides of the belt, rather than the back.

Ángel's cheeks burned as he buckled the thick leather belt around his waist and locked it shut. At Jesenia's direction, he locked his right wrist into its cuff as well. Only then did she relax and move forward, finishing the job by securing the remaining cuff around his left wrist. She hooked a length of chain to the D-ring on the back of the belt and fastened it to yet another cuff that she locked around the side rail of the metal bed frame closest to the bathroom, which was on the opposite side of the room from the door. The end result left him enough slack to easily reach the bathroom, but nowhere near enough to get to the door, especially with two beds in the way.

Ángel remained seated on the bed, his shoulders hunched with sick humiliation. Jesenia might believe that her obsession wasn't sexual, but her choice of restraints said a lot. He had no assurance that things wouldn't change somewhere down the line.

"Good boy," she said, patting his shoulder. "You should be able to use the bathroom like this, with a little effort, so I think you'll be okay for a few hours. I'm going to go get us a new car, and I'll be back as soon as I can."

As she walked away, Ángel made a muffled noise of outrage, jerking his head to indicate his gag.

"I'm sorry, I can't leave you here with your mouth free," Jesenia said with a genuine note of remorse. "Do you want to drink some water before I leave?"

Ángel stared at her incredulously. She was going to leave him alone in a motel room, bound and gagged, for *hours*? For fuck's sake, what if there was a fire?

Jesenia took his silence as refusal. She spent a few minutes unloading supplies from the car—several more duffel bags, cases of water, whole crates of nonperishable foods—and then unplugged the phone from the wall and took the cord with her when she left, promising again to return soon.

She'd turned off the lights, so Ángel was left sitting in darkness, gazing down at his restrained body. There was no hope of getting out of these, so he'd have to plan for the future instead. At some point, Jesenia would have to leave him unbound, even if just to shower.

As he continued coming off the sedatives, he would have size and strength to his advantage—but he and Jesenia were equally well trained, and she was much better armed. He'd have to find some kind of weapon, try to level the playing field a bit.

There was sure to be a pen in the desk that could serve as a crude shiv. He didn't much like the idea of wielding a pen against a stun gun, though, let alone an actual knife. It wouldn't do enough damage without insane accuracy on his part.

His injured finger twinged, and Ángel shook it out, contemplating the angry red line bisecting his fingertip. He'd been able to hide the small wound from Jesenia; she had no idea he'd slashed his finger open to leave a message.

He rubbed his thumb thoughtfully over the cut. Glass. He needed broken glass.

Easing himself to his feet, he very, very carefully hobbled to the bathroom, sliding his weight from one foot to the other at a measured pace. If he lost his balance like this, with his legs locked into a spreader bar and his wrists chained to his waist, he wouldn't be able to break his fall.

Inside the bathroom, Ángel nudged his shoulder against the light switch and glanced around. He couldn't break this mirror, obviously—Jesenia would notice right away. But maybe . . .

Oh, *yes*. He leaned against the vanity, twisting his body until he was able to snag the tumbler beside the sink with the tips of his fingers. He breathed a sigh of relief when he found that it was indeed glass and not plastic.

Tumbler in hand, he backed away from the sink. His main obstacle was that the chains kept him from moving his hands too far from his waist, which gave him little leverage to work with. Still, he did his best, lifting his hand to the limits of the chain and then whipping the tumbler at the ground with all his strength.

The glass cracked but didn't break. Groaning, he slowly squatted down and scooped up the tumbler, then rose to his feet and threw it again—and again, and again, until the tumbler finally shattered on his fourth attempt, sending chunks of glass skittering across the bathroom tiles.

Ángel took a moment to rest, fatigued by the demands of moving his body within such strict restraints. He scanned the floor and found a piece of glass that met his needs—a hefty shard, well-sized to hold in one hand, which narrowed to a jagged point on one end.

Pulling a hand towel off the rack, he crouched and used it to sweep up the broken glass, plucking the piece he wanted out of the mess and setting it aside. If he left even a single pebble on this floor, there was a chance Jesenia would find it and figure out what he'd done, so he was meticulous in his cleanup. Bit by bit, he gathered the glass in the towel, shaking it out over the wastebasket whenever he had a good handful.

Bound this way, it took him ten times longer to clear away the glass than it would have unrestrained. He was panting and dripping sweat by the time he'd finished, his quads aching like they'd been set on fire. He moaned as he heaved himself upright and placed his shiv next to the sink. When he made to return the towel to the rack, he realized there was no way he could manage that with his hands so close to his body.

He sidled into the narrow gap between the toilet and the vanity to grab the bar of soap in the corner, unwrapping it and tossing the paper into the wastebasket on top of the broken glass. Pressing his hip bones against the edge of the sink, he was able to lean forward far enough to snag the faucet handle and run his fingertips under the water by rotating from side to side. He dried his hands on the towel and then dropped it on the counter where he would have naturally.

A quick glance into the wastebasket proved that the glass was still visible, so Ángel grabbed a few tissues, crumpled them up, and let them fall on top. Much better.

For half a second, he considered trying to cut his way out of his restraints, but cheap broken glass would never make it through this high-quality leather. He would get a better opportunity to use the shiv; for now, he had to conceal it, and there was only one feasible hiding place.

He had to hunch his shoulders and curve his body into an exaggerated C to unbutton and unzip the fly of his jeans, but Jesenia had been sincere in her intention to allow him to use the bathroom under his own power. The problem that arose, once he had his jeans open, was that he couldn't use his left hand to hold his clothing away from his body while he snuck the shiv inside. Instead, he was forced to press the glass hard against his hip to get it under the tight waistband of his boxer briefs.

"*Nnnn,*" he grunted behind his tape gag. He huffed sharply through his nose as he worked the serrated glass into his underwear, scraping it against his skin.

Once the shiv was all the way inside, the form-fitting fabric held it right in place against the meat of his hip. He turned from side to side a few times, ensuring that the glass wouldn't shift around. He'd need to be careful with how he moved his body, but the restraints would require that anyway, so it wouldn't look unnatural.

His right palm and fingers were a little grazed from handling the glass, but that could be easily hidden. Satisfied that he'd finally taken a productive step toward escaping, he refastened his jeans and returned to the bed to wait for Jesenia.

"You should have taken your earpiece with you," Jade said when she called Charles in Eva's car around eleven o'clock.

"I know, I wasn't thinking," said Charles. He'd paired his cell phone to the car's Bluetooth so he could talk hands-free, but it wasn't the same. "What's up?"

"You were right—the sheriff's department found blood on the mirror in the gas station bathroom. It spelled out the letters WY."

Charles frowned. "WY? The state code for Wyoming?"

"That's the only explanation that makes sense to us," Eva chimed in, indicating that Charles was on speakerphone back in the office. "We're tearing through all of Jesenia's aliases, looking for any connections to property or contacts out there."

"Yeah, but this shit is a maze," said Sakura. "Jesenia's been in and out of undercover her entire career. She's got aliases she used working for the DEA, ones she used working for cartels, ones she used working inside the cartels *for* the DEA . . . We're talking dozens of different identities, everything from straw puppets to bulletproof covers that we'd never realize were her if we didn't already know what she looks like."

"Why so many?" Charles asked. Thanks to the bubble light on the roof of the car, he was making good time, zipping down the highway as the other cars scattered out of his path.

"She's been moving millions of dollars around between them. Wire transfers back and forth, bank accounts opened with small, frequent cash deposits and closed a few months later—girl's swimming in dirty money."

"Jesenia's been playing both sides of the fence for a long time," Shane said grimly. "Much longer than she's known Phoenix."

Charles blasted his horn as he came up behind a sedan that was moseying along in the left lane, apparently oblivious to the flashing blue lights. "Why do people drive in the left lane if they're not fucking passing?" Charles said, swinging his car over to the right.

Jade ignored his road rage. "It'll take us forever to untangle all of Jesenia's aliases. Now that I know their general destination, it'll be faster for me to work backward. I'm searching records of real estate transactions in Wyoming over the past couple of years, looking for any red flags."

"You think it'll be faster to search those records for an entire state?" Charles said, blazing past the idiot in the sedan.

"Uh, yeah," Jade said. "The population of Wyoming is less than half the population of San Diego alone. When someone moves into the state, it's basically front-page news."

Though Charles rolled his eyes at the hyperbole, he did agree with her approach. "Jesenia would want to keep Phoenix somewhere isolated—a good distance from any neighbors, as far off the grid as possible. Definitely rural."

Shane groaned. "Bro, that doesn't exactly narrow it down. This is Wyoming we're talking about; it's mountains and prairies for days out there."

"It's a good start," said Eva. "We'll need more than that to make a concrete match, though."

Charles glanced at the GPS on the dashboard. He was closing in on the gas station where Jesenia and Ángel had been spotted—by taking a direct route via major highways and driving well over the speed limit, he would arrive much faster than Jesenia had. It wouldn't do him much good, however, if he didn't know where to go once he got there.

"What exactly are you planning to do, Griffin?" Sakura asked, echoing his thoughts. "There haven't been any reported sightings of Jesenia or Phoenix since the last one, we have no idea what route they're taking—"

"I will drive all the way to Wyoming and knock down every door in the goddamn state if I have to!" Charles snapped.

A shocked silence fell on the other end of the line. Charles clenched his fists around the steering wheel and cracked his neck from side to side.

"Oh," Jade said, a quiet exhalation. "You're in love with him, I didn't realize—"

"Just figure out where she's taking him," Charles said, and then softened it with a heartfelt, "*Please.*"

"I will. You wanna stay on the line?"

"Yeah."

Listening to his team chatter as they worked kept Charles calm and focused on the drive. He blew past one mile marker after another, getting closer and closer to what could prove to be an enormous dead end.

"Here!" Jade shouted, so loudly Charles jumped in his seat and almost swerved off the side of the road. "Here, here, here!"

Charles steadied the car with his heart in his throat. "Jesus Christ, Siren, what is it?"

"Twenty acres purchased in foreclosure, *with cash*, in Owl Creek, Wyoming, which has a population of—wait for it—*five.*"

"And?" Eva asked.

"And the property was purchased by a Sara Martin," said Jade. "Sara's bundles and bundles of cash came via wire transfers from Lauren Diaz, who got *her* money in various installments from Christina Ruiz and Donna Parker, both of whom can be traced back to the same banks in Ciudad Juárez where Monica Ochoa, aka Jesenia fucking Santos, participated in low-level money laundering for the Esparza cartel under the auspices of the DEA."

"Holy shit," Shane said, impressed.

"I'll bring this next door," Eva said. "We'll make sure the FBI secures that property ASAP."

Jade made a humming noise. "That'll help in the long run, but Jesenia won't get there tonight—probably not even tomorrow. It's at least a seventeen-hour drive as a straight shot; avoiding highways and tolls, it's more like twenty-five, and that's without any breaks or working around the complications of a captive of Phoenix's size and strength."

"So which way should I go from the gas station?" asked Charles.

"How the hell should I know?" Jade exclaimed.

"I know you don't *know*," Charles said, steadier now that they had a solid handle on Jesenia's plan, "but you can map it out, can't you? We know Jesenia's point of origin, a place she stopped along the way, and her final destination. Isn't that enough to suggest her most likely route?"

"It . . ." Jade hesitated. "In theory, yes. Like I said, Jesenia would want to stay away from highways and tolls, and she'd also want to avoid traffic cameras and areas with a significant police presence. But she wouldn't just be lollygagging around, because the longer she's in transit, the greater her risk of exposure."

"Okay, that sounds like a good start."

"There are a ton of other variables, though," Jade said, a thread of anxiety running through her beautiful voice. "Things I couldn't possibly anticipate or account for—"

"Siren," Charles said, cutting her off. "At some point, Jesenia sat down with a map and plotted out the best way to get from San Diego to Owl Creek, using the same criteria you have now. Are you telling me that Jesenia Santos is smarter than you are?"

Jade blew out a breath. "Fuck no."

Charles nodded, even though she couldn't see him. "*I trust you.* You tell me where I should go, and I won't second-guess you."

"Okay," Jade said, and then with firm resolve, "*Okay.* Keep the line open, and I'll see what I can do."

While he waited for Jade's directions, Charles kept driving, his mind jumping ahead to the future. Now that they knew where Jesenia was headed, she would never get away with this, even if Charles wasn't able to catch up.

If Jesenia realized she'd been burned, though—if she felt cornered, trapped—then in the grips of her psychotic obsession, she might decide that a murder-suicide was her only way out.

Charles gunned the accelerator and barreled down the highway into the darkness.

CHAPTER NINETEEN

Á ngel hadn't meant to fall asleep, but his fear couldn't hold up against the combined effects of exhaustion, boredom, and a dark, silent room. He startled awake when the lights came on, so disoriented that he forgot his restraints and tried to bolt upright, nearly toppling off the bed in his sudden rush of anxiety.

Jesenia hurried to his side and caught him, steadying him on the edge of the bed. "It's okay, it's just me," she said, as if that were supposed to be *reassuring*.

A sharp, hysterical laugh burst out of his throat, muffled by the gag. He blinked a few times and shook his head, regaining his bearings. Then he lifted his chin and made an impatient noise.

"Hang on," she said. She unwound the bondage tape from his head, freeing his mouth. "There you go. *¿Estás bien?*"

"*Agua,*" Ángel said, his voice hoarse.

She jumped up and grabbed a bottle of water from one of the cases she'd brought. She held it for him while he drank, tenderly wiping away with her thumb the stray droplets that rolled down his chin.

"Are you hungry?" she asked once he'd had enough.

He nodded. He didn't want to accept anything from her, but he needed strength to have any hope of a successful escape.

Rather than free his hands, Jesenia insisted on hand-feeding him like a child. He submitted without protest; presenting himself as helpless would fuel her delusions, and though that might be dangerous in the long term, it would mollify her for the time being.

She was so pleased by the opportunity to coddle Ángel, in fact, that she did unbind his left hand and allow him to brush his teeth on his own. When it came time to sleep, however, she laid a T-shirt and a pair of sweatpants out on the bed and said, "You'll need to stay out here where I can see you."

"No," he said.

"Ángel," she said, with an air of exaggerated patience, "I can't have you unbound *and* out of my sight. The gas station was a big enough risk as it was."

"I'm not changing in front of you," Ángel said firmly. He was less concerned about her seeing him undressed, and more about her realizing he had a shiv on him—the lump of glass would be visible through his boxer briefs, if it hadn't already started to tear through. Plus, the jagged edges scraped his skin every time he moved the wrong way, and there was no way she'd miss the blood welling along his hip. His jeans offered his only defense against discovery.

She shrugged. "Then you'll have to sleep in the clothes you have on."

"That's fine."

"Stubborn," she muttered under her breath, turning away. Ángel watched with growing apprehension as she spread a sleeping bag out on the second bed. It didn't look like any sleeping bag he'd ever seen, though—it fastened along the bottom and sides with a series of Velcro strips, rather than a zipper.

"What the hell is that?" he asked.

"It's a suicide-prevention sleeping bag." She opened it up and smoothed it out. "Once you're inside, you won't be able to get out by yourself. This way, I can put you in gentler restraints while you're sleeping so you'll be more comfortable."

Gentler restraints proved to be two pairs of more-flexible leather cuffs and soft fabric tethers as might be found in a hospital. Jesenia swapped out the spreader bar first, binding his ankles and tying them together, then removed the bondage belt and did the same to his wrists. She left him enough slack in both ties that he would be able to keep his feet shoulders-width apart and his arms along his sides while lying down.

She guided him to the bed, helping him into the sleeping bag. Ángel's breathing sped up as she closed it around him. It was a tight fit—not painfully so, but it would have severely limited his range of motion even without the restraints, and in his heightened state of anxiety, it felt like being mummified alive.

He made himself breathe deeply, not wanting to hyperventilate, but he couldn't resist pushing against the top of the bag once she had fastened the last strip. The Velcro held so tightly that the bag might as well have been welded shut.

At his inadvertent, panicked whine, Jesenia smoothed a hand over his forehead and said, "I know, it's not fun. You'll get used to it though."

Ángel kept a close eye on her as she moved around the room, getting ready for bed herself. He paid particular attention to the distribution of her weapons—she left her knife in the pocket of her jeans, which she folded on top of the chair, and the sedative-loaded syringe was zipped into a small case and placed in the nightstand drawer beside the bed. The stun gun and pistol, however, Jesenia brought right into bed with her.

"*Buenas noches, cariño,*" she said, switching off the lamp.

Staring up at the ceiling, he said nothing.

This was his best opportunity for escape, while Jesenia was asleep and she had him in his least restrictive restraints so far. Though the sedative still lingered in his system, giving him terrible dry mouth and occasionally blurring his vision, he felt stronger and more focused after eating. These cuffs were padlocked like the ones before, so he wouldn't be able to remove them, but he should be able to use the glass to cut his way through the fabric tethers and the sleeping bag itself.

Ángel waited for Jesenia's breathing to deepen and even out before he started. It was easy to get his jeans open inside the bag, and required only a bit of tricky maneuvering to get his hand down the side of his pants and underwear to retrieve the shiv. Though he accidentally sliced a cut into his hip as he pulled the glass out, he ignored the pain and settled the shard on his stomach, wiping the excess blood off on his shirt.

Freeing his wrists would be his first step. Though hindered by his lack of leverage—not to mention the fact that he couldn't see what he was doing—he pulled the tether taut with his left hand and sawed through it with the other within a couple of minutes.

As the last few threads snapped, he let out a small gasp that was equal parts relief and terror. There was no turning back now. If he didn't escape tonight, Jesenia would discover the broken tether tomorrow morning, and he'd never get another chance.

He set the glass shard down and shook out his stinging hand. He allowed himself a minute to recover while he looked down at the sleeping bag, searching for weak spots. The seam along the closed side was heavily reinforced, and the industrial-strength Velcro on the other side wasn't an option, either. Even if he could cut it open, the sound of tearing Velcro would wake Jesenia up right away.

He'd have to go out the top.

Taking a deep breath, Ángel lifted the shiv and dug it into a spot on the panel right above his chest. The material resisted much more than he'd expected, so he gave it a little more muscle—then froze in horror as the bag made a loud ripping noise and gave way only slightly.

Jesenia murmured in her sleep, rolling over. Ángel dropped the glass and felt out the hole he'd made.

It was *tiny*. He hadn't anticipated how thick this material would be—at least two layers of heavy-duty fabric, padded for warmth and security. This bag was designed to withstand shredding. He could cut through it eventually, but it would take time, and it wouldn't be the quiet, subtle endeavor he'd been banking on.

Shit. Mind racing, Ángel closed his eyes. If he was going to wake Jesenia up either way, he might as well go for the Velcro. Though it would be a lot louder, it would also be faster. He would see how far he could get before she realized what was happening. Jesenia didn't know that his arms were free, or that he had a weapon—

The air conditioning unit against the far wall kicked on, filling the room with droning white noise.

Ángel's eyes flew open. He set the glass against the small hole in the bag and cautiously chipped away, straining his ears. The sound of tearing fabric was swallowed up in the mechanical rumble.

All of his desperate planning and sneaking around, and his saving grace was a crappy, inefficient motel air conditioner.

He set his jaw and got to work. Because the night was warm and the air conditioner was a piece of shit, it turned off and on frequently, and he had to stop and start around its vagaries. At least the breaks gave him a chance to rest his hands; he switched back and forth, but the jagged edges of the glass gashed up his palms and fingers more with every pass. Blood trickled down his forearms to drip onto his shirt and jeans.

Cutting through the bag took an excruciatingly long time. Once he had enough room to wiggle free, he looked over at the door and considered his route. He could probably get out of the bag without waking Jesenia, but he was sure she'd hear the heavy door open and shut no matter how careful he was, so he'd have to make a run for it once he was outside. He'd be doing it barefoot too, because Jesenia had stashed his shoes under her bed and there was no way he could get to them.

He had originally intended to take the shiv with him, but that was no longer an option; his hands were too damaged. However, he might be able to snatch Jesenia's pocketknife on his way out.

He rested through one more cycle of the air conditioner, gathering his strength, running through his plan in his mind over and over.

Under the cover of the new wave of white noise, he eeled out of the sleeping bag and onto the bed. He blotted his bloody hands on his jeans and picked up the shiv again, biting his lip to hold back a cry of pain. He reached between his legs to cut the tether binding his ankle cuffs, then immediately dropped the glass and panted through the agony throbbing in his palms.

After the wave ebbed, he eased himself off the side of the mattress, using every ounce of experience he'd gained sneaking out of bed with Raúl. He crouched low to the floor as he made his way toward the table and chair in the middle of the room.

He slipped his thumb and index finger into the pocket of Jesenia's jeans and tugged the knife free. Unfolding it to expose the blade, he snuck over to the door and straightened up halfway. Jesenia lay asleep, unaware that he stood free only a few feet from her unconscious body.

He could kill her now, slit her throat—she'd never react in time to defend herself.

He held still, paralyzed by the thought. Killing Jesenia was the safest and most logical strategy. She would hear him leave the room, and she'd run him down to her last breath. None of the odds were in Ángel's favor; he was drugged and injured, and Jesenia had a gun and a willingness to cause collateral damage that he didn't share. If he took her out now, he wouldn't have to worry about any of that.

But killing someone while they slept, even in arguable self-defense . . . that was murder. While it might be the safest choice, it wasn't a choice he would be able to live with.

He could disable her, though, give himself some sort of advantage. The syringe— No. Even if he could get it out of the drawer and the zippered case without waking her, he didn't trust that his cut-up hands would have the dexterity to operate it. One fumble, one slipped needle, and this would all be over.

Studying the nightstand between the two beds, Ángel noticed that, while Jesenia had removed the cord from the motel telephone, she'd left the phone itself out on the surface.

His pulse thundering in his ears, Ángel crept to the nightstand and lifted the big, clunky hunk of plastic in his free hand, gritting his teeth against the pain. He stared down at Jesenia's sleeping face and hesitated a second too long.

She stirred, blinking up at him, and her eyes widened. "What—"

Ángel smashed the telephone into the side of Jesenia's head, pulling the blow at the last moment to be sure it wouldn't kill her. Her head whipped to the side with a strangled grunt.

Dropping the phone, he spun on his heel, vaulted right over her bed, and bolted out the door.

He raced across the motel parking lot, bare feet slapping against the asphalt and broken tethers trailing from his wrist and ankle cuffs. His options were limited here—he couldn't appeal to the motel's other residents for help, since that would put their lives in danger. He'd scare the hell out of them looking like this, anyway. Ángel's arms were streaming blood from fingertips to elbows, more soaking the front of his shirt and jeans, and he still held the knife in one hand.

There was a pay phone in front of the motel office, by the vending machines and ice maker. Ángel made a beeline for it, half expecting to be shot in the back any moment.

He skidded to a halt in front of the rickety plastic contraption and grabbed the receiver. It slipped through the blood covering his hand and fell, hanging from its cord. Ángel groaned, snatched it back up again, and jabbed the buttons for 911.

The emergency call went through without requiring payment. "Nine-one-one, what's your emergency?" the operator said.

"My name is Ángel Medina, I'm a special agent with the ATF," Ángel said, the words coming out in a panicked jumble. He swallowed and said more clearly, "I've been abducted. I'm being held at the address this phone is registered to—"

On the other side of the parking lot, the door to their room slammed open and Jesenia lurched outside. She tottered on her feet, her Glock held in one hand.

"*Ángel!*" she shouted, and raised the gun.

Ángel whipped around, taking cover behind the side of the phone booth as she fired. Whether due to the head injury or because she wasn't truly trying to hit him, the shot went wide, cracking into the side of the building with plenty of space to spare.

Still, Ángel couldn't stay here. "*Shit,*" he said with feeling, and dropped the phone. He should have hit Jesenia harder.

"Sir?" the operator's voice came urgently from the dangling receiver. "Sir, was that a gunshot?"

Ángel took off again, with Jesenia in hot pursuit. The blow to the head would slow her down, but not enough, and they were in the middle of fucking nowhere, with no cover anywhere except—

Except that restaurant they'd driven past, a quarter mile away.

Ángel sprinted out of the parking lot and into the sand along the side of the road, running for his life.

Charles had been driving in the dark for what felt like days, his only company the background noises of his team working in the office as they fielded reports from law enforcement agencies across the state and in Wyoming, when Jade said, "Charles!"

"I'm here," he said, his heartbeat picking up at the excitement in her voice.

"I just got off the phone with the California State Police," she said. "Ángel called 911 from a motel not far from where you are now."

Charles's hands tightened on the steering wheel. "Are you sure it was him?"

"Yeah, I listened to the call myself. It . . ." Jade hesitated. "It ends abruptly, and I heard a gunshot in the background."

"Jesenia wouldn't shoot to kill, not at Ángel," Charles said, as much to reassure himself as Jade. "Not unless it was an absolute last resort." He had to believe the situation hadn't reached that point yet. "Do you have the address?"

Jade read it to him, and Charles programmed it into the car's GPS. As it turned out, the route Jade had extrapolated was impressively close to the one it seemed Jesenia had taken, running almost parallel. With a few not-quite-legal shortcuts, Charles could make it to the motel before one thirty.

"The state police will get there first," said Jade. "Hopefully they'll have the situation contained before you show up."

"I'm not betting Ángel's life on it," Charles said, swinging the car into an ill-advised U-turn.

Ángel reached the diner a few minutes ahead of Jesenia, but he was under no illusion that she wouldn't figure out what he'd done—there was nowhere else he could have gone. Still, he didn't have to make it blindingly obvious, so he circled around the building until he found the side door.

The restaurant was closed for the night, locked up with the lights off. A thrown rock took care of the glass pane in the door's top half, and he used a second rock to knock the rest of the glass away so he could reach in and unlock the dead bolt. With any luck, he'd set off some kind of alarm.

The side door entered into the vestibule outside the restrooms. Moving carefully in the dark, Ángel pushed through the swinging doors into the kitchen and glanced around. This was a classic diner setup—the kitchen fronted by prep and pickup areas, beyond which stood a service counter lined with barstools. As his eyes adjusted, he could make out the shadowy bulk of vinyl booths ringing the front half of the restaurant.

Jesenia would catch up any moment. He hurried over to a little desk tucked in the corner of the kitchen, fishing a pair of scissors out of a pen cup. One by one, he snipped the trailing tethers off his wrist and ankle cuffs so they couldn't be used against him in a fight. Then he moved to the sink, hissing through his teeth as he ran his hands under cold water, washing the blood from his skin and the handle of the pocketknife. His hands still oozed blood after he'd blotted them with paper towels, but at least he wouldn't lose his grip on the blade the way he had on the pay phone.

"Ángel!" Jesenia called—from outside the diner, but not far.

The kitchen's back door was clear on the other side of the building from the side door. Ángel unlocked it but left it shut, crouching down beside the massive flattop. From here, he'd have cover from gunfire as well as a straight shot to the back door if he needed a quick exit.

"Ángel," Jesenia said, much closer this time; he guessed she was standing by the door he'd entered through. "I'm not chasing you down in there like a child."

He stifled a snort. She wasn't willing to come in here because he had the advantage of surprise and familiarity with the environment.

"Come out now, and I'll forgive you."

He didn't speak. Any noise from him would give away his position.

Her heavy sigh was audible all the way across the diner. "Ángel," she said, her voice stern, "if you don't come out now, I'll go back to the motel, start knocking on doors, and shoot anyone who answers."

Oh God. Ángel steadied himself against the side of the flattop as he considered her threat. She was bluffing; she had to be bluffing. She'd never escape after something like that.

Maybe she didn't care, though. Maybe she found capture or death preferable to not having him the way she wanted him.

He couldn't let her return to the motel, but he couldn't just surrender either. He would have to initiate a confrontation himself— and that was exactly what Jesenia wanted, for him to give up his cover.

Torn by indecision, he flexed his fingers on the knife handle. He was debating his few unappealing options when approaching police sirens split the air.

"Oh, Ángel," said Jesenia. "So you *did* call the police. Bad boy. Now I have to take care of them too."

The police would respond to the motel first, to the pay phone from which Ángel had called 911. They'd find it smeared with blood, and he had been bleeding while he ran; he'd left a blazing trail along the sand all the way from there to here. The cops would find their way to the diner in a matter of minutes, with no idea what they were walking into.

"You're causing me a lot of problems," Jesenia said. The crunch of gravel signaled her retreating footsteps.

Cursing under his breath, he crept out of his hiding place. He grabbed a bottle of degreaser with his free hand and padded back to the side door, watching Jesenia stride away across the parking lot.

Unfortunately for him, there was no quiet way to move across gravel. He bounced on the balls of his bare feet and then took off as fast as he could, rushing Jesenia from behind.

She heard him coming and turned around, lifting her pistol, but she couldn't get off a shot before Ángel bulldozed into her and brought them both to the ground. She gasped as she landed hard on her back, and he capitalized on her disorientation by spraying the degreaser into her eyes.

Screaming, Jesenia lashed out blindly with the Glock. He dropped the can to block the blow, but he made the rookie mistake of leaving his face wide open. She smashed the heel of her hand into his nose hard enough to drive him off her and onto his ass.

She struggled to her knees, her eyes bleary and bloodshot, her temple gashed open from where Ángel had hit her with the phone. Ángel shifted his weight backward and kicked out one foot, striking her wrist. As she yelped and dropped the pistol, he lunged forward with the knife.

She grabbed his attacking wrist and yanked him off-balance, seizing the nape of his neck with her other hand and hurling him face-first into the gravel. Ángel coughed, dust clogging his nose and mouth, and struggled to throw her off. She had a good grip on him though, squeezing his neck and wrist to ensure pain compliance.

He let go of the knife. When her hold loosened in response, he slammed his elbow back into her gut. She backed off and he squirmed free, spinning around to face her on his knees.

With an enraged cry, she flung herself at Ángel, wrapping both hands around his throat. She shoved him onto his back and straddled his waist, her face screwed up in concentration as she strangled him.

He locked his left foot around her ankle and plucked hard at her hands, releasing the choke. She unbalanced, falling forward, and he thrust his hip up to roll them over. Jesenia was an experienced fighter though, and wrapped her free leg around his waist so he couldn't disengage.

Grunting with the effort of holding down her thrashing body, Ángel turned the tables and clutched her throat, even as his battered hands screamed their protest. Jesenia glowered up at him, shifting with one hard undulating movement.

Too late, Ángel realized she was still armed.

She pulled the stun gun out of her pocket and jammed it into his side. His scream cut off in his throat at the all-encompassing pain, every muscle in his body locking up and convulsing as his nervous system flooded with electricity. He toppled off Jesenia to sprawl out on the gravel, twitching uncontrollably, his breath coming in frantic, shallow gasps.

She pushed him all the way onto his back and punched him in the face. He couldn't even cry out.

"Stay here," Jesenia said. She staggered to her feet, retrieved her Glock from where she'd dropped it, and started back toward the motel.

Ángel didn't have a choice—he couldn't move. He had no control over his body, jerking like a beached fish, pain sparking all up and down his nerve endings. He stared up at the night sky and concentrated on breathing through it.

Once his muscles were obeying his brain again, he rolled stiffly onto his stomach. He was just easing himself onto his hands and knees when he heard two gunshots in quick succession from the direction of the motel.

"No," he moaned, knowing deep in his gut that neither of those shots had taken out Jesenia. With every inch of his body pulsating with agony, Ángel began to crawl, dragging himself toward the diner.

He had to get to cover before she came back for him.

Charles careened into the motel parking lot with squealing tires, barely remembering to pull the key from the ignition before he jumped out. A state police car was parked a few feet away, its swirling lights bathing the lot in red and blue, but the cops themselves were nowhere to be seen.

Some of the motel residents had emerged from their rooms, gathering on the sidewalk and the second-floor balcony, whispering among themselves—but they were all facing *outward*, as if the emergency wasn't taking place inside the motel itself. Frowning, Charles scanned the surroundings until he found the pay phone by the office. Its receiver hung from the cord, coated with blood, and more blood was smeared along the box and on the ground.

His stomach lurched. Fuck, he had to get these people out of the possible line of fire.

Jogging over to the cop car, he pulled his badge from his pocket and flashed it at the small crowd. "ATF!" he said, raising his voice loud enough to be heard on the second floor. "Everybody please return to your rooms and lock your doors. Don't answer for anyone but a uniformed police officer."

Though a few people obeyed, the others shifted restlessly on their feet, exchanging uncertain glances.

"*Now!*" Charles barked with every ounce of fury and anxiety boiling inside him.

Several people jumped; one by one, they turned and scattered back to their rooms. Once he was sure all the civilians were safely locked away, Charles drew his gun and headed for the pay phone.

This had to be Ángel's blood. He'd called 911 from this phone, and Jesenia had interrupted him with a gunshot—though if she'd managed to hit him, there would have been more blood than this. The spatter on the ground was more indicative of a small, dripping wound. It led away from the motel, of course; Ángel would have wanted to get her away from innocent people.

Where would he have gone, though? Charles had a vague memory of passing a diner down the road, but it had been dark, empty. If the responding police officers had come to the same conclusions he had, they should have caught up to Jesenia and Ángel already. Unless . . .

"Oh fuck," Charles said. He took off into the sand, following the blood trail, gun held at the ready.

Thanks to the flat ground, Charles saw the huddled shapes long before he reached them. Putting on a burst of speed, he sprinted toward the crumpled bodies of two uniformed state police officers. There was nobody else around and nowhere an attacker could hide, so he dropped to one knee and felt for the first cop's pulse.

Nothing.

"Shit." Charles shuffled over to the second cop, relieved to see that she was still breathing, albeit shallowly. Her lips were flecked with blood, though, and her pulse was thready.

She'd been gutshot in the side of her abdomen. Charles pulled off his jacket and wadded it up, packing it around the wound to try to stem the bleeding. He grabbed the radio off her belt.

"Dispatch, come in."

"Proceed."

"This is Special Agent Charles Hunter with the ATF," Charles said. "You have two officers down near the scene of a response call at the Desert Wind Motel. The perpetrator is still at large and she's almost certainly still armed. You need to get backup and a medevac out here *immediately*."

"Roger that, Agent. Do you have an exact location?"

He holstered his gun and fumbled one-handed with his phone, reading off their current GPS coordinates. As he spoke, the cop beneath him stirred and opened her eyes. She blinked down at her bleeding stomach and then let out a small, frightened gasp.

The dispatcher promised that backup and medical assistance were en route, only a few minutes out. Charles let go of the radio and took the cop's hand.

"Help is on the way," he said. "Hang in there."

He looked up at the darkened diner, which was well within sight now. Seconds later, a shot rang out in the distance and a bright muzzle flash blazed behind the windows.

He stiffened, preparing to jump to his feet, but he caught himself and glanced down at the injured cop.

"Go," she said.

"I can't—"

"*Go*," she said again, pushing weakly at his arm.

He folded her hands over the jacket, instructing her to keep pressure on the wound. Then he leaped up and drew his gun in one motion, running for the diner.

Around the side, a large section of the parking lot's gravel was disturbed and stained with blood, dark wet patches glinting under the sickly yellow light thrown off by the lampposts. A stun gun lay abandoned near the mess. Charles snatched it up as he passed, approaching a side door that hung open, its window broken.

He heard fighting inside, grunts and curses and the thud of flesh impacting flesh and hard objects. At least that recent shot hadn't been fatal.

Moving warily in the dark, Charles entered the vestibule and crept into the kitchen, then eased around the corner behind the service counter. He saw Ángel and Jesenia locked in a life-or-death struggle for a gun, trading blows and banging into the booths and the walls as they stumbled across the floor. Neither gained any advantage.

Charles's initial exhilaration at seeing Ángel alive was swamped once he took in Ángel's poor condition. He was bleeding from the face and hands and feet, and there was something off about his body's movements, a sluggishness that Charles had never seen in him before. It was a small consolation that Jesenia wasn't faring much better, her face streaming blood from a nasty head wound.

Charles aimed his Glock, but he couldn't shoot—they were too close together and moving around too quickly. Even if he were able to hit Jesenia accurately, the bullet could go right through her into Ángel.

Shoving the pistol back into its holster, Charles readied the stun gun and came out from behind the counter, bearing down on Jesenia from behind.

Ángel saw him first, his face going slack with shock. Unfortunately, this warned Jesenia, and she spun around. The gun she and Ángel had been fighting over went flying, clattering onto the linoleum floor and sliding away under a nearby booth.

Charles lunged at Jesenia with the stun gun. She blocked him with a hard chop right at his wrist that numbed his hand, throwing a simultaneous punch at his throat. Though Charles was forced to drop the stun gun, he jerked back in time to evade the bulk of the punch's force. Still, the pressure was enough to send him stumbling away in a coughing fit.

When Ángel tried to reengage Jesenia, she nailed him in the groin with a hard side kick that slammed him into the table behind him. Ángel yelped as his hips cracked against the edge and he tumbled sideways, crumpling to the floor in a ball.

Jesenia faced Charles in a defensive posture, her blood-streaked face twisted with rage. He had to get her away from Ángel, who was in no physical condition to be fighting and seemed to be weakening further by the moment.

Seizing one of the barstools at the service counter, Charles swung it in a wide arc and smashed it into her with all his might.

As well-trained as she was, she couldn't rival Charles's raw strength; the blow knocked her right off her feet. She landed hard but rolled with the momentum, picking herself up halfway across the room. Charles dropped the stool, moved around to interpose himself between Jesenia and Ángel, and reached for his Glock.

Time to finish this.

Ángel groaned and uncurled his body, squinting at Charles and Jesenia on the opposite side of the diner. His body shook, leaden with the cumulative effects of sedation, blood loss, and electric shock. He could barely feel his cut-up hands anymore, and his nose had bled into his mouth, filling it with that nauseating sickly-sweet taste.

The blow he'd taken to the groin wasn't helping him recover from his incredulity at Charles's appearance, either. What the *fuck* was he doing here?

Ángel watched as Charles tried to draw his gun, only to be thrown off-balance when Jesenia began pelting him with objects from nearby tables—ketchup bottles, saltshakers, sugar canisters. Charles had to lift both hands to protect his face from the constant barrage.

Jesenia's own gun had gone . . . somewhere. They'd both lost their grip on it when Charles surprised them, but it had to be nearby.

Spotting the familiar shape under one of the tables, Ángel marshaled his strength and shuffled over on his hands and knees, retrieving the Glock with a trembling arm. It didn't do him much good though—he didn't have a clear shot at Jesenia, and with his hands in their current state, it was all he could do to hold the goddamn thing anyway.

Charles gave up on his own gun and let out a frustrated shout, rushing forward to close the distance between himself and Jesenia. He grabbed her when she tried to dodge and shoved her up against the edge of a table, getting in a few good blows to her face and stomach, his fists driving into her body with sickening thuds.

Ángel pushed himself onto one knee, but that was as far as he got before a wave of dizziness overtook him. He steadied himself and straightened up, doing his best to wrap his hands properly around the Glock. This was the only way he could help now; he'd be nothing but a liability if he tried to rejoin the fight. But it wouldn't matter if he *couldn't get his fucking hands to work.*

Charles drew his arm back for a game-ending punch. But as his fist flew toward Jesenia's face, she smacked his arm sideways and darted in the opposite direction to counterattack with a brutal punch to Charles's cheekbone. She slid smoothly around him, grabbed the nape of his neck, and slammed his forehead into the Formica table.

Ángel flinched at the horrifying *crunch* that echoed through the diner.

Holding Charles's stupefied body in place against the table, Jesenia snatched up the metal napkin holder and reared back—God, she was going to smash in Charles's head—

Ángel raised the gun and fired.

The bullet traveled through Jesenia's shoulder and cracked into the plate glass window beyond. She screamed, toppling off Charles to collapse on the floor, but her scream was lost in Ángel's own as the gun recoiled against his damaged hands. He dropped it immediately and hunched forward, clutching his hands to his stomach.

Even as Ángel gasped through the agony, he watched Charles slump to his knees, clinging to the edge of the table. A few seconds later, Charles turned around—wobbling like a drunk, but at least he was conscious.

Charles reached out for Jesenia, who lay sprawled on the floor with her eyes shut, and felt for her pulse. Then he grabbed a pair of handcuffs off his belt and snapped them around her wrists.

Ángel hadn't killed her, then. Jesenia was still alive—for now.

Charles lurched to his feet, staggered, and made his unsteady way toward Ángel, where he fell onto his knees again. "Ángel," he said, cupping Ángel's face with both hands. He wiped the blood away from Ángel's nose and mouth.

"*Charles*," said Ángel.

Wrapping him in a bone-crushing hug, Charles buried his face in the crook of Ángel's neck. Ángel slumped against him and let Charles take his weight, even though Charles was shaking as badly as he was.

"It's okay," Charles said. "I've got you. You're gonna be okay."

Over Charles's shoulder, Ángel watched the blood pooling from Jesenia's motionless body seep across the linoleum floor.

"No," he said quietly. "I won't."

CHAPTER TWENTY

"How's the pain?" asked the resident who was stitching up Ángel's hands.

"It's fine," said Ángel, his blank eyes fixed on the opposite wall.

When the resident shot Charles a concerned glance, he nodded for her to continue and rubbed one hand up and down Ángel's back. Ángel had refused a local anesthetic, and his terrified reaction to the proffered needle had been his first and only real emotional response since they'd left the diner. Once they'd calmed him down, neither Charles nor the resident had argued with him about it, wary of provoking him again.

The ambulance had whisked them away from the diner to the nearest community hospital, where the ER physician had checked out Charles's head and concluded that no treatment was necessary, so long as he was monitored closely for the next twenty-four hours. Charles cared little about his own injury—all of his focus was on Ángel, from whom he refused to be separated. None of the hospital staff had objected.

Ángel himself was in better physical condition than Charles had feared. His nose was bruised but not broken, and the scratches on his feet had only needed cleaning and bandaging. His hands were another story though—he'd torn them to shreds on broken glass trying to escape, then ripped the wounds open further with everything he'd done afterward.

Broken *glass*. Charles was sick with rage just imagining it.

He wasn't sure he should even be touching Ángel like this, but whenever he backed off, thinking it might be too much, Ángel swayed toward him in silent entreaty. So Charles remained by Ángel's side, stroking his hair and back, watching with morbid fascination as the resident carefully sewed the horrific gashes in Ángel's hands back together.

Ángel didn't so much as flinch throughout the entire procedure. There were moments when Charles doubted Ángel was aware of what was happening at all; he had the same empty, disconnected expression on his face he'd had after they found Warner's body. From the few jumbled sentences Ángel had spoken in the ambulance, Charles had worked out that Ángel was still under the influence of some kind of drug, which couldn't be helping his tendency to dissociate in the aftermath of trauma.

Once the resident had finished placing bandages over Ángel's stitches, she said, "You're going to have trouble using your hands for a while, and you'll need to have the sutures removed in about seven to twelve days. Follow-up care for hand injuries like these is really important, okay?"

Ángel didn't respond. Charles nudged him gently.

"Uh-huh," Ángel said.

"Go ahead and take these for now," the resident said, holding out a small plastic cup, "and I'll write you a—"

"What is that?" Ángel interrupted, snapping to sudden attention. He stared at the cup as if it were a loaded gun.

"Tylenol."

Ángel jerked backward, the paper beneath him rustling as he pressed himself against Charles. "I don't believe you."

"It's the same thing you'd get at the drugstore—" the bewildered resident began.

"You could be lying." His voice ragged with fear, Ángel twisted around to look up at Charles. "That's how she took me, she tricked me and she knocked me out and—and she had a needle, she said she'd do it again if I didn't cooperate—"

"Nobody's going to make you do anything you don't want to do," Charles said, holding Ángel by both shoulders and looking him in the eye. "We talked about this before. You know you're in a hospital, right?"

Ángel nodded tightly. A muscle in his jaw jumped with stress.

"And you remember they can't force you to accept treatment you don't want?"

"Yeah," Ángel said. Some of the panic receded from his face, and his breathing evened out.

"If you don't want to take the pills, you're not gonna take them," said Charles. "That's all there is to it."

The last time Charles had genuinely wanted to kill another human being, he'd been a child watching news reports on the arrest and trial of the cokehead gangbangers who'd shot up the convenience store where his parents had been caught in the crossfire. If Jesenia didn't die from Ángel's bullet, Charles would be sorely tempted to finish the job himself.

The resident, who'd watched their exchange with wide, sympathetic eyes, said, "What if the nurse gave you a sealed bottle from the pharmacy instead?"

"Thank you," Ángel said, already shutting down again.

"I'll ask her to bring it in when she goes over your discharge instructions. It shouldn't be more than a few minutes." The resident reached out to Ángel, hesitated, and dropped her arm before she made contact. "Take it easy on those hands."

She slipped through the curtains that partitioned them from the other ER patients. *A few minutes* in ER lingo could mean a half hour or more, so Charles snagged the rolling stool the resident had been using and wheeled it over beside Ángel to sit on it himself. His headache was starting to get the better of him.

After several moments of silence punctuated only by the background noises of a bustling ER, Ángel said, "Is she dead?"

"I don't know," Charles said. Jesenia had still been alive when her ambulance reached the hospital, but that was the last he'd heard.

"Would you tell me if she was?"

"Of course I would. But they won't tell *me*; you know that. We'll have to hear it from Ed."

"What if she dies?" Ángel said, gazing down at the thick, pure-white bandages swaddling his hands. "I've never killed anyone before. What if I have to spend the rest of my life knowing I killed someone I once considered a good friend?"

As harrowing as the stalking and abduction had been, it was Jesenia's bone-deep betrayal that made her crimes particularly heinous. She'd deceived Ángel completely, cultivated his trust and friendship, and then used those things to harm him. Charles could barely begin to comprehend the monstrosity of it.

"I don't know what to say," Charles said, figuring blunt honesty was the best policy. It would be a refreshing change from their usual mode of communication, anyway.

"I do. I know exactly what to say to someone in my situation." Ángel's eyes were unfocused, dreamy. "It wasn't my fault. She was going to kill us both, and I had to shoot her. I couldn't have known she was the stalker. Nothing I did or didn't do encouraged her obsession with me, and I'm not responsible for her actions. It's not my fault."

Ángel closed his eyes. When he opened them again and looked at Charles, he was abruptly, painfully present.

"I know in my head those things are true," he said. "But they don't *feel* true, Charles. It is my fault. All of the things she did, the people she killed—she did those things because of me. And I had no idea. For two years, I missed every sign there must have been along the way. I trusted her, I . . . I *liked* her . . ."

Charles squeezed Ángel's knee, cutting off his distressed rambling. "It isn't your fault. I know you know that, but I'll say it as many times as you need to hear it to believe it with more than just your head."

"If she dies, she'll have made me a killer," Ángel said. He looked not one bit reassured. "And if she lives, then one day I'll have to get up in front of a room full of strangers and tell them what she did to me, with her watching me the whole time. I can't do that, Charles, I *can't*—"

He started shaking, his voice cracking with anxiety. Charles pulled him close and rubbed his back again, letting Ángel lean heavily against him. Because how else could he help, really?

Ángel pulled himself together when the nurse came in with his discharge paperwork, and took the acetaminophen she handed him without complaint—though he did inspect the pills first. Since neither Charles nor Ángel could drive in their conditions, a state police officer had offered to drive them home in Eva's car and catch a ride back. Charles escorted a listless Ángel out of the hospital and sat in the middle of the backseat so they could stay close.

After half an hour on the road, Ángel fell asleep, slumped on Charles's shoulder. Charles kept himself awake by picturing all the creative ways he'd enjoy hurting Jesenia for subjecting Ángel to this nightmare.

They pulled up the driveway of Eva's charming suburban house shortly after sunrise. She waited for them on the porch, wrapped in a thick robe and cradling a mug in her hands.

The state cop stayed in the car while Charles walked Ángel to the door. It would have been more efficient for him to drop Charles off first, because he'd have to bring the car back here later, but Charles hadn't wanted to leave Ángel alone with a stranger.

"Hey," Eva said as they climbed the front steps. She smoothed a gentle hand from Ángel's shoulder to his elbow. "It's good to have you back."

"Thanks."

"You're going to stay with Eva for a while," Charles said. Then, realizing how insensitive it was to give orders to someone who'd recently been abducted and held captive, he added, "If that's okay with you."

"Yeah, of course," said Ángel.

"I'll see you later, then." Charles turned to step off the porch.

Ángel caught his arm. "You're not staying too?"

Striving for a lighthearted tone, he said, "Three kids—kind of crowded."

"You have a concussion," Ángel said, rallying for the first time in hours. "You can't be alone; you need somebody to watch you—"

"I'm going to Sakura's." Charles pressed a kiss to Ángel's cheek, lingering for a moment with their faces close together, loath to pull away. "I'll see you soon. Get some sleep, okay?"

Charles nodded to Eva and hurried down the steps before he could give in to the temptation to insist on staying behind and sitting vigil by Ángel's bedside.

Ángel woke up in a lush purple room with fairies on the wall.

He blinked a few times, his vision blurred with sleep and confusion, before he remembered that he was in one of Eva's daughters' bedrooms. It was decorated with an enchanted woodland theme—very *Midsummer Night's Dream*—including a beautiful mural of dancing, smiling fairies that took up an entire wall.

Ángel lay in the small twin bed for a long time just staring at the mural, picking out every detail. Eventually, the pain and itching in his hands grew bothersome enough to force him upright. He reached for the bloodstained clothes he'd dropped on the floor last night—early that morning, rather—only to find them missing.

A fresh set of clothing had been set out on the dresser. They were his own clothes too, ones he'd brought to Charles's apartment after he'd retrieved them from the moving van with—

Ángel jerked violently away from the memory and heaved himself out of bed.

Dressing was a laborious and painful process, given his fucked-up hands, but he persevered. Relying on his vague recollections from earlier, Ángel shuffled out of the bedroom and down the stairs, making his way to a spacious, airy kitchen with pale-gold walls and white woodwork.

"Good morning," Eva said from the kitchen table, though the clock on the oven read 12:53.

"Morning." Ángel hovered behind one of the chairs, feeling awkward. Eva's kids must have left hours ago for school, her husband for work; he hadn't met any of them when he came in. He barely knew Eva herself, when it came down to it.

"Do you want some coffee?" Eva asked.

The words struck such a deep nerve that Ángel doubled over, grabbing the back of the chair for support. For a few dizzying seconds, he was back in that motel room, drinking Jesenia's drugged coffee like a naïve, trusting idiot—

Eva jumped to her feet and rushed to his side, putting a hand on his back. "What's wrong? Do you feel sick?"

"No, I . . ." Trying for subtlety—and failing miserably—Ángel slipped sideways to evade her touch. "I'm fine. Sorry."

She backed off, returning to her seat, and studied his face for a moment. "The machine's over there if you're interested," she said. "It takes K-cups, so it shouldn't be too rough on your hands."

"Thank you," Ángel said, grateful that she wasn't the type to push.

He followed Eva's directions to make and pour himself a cup of coffee, then joined her at the table. After Ángel had taken a few sips, Eva set her tablet aside and said, "Ed called me a couple of hours ago."

Every muscle in Ángel's body clenched tight. He couldn't bring himself to look up.

"Jesenia made it through surgery," said Eva. "She's in critical condition, but she is stable."

"Oh," Ángel said. He traced his thumb around the rim of his mug. "Good."

He didn't regret shooting Jesenia, not when the alternative would have been Charles's death, but he was glad she'd survived—or, more precisely, he was glad he hadn't killed her.

"You'll need to go into the office to be debriefed, but you can put that off for a day or two if you'd rather."

Ángel shook his head and pushed the mug away, no longer able to stomach the coffee. "No, I just want to get it over with. Can we go today?"

"Sure. Let me know when you're ready."

It was no surprise to Ángel that Eva and Charles got along so well; they had the same aura of calm, gave the same impression that they couldn't be flustered or discomposed. Of course, no human being was one hundred percent unflappable—Charles certainly wasn't—but Ángel found that steady presence reassuring nonetheless.

Eva drove Ángel to the office shortly afterward and walked with him to Ed Campos's office, her icy glare fending off well-wishers and nosy busybodies alike. She left him at the door with a murmured, "Good luck," and Ángel breathed deeply before letting himself inside.

"Ángel," Campos said, greeting him with a broad smile. "Come on in."

"I need to take a leave of absence," Ángel said. He couldn't take one more step without making that clear.

Campos nodded and gestured to the empty chair in front of his desk. "Have a seat. Let's talk."

Ángel emerged from the building a few hours later. He paused at the top of the steps, bandaged hands shoved into his pockets, and realized that he had no idea what to do next.

He had no home base, no job demanding his presence, no family he had any desire to speak to again. No commitments, zero obligations.

Had Ángel been himself, he would have relished the opportunity, looked forward to the adventure of striking out on his own without knowing where the road would lead him. Now, he just felt lost and afraid.

His eyes fell on an unfamiliar SUV parked at the curb, and he frowned when he recognized Charles sitting on the hood, engrossed in his phone. Charles chose that moment to look up, meeting Ángel's gaze.

As Ángel slowly walked down the steps, Charles hopped off the car, moving to stand on the curb. Ángel stopped a few feet away.

"You're not working?" he asked. Ángel had gone straight to and from Campos's office without stopping by the team's cluster, exhausted by even the thought of talking to anyone. He figured he was allowed to be a little selfish today.

"I took the day off," said Charles. "I've got a concussion, you know."

A smile tugged at Ángel's lips. He and Charles watched each other across the concrete expanse of the sidewalk. Bruises were blossoming on Charles's cheekbone and forehead where Jesenia had struck him, and while they weren't as glaring on his dark skin as they might have been on a man with a fairer complexion, they were still brutal.

"Why'd you come after me?" Ángel finally said.

"Because I love you," Charles said steadily, "and I made you a promise."

Ángel rocked back on his heels. While Eva helped him change his bandages that morning, she'd filled him in on last night's events, sharing the details he'd been too devastated to ask for then. The last time Ángel saw Charles before his abduction, he'd confessed two agonizing secrets, and Charles had given him nothing in return.

Then Charles had gone to extraordinary lengths to find him, hunted him down against overwhelming odds, risked his own life to protect Ángel's, and stayed with him for every horrible moment afterward. His actions spoke the truth, but Ángel hadn't expected to hear him say the actual words.

"Let me take you away," Charles said, before Ángel could respond to his declaration.

Ángel tilted his head, not understanding. "What do you mean, like for dinner?"

"No, I mean *away*." Charles stepped closer. "Let's get out of here, Ángel. Just me and you, anywhere you want to go. I know you took a leave of absence, and I've accumulated a shit-ton of paid time off. We could get away from all this, go somewhere quiet where we can be alone and you can . . ."

"Recover?" Ángel said, arching an eyebrow when Charles hesitated.

Folding his arms, Charles said, "Are you going to tell me that's not what you need?"

Ángel sighed. Of *course* that was what he needed. The true question was whether it would be better or worse with Charles by his side.

"We can do whatever you want," Charles said. His expression was open and honest, with a hint of anxiety that twisted Ángel's heart. "*Talk* about whatever you want. I'm not going to fuck up with you again. I won't let you down."

"*Charles*," he said. "You didn't let me down. You saved my life."

"I'm not just talking about yesterday."

"I know." The more Ángel thought about it, the more appealing it sounded to just fuck off out of San Diego, hole up somewhere private with Charles, lay all their cards on the table, and just . . . let whatever happened happen.

He pulled his hands out of his pockets and slipped his arms around Charles's waist. Charles returned the hug, resting his uninjured cheek against Ángel's.

"Yeah," Ángel said, "let's get the hell out of here."

They ended up heading about four hours north along the coast, past Santa Barbara, to a rustic beach town that was long past its prime. Charles checked them into a shabby hotel right on the beach, where the incredible views of the water more than compensated for the scratchy sheets and fading wallpaper.

Ángel didn't speak for two days.

He stayed in bed for most of that time, in fact, only occasionally venturing out onto their balcony. Charles didn't push. He was content to bring food back to the room as necessary, to sit and read or people-watch in silence, to lie beside Ángel and rub his back when he woke up gasping.

On their third night, Ángel turned to Charles long after they'd turned out the lights and started kissing his face and neck, one hand sliding into Charles's boxers to stroke his cock. Charles let Ángel climb on top of him and hold him down while they fucked hard, then held him afterward in the dark and listened to his halting, disjointed story about what had happened in the hours he'd been alone with Jesenia.

After that, it was as if a dam had broken. They talked and fought and fucked each other's brains out, then fought some more. The fights they had in that hotel room were the most vicious they'd ever had, but unlike their previous confrontations, which had left Charles sick and self-loathing, this lanced infected wounds and let the corruption bleed out. These injuries would heal clean and leave them stronger; each time they reached a new accord, Charles's understanding of Ángel deepened, their connection reinforced. They were getting to know each other all over again.

At night, Charles thrust into Ángel and panted, "I love you, I love you," against his skin while Ángel shuddered beneath him and cried out his name.

Charles took three weeks off work—it was all he could afford, though Ed Campos had apparently hinted that he was willing to arrange for more. Ángel knew he wouldn't take it; Charles couldn't be away from the action that long. That he'd been willing to spend these past few weeks hidden away with Ángel spoke volumes.

Their last night in the hotel, Ángel stood alone on the balcony, watching the sun set over the ocean. He turned his hands palm up on the railing and grazed one thumb over the jagged lines slashing his skin. The stitches had come out a while ago at a nearby urgent care, but there would be scarring.

"Here you go," Charles said, stepping out onto the balcony and handing him an open bottle of beer.

"Thanks." Ángel hesitated for only a moment before he took a sip. He didn't know if he'd ever be willing to accept a drink from most people again, but Charles was the exception.

Charles joined him at the railing, propping his elbows on the rusted metal, his own bottle dangling from his fingers. "Are you coming back with me tomorrow?" he asked after a while.

Ángel had been dreading this question all day. "No," he said.

Charles nodded, as if he'd been expecting that. He rolled his beer between his palms and opened his mouth, then shut it, then opened it again without saying anything.

"What?" Ángel said.

"I want to ask you to stay," Charles said, "but I don't want you to stay because I asked you to. Does that make sense?"

"Yeah," Ángel said with a rueful twist to his lips. He understood Charles's conflict, particularly given their history.

Pushing himself upright, Charles said, "If you want to leave because you honestly believe that's what's best for you, I'd never try to talk you out of it. But if you want to leave because you think things would be like before if you came back with me—that's not something I could live with."

He took Ángel's beer and set both bottles on the floor, then put his hands on Ángel's hips. Ángel hooked his own fingers in Charles's belt loops.

"Even if Jesenia hadn't outed me, I'd want things to be different now," Charles said, his voice soft. "My life is better with you in it, and

I don't want to lose you again. I think we could have something great if we give this a real, honest shot. But I'm still not sure if you want the kind of commitment I do."

Ángel was quiet for a moment. "When we fought the day . . . the day she took me . . . you said that nothing in my life has ever been long-term."

"I—"

"You were right," Ángel said. His fingers tightened where he held on to Charles. "I don't have any real family. I've never had any friendships that lasted longer than it took for me to move from place to place, and I've never lived anywhere for more than a couple of years. I've never made a serious commitment to anything except my job."

He had to stop to work up the nerve to say what came next. Charles waited for him without interrupting.

"She was counting on that." Even three weeks later, Ángel couldn't bring himself to say Jesenia's name aloud. "She said it herself—if you hadn't been on my extraction team, I wouldn't have had anyone but her to turn to when I came out of the cartel. It would have been so easy for her to take me."

"Nobody else would have noticed you were gone for days."

Shaking off the ghost of Jesenia's words, Ángel said, "I spent two years of my life pretending to be another person, and when I finally got out, when I could finally be myself again, I didn't have anything to go back to."

Charles rested his forehead against Ángel's, offering silent support. Ángel closed his eyes and breathed out.

"I don't want to ever feel like that again," he said. "I want to put down roots; I want to be around people who won't let me go without a fight. I want somewhere I can call home." Opening his eyes, he met Charles's gaze. "I want all those things with *you*."

"So do I," said Charles.

Ángel sighed. "But if I go back with you tomorrow, I'll never know if I only want it because you helped me escape the worst thing that's ever happened to me. If we're going to have a real future together, that can't be the way it starts. I need more time to be sure—time by myself, away from you."

"I understand." Charles kissed Ángel's lips. "I'll wait for you."

"You don't have to—"

"I'll wait for you," Charles said firmly.

Ángel wrapped his arms around Charles's waist and kissed him, turning them sideways to shove Charles up against the balcony railing and get a thigh between his legs. Charles groaned, sinking his fingers into Ángel's hair.

"Let's go to bed," Ángel said against Charles's mouth, even though the sun hadn't finished setting. He intended to make the most of tonight.

Charles waited with Ángel outside the hotel the next morning, quiet and subdued, though not in a sulky way. Ángel came so close to reversing his decision that he had to bite the inside of his cheek to stay silent.

He heard the bike long before it entered the parking lot, the purr of the engine bringing a smile to his face. Sakura parked Ángel's motorcycle close by, jumped off, and removed the helmet, combing her fingers through her spiky hair as she walked up.

"Thanks for driving her all the way up here," Ángel said, taking the helmet with one hand and shaking Sakura's hand with the other.

"My pleasure," said Sakura. "My mom begged me to get rid of my own bike years ago. It was awesome to get back out on the road."

Ángel picked up his bags and moved to strap them to the bike, letting Charles and Sakura speak privately. Once he'd gotten everything squared away, he returned to the sidewalk.

"All set?" Charles asked.

"Yeah." Ángel bounced on the balls of his feet, itching to get going while at the same time reluctant to leave Charles, not knowing when or if they'd see each other again.

He didn't know what kind of good-bye Charles would be comfortable with in front of Sakura, either. Did they shake hands, did they hug, did they—

Charles stepped forward, cupped Ángel's face with both hands, and kissed him full on the mouth. There was no tongue, but the kiss lingered, and Ángel's resolve was weaker than ever when Charles pulled away.

"You can call me if you need anything," Charles said.

Ángel grabbed Charles's hand and squeezed hard, just once. "Bye," he said, smiled at Sakura, and headed for his bike.

He swung himself into the saddle, zipped up his jacket, and pulled on his helmet and gloves. The bike jumped to life beneath him as he started her up, and Ángel gave her some gas, driving out of the parking lot without looking back.

Two Months Later

"Explain to me again why you didn't pay for delivery," Eva said, straining under one side of the heavy table they were carrying into Charles's new apartment.

"The delivery charge was almost half what I paid for the furniture itself." Charles readjusted his grip on his end of the table and said, "Hey, watch your step."

"Shit." Eva, who was walking backward, caught herself before she tripped over the threshold and stepped up carefully instead.

The two of them lugged the table into the kitchen and settled it in place. They were followed by Shane and Sakura, each carting heavy boxes that they dumped on the counters. Jade, meanwhile, sat on the edge of the kitchen island, eating a doughnut and texting one-handed.

"Are you planning to help at all?" Sakura said to her.

"I'm taking a break."

"From what? You've been on your phone all morning."

Jade slid her phone into the pocket of her hoodie. "From appreciating this view," she said and grinned at Charles.

Charles rolled his eyes and lifted the hem of his tank top to wipe the sweat off his forehead. "I could use a break too, actually."

He'd stocked the fridge in advance with a case of water, and he cracked it open now, passing bottles out and keeping one for himself. After taking a few deep chugs, he looked around the apartment with a pleased eye.

When his lease expired, Charles had decided to downsize to a smaller, one-bedroom apartment in the same complex, enlisting his team to help him move. It was a first-floor unit with the same basic layout, but it felt warmer somehow, more welcoming. Charles had waited until the move to buy himself new furniture, figuring it made more sense to only transport the stuff once. The apartment was still a little bare, but at least he had a pair of armchairs to complement the couch, a coffee table, and a kitchen table with a full set of chairs. Sunlight streamed through the open blinds on the sliding glass door to brighten the room.

"All right, break's over," Charles said once he'd drained his water bottle. He pinched Jade's side, prompting her to squeak and jump off the island. "Come on, you."

It took another hour for them to finish moving everything. Afterward, as his exhausted team flopped out around his living room and kitchen, Charles ordered a few pizzas for delivery as thanks.

"Hey, Shane," he said, hanging up his phone, "do you want to—"

He cut himself off midsentence at the rumble of a nearby motorcycle engine, his shoulders tensing. For the most part, the others pretended not to notice, though Eva and Sakura exchanged a quick glance.

Charles hadn't heard from Ángel since they'd parted ways at the hotel. He'd respected Ángel's request for space, never texting or calling him, and he had no idea where Ángel was now—but that didn't stop his heart from giving a hopeful bound every time he heard a motorcycle.

Clearing his throat, Charles picked up his thought where it had left off. "Want to come with me on a beer run?"

"Sure," Shane said, rising to his feet.

Everyone in the room paused as the sound of the motorcycle grew louder, clearly heading in their direction. Nobody living in this complex owned a motorcycle; Charles would have noticed.

Sitting in one of the new armchairs, Jade chewed her thumbnail and avoided eye contact, her foot tapping against the floor.

"Jade," Charles said, "who were you talking to earlier?"

Jade sighed. "It was supposed to be a surprise," she said. "I told him he'd be better off taking a cab—"

Charles spun around and all but ran out the door, stopping on the edge of the sidewalk as that familiar red bike glided into one of the visitors' parking spaces. He watched dumbly while Ángel got off, set down his helmet, and shook out his hair, smiling at Charles across the lot.

Ángel looked good—not the blithe, happy-go-lucky man Charles had once known, but the hollowed-out devastation in his eyes had faded, replaced with a quiet alertness. He held himself comfortably, his shoulders straight under his leather jacket, and his steps were confident when he started walking.

Charles strode forward to meet him halfway, ignoring his friends as they spilled out of the apartment behind him. He opened his mouth, searching for something to say, anything that could encompass the desperate, yearning hope Ángel's return had kindled within him.

"Are you sure?" Charles asked.

Ángel's smile widened, lighting up his face. "I'm sure," he said, under a sun that suddenly shone a little more brightly.

Dear Reader,

Thank you for reading Cordelia Kingsbridge's *Can't Hide from Me*!

We know your time is precious and you have many, many entertainment options, so it means a lot that you've chosen to spend your time reading. We really hope you enjoyed it.

We'd be honored if you'd consider posting a review—good or bad—on sites like **Amazon, Barnes & Noble, Kobo, Goodreads, Twitter, Facebook, Tumblr,** and your blog or website. We'd also be honored if you told your friends and family about this book. Word of mouth is a book's lifeblood!

For more information on upcoming releases, author interviews, blog tours, contests, giveaways, and more, please sign up for our weekly, spam-free newsletter and visit us around the web:

Newsletter: tinyurl.com/RiptideSignup
Twitter: twitter.com/RiptideBooks
Facebook: facebook.com/RiptidePublishing
Goodreads: tinyurl.com/RiptideOnGoodreads
Tumblr: riptidepublishing.tumblr.com

Thank you so much for Reading the Rainbow!

RiptidePublishing.com

ACKNOWLEDGMENTS

Endless gratitude to my amazing parents and sister, who have been a constant source of unconditional love, support, and encouragement, and without whom I would never have had the courage to pursue my dreams and make them reality. I love you guys!

Big thanks are due as well to all of the readers who have supported me throughout my journey as an author, from my early LiveJournal days to the present. Your faith and enthusiasm mean the world to me!

ABOUT THE AUTHOR

Cordelia Kingsbridge has a master's degree in social work from the University of Pittsburgh, but quickly discovered that direct practice in the field was not for her. Having written novels as a hobby throughout graduate school, she decided to turn her focus to writing as a full-time career. Now she explores her fascination with human behavior, motivation, and psychopathology through fiction. Her weaknesses include opposites-attract pairings and snarky banter.

Away from her desk, Cordelia is a fitness fanatic, and can be found strength training, cycling, and practicing Krav Maga. She lives in South Florida but spends most of her time indoors with the air conditioning on full blast!

Connect with Cordelia:
Email: cordeliakingsbridge@gmail.com
Tumblr: ckingsbridge.tumblr.com
Twitter: @c_kingsbridge

Enjoy more stories like
Can't Hide from Me
at RiptidePublishing.com!

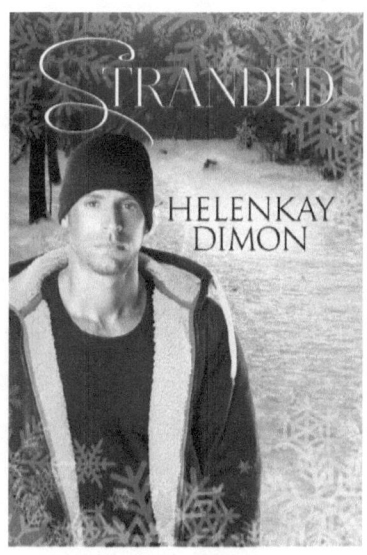

Stranded
ISBN: 978-1-62649-364-3

Free Falling
ISBN: 978-1-62649-137-3

Earn Bonus Bucks!

Earn 1 Bonus Buck for each dollar you spend. Find out how at
RiptidePublishing.com/news/bonus-bucks.

Win Free Ebooks for a Year!

Pre-order coming soon titles directly through our site and you'll
receive one entry into a drawing for a chance to win free books for
a year! Get the details at RiptidePublishing.com/contests.